ROWE IS A PARANORMAL STAR!" ~J.R. WARD

PRAISE FOR NOT QUITE DEAD

"[Rowe] has penned a winner with *Not Quite Dead*, the first novel in her new NightHunter vampire series...an action-packed, sensual, paranormal romance that will captivate readers from the outset... Brimming with vampires, danger, resurrection, Louisiana bayou, humor, surprising plot twists, fantasy, romance and love, this story is a must-read!" ~ *Romance Junkies:*

PRAISE FOR DARKNESS POSSESSED

"A story that will keep you on the edge of your seat, and characters you won't soon forget!" - Paige Tyler, *USA Today* Bestselling Author of the X-OPS Series

"*Darkness Possessed*...is an action-packed, adrenaline pumping paranormal romance that will keep you on the edge of your seat... Suspense, danger, evil, life threatening situations, magic, hunky Calydons, humor, fantasy, mystery, scorching sensuality, romance, and love – what more could you ask for in a story? Readers – take my advice – do not miss this dark, sexy tale!" ~*Romance Junkie*s

PRAISE FOR DARKNESS UNLEASHED

"Once more, award winning author Stephanie Rowe pens a winner with *Darkness Unleashed*, the seventh book in her amazing Order of the Blade series...[an] action-packed, sensual story that will keep you perched on the edge of your seat, eagerly turning pages to discover the outcome...one of the best paranormal books I have read this year." ~*Dottie, Romancejunkies.com*

Praise for Forever in Darkness

"Stephanie Rowe has done it again. The Order Of The Blade series is one of the best urban fantasy/paranormal series I have read. Ian's story held me riveted from page one. It is sure to delight all her fans. Keep them coming!" ~ *Alexx Mom Cat's Gateway Book Blog*

Praise for Darkness Awakened

"A fast-paced plot with strong characters, blazing sexual tension and sprinkled with witty banter, Darkness Awakened sucked me in and kept me hooked until the very last page." ~ *Literary Escapism*

"Rarely do I find a book that so captivates my attention, that makes me laugh out loud, and cry when things look bad. And the sex, wow! It took my breath away... The pace kept me on the edge of my seat, and turning the pages. I did not want to put this book down... [Darkness Awakened] is a must read." ~ D. Alexx Miller, Alexx Mom Cat's Gateway Book Blog

Praise for Darkness Seduced

"[D]ark, edgy, sexy ... sizzles on the page...sex with soul shattering connections that leave the reader a little breathless!...Darkness Seduced delivers tight plot lines, well written, witty and lyrical - Rowe lays down some seriously dark and sexy tracks. There is no doubt that this series will have a cult following. " ~ *Guilty Indulgence Book Club*

"I was absolutely enthralled by this book...heart stopping action fueled by dangerous passions and hunky, primal men...If you're looking for a book that will grab hold of you and not let go until it has been totally devoured, look no further than Darkness Seduced."~*When Pen Met Paper Reviews*

"[a] thrilling entry into romantic suspense... Rowe comes through with crackling tension as the killer closes in." ~ *Publisher's Weekly*

PRAISE FOR CHILL

"*Chill* is a riveting story of danger, betrayal, intrigue and the healing powers of love… *Chill* has everything a reader needs – death, threats, thefts, attraction and hot, sweet romance." ~ Jeanne Stone Hunter, *My Book Addiction Reviews*

"Once again Rowe has delivered a story with adrenalin-inducing action, suspense and a dark edged hero that will melt your heart and send a chill down your spine." ~ Sharon Stogner, *Love Romance Passion*

"*Chill* packs page turning suspense with tremendous emotional impact. Buy a box of Kleenex before you read *Chill*, because you will definitely need it! …*Chill* had a wonderfully complicated plot, full of twist and turns. " ~ Tamara Hoffa, *Sizzling Hot Book Reviews*

PRAISE FOR NO KNIGHT NEEDED

"*No Knight Needed* is m-a-g-i-c-a-l! Hands down, it is one of the best romances I have read. I can't wait till it comes out and I can tell the world about it." ~*Sharon Stogner, Love Romance Passion*

"*No Knight Needed* is contemporary romance at its best….There was not a moment that I wasn't completely engrossed in the novel, the story, the characters. I very audibly cheered for them and did not shed just one tear, nope, rather bucket fulls. My heart at times broke for them. The narrative and dialogue surrounding these 'tender' moments in particular were so beautifully crafted, poetic even; it was this that had me blubbering. And of course on the flip side of the heart-wrenching events, was the amazing, witty humour….If it's not obvious by now, then just to be clear, I love this book! I would most definitely and happily reread, which is an absolute first for me in this genre." ~*Becky Johnson, Bex 'N' Books*

"*No Knight Needed* is an amazing story of love and life…I literally laughed out loud, cried and cheered…. *No Knight Needed* is a must read and must re-read." *~Jeanne Stone-Hunter, My Book Addiction Reviews*

Acknowledgements

Special thanks to my beta readers, who always work incredibly hard under tight deadlines to get my books read. I appreciate so much your willingness to tell me when something doesn't work! I treasure your help, and I couldn't do this without you. Hugs to you all!

There are so many to thank by name, more than I could count, but here are those who I want to call out specially for all they did to help me with this book: Alencia Bates Salters, Kayla Bartley, Alyssa Bird, Jean Bowden, Shell Bryce, Holly Collins, Ashley Cuesta, Kelley Curry, Denise Fluhr, Valerie Glass, Christina Hernandez, Heidi Hoffman, Jeanne Stone Hunter, Rebecca Johnson, Dottie Jones, Janet Juengling-Snell, Deb Julienne, Bridget Koan, Felicia Low, Phyllis Marshall, Suzanne Mayer, Sandi McCoombe, D. Alexx Miller, Jodi Moore, Judi Pflughoeft, Carol Pretorius, Kasey Richardson, Karen Roma, Caryn Santee, Julie Simpson, Summer Steelman, Nicole Telhiard, Regina Thomas, Linda Watson, and Denise Whelan.

And lastly, thank you to Pete Davis at Los Zombios for another fantastic cover, and for all his hard work on the technical side to make this book come to life, and for the most amazing website. Mom, you're the best. It means so much that you believe in me. I love you. Special thanks also to my amazing, beautiful, special daughter, who I love more than words could ever express. You are my world, sweet girl, in all ways. And of course, to my awesome dog, who endured such hardship sleeping next to me in his big armchair while I worked, just so that I would have company. What a dog!

DEDICATION

Special thanks to Lynne Griffin and Katrin Schumann at GrubStreet Writers for all their guidance, support, and generosity, and to the all the amazing authors in Launch Lab 2014 for turning the solitary author journey into a band of camaraderie, laughter, support and pure genius: Lori Jenkins Reisenbichler, Ellen Herrick, Lenore Myka, Ann Sussman, Robin McLean, Alice LoCicero, David Marshall Hunt, Mark Day, Nadine Lynn, and Stephanie Kegan.

NOT

QUITE

DEAD

A NIGHTHUNTER NOVEL

STEPHANIE

ROWE

CHAPTER 1

The ancient burial ground was not where Eric Hunter wanted to find his brother, but not for the obvious reasons. Dead bodies, ancient spirits, and decaying graves were all well and good, but not when his twin brother, Tristan, was around them.

Eric slogged soundlessly through the Louisiana swamp, his hiking boots flooded with murky water that reached his knees. Tendrils of mist were winding through the trees, hovering inches above the surface of the water. The full moon cast an unearthly glow on the mist, illuminating an iridescent silver reflection upon it. The air was thick with the stench of dampness and stale water, laced with the more subtle beauty of nature undisturbed by the intrusion of humans.

A low whine, like that of an animal on the hunt, drifted through the night. Eric went still, straining to hear any indication that the stories of werewolves, vampires, and shapeshifting panthers were about to be proven true, just in time for his fairly immortal, but not entirely indestructible, body to be torn asunder. He could fight the good fight, but he really didn't have time to engage right now. This part of the Louisiana bayou was replete with tales of voodoo, deadly creatures, and magic that took lives with ruthless abandon. He'd seen enough and done enough in his life to know the odds were high that every single whisper of lore was steeped in truth. Hell, if he lived here, stories would soon start to circulate about what he could do and what he was.

In truth, a lone werewolf probably wouldn't win a battle with him, but a pack of particularly impressive ones could be another story. And vampires? Yeah, well, Eric had a feeling it might depend on the vampire. A battle with a powerful one might take him where he didn't want to go.

Preferring his throat to be attached to his body instead of set out on a silver platter as an entrée for a bloodsucker, Eric silently grasped the hilt of his knife as he mentally tracked the animalistic growl creeping through the swamp. Energy pulsed in his palm, generated by the weapon that carried several centuries' worth of secrets in its shadowy green blade. He waited, utterly still as he listened for the whine again.

Sweat slithered down his temples, and steam rose from his skin, which was suffocating beneath his tee shirt. Even the air he breathed was so thick with humidity it seemed to weigh his lungs down, and he had to fight to get enough oxygen with each breath.

Though he wasn't moving, the dark swamp was teeming with life. He could hear the scrabble of claws, the croaks of frogs, the splashes as alligators slid into the dank water, and the rasp of snakes stalking their prey. Again, he heard the low growl, and it was deeper this time. Not a small animal. A large one, in the nearby vicinity. For a brief moment, he wished he'd disregarded his gut and had opted to strap his gun beneath his arm for tonight's trip, but he knew that would have been a poor choice.

The swamp didn't like those who entered its realm armed with guns, or at least this part of the swamp didn't. He'd stick with the knife unless the situation became dire. Knife first, gun not allowed, magic as a last resort.

When nothing leapt out of the woods to try to sever his head from his body, Eric grew impatient. Unwilling to waste any more time, he moved forward again, keeping his blade ready.

As the water swirled restlessly around his calves, he cast a glance at his watch and grimaced. He was already late. Would she wait for him? Anticipation rippled through him at the thought of the woman who had texted him right before he'd walked into the swamp, letting him know that her plane had touched down. After weeks of delay, Jordyn Leahy was finally in town. He was going to see her *tonight*.

What would it be like when he saw her again? The same? More? *More.*

He wanted more. Much more. Women didn't generally intrigue him these days. He'd trained himself out of the need to connect with females a couple hundred years ago. Yeah, sure, he entertained their flirtations and their attentions, but he never allowed himself to *notice* them. But Jordyn was different.

The first time he'd seen her, she'd been hiking through the Brazilian jungle wearing a hot pink tank top, jeans, and a brand new pair of boots. When she'd stepped from behind a tree with a bazooka aimed at his head, he'd been riveted by her. She'd rebuffed every one of his attempts to seduce her, which made him even more intrigued. Add in the fact that his brother had nearly sacrificed his life to save hers? That meant she was important to his brother, which made her important to Eric. It also made her off-limits, but his fantasies and certain parts of his anatomy were having a little trouble with that concept.

Not that it mattered. She'd come to Louisiana to help him find Tristan, and that's what they were going to do.

But there was no denying the fact that Eric's entire body had been humming in anticipation of seeing her again. And now, she was in town. Less than ten miles away. At that very moment, she was waiting for him at the bar where they'd agreed to meet. And where was he? Slogging through a swamp after what he suspected would be another dead end in the hunt for Tristan, who had been missing for a year.

For a moment, he almost considered ditching the rank water and heading out to meet Jordyn. The thought was tempting as hell, and if he weren't so deep into the swamp already, he might even think about it.

But he needed to find his twin, and soon. He was far enough along this particular trail that he'd be able to wrap up this lead in a few more minutes.

Tristan couldn't be dead, because Eric would know if he was. Yeah, he'd know because they had that twin bond. They were also both connected to the metaphysical world in a way that neither of them fully understood. But the most damning indication of his brother's death would be the fact that Eric would keel over and die shortly after Tristan did. Since he was still alive and kicking, he knew that Tristan wasn't six feet under a pile of dirt somewhere, but Eric had a bad feeling that death wasn't far away. And even if Tristan wasn't teetering on the edge, the brothers could survive only so long without being near each other, and the clock was ticking on that one.

It was time to find his twin, and now that Jordyn was here, Eric had a chance to make it happen. Although she hadn't lived in town for years, Jordyn was a local, bringing with her the inside knowledge of the town that had apparently swallowed up his brother a year ago. He needed her familiarity with the locale, and since she owed Tristan her life, she'd been determined to find Tristan as soon as she'd learned he was missing.

Anticipation rushed through him. He was finally going to track down his brother, and he was going to do it with the woman he couldn't get off his mind. He could still remember exactly what Jordyn smelled like: a faint hint of vanilla, sprinkled with something lighter, something so decidedly female that his cock got hard every time he thought about it. He could still recall the highlights in her hair when the sun had slipped through the thick jungle canopy and brushed over her slightly crooked ponytail. And those two kisses. Those two brief, incredible kisses that he couldn't get out of his mind, not even for a moment.

And now, she was back in his life. She was waiting for him. And he was late.

The spirit he'd been following to the grave flickered suddenly, jerking his mind back to the present. Swearing, he sent a careful pulse of magic at it, pulling it back into the physical world just as it started to fade. It surged back into sight, a slippery, silvery-gray presence fighting his grasp. The glittering shadow hovered restlessly between two trees, waiting impatiently. It swirled in and out of sight as if it were still alive.

Eric loosened his grip on it just enough to allow it to move again. With a sudden surge of energy, it burst into action, streaking toward the burial ground that would empower it to break Eric's hold.

Eric pushed onward relentlessly, knowing that he wouldn't be able to hold the spirit in this world for much longer. Once his guide dematerialized, he would have no way to find the cemetery that had once been a holy burial site, but which had been consumed by the swamp over two hundred years ago.

The spirit traveled swiftly, and Eric had to break into a run to keep it in sight. He slogged through the swamp to solid ground, and then was able to move more quickly as his feet found purchase in the mucky soil. His body moved with the same grace it always had, and it felt good to unleash the power he usually had to keep contained in mainstream society. His stride lengthened, and his muscles elongated as strength surged through him. The thick, steamy air weighed on him as he ran, but he kept his pace even, tracking the spirit as it led him deeper and deeper into the swamp that the locals refused to enter.

Then, finally, Eric felt his body suddenly go taut, as if his muscles were made of wire strung so tightly they were about to snap. *The spirits of the dead were nearby.* He eased to a stop, his skin humming with the energy of dozens of spirits, entities who had feasted upon the life that still existed in this world.

His weapon ready, he slipped between the trees, his senses open wide as he searched the night for all the information he could find. The spirit he'd been tracking ducked behind a massive cypress tree, and then vanished, but he didn't need it anymore.

He was close.

He could feel it.

Forcing himself to approach more slowly than he wanted, he eased through the overgrowth, calling upon his deeper skills to move with absolute silence. He passed the cypress tree, and then froze. Ahead of him, covered in moss and dampness, were seven ancient, crumbling headstones. He could feel the weight of the spirits in the area...all of them heavy with malice and darkness.

The burial site of the damned.

In this region, most bodies were buried above ground because the water table was too high, but these had been buried deep beneath the earth, cut off from any chance of them reconnecting with the human society they had terrorized. In front of the first headstone was a burned patch of soil centered around a small, black stone.

He knew instantly what it was, and adrenaline surged through him. Anticipation and triumph, marred by a dark foreboding. *Tristan had been there.* It was his altar.

Eric had seen Tristan build hundreds of altars as a kid, until they'd discovered the dark side of his brother's abilities. Tristan didn't do it anymore, and yet the signs were unmistakable. Tristan had been there, trying to resurrect whoever had been buried in that grave. "Tristan. You around?" His voice was low, drifting through the mist for only his brother to hear.

There was no response, and he tried again, this time reaching out telepathically over the bond he and Tristan had shared since they were kids, though it hadn't worked since Tristan had gone missing. *Tristan? You here?*

Again, no response, but once more he heard the deep whine of a large, wild animal. It was in the distance, but the menacing sound made his muscles tense with readiness. Moving quickly, he strode out into the clearing, staying low and ready as he swiftly approached the altar his brother had abandoned.

He crouched in front of the headstone and shined his flashlight on the burned patch of dirt. Instead of the single stone he'd expected to see, there were dozens of small, rounded rocks, all filthy, so covered in soot that they had blended into the ground from a distance. Tristan never used more than one stone, and yet there were close to two dozen in this one spot. Had he tried more than once, or had all the stones been used for a single, massive burst of power?

During the year he'd been searching for Tristan, he'd refused to give up hope that his studious brother was holed up in a library somewhere, consumed by some massive research project that had made him forget that the rest of the world existed. But this site destroyed that delusion. His brother was in trouble, serious trouble. "What the hell were you trying to raise, Tristan?" Eric whispered as he picked up one of the stones.

The stone was dead and lifeless, which considerable time had passed since Tristan's magic had run through it. It was also intact, which meant his brother hadn't been successful in the resurrection. He picked up another. The surface was rough, and it flaked off under his thumb, but this one was also intact. Eric began to relax. If Tristan had failed, then he might still be okay—

He suddenly noticed a large stone to the right of the

grave marker. Unlike the others, it was streaked with a blood-red spatter that appeared to be sunk deep into the rock...and it was cracked in half, splayed open on the ground in two parts.

A dark shadow of unease crept down Eric's spine. The broken stone could mean only one thing: Tristan had successfully resurrected whoever had been buried in that grave. Who was worth the cost it would have taken on his brother to call upon so much magic?

Eric flashed his light onto the crumbling headstone. The carvings in the granite were faded and chipped away, making the name unreadable, but there was no doubt that the year was 1621.

For his brother to resurrect someone or something that had been dead for almost four hundred years, the cost to Tristan was unimaginable. Why had he done it? And what had happened in the time that had passed since then?

Then the thin beam of his light settled upon a marking at the top of the headstone, a carving so deep and violent that it had survived four hundred years so well that it was almost blinding in its intensity.

It was three intersecting triangles bisected with a stake, the ancient warning symbol that the locals had once used to warn that it was a gravesite of the damned.

It was the symbol of a vampire.

Tristan had raised a vampire?

No. He would never do that. *Ever.* There had to be another explanation.

Eric plunged his hand into the dirt and opened his mind, searching for the truth of what had happened. The moment he dropped his mental shields, the dark energy of the spirits in the vicinity converged upon him. Images flashed through his mind of bloodied corpses, ravenous hunger, and the gaping emptiness of souls long missing. There was no doubt that the creatures buried there were every bit the predators they'd been accused of being. Evil plunged deep inside him, seeking a foothold to anchor itself to, as the spirits trapped in the burial ground swarmed him.

He closed his eyes, knowing he had only seconds left to raise his shields before the spirits of the dead would consume him. He plunged his mind deep into the soil beneath him, sending out tendrils in every direction. Deeper and deeper he went, searching for the vessel of the body that was supposed to be in the grave.

The soil was thick with maleficent violence, tainted with the shadows of the creature that had once lain there, but Eric could find no physical remains lingering. The body was definitely gone. Tristan had brought it back to life.

Eric gritted his teeth. "What the hell have you done, Tristan?"

But it was pretty obvious what Tristan had done. He'd resurrected a vampire that had been dead for almost four hundred years, one so evil that it had been buried in this remote site, its grave marked with ancient runes to protect against it coming back to life or causing any more harm.

Tristan had brought it back to life. *Hell.*

Sudden, spine-chilling malevolence knifed through him, and he slammed his mental shields closed just as invisible claws gripped his heart. For a split second, he couldn't breathe, and he thought he'd reacted too late, but then the menacing presence fled his body.

He sucked in a deep breath, reinforcing his psychic walls as the evil of the dead continued to circulate around him. He could feel them pushing at him, trying to take advantage of the connection that they'd just shared, seeking access to him.

He needed to get out of there and rebuild his protections properly. Knowing he had very little time, he pulled his hand out of the dirt and grabbed his phone to take a picture of the headstone. Moving with ruthless efficiency, he took snapshots of each crumbling carving, hoping that he'd be able to decipher the name of the interred and get a clue as to why Tristan had done it. Sweat poured down his back as he canvassed the rest of the burial ground. No more graves had been tampered with. That main one was the only one Tristan had wanted.

Nevertheless, Eric snapped pictures of the other headstones, all of which were crumbling as well. The vampire mark was on the top of each headstone. Why had Tristan chosen this one? Why had he left the others? Eric worked quickly, an increasing sense of foreboding weighing on him. He needed to get out of the area, and fast.

Just as he snapped his final picture, he heard a low growl again, this time, to his right, and close. He spun fast, shoving his phone in his pocket as he readied his knife. He went into a crouched position, using the headstone to shield his right side as he stared into the thick woods.

He shone his light into the dark, and two large, red eyes reflected back at him. He caught a glimpse of a shadowed body and white canines, and then it bolted, disappearing into the darkness.

He had less than a split second of relief, when he heard a sudden scream. It was a woman's voice, and it was coming from the direction the animal had just taken. Fear tore through him. Jordyn? Had she followed him into the swamp? Earlier today, he'd texted her about the burial site he'd been planning to investigate. Had she taken it upon herself to come here? That was something she would do. "Jordyn!"

He reacted instantly, without even thinking. He sprinted straight into the woods after the animal, toward the woman it was hunting. He caught a glimpse of movement ahead, but it was gone before he could identify it. "Hey!" he shouted. "Come back and get me! Leave her alone!" He hurled a rock in the direction of the creature, but it fell with a thud on the ground as the creature vanished through the trees. "Hello? Is anyone out here? Jordyn!"

Ominous silence greeted him. The woman whose scream he'd heard didn't respond. Fear thick in his throat, he surged forward, scanning the swamp for her, for the animal, or even for a broken twig. Anything to tell him where they'd gone and what had happened.

He found nothing. Not one single indication that anything had been there. He wanted to lower his mental shields to search on the spiritual level, but the air was still so thick with malevolence he knew he couldn't risk it. He'd do no one any favors if he became a vessel for the evil trying to take root in his body.

As he searched, he texted Jordyn. *Where are you?* He had

to know it wasn't her, that she wasn't dead ten feet from him, invisible even to his enhanced senses.

She didn't reply.

Jordyn. You okay?

No response.

His fingers itched with the need to call her, but they'd never spoken on the phone before. Their only contact had been brief texts arranging the logistics of her arrival. After their two-day trek through the jungle in search of her friend, they'd parted ways. She'd returned to Boston to make arrangements for long-term coverage of the battered women's shelter she owned, and he'd come to Louisiana to start tracking Tristan again.

During the entire time they'd been apart, there'd been no calls. No familiarity. She'd put up the emotional barriers, refusing to acknowledge any text where he even mentioned sex. Business only. Text only.

Screw that. The rules changed when a woman was attacked in the swamp. He didn't hesitate as he hit that green button on his screen and called her.

The phone went right into her voicemail, and an automated recording requested he leave a message. Disappointment surged through him at the computerized voice, and he realized that he'd been expecting to hear *her* voice. He left her a brief message. "It's me. Call if you get this. Now." He hung up, frustration and fear hammering through him as he widened his search. "Jordyn!" He shouted again, his voice dampened by the heavy growth of the bayou. "Hello? Is anyone there?"

He found nothing. Swearing, he knew he had no choice but to expose himself to the darkness hunting him. Keeping a tight focus on his mind, he lowered his mental shields slightly and reached out to touch the spiritual energy of the area. He didn't find even a whisper of the woman's spirit, not a footprint from the animal, and no more signs of his brother.

It was as if it had never happened.

But he knew it had.

What the hell was going on? And why hadn't Jordyn called him back?

CHAPTER 2

Jordyn Leahy stood in the doorway of the fifth bar she'd visited over the last two and a half hours, debating whether or not to try one more place or check into her hotel and crash. She was tired. Her feet hurt from wearing heels. She needed a shower, and she'd had enough of the lascivious approaches she'd been fending off all night.

Eric had never shown up at Mack's Diner. She'd waited over two hours, and he'd never appeared. No text. No call. Nothing. After traveling all day, her phone battery had been dying. She'd contemplated leaving it on in case he needed her. But what if he'd never called and her phone had died? There was no way she was foolish enough to strand herself without a phone, so she'd finally shut it off after an hour. Once she'd cut him off, she actually felt better and more empowered. Why should she wait around for a guy who couldn't be bothered to keep a date they'd had for a month? Not a *date*, but still.

She didn't need him. She'd immediately decided to give up her vigil and take action on her own, and had headed out to canvass the local bars to start the search for Tristan herself.

As she'd walked out of Mack's Diner, she'd been a little annoyed with herself for waiting even that long for Eric. She knew what he was like. She knew better than to count on someone like him. Even for Tristan, she would not align herself with a man like Eric, who seemed to be obsessively focused on convincing her to have sex with him. The one thing she didn't do anymore was get involved with men on any level. Been there, done that, time to find some new experiences in life.

But even as she thought it, she couldn't help the smile that flickered over her face at the thought of how many times Eric had suggested they get horizontal. His audacity was actually completely charming, and she was fascinated by the fact that a part of her almost wanted to scream "yes" and leap into his arms so he could show her exactly how great a lover he really was.

But the other part of her would rather stick splinters under her fingernails than get naked with him, or any other man.

Eric had told her Tristan was missing, and that her hometown, Parrish Creek, was the last place he'd been seen. Now that she knew that, she didn't need Eric anyway. She could search for Tristan on her own. She owed him that much. No, she owed him *everything*. She owed him her life. Eight times, in fact.

But even as she'd trekked around from bar to bar, she couldn't help wondering what had kept Eric. Yes, he was an incorrigible flirt, but he'd risked his life to help find her friend, and she knew how much his brother meant to him. Despite his best efforts to convince her otherwise, she knew he wasn't only the shallow playboy he liked to present himself as. So, where was he? Fear flickered through her, and she tried to shove it aside. She'd seen glimpses of what Eric could do, and she knew he could take care of himself. He wasn't her concern.

With a sigh, she adjusted her purse over her shoulder, surveying the low-ceilinged bar that was mere yards from the swamp. One more bar, and then she was calling it a night. The sooner she found Tristan, the sooner she could go back to her life.

The windows were wide open, but thick screens held the insects at bay. The stench of overheated bodies and humidity was thick and almost toxic. Would Tristan ever have come here?

Maybe, if he thought there was something or someone here of interest. Tristan's project had been important to him, and he'd been willing to do anything to get answers. Was this the place where she would finally get a break? Someone must have seen him. The last time she'd been with him, he'd been in this town, researching ancient cemeteries. He'd said it would take at least two years to finish his project, and yet, he was gone.

Someone in this town had to know something. They

might not tell a stranger like Eric, but she wasn't a stranger. Not by a long shot. This used to be her town.

Two men were at a nearby table, their jeans and tee shirts doing little to hide the sheer mass of muscle that both of them carried. Their gazes were bold as they roved over her, their eyebrows lifted in an unspoken invitation that even an antisocial woman like herself couldn't fail to recognize. She also recognized, however, the faces of both of them. The Gaston brothers, who had both been several years ahead of her in high school, were the kind of guys who dominated every room they walked into, who had exuded power even when they were teenagers. Boys that, even then, she had instinctively stayed away from.

There was no recognition in their eyes as they watched her. Though she had seen many people from her past tonight, not a single one had realized who she was. They hadn't noticed that she had once been the skinny, gawky child that ran wild through the fringes of the bayou, playing with the neighbors' kids while her father passed out on their back porch after a night of binge drinking.

Granted, the entire point of Eric asking for her help was for her to use her local influences to assist him, but the moment she'd driven her rental car across the town border, something inside of her had shriveled up, creating the same hard knot in her chest that she'd had when she'd lived there. She wasn't ready to reveal her presence to the town. Not yet. So, she'd simply posed as a stranger from out of town in each bar she'd entered, and the result had been educational, to say the least.

Tonight, the men in the bars had noticed only her breasts, and they'd seen her as only a possible chance to get laid. If she'd walked in the door in jeans and sneakers, with her hair in a ponytail, she was pretty sure everyone would have known who she was. But clad as she still was in her narrow work skirt and her silk tank top, no one was looking past her boobs to her face...which was why she'd chosen not to change her clothes after she'd arrived here. She wasn't ready to be the Jordyn Leahy she used to be. And quite frankly, it was somewhat illuminating to see how the men in her town treated a woman they thought was a stranger. They weren't very helpful, and they had an annoying fascination with her breasts. Was this really what the men she'd grown up with had become? Or maybe she was just bitter and suspicious?

She laughed to herself as she walked further into the bar. Yes, it was probably the latter. She definitely carried enough baggage when it came to men to justify keeping even the nicest guy at a distance. They were just being guys reacting to a single woman waltzing into seedy bars at one in the morning. She knew this world, and she knew her way around it.

With a weary sigh, she shook out her shoulders as she walked up to the bar and eased onto a stool beside a guy she didn't recognize. He was tall, with wide shoulders, and a face that looked gaunt and gray, as if he'd been sick for a long while.

He turned his head as she sat down, and she was struck by the anguish in his gray eyes. Instinctively, she touched his shoulder to offer comfort. The moment her fingers brushed over his shirt, a sharp tingle of pain shot through her. She jerked her hand back, a chill of fear rippling down her spine.

She stared at him, her heart pounding. "Are you okay?" she blurted out.

One dark eyebrow went up, and he shrugged. "I might be," he said in that Cajun drawl she hadn't heard since she'd moved away. He flashed a smile that showcased a dimple and perfect white teeth, but no warmth. "Evenin'."

She managed a smile. "Hi." She cleared her throat, resisting the urge to move away from him. Instead, she stayed where she was and scanned the bar, even though she knew there was no chance she'd find Tristan sitting there, sprawled on a bench, waiting for her to march up to him.

"Can I get you a drink?" the bartender asked.

She swiveled around on the stool to answer him, and then her heart lifted when she saw deep blue eyes studying her, azure eyes she knew so well. "David?"

His dark eyebrows went up, and he narrowed his eyes. "Yes?" His reddish-brown hair was cut short, and he had a half-grown beard on his jaw, making him look so much older and more masculine than the last time she'd seen him, almost ten years ago. His bright orange tee shirt was more flamboyant than the David she knew, but the quirk to his eyebrows, as if he were about to laugh at a joke, was the same. The same black and red cross was even dangling from his left earlobe, as if he'd never taken it out after all those years.

She knew it was him, the gangly boy who had pulled her out of hell the night her father had almost killed her. Unable to stop the smile building inside her, she leaned forward and grinned at him. "Yes?" she teased. "That's all I get is a 'yes?'"

He stared at her blankly. "What?"

She hesitated. Did he really not remember her? How could he not know who she was? Yes, it had been a decade, but she hadn't changed that much...had she? He had once been her best friend. "David—"

A warm grin lit up his face in sudden recognition. "Jordyn Leahy? No shit? It's you?" He didn't even wait for an answer. He just reached across the bar and wrapped her up in a huge hug that had a lot more muscle than the last time she'd seen him. For a brief moment, she wanted to cry, it felt so good to be hugged. Just hugged, not fondled or harassed, or anything. Just hugged.

But then, quickly, too quickly, that good feeling fled, and a rising sense of tension gripped her. He was holding too tight, and she suddenly felt trapped. She pushed at his chest, and he let her go.

He frowned at her. "What's wrong?"

"Nothing."

"You lie." He set an empty glass down on the bar in front of her, and poured her favorite drink into it. Raspberry-lime flavored water, with fresh strawberries. After all these years, he hadn't forgotten. "I've known you since you were four," he said. "You can't lie to me. What's wrong?"

She wrapped her hands around the cold glass. "I haven't seen you in ten years, and the first thing you do is harass me? What about asking me how life has been? Or what I've been up to?" But even as she said it, she felt herself tighten up. She didn't want him to ask how her life had been. How could she possibly explain to him what she'd been through?

He shrugged, apparently blissfully oblivious to the ugliness of the images in her mind. "What life has been like for the last ten years doesn't matter, because something's wrong right now, so that's what I care about. What's going on?"

Her throat tightened at his reply. He was so David, exactly as he'd been for all the years that he'd been her best friend. It felt like no time had passed between them. God, she'd missed the feeling of belonging, of having someone in her life who knew every flaw she had and loved her anyway. For a moment, she was tempted to pour everything out to him, but then she shook her head. She wanted to be different from the woman she'd been when she'd grown up here. She didn't want to be a victim. She wanted to be strong and together. "It's nothing," she lied, "but I do have something you could help me with."

"It *is* something, but I'll let it go for now." He raised his brows as he grabbed another glass and began to fill it from the tap. "What's up?"

"Did a man named Tristan Hunter ever come in here?" She held up the picture on her phone, showing him the blond-haired man who had done the unthinkable and brought her back from the dead eight times, at an unspeakable cost to himself. Although Eric had said that he and Tristan were twins, the brothers didn't look at all alike. Tristan was blond and fair, while Eric was dark and penetrating.

David peered at the picture. "Nope. Never seen him. He live around here?"

"No. He was in the area for a while doing research. He seems to have vanished, and this was the last place he was seen." What would she have done if she hadn't met Tristan that night so long ago? Her life would have gone in such a different direction. Well, she'd be dead, for one thing, but there were so many other ramifications of their brief time together. He was the one who'd taught her exactly how strong she could be.

"Recently?" David asked.

She shook her head. "A year or so ago." She'd been back in town then, but she'd stayed low profile that time, not talking to anyone. Tonight, she'd been forced to get out and immerse herself in the town, and it had been more difficult than she'd expected. It felt weird, both reassuring and isolating at the same time.

Now that she had reconnected with David, however, she felt the loss of having kept herself isolated for so long, yet another cost of her relationship with Walter, the Calydon warrior she'd been bold enough, foolish enough, weak enough, and strong enough to fall in love with.

"That long ago?" David finished filling the beer. "I wasn't around back then. I was traveling."

She frowned at his evasiveness. "Traveling? Traveling where?" As far as she knew, David was a lifer in this town. He was part of the fabric of this community all the way back for six generations. Where would he go?

He shrugged. "Around." Someone called for his attention, and he nodded at her. "Don't take off. There's something I want to talk to you about. Can you stay around?"

"Yes, sure." But as she watched David head off to deal with customers, she regretted agreeing to it. Her pleasure at seeing him again faded, and the familiar sense of isolation settled over her. She didn't belong here anymore. What did she and David have to talk about? She was tired, so tired. She was weary from life, not just from being on the run for the last month. Not that the last four weeks had been easy, of course. It had been a time of insane rushing around getting organized so she could leave town, fueled by the frenzied anticipation of getting down to Louisiana to help Eric find Tristan.

She didn't know what she'd thought would happen when she finally arrived, but suddenly, she felt drained. No Eric. No Tristan. Besieged by a past she'd walked away from so completely. She had no idea where to turn or how to help Tristan. What was she doing here? It had felt good to see David at first, but now, she just wanted to leave and return to Boston, to the world that she'd carved out for herself. In Boston, she felt safe, confident, and connected, so different from this place of her past that reminded her of who she used to be.

But she owed Tristan.

She couldn't leave until she found him.

With a sigh, she spun her stool toward the room. She propped her elbows on the bar and leaned back against the battered wood. Slowly, she examined every person in the room, going through the same process she'd used at every other bar she'd visited to see if the man she was looking for was present.

Even as she did it, she was aware of the low odds of success. Did she really think she'd find Tristan this way? No, she didn't, but he'd lived here for a while, and he had to have had an impact, right? Somewhere in this town, he'd left a clue before he'd disappeared.

Her gaze wandered to the Gaston brothers, and then the door to the bar swung open, drawing her attention. The screen door slammed against the wall, and a dark shadow filled the doorframe. The man who stepped inside was tall and broad-shouldered, with dark hair. His presence was so powerful that the energy in the room actually shifted, rippling as it tried to accommodate the sheer force of his being. She sucked in her breath and sat up, chills racing down her spine.

Eric.

He'd arrived.

She stared at him, her fingers clenching the seat of her stool. He was so much bigger than she remembered. Taller, wider shoulders, a more dominating presence. He seemed to loom over the entire bar, an unstoppable force of power. He scanned the room slowly, starting with the Gaston brothers.

A part of her wanted to leap up, race over to him, and throw herself into his arms. She was riveted by the raw strength of his body, and she knew exactly how powerful he was. He'd been wild and untamed in the jungle, but here, it was as if he were part predator, a feral beast constrained by no one and nothing, stalking through civilization in search of prey to conquer. She recalled his claim that he wasn't a man, and she suddenly believed him. Yes, he was a man, but there was something else as well. Something more visceral and dangerous. Something so graceful and lethal, physicality far beyond that of an ordinary human.

His hair was longer now, disheveled and ragged. His eyes were blazing and dark, his jaw taut, his muscles flexed. The man standing in the doorway was nothing like the flirtatious, irreverent man she'd met a month ago. This man was moody, dark, and pulsing with sensual energy that slid down her spine and settled right in her lower belly. This man was a warrior, and he was pure, unbound *male.*

Her heart started to hammer, thundering against her ribs, as she watched his gaze slide over the inhabitants, moving inexorably toward her. She knew then why she was still wearing her business suit. It hadn't been to prove herself to the town that had once been her home. It had been for Eric.

The only time she'd met him, they'd been deep in the Brazilian jungle, and she'd been wearing boots, jeans, and a ponytail. He'd overpowered her with the sheer force of his being, and she'd wanted to reinforce her shields this time by putting on her work persona, the one that was about the power and strength of a woman.

It wasn't working.

She felt sucked into the vortex of his power, every cell in her body tightening with each passing second as she waited for him to notice her. In the jungle, she'd been so worried about finding her friend that she'd had no emotional space to really let Eric affect her, but now it was different.

Now, she was so deeply aware of him that she couldn't stop thinking about how it had felt those two brief moments when he'd kissed her in the jungle. Fast. Passionate. Sexual.

His gaze penetrated the darkest corner of the bar, his brown eyes alert and vibrant. He'd looked rugged and athletic before, but now, he looked rougher, like he'd been spawned by the earth itself. His jeans sat low on his hips, dripping wet, as if he'd been submerged in the bayou for hours. His boots were thick with mud, and there was dirt streaked across his face. His dark hair was damp and tangled, shoved ruthlessly off his face so it was spiked and messy. Droplets slid in a wet sheen across his forehead, the sweat of a man who'd been working hard at something, even though it was the middle of the night. Whiskers were heavy on his jaw, and she had a sudden ridiculous urge to run her fingers over them.

So much for thinking that four weeks in Boston was going to make her immune to the effect he had on her. It had gotten worse, exponentially more intense since they'd parted ways.

She wasn't ready for this.

She wasn't ready for him.

She wasn't ready for any of it.

Jordyn swallowed, her heart almost leaping out of her chest as he finally turned his head toward her. His eyes met hers, and she knew instantly that, unlike the town that had known her for the first sixteen years of her life, *he* didn't have any trouble recognizing her. The flash of awareness was instant, and she felt like her skin was on fire. She swallowed, her mouth suddenly dry, and her fingers tightened around her stool, as if she could keep herself from tumbling off it and into his arms.

Instantly, he shoved away from the doorway and headed straight toward her. His jaw was tense, and his stride was long and purposeful, rippling with languid strength. His gaze was fixed on her so intently that she wanted to look away...except she couldn't take her eyes off him.

She tensed as he neared, sitting up straighter and trying to get a cool expression on her face. "Where have you been—?"

He gave her no time to finish her sentence. He just swung his arm behind her lower back, hauled her up against him, and kissed her.

CHAPTER 3

Jordyn knew that she should stop Eric from kissing her. She *knew* it in every cell of her body, and yet the moment Eric's mouth descended upon hers, all thought fled her mind. She was instantly overwhelmed by the taste of his mouth, by the decadent softness of his lips, and by the white-hot yearning that gripped her with ruthless intensity.

She froze, too shocked by the kiss to react, to stop him, or to pull away.

In her brief lapse of self-discipline, Eric took over. He slid his hand through her hair, angled his head, and consumed her. His kiss was sinfully hard and rough, penetrating all her defenses. He locked his other arm around her back, and hauled her against him until her breasts were crushed against his chest. She could feel the wetness from his clothes saturating her thin blouse, and the heat from his body was like an inferno blazing through her.

Desire leapt through her, an irrational need for *him*. Instinctively, her hands went to his shoulders, gripping him tightly even as she fought to keep her senses. But his kiss was devastating, an assault on her senses that she couldn't begin to fathom. It was as if every part of her soul had ignited, burning for his touch and his kiss.

Their bodies were plastered against each other, and it still wasn't close enough. With a low growl, he deepened the kiss, and suddenly, his tongue was dancing with hers, stoking fires within her that were so vibrant she felt like she would catch fire right there. Her fingers dug into his muscles, and suddenly, she was kissing him back. The moment she began to respond, he growled low in the back of his throat, and broke the kiss, severing the connection between them so abruptly she felt as if he'd cut off her oxygen.

She stared at him, barely able to breathe, her hands still clenching his shoulders. His arm was still wrapped around her lower back, pinning her against his chest as he stared at her.

For a moment, he said nothing, and silence coiled between them, becoming more and more tense. What was she supposed to say after that kiss? *More, please, more?*

God, no. *No.* She wrenched her hands off him and pushed at his chest, demanding space.

He didn't give it to her.

He just kept staring at her, his brown eyes searching her face as if he would find the answer to humanity's greatest questions in her cheekbones. She swallowed. "You weren't there."

A slow grin spread across his face, and for a moment, she thought she might melt right then. Damn the man. His smile hadn't lost its high-voltage charm. "No, I wasn't. Sorry about that." He studied her more closely. "You're alive."

There was an edge to his voice that stifled the smart remark that she was going to shoot at him. She frowned, her hands softening against his chest. "You thought I was dead?"

"I think a woman got murdered in the bayou tonight. I thought it might be you." His gaze went to her hair, and he brushed it back from her face in a gesture that was more intimate and tender than she was ready for.

She tried to push back from him, and this time, he let her, his hand sliding over her hip as she stepped back. "Murdered? You're serious?" His words sank in, filtering through the flush of attraction still ringing through her.

"Yeah." He brushed his fingers over her cheek, and she had a sudden feeling that he was checking to make sure she was really there. It was as if he couldn't keep his hands off her, not because of pure, bold lust, but because he needed to connect with her. "I couldn't find anything, but something happened out there in the swamp."

An involuntary shiver rippled over her. She'd seen and

heard too many strange things in the bayou at night not to realize that he might be right about what he'd heard. "Something probably did happen," she agreed, barely resisting the urge to run her hand over his chest, as if she could quiet the tension radiating through him. "This place is like that. Did you call the police?"

"No." He was still studying her as he sifted his fingers through her hair, untangling the ends of the strands, a restless, vulnerable move that wasn't about seduction as much as a need to simply touch.

The physical intimacy between them was unexpected, and it had no foundation. It shouldn't be like this between them. She knew she should push him away, but somehow, it felt so right. "No?" She couldn't remember what she'd asked him.

"No, I didn't call the police." He tucked her hair behind her ear.

"What?" She batted his hand away, startled by his comment. "You heard a woman possibly being murdered, and you didn't call the police? Why not?"

"What could they have done? I searched the area for an hour. I was there, and if I couldn't find her, no one else could." He shrugged, and something flashed in his eyes. "Trust me. I searched the swamp very thoroughly. I thought it was you."

She blinked at the unexpected turn to the conversation. "Me? Why would it be me?"

"Because you didn't answer your phone, and you knew that's where I was planning to go. It was a logical assumption, when I'm dealing with you, the woman who charged into a South American jungle to find her missing friend." He raised his brows. "Why didn't you answer your phone?"

She lifted her chin. "I turned it off after you were an hour late. I got tired of waiting on you." She didn't feel like mentioning that she'd also turned it off because the battery had been dying. Eric unsettled her, and she needed both of them to believe that she was strong and immune to his charms. She knew enough about Eric to know that the best way to manage him was to retain the power in the relationship.

Not that they had a relationship. Really. Seriously. And she didn't want one either. She *really* didn't.

His lips thinned, and he leaned forward. "Do me a favor," he said roughly. "Never turn your phone off again, okay? Not when I might need you."

She swallowed as his voice rolled through her, making her belly tighten. He'd paused just long enough over the word *need* to make heat plunge through her. She set her hands on her hips and gave him a steady glare. "Don't be late again, and I won't."

"I wasn't late. I was looking for you." His voice was haunted with an edge that made her heart pound. He looked right at her, his gaze boring into her. "I had to find you. You come first."

His words were so simple, so matter-of-fact, and yet they seemed to strike right past her shields. *I had to find you.* Suddenly, all the independence and self-sufficiency she'd cloaked herself in for so long shuddered, and she wanted to stop fighting so hard, and let herself lean on him. It just felt *good* to have someone care if she was dead.

No, no, *no.* She didn't want to feel like this. She couldn't go down this road again. Falling in love with Walter had led to terrible things. She wasn't getting involved with a man again. Not with Eric. Not with anyone.

Eric said nothing, but he leaned past her to order a beer from David. She held her breath as his shoulder brushed against hers, making her jump. She didn't want to come first to a man anymore. She wanted to be left alone.

But even as she thought it, Eric turned his head slightly so his lips were next to her ear. His breath was warm against her neck, making chills run down her spine, belying her own thoughts. "I missed you," he said softly. "Four weeks is a long time not to hear your voice."

Damn him. He wasn't going to leave her alone, not for one minute.

She scowled at him. "Don't start with me," she said. Heaven help her, she really did not want to hear him suggest they have sex, like he'd done a dozen times already in the jungle. And the reason she didn't want him to suggest it was because a little part of her wanted him to keep trying. She didn't want him to give up on her, even though she absolutely was *not* interested in getting physical with him, because as long as he kept trying, it meant that at least one person in the world believed that she had a chance to become whole again. His relentless, irritating, and annoying flirtation gave her hope, and she hadn't had that in a very long time.

He grinned, that same wicked gleam in his eyes that she knew all too well, that still made her belly tighten. "Oh, Jordyn," he said softly, his deep voice rolling over her like a seductive caress, "you'll know when I start with you, I promise you that."

And she could tell he meant every word.

⌧⌧⌧

Jordyn was safe.

The words kept tumbling through Eric's mind, again and again. He couldn't get them out of his head. The relief had been so visceral the moment he'd seen her sitting at the bar, looking so proper and dignified in her business suit. She'd looked cool and reserved, and for a split second, he'd wondered whether he'd imagined the fiery woman who had been haunting him since they'd parted ways. But the moment she'd locked gazes with him, the heat in her eyes nearly set him aflame.

Jordyn turned toward him as she slipped off the stool, the slit in her narrow skirt showing the slightest tease of smooth thigh. Her white blouse was damp from him, revealing just the faintest hint of lace on her beige bra. "I'm tired. I think I'm going to head to my hotel—"

"Not yet." There was no chance he was letting her ditch him. Not now. Not when his entire body was roaring with his need for her. Lace. His badass warrior woman was wearing *lace*, the ultimate in femininity. Shit. He was in over his head before, but now? He was a goner. "Let's sit in back. We need to talk about Tristan."

She grimaced, but nodded, a rare concession from her that made his body tighten. Hell. He was turned on by a simple nod from her? Yeah, apparently.

"Just for a few minutes," she said, reaching past him to retrieve her pink, fruity drink from the bar, holding it between them like a shield.

"Agreed." Musing that she seemed way too tough to

allow herself to be seen with a drink that was a girly rose color, he set his hand on her elbow and guided her through the bar toward a table in the rear corner. Her shoulders were stiff beneath her silk blouse, and she was trying desperately to keep their bodies from bumping together as they wove through the tables, just like she'd done in the jungle. The woman wanted distance from him, but there was no way that she could hide her response to his kiss.

He hadn't meant to kiss her just then.

He hadn't intended to haul her up against him and feel the soft curve of her breasts against his chest.

All he'd wanted to do was make sure the woman who would help him find his brother was safe. But when he'd seen her...his brain had completely stopped functioning, and all that mattered was *her*.

That was the third time he'd kissed her, and not a single kiss had been planned. But he'd done it, and each time, she'd kissed him back with an intensity that had nearly shattered all his self-control. She wanted space from him, that was obvious, but there was something between them that neither one of them could deny.

Which was a major problem, because there was something going on between Jordyn and his brother, and he *never* coveted one of his brother's women. *Ever.*

So, that kiss was just going to have to haul its pretty little memory out of his brain and take a hike, because it wasn't going to happen again. He was going to have to shove all that lust right back where it came from, and deny his need for her. He laughed softly at the irony. He was the man who never denied his need for anything. And now, here he was in the presence of the first woman he'd truly wanted in several centuries, and he was going to shut himself down before he got started.

All for his bro? Yeah, all for his bro. Tristan was all he had, and he wasn't going to let a woman come between them. So, as of now, he and Jordyn were a platonic team on a mission to find his brother before things went irretrievably south.

True, he felt insanely protective of her. So what? It was only because of her connection to his brother...because he was a dedicated family guy. Amen, brother.

Eric glanced around the bar as they reached the table,

instinctively checking to make sure no one was eyeing Jordyn the wrong way as he pulled out a chair for her. The two men by the door were watching, and he glowered at them until they looked away.

She glanced up at him as she sat down. "You pulled out my chair?"

He had? He looked down at his hand still wrapped around the wooden back of the chair, and shrugged. Apparently, he had. That was a new thing for him. He wasn't sure what to make of it. "I'm a gentleman," he said as he sat down across from her.

She laughed softly, a lighthearted sound that seemed to reach right through his tension and crack it. "You're not a gentleman," she said. "You're arrogant, and all you think about is sex."

He grinned at her, enjoying the lightness of her tone that belied her accusation. "I'll grant you the arrogance, but it's only you that makes me think about sex." Well, hell, what was that? Hadn't he just finished putting her off limits when it came to nakedness? He was pretty sure he had.

Her cheeks turned red. "Shut up."

His smile widened as she tossed the familiar phrase at him, the one she used every time he crossed a boundary that made her uncomfortable. It felt good to hear her say that, and he finally relaxed. She was really here. She was really okay.

She was safe.

He'd never felt such an extreme sense of rightness as he had when he'd seen Jordyn across the dingy bar. It was as if the rest of the world had disappeared, sucked into a vortex that was occupied only by her.

Shit. He was in trouble, wasn't he? She was *his brother's woman*...wasn't she?

He leaned forward, studying her. "What's up with you and Tristan?" He didn't bother with subtlety or finesse, neither of which had ever been a particular skill of his. He had to know. He had to hear it from her lips that she and Tristan were involved, otherwise his damned libido was not going to shut up.

Her face grew shuttered, and she glanced away.

"No. You don't get to shut me out when it comes to my

brother." He leaned closer, into her space, just close enough to catch a whiff of the scent that he knew so well. Vanilla and some sort of faint flowery scent. God, she smelled good. Not that he was thinking about it.

He glared at her. "My brother's extremely important to me. You're my only link to him, sweetheart, and I need to know everything about you and him. You might have been the last person to see him." Yeah, okay, he'd made it sound good, like his need to know about the two of them was because he needed to find Tristan. It was, but he also needed to do something about the fact that he couldn't keep himself from appreciating the curve of her collarbone and wondering how soft her skin really was.

Jordyn looked back at him, and, engaging in her typical modus operandi, attempted to regain control of the conversation by changing the subject. "Don't you need to call the cops about the missing woman?"

He shrugged. "I called on the way back. If I didn't find anything, they won't either, because I'm really good at things like that. But I figured they might want to know in case someone is reported missing. Why won't you talk about Tristan?" he pressed. "What are you hiding?"

Her face tightened. "You called the police? You said you didn't contact them. You said you were so worried about me that you forgot to call." She sat back in the chair and folded her arms over her chest, completely ignoring his questions.

He'd forgotten how much he liked the fact she refused to give him what he wanted. He grinned, stretching back in the chair. His wet jeans were getting uncomfortable, but there was no chance he was going to cut this conversation short to change his clothes. "I *was* looking for you. You were the only thing I was thinking about, so yeah, it didn't occur to me to call them when I was there and could search myself. I'd never trust them to find you. By the time I got in my truck, I finally thought of calling them. When you asked earlier, I thought you were asking whether I'd called the cops *at the time*." It was a bit of a lie, because he hadn't thought clearly about her question one way or the other. The truth was, when she'd asked him the question, it had thrust him back into those moments in the swamp when he'd thought she might have been dead, so that was how he'd answered. "Why are you so important to Tristan? Why did he risk himself to save you?"

She shrugged. "We're friends."

Friends? She and Tristan were only *friends*? For a second, he contemplated jumping out of his seat and pounding his chest in victory at that news, but he managed to restrain himself, mostly because he was distracted by the thought that if she and Tristan weren't hot and heavy, then why had Tristan resurrected her eight times? "Then why did he save you?"

"Real friends do nice things for each other. I'd think even a guy like you would understand loyalty that isn't related to sex."

He bristled. "I understand loyalty," he said. "But Tristan's powers are different. They come at a great cost, and I assume you know that. Didn't you ever wonder *why* he was willing to do that for you?"

Doubt flickered in her eyes, and he realized she'd asked that same question many times, and hadn't liked the possibilities. Shit. What was going on with his brother? The more questions he asked, the murkier the situation became.

Jordyn leaned forward, pinning him with her intelligent, relentless gaze. "Why did you ask me about vampires when you first mentioned he was missing? Back when we were in the jungle?"

He thought back to that woman's scream, and the animal he'd heard. "Do you believe in werewolves? Werepanthers? Monster beasts from hell? Vampires?"

Her gaze met his, and he didn't see the amusement he'd been hoping for at his mention of mythical beasts. "I don't know what exactly I believe," she said softly, blessedly giving him a direct answer to one of his questions, "but I've seen a lot of things in the swamps that I can't explain. People see things. People disappear. Nightmares come alive. Everyone who has lived here for a long time has stories. But yes, I believe vampires are real."

"You do? Damn." He rubbed his jaw thoughtfully, digesting her response. It was getting less and less likely that there was an easily solvable explanation for what had happened in the swamp tonight. "Jordyn, I know my brother, and I know that he'd never risk resurrecting someone, let alone do it eight times. But he did it for you, and then he resurrected someone else, possibly a vampire. I need to understand what's going on with him. Tell me what happened between you and Tristan. Start from the beginning. How do you know him?"

Jordyn took a sip of her drink, and sighed in capitulation. "Do you want the short answer or the long one?"

"Don't leave anything out. It might help me figure out why he decided to help you." Satisfaction settled in him, and he clasped his hands on top of his head, letting her voice roll through him as he leaned back to listen. He hadn't been lying about missing the sound of her voice. He had. Sitting with her and listening to her talk felt good.

She shrugged, spinning her glass between her fingers restlessly, as if she were uncomfortable getting personal. "I left here when I was sixteen. I didn't want to be a part of this world. I wanted out." There was a tinge of vulnerability in her voice that caught his attention.

She wasn't giving him a direct answer about Tristan, but she was talking, and that was good. Really good, in fact, because as she spoke, he realized he was more than a little interested in finding out more about her. He wasn't going to lie: it wasn't simply so he could figure out why Tristan had bonded with her. He wanted to know because he was intrigued by her.

He watched her play with her drink, and he realized he liked the fact it was pink, revealing the softer side that she tried to keep buried. "Why did you want out?"

She gave him a hard stare. "I didn't have an idyllic childhood," she said defensively. "But that's not the point. I left here, and I met a Calydon warrior. He was sexy, and tough, and he thought I was amazing." Her voice softened, and a stab of jealousy shot through him. "I fell in love instantly, and then later discovered I was his *sheva*." She looked at him. "Do you know what that is?"

He stared at her in shock, denial raging through him. She was another man's *sheva*? It had been bad enough when he'd thought that she and his brother had something going on, but for her to be metaphysically bonded with another male, unable to see or feel anything for any other man? *Shit.* Even as he thought it, he vaguely recalled her mentioning it before in the jungle. He hadn't really been paying attention back then. He'd been more concerned about the other things they'd been dealing with, and, at that point, Jordyn had been more of an interesting challenge to his seduction skills. Now, she was a woman to him, and it was different. He didn't like that she had been a *sheva*. Not one bit. "I know what a *sheva* is. It's a soul mate," he said, unable to keep the edge from his voice. "A physical, emotional, and metaphysical bond that locks a Calydon and his woman together for all time. Nothing can come between them."

She met his gaze. "Nothing, except murder."

"Murder?" He'd been expecting declarations of true love, eternal bliss, and deep, passionate intensity that had ruined her for all other men.

He had not been expecting *murder*.

CHAPTER 4

Eric's face went blank, as if he were hiding his emotions, but his eyes were intelligent as he rapidly processed her statement. "Your soul mate was murdered?" he asked.

Of course he would have figured it out. She'd be traveling the world alone only if her soul mate was dead. Nothing else could tear them apart. "Yes, he was murdered." *Yes, yes, yes.* The words hammered at her.

His expression suddenly softened, and she saw empathy in his face. Empathy. The first soft emotion she'd ever seen on his face, and it was empathy for the fact her soul mate had been murdered? Guilt flashed through her. "Don't feel sorry for me," she said quietly. "I was the one who killed him."

She waited for the condemnation, for the disgust to flash across his face. What woman murdered her soul mate? The reason was never enough, not even the fact that the *sheva* destiny was supposed to result in a *sheva* killing her soul mate. What was fate? A mindless excuse not to take control of her own life. She didn't believe it gave her an excuse for what she'd done.

His face hardened, and anger flashed in his eyes. His jaw stiffened, and she tightened her fingers around her glass, waiting for the accusation.

"Why?" he asked.

She lifted her chin defensively, preparing to launch into the sordid details of what had happened. Not that the facts changed anything or excused her, but because she had to tell him the whole story, as if maybe, just maybe, he would see something besides a cold-blooded murderer. "Because—"

"You mentioned this in the jungle, didn't you? When we were with Rohan's team?"

She frowned, trying to remember what she'd told the crew. She'd been so consumed with finding her friend and facing down an entire team of over-testosteroned Calydons, as well as trying not to notice her reaction to Eric, that she hadn't really thought about it. But now that he pointed it out, she realized she had. "I guess I did." She lifted her chin, preparing for him to give her a hard time about it, now that he was actually paying attention enough to register it. It was almost comforting to realize that she wasn't the only one who'd been so distracted in the jungle.

"When you told us about it," he said, his voice edged with razor sharp lethalness, "you never told us what the bastard did to deserve it."

"What?" She was startled by his statement. There had been no accusation in his tone. Not toward her, at least. His anger was directed at her soul mate, as if he'd automatically assumed it wasn't her fault. Suddenly, she had to look away, fighting against a surge of emotions she couldn't afford to feel. The bar was dark, and the patrons had started clearing out. There were only a few left, including the man at the bar who'd looked so haunted and ill.

"Jordyn?" Eric touched her arm, jerking her attention back to him. "What did he do to you?" His jaw was tense. "Did he hurt you?"

Electricity seemed to jump through her at his touch, and a part of her wanted to put her hand over his so he couldn't break the contact between them. Instead, she clasped her hands in her lap, refusing to let herself be weak enough to ask for help. "He went rogue," she said.

Rogue. What a simple word to describe a hell worse than anything she could have envisioned. On a literal level, a rogue Calydon was one who had lost his humanity and surrendered to the demon blood circulating through them all. Red eyes, deadly rage, and an utter loss of morality. A mindless beast who slaughtered at random, whatever was within his reach. But it was so much more. To see the man she had loved consumed by the monster had been horrific. To hear the screams of their family, friends, and daughter as he tore through them had been devastating. She could still smell the coppery blood of those she loved. She'd been surrounded by carnage where there had once been safety, and by blind hatred where there had been love. That night had been the utter betrayal and loss of everything that mattered

Eric's fingers tightened on her arm, and understanding softened the hard lines of his face. "The *sheva* bond was completed? And then he went rogue and destroyed everything that mattered to you both? Just like the *sheva* destiny commands will occur?"

She nodded, biting her lip as memories of that horrible night flashed in her mind. She'd tried to put it out of her mind, but the images were too strong. She had to tell him. She had to talk about it. She'd never spoken about it, not even to Tristan, but for some reason, she wanted Eric to know, as if maybe he could understand the depths of what had happened and it would expunge the stain from her soul. "We were having a party," she said softly. "It was our wedding anniversary. We'd worked hard not to complete the bonding stages, and trigger the *sheva* destiny. I was so in love." She looked away, her throat tightening. "And then, he got drunk." Drunk. *Drunk.* She would never forget the chill that went down her spine when she'd realized he was drunk. After all the hell with her father, she was terrified of men who drank. Walter had always had drinks, but he'd never been actually drunk, until that night. *Until that night.*

"Why do men get drunk?" she asked, turning back to Eric. "Why do they have to do that?"

"They don't all get drunk." Eric looked down at the beer in front of him, and then he slid it away from him. "But yeah, some of them do."

She studied his glass, now on the other side of the table from him. "You're not drinking it?"

"No. It makes you uncomfortable. I don't need it." He drummed his fingers on the table, the only outward indication of the tension radiating through him. "What did he do?"

"The blood bond," she said, still staring at the beer. He really wasn't going to drink it, just because she didn't like it?

He didn't even know her. He owed her nothing. And yet, there his beer sat, on the far end of the table, untouched. Walter had always drank, never crossing the line to intoxication, but he'd always enjoyed that pleasure in life, telling her to trust his ability to handle it.

She had. Big mistake.

Eric touched her arm. "It's not going to bite you," he said. "Ignore it. I want to hear what happened."

She pulled her gaze off his abandoned beer and looked at him. "Once Walter was drunk, he had no willpower to resist the call of our connection. He grabbed me and pinned me down in the kitchen. He called out his weapon, ripped it across his chest and my hand, and then completed the blood bond with me. I couldn't stop him. He was insanely strong, a thousand times stronger than I was."

A muscle ticked in Eric's jaw. "Of course he was. He was a Calydon. He had no business using his strength against you." A dark energy seemed to roll off Eric and over her skin. It was a cold, hard energy that sent prickles over her skin. "Worthless piece of shit."

Jordyn couldn't help the smile that flickered across her face at Eric's words. He was so outraged that it felt good. "The blood bond was the only stage of the bond we hadn't completed. It had been calling to him for so long, but he'd held off. But once he was drunk..." She shrugged. "You know the old saying, how inhibitions vanish when the alcohol gets flowing?"

"He had no business drinking in that situation. He deserved to die. How dare he endanger his soul mate like that?" Eric looked so furious, which should have scared her, but it didn't, because she could sense it was contained, unlike Walter's insanity. Somehow, for some reason, she trusted Eric.

During those years with Walter, she'd always lived with the fear of the *sheva* destiny. She spent every minute looking over her shoulder, wondering when and if the man she loved was going to become a monster, which, of course, he eventually had.

But with Eric, it felt different. He was even less refined than Walter had been. He had an edge of untamed wildness. He was arrogant and too sexy for anyone's good. He was flippant and irreverent. He was strong, so much bigger and stronger than she was, easily able to overpower her. And yet...for some reason, she wasn't afraid of him.

She took a deep breath, needing to finish her story. She hadn't told anyone the details before. It was too gruesome, something she didn't want to remember or think about, but somehow, finally putting it into words for Eric seemed to be taking some of its power away. "The minute it was finished, he went rogue." Memories of bright red blood spraying through the air flashed in her mind, and she flinched. "There was so much blood. The bodies of my friends, literally torn apart. My poor daughter." Tears began to trickle down her cheeks, and she couldn't stop them. "He went crazy. I'd heard about Calydons going rogue, but nothing had prepared me for it. It was...it was like a scene from a horror movie. I couldn't stop screaming. I was just screaming at him to stop, and it was as if I didn't even exist. I couldn't do anything."

Eric swore viciously, and he moved his chair around the table, invading her space. He set one arm over the back of her chair, and leaned into her. His gaze was dominating, and unyielding, sending shivers down her spine. She knew she should tell him to back off, but there was something about his overpowering presence that was incredible and felt amazing.

"Listen to me, Jordyn," he said. "It's not your fault. A rogue Calydon is a monster that only specially trained warriors can defeat. Only the elite warriors in the Order of the Blade can stop them. It's not your fault you couldn't protect them."

He was so adamant that, for a moment, she wanted to believe him. She wanted to retreat back into her naive world and believe him, but she couldn't. She knew too much. Sadly, she trailed her finger down his jaw, sliding over his rough whiskers, somehow wanting to convey to him that she was touched by his support, even though she couldn't accept it. "No," she said. "It was my fault. I have to take responsibility. Tristan warned me, but I didn't listen."

"Tristan?" He frowned, his forehead furrowing with wrinkles that made him more human than she wanted him to be. "What does Tristan have to do with your soul mate going rogue?"

She dropped her hand from his jaw. "I came back here

six months before Walter went rogue. My father had finally died, and I needed to arrange the funeral. I met Tristan in the graveyard when I was looking at gravesites, and we became friends." She smiled faintly, remembering that moment. "He was so nice to me. He had this great smile, with dimples." She glanced at him. "Like yours. He was working on some project relating to ancient cemeteries, and we wound up talking for hours in the graveyard. I didn't want to go back to the house I grew up in, or socialize with the people from my past, and he wanted company. We hit it off, hiding in the graveyard away from real life."

A muscle ticked in Eric's cheek. "He's a good guy."

"He is." She took a sip of her drink, letting the cool liquid slide down her throat. It was her favorite beverage, but it tasted almost bitter in the face of so many ugly memories. "I told Tristan about my upcoming anniversary, and he told me that there was no way I'd be able to fend off the final stage of the bond forever. He told me I couldn't go back, but I loved my husband, and I refused to listen to him." She laughed softly. "Do you ever wish you could redo one decision in your life? That if you could do one thing differently, it would change everything?"

Eric shook his head. "Thoughts like that will destroy you. You can't change the past."

She rolled her eyes at him. "I'm not an idiot. Of course I know that. I suppose you're above such mundane and human things as regret and guilt?"

His dark brown eyes studied hers. "No. I'm not."

The gritty intensity of his words caught her attention, and she looked sharply at him. Something dark roiled in his eyes, a grief so heavy she sucked in her breath. "What happened?"

He shook his head, denying her request. "Tell me the rest."

"The rest?" She shrugged. "There's not much more. I thought I loved Walter enough to save him from his destiny. I thought that my love was this great saving grace. It's like the ultimate reforming of the bad boy, you know? Save the rogue warrior from a living hell, just by loving him." It hadn't worked with her derelict father, and it hadn't worked with Walter. "I'm the worst stereotype ever. Isn't it pathetic?"

Eric's gaze bore into her. "Pathetic isn't the word I'd

select, no."

"Naive? Is that better?" She shook her head. "Maybe just stupid. Whatever it was, I was determined to go back. Tristan said I would die if I did. He said others would die. I didn't care. I thought I could be strong enough for us both. So, he gave me a gun loaded with powdered demon bile. He said that was the only thing that would kill a rogue Calydon. He told me to use it on Walter as soon as I got home, before he went rogue."

Understanding flickered in Eric's eyes. "You waited, didn't you? That's why you blame yourself?"

She met his gaze. "I didn't use it, and Walter went rogue. By the time I ran into the basement and got the gun, people I loved were dead, because I was too selfish, stupid, and arrogant to stay away, or to kill him before he could turn."

Silence hung in the air, and then Eric nodded slowly. "And then you succumbed to the final stage of the *sheva* destiny, and you killed yourself because you were so distraught over his death. That's when Tristan resurrected you?"

"Yes." Oh, yes. God, she never wanted to feel that much anguish again. She'd felt like her soul had been wrenched from her body and sucked into a bottomless hell of torment and agony. Never had she understood what true despair was until she'd killed her soul mate and watched her daughter die. "It was horrible," she said. "It was as if a demon had gripped my mind and my heart and drained them of everything but darkness. It consumed me. Darkness. Agony. Grief. The most debilitating loneliness ever. I felt like I was standing in a vast wasteland of destruction, with this arid wind howling through me, ripping pieces of my soul apart as it blew." As she spoke, that familiar haunting came back, tightening in her chest until she had trouble breathing. She coughed, unnerved by how dark the bar suddenly seemed. That same haunting darkness was falling over her, that agonizing loss. Oh, *shit.*

Eric frowned. "What's wrong?"

She closed her eyes, and tried to take deep breaths. "Sometimes the desolation tries to come back. The last three times Tristan resurrected me, I thought I had it managed, then it would return with a howling vengeance. Like now." Sharp pains began to echo in her chest, and she set her hand over her heart.

"I shouldn't have talked about it. It's making it come back." Her eyes filled with tears, and she shoved her chair back from the table. "I can't do this. I can't let this take me again. I can't—"

"Jordyn." Eric caught her hand, as she tried to back away. "Stay with me."

"No. I can't." She stumbled to her feet, gasping for air as the grief started to pour down upon her. Walter's face flooded her mind, and she saw him reaching for her as he fell, dying from her blow, his face twisted in the agony of her betrayal when he realized that she'd killed him. "Oh, God—"

"Jordyn." Eric grabbed her around the waist and pulled her against him. "Look at me."

She fought against his grip as the darkness began to close in around her. She heard the distant howl of the wasteland of her soul, and a cold chill settled in her bones. It was coming back again, attacking her, that insurmountable darkness from which the only escape was death...and Tristan wasn't around to save her this time.

"Jordyn!" Eric framed her face with his hands, forcing her to look toward him. His dark gaze pinned her with its intensity, and she went still, shocked by how steady they were in the blackness that was trying to consume her. His eyes were like an anchor, plunging through the abyss to grab her.

"Eric!" Instinctively, she gripped his wrists, trying to focus on the feel of his skin beneath her fingers. He was so alive, so strong, so warm, and so *present*. She tried to cling to his strength, and the sheer magnitude of his life force, but it wasn't enough. The darkness continued to build, an anguish so deep it wanted to tear her apart—

He sighed. "You're faking it just so I'll kiss you again, aren't you?"

Her legs started to tremble. "What?" His words were a distant blur in her mind, drowned out by the emptiness howling through her. "Kiss me?" The idea was preposterous. She was about to fall into the pit again, and he was talking about kissing her?

"All you have to do is ask. I've been wanting to get you naked since the first moment you pulled that damned bazooka on me. I'm a good guy, so I'm willing to sacrifice my self-respect and honor and kiss you."

His tone was so flippant, that same edge that he'd used in the jungle, that same subtle humor that was so good at prying her out from under the grip of stress, and suddenly, she realized he was her chance for survival, for hope, for redemption.

He'd kissed her before, but she hadn't wanted it. She'd wanted space, not seduction, intimacy, or connection with another man. And yet, when he'd kissed her, each time it had been this great salvation, ripping her from her isolation and plunging her into a world where she felt vibrant and alive. Eric and his kisses could reach her in a way that nothing else could. Could he save her from this? She gripped his arms. "Eric?"

His smile faded into a look of such unabashed thirst for her that her stomach clenched. "Just say the word, Jordyn, and I'm all yours."

I'm all yours. The promise disintegrated the last remnants of resistance, and she looked up at him. "Kiss me," she whispered. "God, yes, kiss me. Kiss me like you want to own every last piece of my body and soul."

"Now that sounds like a kiss." He grinned, a wicked smile of such promise and temptation that she wanted to run... right into his arms. "As you wish." Then he slid one hand behind her head, lowered his head, and let his mouth descend onto hers in the first kiss she'd ever wanted from him, or from any man, in far too long.

CHAPTER 5

Eric knew that he wanted Jordyn.

He was well aware that his attraction for her ran at a fever pitch higher than anything he'd ever experienced.

He knew damn well exactly what those few kisses they'd shared had done to him.

But *nothing* had prepared him for how different it would be when she kissed him back without reservation.

The moment his lips descended upon hers, she melted against him so completely it was as if their bodies had suddenly become one. Her hands slid around his neck, holding him close as her mouth opened to his. The kiss became a heated dance of tongues, ravenousness, and passion that wound through his body like a chain of fire trapping him in its searing heat. The lust that he'd held in check since they'd met exploded out of his grasp with no mercy.

He wrapped his arms around her and hauled her up against him, but she was already there, her body as tight against his as it was possible to get. The kiss was desperate, flooded with emotion that spun through his mind. For a split second, he wanted to pull away. He wasn't ready for a kiss that was so wrought with emotional need. He wanted light and irreverent—

"*Eric.*" She whispered the word, and the sound of his name on her lips undid all his resistance.

With a low rumble, he angled his head and deepened the kiss. What had been hot and desperate a moment ago, took on an entirely new level of intensity. He couldn't touch enough of her, his hands roaming her lower back, her hips, and the curve of her butt. Her arms were wrapped so tightly around his neck it was as if she would never let him go. The heat burning between them was electric, pouring off them in batches of steam that made the humid, sweaty night even more intoxicating.

Her shirt was damp with perspiration, her skin so hot that it felt like she was a living, breathing inferno wrapped around him. He slid his hand down her thigh and pulled her leg up against his hip. Her skirt slid up her thigh, giving him access to a broad expanse of flesh so tempting that he wanted to throw her down on the table and—

The table? Holy crap, he'd forgotten that they were in public.

Swearing, he broke the kiss and lowered her leg, tugging her skirt back down over her thigh. He kept his other arm locked around her lower back, and she didn't let go of him either. She looked up at him, beads of perspiration shining on her upper lip, her cheeks flushed.

Unable to summon the willpower to resist, he slid his thumb over her lip, wiping away the droplets in a sensual move that seemed to crackle with intensity.

She swallowed, and then cleared her throat. "Wow."

Wow. It was one word, but it made him grin. His loquacious woman had been kissed into wordlessness. Yeah, he was good. Or at least, he was good with her. He wasn't going to lie to himself. She brought out a side of him that no other woman ever had. "I have a lot more where that came from."

She took a deep breath. "Why doesn't that surprise me?" She slowly untangled her fingers from around his neck, sliding her hands over his shoulders and down his arms, as if she couldn't quite make herself break contact. "Well, that worked."

"It worked?" He frowned, and then recalled that he'd kissed her to ground her when the memories had become too overwhelming. Funny how the kiss had gone from therapy to pure sex in a fraction of a second. Not a surprise, given the intensity of what was developing between them. "See? If you'd had me around to kiss you, you wouldn't have needed Tristan." As he said the words, a flicker of envy rippled through him. Yeah, the fact that she'd still been with Walter when she'd met

Tristan made it apparent that there'd been no naked, sweaty nights between Jordyn and his brother, which was good. No, more than good. It was *great* news. But it was also apparent that she and Tristan had a bond, and his brother had been there for her when she'd needed someone.

He wanted to be that guy for her.

Shit. What? He wanted to be a go-to guy? No. He didn't. He wanted to be her hot sex guy. That was it. Nothing else. He didn't do the go-to-guy thing anymore.

She laughed softly and finally stepped back, and he reluctantly released her. "As magnificent as your kisses are, I don't think they would have been sufficient back then. The grief was pretty debilitating." She sat back down in her seat, and he eased down across from her.

He didn't want to be sitting across from her. He wanted to haul her into his arms and kiss her until neither of them could think. He wanted to slide his hands over her skin, and kiss his way across her body. He wanted to hear her breath catch as he touched her. He wanted to feel her hands in his hair. He wanted to taste the salty sweat on her body. He needed to hear her whisper his name as he sank between her thighs and—

"It got better after the eighth time," she said, interrupting his thoughts. "I was able to manage it better."

"Yeah?" He could barely remember what they were talking about, and he was a little cranky that she seemed to have recovered so completely from the kiss, while he was still fixated on how insanely good her mouth had tasted.

"I thought I was over it, but apparently, it can still come back." She grimaced, and her gaze went to his mouth. "But apparently, it can be averted by a kiss from the right guy."

Yeah, he was the right guy. He liked the sound of that. "I'm here for you whenever you need it."

She laughed softly, clearly aware of his thinly veiled offer. "You never give up, do you?"

He took a deep breath and finally leaned back in his chair. "It's just you. No other woman affects me like that. It's a little distracting."

She met his gaze. "I know what you mean."

For a long moment, silence hung between them, a

silence beating with the pulse of desire and need.

After a moment, she cleared her throat. "It seems like the *sheva* destiny can be overturned by killing yourself eight times. After that, the compulsion fades enough that it's manageable, and you get a second chance at life." She spread her hands on the table. "So, that's why I owe Tristan. He gave me the chance to live, so I owe him everything. I have to make sure he's okay."

"Yeah, I can see that. I like your loyalty to him. It says a lot about you. He chose well." It felt a little strange to be going back to simple conversation about his brother after that kiss. Had she really just turned it off? Because his jeans were so tight he wasn't going to get any breathing room in them until he took some time for himself to deal with it. Was it a woman thing, to be able to experience a kiss like that and then just turn it off? Because it sure wasn't a guy thing.

She smiled faintly and began to swirl her straw around in her drink. "Thank you," she said quietly. "I know he sacrificed a lot to help me. I know what he endured."

"Why do you think he helped you? I'm assuming you weren't romantically involved with him, given that you were still with Walter." He watched her toy with her drink. She was restless, and she wouldn't meet his gaze. Was she embarrassed because of her reaction to the kiss? Eric leaned back in his chair, drumming his fingers on the table as he studied her.

"I don't know. I actually have no idea why he helped me." She still didn't look up. "I wasn't in any shape to ask. I'd kill myself, he'd resurrect me, and then I'd kill myself again. It was sort of a challenging time. Not a lot of opportunity for talking. I asked him once or twice, and he wouldn't tell me. So, I don't know."

He said nothing, contemplating her story. He knew his brother well enough to know that Tristan would not have sacrificed himself for her without a significant reason. What was it? True love, or mind-blowing lust, might have been enough, but with those off the table...he didn't know. And how much damage had been done to Tristan as a result of saving her?

She shifted restlessly, then finally looked up at him. "Just say it."

He blinked, not sure what she was talking about. "Say

what?"

"That I was weak and selfish for going back to Walter after Tristan had warned me. That I was so weak that I killed myself eight times, forcing Tristan to sacrifice so much to save me. Because I was so selfish and pathetic, many people died, and now something terrible has happened to the man who saved me. It's my fault. Just say it. I know it."

Shit. Was that what she thought? He leaned forward and took her hand.

She immediately stiffened and tried to pull back, but he didn't release her. Instead, he ran his thumb over her palm, tracing the lines on her skin. He said nothing. He just touched her, an unrelenting caress that sent chills down her spine and spread warmth through her belly.

After a moment, Jordyn sighed and stopped trying to pull away. She realized his touch felt good. More than good. She was unsettled by how incredibly amazing it felt to be touched by him. His skin was warm, and his touch was so gentle and intimate. She didn't want to be connected to him, or any man, ever again. His kiss had almost undone her, and now she wanted space, not intimacy. "Let go of my hand," she said.

"You believed in the power of love," he said quietly. "How can you ever fault yourself for that? That kind of faith is all that keeps our world from crumbling into depravity and ruin." He continued to caress her palm in a sensual massage that made her belly tighten. Her lips were still tingling from his whiskers, and her nipples were still taut from being pressed up against his chest. She didn't want to react to him like this. She was here for Tristan, not to be cajoled into something she never wanted to get near again.

"People died and suffered because of my choice," she felt compelled to point out. "My *daughter* died."

He raised his gaze to hers. "People die and suffer every day, no matter what we do. Some who we love, some who are strangers. Most people live, die, and suffer alone. You walked through life making choices because you believed in love. That's bravery, Jordyn. That's the kind of thing that should make you hold your head up and be proud."

Tears threatened in her eyes. "Love isn't good when

it's stupid and naive, and results in people dying. If you don't understand that, then you don't understand love at all."

He snorted. "Sweetheart, I know shit about love. I don't even know what the hell it is, let alone understand it. But I hear it in your voice and see it in your eyes, and I'll never condemn you for that. Ever."

She bit her lip. "My daughter died at his hands. My best friend had her head torn off her body in front of me because I refused to see the truth about my relationship with Walter. I wanted love more than I was willing to be responsible." She shook her head. "It was unconscionable," she said. "I will have to live with that forever." She stared at their entwined hands, at the way his thumb was still caressing her palm. It felt so good that she wanted to cry. He knew what she was like, and yet he refused to judge her? He was wrong, but at the same time, it was such a gift.

A gift that would tempt her into making bad decisions again. She didn't want comfort from him. She wanted space. She needed to keep her emotions under control, so that she never hurt anyone else again because she made a choice based on selfish emotions. "Let me go."

He tightened his grip on her. "If you want me to let go of you, you're going to have to be the one to pull away."

She swallowed, heat suffusing her cheeks at her inability to make herself pull back from him. "I don't want this. Not with you. Not with anyone."

He met her gaze, his face so close to hers that she could see the auburn highlights in his whiskers from the dim light of the bar. "Listen to me, Jordyn. I lived with Calydons for a year. I know all about the *sheva* bond. It's stronger than the most powerful warrior. If you hadn't gone back to Walter, he would have come after you. It was inevitable that it would end the way it did. The bond is too strong, and the *sheva* destiny always wins. So, ditch the guilt, and instead, be proud of the fact that you did what you had to do and somehow survived after it was all over. Your mate wasn't disciplined enough to stay sane, and *he* wasn't strong enough not to run around murdering everyone, but *you* were strong enough to stay alive. He's the one who made the choice to kill, and you were the one who made the choice to defeat a destiny that has claimed thousands of women over the centuries. You *impress* me."

Sudden tears filled her eyes, and she pulled her hand away, her heart aching from the kindness of his words. "Don't be nice," she said.

"Why not? You want me to be an ass? Just because you blame yourself for what happened? Well, too bad. I don't agree, so you're not going to get me to vilify you and string you up by those sexy-as-hell ankles of yours."

"No, it's not that." She saw the furrow in his brow, and realized he genuinely didn't get it. She sighed, trying to articulate a jumble of emotions so confusing she didn't even understand them herself. "Eric, I choose to love the wrong men. My dad. Walter. It leads to terrible things, and people dying. I don't want to ever get close enough to a man for those things to happen again." She gestured at him. "There's no room for love anymore. Don't you understand?"

"Love?" He blinked. "I think you're impressive as hell, and I want to get you naked, but I'm not talking about love. I'm sorry if I misled you, but—"

"I know you're not proclaiming love," she interrupted. How dumb did he think she was? She knew a man like Eric didn't do the love thing, but that didn't change her reaction to him. "But you tempt me," she said. "I don't know what it is about you, but you appeal to me on a thousand different levels. I don't want to be tempted. I want to be safe and alone. I want all the men in my life to be just friends. But you—" She gestured at his chest, unable to keep the annoyance out of her voice. "You're so incredibly sexy that I don't want to be just friends with you. I want you to ravage me."

His eyebrows nearly shot off his forehead. "I'm okay with that—"

"Of course you would be. You're a guy." She poked him in the chest, pausing for a fraction of a second to marvel at his muscle tone, then glared at him. "But if it was simply hot sex, that would be fine, because empty sex can't hurt me, right?"

He grinned. "Yeah, so you want to—"

"However," she snapped, "when you're all nice and understanding, you wake up that side of me that I don't want to hear from. The one that makes me see you as more than a nice set of pecs, the one that reminds me that I'm a woman with emotions and vulnerabilities. So, be the arrogant jerk you were in the jungle, make lewd suggestions that annoy me, and stop being nice. Got it? Don't tempt me into becoming emotionally attached to you!"

She finished her speech, and then realized she was standing up, still poking his chest, almost shouting at him. He was leaning back in his chair, a small, arrogant grin playing at the corners of his mouth, which made him look even sexier than when he'd been all nurturing and nice. "Oh, come on! Just stop it!"

"Everything okay, Jordyn?" David's question jerked her attention back to the room, and she looked over her shoulder. The entire bar was watching her, and David was on his way over to them with a baseball bat, eyeing Eric like he was about to use him for batting practice.

Oh, *crud*. She hadn't realized how vehement she'd gotten. "Yes, yes, it's fine." She hurriedly moved to put herself between David and Eric, but Eric moved even faster. One second, she was in front of him, and the next second, he was on his feet, shoving her behind him, and using his body to shield her from David.

"Back off," he said, his voice a quiet menace as David approached.

David stopped immediately, his fist tight around the bat. "Get away from Jordyn."

A barroom brawl was not what she wanted right now. "Stop it, both of you!" Jordyn tried to shove Eric aside, but he didn't move. Damn the man for being built like a brick wall, for heaven's sake! "David, I was just venting. Eric's helping me find Tristan Hunter, and he's on my side. Eric, this is David Savoy, my best friend from childhood. He's just looking out for me because you look like a thug and I'm yelling at you. So, both of you, calm down!"

Again, she tried to get past Eric, and again, he blocked her path with ease as he continued to trade hostile glares with David.

Then suddenly, David grinned and lowered the bat. "She must think you're okay if she's yelling at you when she's not mad at you."

Eric's frown dissolved, and he grinned back. "She insults me constantly."

David nodded knowingly. "Does she tell you to shut up?"

"All the time. Is that a good thing?"

"It is when it comes to Jordyn. That's her way of telling you that she thinks you're hilarious, and you make her life better."

Eric glanced over at her, and his right eyebrow went up. "So, you really *are* in love with me then? That's why you got all worked up?"

Her cheeks heated up. "Oh, shut up." The words came out before she could stop them, and both men laughed.

"Looks like you're all right, man." David held out his hand, and the two men shook hands heartily, instant best friends when they'd been ready to kill each other moments before. She scowled as they exchanged amicable greetings. She didn't understand how men could go from enemies to best buddies instantly. How could they be so sure they could trust each other?

Sighing, she sat back in her chair, watching David's expression as he talked with Eric, who was grilling him about Tristan. David looked serious and interested, and not at all wary. David, who was so protective of her in high school that he'd beat up more than one of her dates for looking at her the wrong way, clearly sensed no threat from Eric...which made it all the more frustrating because she didn't want to be stupid enough to trust Eric or like him. Having David like him made it harder to be smart and keep her distance.

After a moment, the men shook hands again. David turned away to answer a question from a patron at the next table, and Eric sat down in his seat, studying her with great interest. No longer was he all about languid sex, or the relaxed chumminess she'd seen with David. He was alert and interested. The expression on his face was almost curious.

"What?" she asked.

He cocked his head, studying her. "He's not the kind of person I'd have thought you'd pick for a lifelong best friend. He's too—" His body suddenly changed. He became rigidly tense, and sat up abruptly. He scanned the room, looking past her, as if there was something hunting her. "Let's go."

"You want to leave?" At his nod, her chest tightened at his visible tension, unsure what had suddenly put him on alert. She glanced at David as he started to head back toward the bar. "Okay, but wait a sec. David? Didn't you want to talk about something?"

He hesitated, then his gaze flicked toward Eric. "Later."

So he didn't entirely trust Eric after all? He trusted Eric with her safety, but not whatever it was he wanted to discuss with her? That didn't make sense. "David—"

"Later," he repeated, with a meaningful shake of his head.

Jordyn glanced at Eric, and saw he was watching the exchange very intently. He was still tense, but for the moment, he'd focused his attention on them. Chills rippled down her spine, and she suddenly felt claustrophobic. She didn't want to be that closely scrutinized by any man, but especially Eric. He was too intense. That was why she had connected so well with Tristan, because he was fun and easygoing, not some testosterone junkie with too much muscle. "Okay, fine. Should I come by tomorrow?"

"No." David shook his head. "I'll call you. What's your cell phone?"

She rattled it off to him, and by the time she was done, Eric already had her arm and was propelling her toward the door. Irritated, she twisted her arm out of his hold. "What's the rush?"

"Do you hear it?"

She shivered at the dark undertone of his voice. Her instincts fired on, and her skin prickled in sudden fear. "Hear *what?*"

He shouldered the door open and stepped out into the dark night, pulling her with him. He shoved the door shut, and the night descended upon them. *"Listen."*

Chapter 6

The screen door swung shut behind them, clattering gently against the battered wooden doorframe. Eric's fingers were light around her elbow, and he scanned the woods around them, his gaze intent, and his entire body taut with readiness.

The night was dark, the moon barely reaching through the thick tangle of trees ahead. Heavy dampness hung thick in the air, clinging to Jordyn's flesh. The parking lot was half-empty, and the remaining vehicles were mostly old pickup trucks, trying to hold together for one more day. Behind them, she could hear the hum of insects in the swamp, a buzzing that reverberated through the dark night. "Listen to what? The insects?"

"No." He moved closer to her, pulling her into the shield of his body.

Something flashed in his hand, and she saw that he was holding a knife against his thigh. It looked like an ancient weapon, with runes carved in the blade and on the handle. There was a black stone embedded at the end of the handle, and it was glistening even though it was dark out. It almost looked like it was glowing with a faint green light...and so did the blade? Frowning, she looked closer, and she saw that there were shadows undulating in the blade, as if it were alive. Her heart started to hammer. "Eric, what is that?"

"Listen."

The edge to his voice made her stiffen, and she looked around again. The dirt road was empty, disappearing on the far side into thick woods and marsh. The shadows loomed dark and menacing, just like they had when she was a kid. Suddenly, memories of the monsters that lived in the bayou came flooding back, and she shut her eyes, cutting off the visual distractions.

For a moment, she concentrated on the feel of Eric's fingers on her elbow, using his touch to ground herself. His grip was light and warm, but solid. She could hear his breathing, and he was so close she could feel the heat rising from his body as he used it to shield her from the night.

Trusting him to keep her safe, she let her focus drift from fear and from him. She allowed her mind to reach out into the dark night. The noises of the swamp seemed to swell, pressing down upon her. The splash of a gator as it slipped into the water. The anguished scream of a mouse as it met its demise. The low hoot of an owl.

And then she heard a sound that made the hair on her arms stand up. A low growl, so faint that it almost blended in with the swamp. A menacing, terrifying sound she hadn't heard since she was a child running from her nightmares. She'd never heard it in real life, but it slithered over her with chilling familiarity. "Oh, my God," she whispered.

"You hear it?"

"Yes." Again, the menacing growl. It was distant, but if she could hear it, maybe it could hear her, too. Her heart started to pound, and a memory flashed through her mind, a memory that she hadn't had to face for so long, but there was no doubt in her mind what she'd heard. Her stomach turned, and her eyes sprang open. "We need to get out of here. Now!"

Eric didn't move. He was staring into the woods, his face grim. "That's the sound I heard in the swamp before that woman screamed."

"You heard the scream? Oh, God." She tore herself out of his grasp and raced down the stairs. "Come on!" She was halfway to her rental car, when Eric caught up.

"My truck," he said.

"But—"

"I need my stuff. Come on!" He pulled her toward a massive black pickup truck parked near the door, ten times the size of her subcompact rental car, and so much more capable of handling the swamp.

"Okay." She raced beside Eric, barely even noticing the high heels that had been killing her feet only moments before he'd walked into the bar. He unlocked the truck remotely, and she flung herself in the driver's side, scrambling across his seat while he leapt in behind her.

He gunned the engine. Dirt sprayed up from the tires as the truck flew backward. Then he jammed it into drive, and it sprang forward.

"Turn right," she said, leaning forward, her hands clenching the dashboard as she searched the road ahead of them. White mist was drifting across the road, smoky tendrils that undulated as if they were alive. "The mist," she whispered, dread gripping her more tightly. "I didn't even think of it."

"Think of what?"

"The mist." She searched desperately ahead of them, praying that she wouldn't see a shadow flit across their path. "Most of the time, it's just innocuous fog, but sometimes, it's more. It hasn't been more for a really long time." Was that what David had wanted to talk to her about? What had he noticed? Of course he wouldn't have wanted to talk about it in front of Eric, an outsider. Who would believe the stories that coated this region? Even she didn't want to believe them, but she knew better. Her grandmother, Oba, had told her too much for her not to believe it.

"What do you mean, more?" The fog grew thicker, winding around the truck until they could barely see the road. Eric slowed the truck, his headlights reflecting uselessly off the water droplets coating the air.

"Don't slow down," she said urgently.

"I can't see—"

"I don't care! You have to keep going!"

Swearing under his breath, Eric obeyed. The truck hurtled onward, the tires spinning ruthlessly on the slippery dirt. Jordyn held her breath, her gaze riveted to the fog closing around them. "We have to get to my house. I mean, the house I grew up in." Even the words sent a chill racing through her. She didn't want to go back there. Ever. But there were things there that she needed, things that had been gathering dust for decades, things that her grandmother had warned her she would need someday.

She didn't want to need them.

"What the hell is going on?" Eric's flirty arrogance was gone, replaced by the steely focus of a man on high alert. "What was that thing growling?"

"I don't know for sure," she hedged.

He glanced over at her. "What do you *think* it was?"

She bit her lip, not even wanting to talk about it. No one in this town would ever talk about it. "Around here, people think it's bad luck to talk about it," she said.

"Talk about *what*?"

She sighed. "Evil." She waited for him to laugh or snort in derision.

He didn't. He simply nodded grimly. "What kind of evil?" He asked the question as if he knew. "A vampire? It was a vampire, wasn't it?"

"Vampire?" She looked out the window into the dark. "No, not *a* vampire. One particular vampire. Le Cicatrice. It means the one with the scar. For over four hundred years, he ravaged the area. He drained mostly young girls, and left them for dead. People started sending their daughters away to live with relatives. Then, the boys started disappearing...and then coming back as vampires. Nighttime became a time of terror..." She looked over at him. "Until he found a way to come out in the daylight. Then the real horrors began."

Tension flashed across Eric's face. "He's dead?"

"Yes." She looked out the window. "But my grandmother always said he wasn't really dead. She said that there are some vampires you can't ever kill. I used to hear that growl in my dreams, and my grandmother said he was trying to find an anchor to bring him back. He knew my name, and would whisper it to me. She always told me to wake up when I heard it, to take my mind back before he could own it." She hugged herself, still watching the fog. "I still don't sleep well," she said. "I'm afraid of sleep." Even in Walter's arms, she hadn't slept well. As powerful as Walter had been, the ancient vampire was something more evil, more powerful, and more terrifying. "The mist forms because the earth is disturbed by his presence." She bit her lip. "He can't be back," she whispered. "He can't be—" But even as she said it, a sudden, horrifying thought occurred to her.

She looked sharply at Eric, whose hands were tight around the steering wheel. "Could Tristan resurrect him?"

"I would have said no."

Oh, God. That wasn't the answer she'd been hoping for. "Except—"

He pulled his phone out of his pocket and flicked to an image. "I found this burial site," he said. "Tristan was there, and I think he resurrected whatever was in the grave."

She took the phone and studied the picture. With growing dread, she flipped through the images, until she came to the last one, a carving that was so battered it was barely recognizable...except that she knew what it was. The jagged tear. The sharp incisors. The drip of blood. "It's the sign of Cicatrice," she said. "It's the ward that one of the ancient voodoo queens created to protect against him." She looked up. "This headstone marks his grave, Eric."

"It's empty now. I checked it carefully."

"Oh, God." She sank back against the seat, holding her breath as the fog began to thin. A respite. A chance to recover. Not that it really mattered, because if Cicatrice was really hunting in the bayou again, there was nowhere safe. Not for anyone, but especially not for her.

"If Tristan resurrected him, what would he do to Tristan?" Eric asked.

She looked over at him. She didn't want to say it. But there was no way around it. "He'd turn him," she said thickly. "Tristan's ability to resurrect the dead would be a powerful asset. A lot of vampires were killed in this area at the time of Cicatrice's death. A reunion would probably be a great time for them." Numbly, she noticed they were coming up to a turn they needed to make. "Make a right up ahead," she said.

Eric swung the truck around the corner, the tires churning relentlessly on the gravel-covered road. "If Tristan has been converted, will he be evil? Can we save him?"

She looked out the window at the dark swamp as the trees flashed by. "My grandmother said there was always a chance."

"To bring him back from being a vampire?"

"No. He'll always be a vampire." God, Tristan, a vampire? She prayed they weren't too late. "But if his will is strong enough, he can fight the evil and hold onto his humanity, as long as he gets an anchor to hold him."

"What kind of anchor?"

She shook her head. "An emotional anchor. Someone he loves. Someone so pure and good, that they can help him fight it off."

Eric looked over at her. "He loves you."

"No." She hugged herself. "We're just friends."

"He resurrected you eight times. How much did it cost him?"

She thought back to how Tristan had been the last time she'd seen him. His face had been gaunt and gray. His hair had lost its luster, and he'd lost so much weight he'd looked like he was on the verge of death. "Almost his life," she said quietly.

"How long had you been dead?"

"Three days, the first time he did it. He came after me. He said he'd felt my death, and he came after me, but it took a few days to get there. After that, he pulled me back within minutes of my death each time."

Eric hit the brakes so hard that the truck skidded across the dirt before it stopped. "He *felt* your death?"

"That's what he said."

Eric swore under his breath and leaned his head back against the seat. "What are you doing, Tristan?" He muttered. "What the *hell* were you doing?"

"What?"

He looked over at her, as he started driving again. "The only way he could feel your death is if he connected the two of you on a metaphysical level. He bound you to him, Jordyn, which means your lives are intertwined. If he dies, you hold him in this life. If you die, he holds you in this life. He made you his anchor. Shit. No wonder he worked so hard to save you. He needed you alive."

"No." Jordyn felt sick, as if there was a noose tightening around her throat. "We were friends. He saved me because we were friends. He wouldn't have trapped me like that." She couldn't be bound to another man. Not to Tristan. She'd trusted

Walter, and he'd trapped her against her will. She'd trusted Tristan as well. "Why would he do that? It doesn't make sense."

Eric looked over at her, his face grim. "By using you as an anchor, whenever he drains himself too much doing a resurrection, he pulls on your life force. If he continues to resurrect people, he will drain you until you die."

She stared at him, her mind swiftly going back to the times over the last year when she hadn't felt well, or had been too tired to drag herself out of bed. No, that hadn't been from Tristan. It was just the ups and down of life, right? "No, he wouldn't—"

Eric slammed his fist into the steering wheel. "No, the brother I know wouldn't have done that, not without a damned good reason." He hit the gas, and the truck sped forward. "I'm going to find out what it is."

Jordyn sank back against the seat, her heart thundering in her chest as she gripped the door handle. Another man had trapped her? Tristan had saved her life. She *trusted* him. And he'd bound himself to her forever? "If he's been turned by Cicatrice and is working for him now—"

"He'll be resurrecting a lot of old vampires, I'm guessing." He didn't state the obvious, but they both knew it.

If Tristan was getting busy raising the dead, it would cost him. She could be dead within days. Hours, even, depending on how much Tristan drained her. A cold fear shivered down her spine. "We have to stop him. Cicatrice. Tristan. All of it." No longer was it about saving Tristan. If he were a vampire who had been co-opted by Cicatrice, there was no salvation for him. She had to kill him. It was the only way to end it. If he was working for Cicatrice, she had no choice. Tristan had to be stopped.

Kill the man who'd given her life, eight times?

How could she do that?

Why would he save her life at great cost to himself, only to then prey on her until she died? It didn't make sense that he'd saved her so he could siphon her life away. "Couldn't he have connected with someone else instead of me, if I'd died?"

"Technically, yes, but it wouldn't be easy. As long as you're alive, his ties are to you."

A chill flickered down her spine. "As long as I'm alive?"

"Yeah."

Oh, God. She didn't like the sound of that. "If he's working for Cicatrice, we have to kill him," she said quietly. "He won't be able to resist Cicatrice, and he's too powerful in his own right. He'll resurrect all the old vampires, the ones that are so dangerous."

Eric's hands tightened around the steering wheel. "We can't kill him."

Jordyn pulled her knees up to her chest. "I don't want to either. God, I don't want to. But we can't let him do this. We can't let him unleash that horror onto my town again." *Her* town? The possessive pronoun had tumbled instinctively from her lips, even though she'd rebelled so completely against the life she'd once had here. It was a place of nightmares and loss, but at the same time, her roots were here. Her grandmother, David, and even a few friends. She thought briefly of the blond-haired Skylar Morgan, who used to hide in the woods with Jordyn when her own dad became too violent. Skye had moved after several years, but they'd carved their initials into a tree in the swamp, forever declaring themselves sisters of the heart. This town was her past, and it had helped define her. The thought of it being torn apart by vampires made her feel sick, as if the loss of it would rip out what little foundation still supported her.

"Tristan isn't just my brother," Eric said grimly, drawing her attention back to the discussion. "He's my twin, and our spirits are intertwined." He looked over at her. "If he dies, then I die as well. We can't live without each other."

Horror congealed in her belly. *"What?"*

"As for him turning vampire..." Grimly, he ran his finger over his teeth, as if checking for fangs. "I don't know what that will do to me." He looked over at her. "We need to find him, and fast."

<hr/>

The silence in the truck spoke louder than words about the gravity of their situation.

Jordyn had fallen quiet after Eric's revelation that he would die if Tristan did. What else was there to say? If Tristan were a vampire, or even if he was simply under Cicatrice's control and resurrecting ancient vampires, she needed Tristan dead to free herself, and her town. He, on the other hand, needed Tristan alive. A conflict with no happy medium, unless they were lucky enough to discover Tristan was actually on vacation in the Caribbean. If that were the case, they could just focus on Cicatrice and call it a day…but yeah, the odds of that happening weren't looking too good.

"Go left here. This is the driveway." She glanced over at him. "Maybe he's not a vampire. Maybe he hasn't been taken over by Cicatrice."

"Yeah, maybe." He'd seen the gravesite, and he recognized his brother's work. The likelihood of a happy ending wasn't too promising. Grimly, he turned on his blinker and then swung into the rutted, dirt driveway.

The moment his tires crunched on the gravel, Jordyn tensed beside him. He glanced over at her, and saw that her face was pale. She was leaning forward, staring through the windshield, her fingers wrapped tightly around the door handle. She was biting her lower lip, and her eyes were wide as she frantically scanned the property.

He was no fool. Jordyn was scared, and he didn't like that. Scowling, his adrenaline surged, and he drew in energy from the air, preparing to do whatever it took to protect her. The magic swirled through him, otherworldly energy gifting him with its power, even as it sought to find a way to penetrate his defenses.

"There it is," she whispered.

Eric followed her gaze, then slowed the truck as his headlights illuminated a ramshackle cabin with broken windows and a boarded-up door. A rusted tin roof looked like it was ready to slide off at any moment, and the yard looked like a cemetery where used-up vehicles went to die. The shanty was on the edge of the swamp. His headlights were reflecting off the stagnant water and the reeds that guarded its shoreline. It was a place of misery and doom.

He eased the truck to a stop, but left the engine idling as he turned his bright lights on the shanty. A small rodent scurried out of sight behind a tire, but there was no other movement. "What is this place?"

"It's where I grew up."

Eric whistled softly as Jordyn opened the door and stepped out. He couldn't believe this confident, sassy woman had come from such hell. How had she dragged herself out of this beginning to become a woman strong enough to take down one of the most powerful Calydons of this century, and then survive the severing of the *sheva* bond? He'd been impressed with her since the first moment they'd met, but now? Shit. She was good. Really good.

"No wonder you're a survivor," he said. "Looks like a tough place for a kid."

She glanced over at him, surprise in her eyes. "It was worse when my father was alive. Now it's just an empty house."

"An empty house with memories. Don't underestimate the power of the past. It can choke the life out of you when you least expect it."

She cocked her head. "You say that like you've lived it."

He managed a cheeky grin. "Sweetheart, doesn't everyone have a skeleton in their closet?"

"Not everyone has a skeleton that can choke the life out of them on a moment's notice," she observed.

"Yeah, well, poor deprived bastards then, right?" Yeah, he knew she was digging for information, but he didn't want to talk about it. Instead, he reached into the back of his truck and pulled two flashlights out of his bag. He handed one to Jordyn as he climbed out. "I assume the electricity doesn't work anymore."

"I think that's a safe assumption." She sounded grim. "It didn't work much when I lived here." She started to walk across the yard, and he kept close behind her, flashing his light over the surroundings.

The light from a nearby house shone through the trees on his right, and he could hear voices laughing. To his left, he could just make out another house, one that was brightly lit and looked huge. "You lived next door to a mansion?"

"It wasn't there when I was a kid. The neighborhood is being upgraded. No developer wants this property though."

"Why not? Money talks, doesn't it?"

"So do rumors. Supposedly, this land is cursed."

He turned the light on her. "Cursed? As in a real curse?"

"Yep. Everyone who has ever owned this property has died in a pool of their own blood." Her face was pale and glowing in his beam. "Guess who owns it now?"

"You."

"Me." She managed a smile that didn't reach her eyes, then turned away to flash her light over a small headstone. "The best dog ever," she said softly. "She bit my dad three times, once so badly that he couldn't use his right hand for a month. I loved her so much. She was part pit bull and part Rottweiler. She used to sleep with her head on my stomach, and once I got her, my dad never messed with me again." She laughed softly. "Well, it wasn't until the third time she bit him that he figured it out. After she bit his thigh, less than an inch from his crotch, he learned his lesson well enough to remember it even when he was so drunk he couldn't recall his own name. He threatened to shoot her, and I just told him that I'd get another one, and that maybe the next one would bite him in the throat instead of the thigh." She grinned. "And I might have taught her to go for his crotch as well. Maybe."

"I can see you doing that." Eric couldn't believe the warm good humor in Jordyn's voice as she spoke of her dog. Clearly, her dad had been a complete piece of shit, and had probably laid a hand on her more than once, but she wasn't dwelling on that. Instead, she was telling stories about her dog and smiling. The woman was resilient and a fighter, no doubt about that. As he said...impressive. Riveting. Compelling. Sexy as hell. Every word out of her mouth heightened his attraction to her.

She deserved a good guy, a better guy than he was even on his best day, but he had a bad feeling that after a few more hours in her company, he wasn't going to care. He couldn't get her out of his head. He couldn't stop picturing her as a skinny kid, hiding from her roaring drunk of a father, hunkering down in the swamp with just a dog to protect her.

Well, that day was over. She didn't have a dog, but she had him. She'd come back to town to help him find Tristan, and there was no way in hell he was going to leave her unprotected, not from vampires or memories. No matter what. He glanced out at the woods around them, and sent a message to his brother. *Tristan, don't you dare hurt her and make me have to choose. You hear me?*

Silence.

After a lifetime of mental telepathy with his brother, there had been radio silence for a year, and he didn't like it.

Apparently oblivious to the protectiveness raging through him, Jordyn ran her toe over the ground in front of the grave. "Such a good girl," she said, her voice tinged with sadness. "I left home the day after she died, when I was sixteen. There was no reason to stay once she was gone."

Eric noted the heart etched on the old wooden headstone. Crooked, as if the hand that had carved it had been trembling with grief. Instinctively, he took a step toward her and set his hand on her lower back. He had no idea how to comfort her, but touching her felt like it made sense. "What was her name?"

She leaned into his touch, just barely, but he noticed. So, yeah, right call then.

"Molly." Jordyn shined the light around, and he saw a tattered tire swing hanging from a nearby tree. "David put that up for me. We used to swing out over the swamp and jump in. David, my friend Skye, and I."

He studied the thick, swampy area. "Seriously? What about gators?"

"The risk was part of the fun." She grinned at him, a sudden sparkle in her eye. "Aren't you a risk-taker?"

He was surprised by the change in her personality. They were in a brutally depressing place, and yet she seemed to be vibrating with more life and energy than he'd ever seen before. How did someone shine when surrounded by such hell? But there was no doubt about it. Something about her had shifted, and she was more confident and more self-assured. Was it the memory of a dog that had kicked ass and taken names on her behalf? Or the friend that had built her a swing? Or the recollection that she'd braved gators and won on numerous occasions? He didn't know, but somehow, in this mire of hell, she'd found strength.

And damn if that didn't make her even more attractive, which was great, of course, because he definitely needed to be even more into her than he already was, right? Not so much.

Shit. He was going to have to get her naked, wasn't he?

He was pretty sure he was.

Jordyn walked across the junkyard, her flashlight skimming over the carnage. "You know," she said, "I didn't want to come back here. I avoided returning to the house when I came back for my dad's funeral, but there's something about being here that feels good." She crouched next to a flat patch of dirt and ran her hand over it. "It just feels like a piece of me that's been missing suddenly came back to me." She glanced at him. "It doesn't make sense, does it? This was a terrible place for me, but I feel more complete being here."

He walked up beside her, still scanning his light over the woods around them. "It's home," he said. "It's your roots. It made you who you are today."

She let some dirt sift through her fingers. "But it was a bad home."

"With a loyal dog and a couple good friends, right?"

She smiled at him. "True." Wiping her hands, she stood up. "Where's your home, Eric? Where do you and Tristan come from?"

He shrugged. "We were dumped on the steps of an orphanage when we were three weeks old with a note that had our names and the fact that I was two hours older than Tristan. That's all we know."

Her brow furrowed. "So, what about Tristan's powers of resurrection? How did you find out about that?"

"The hard way. Little boys like to play in cemeteries." He grinned, remembering that day. "When that old man came out of the ground with a hatchet in his hand, I've never run so fast in my life. We were scared as hell. The dude was half-decayed and he disintegrated the moment Tristan starting running, but it gave us ideas, and after that, we started messing around. We did some cool shit, some really stupid shit, and a lot of stuff that ended up nowhere."

She cocked her head. "What about you? What do you do? Can you resurrect bodies, too?"

"Nope. I'm a spirit guy. Ghosts. Specters. That kind of stuff. I can summon the energy of spirits and use it to do things. It's kind of like magic, but my power comes from spirits. What I can do depends on the nature of the energy I harvest at that time. It can be a little dicey, but it usually works pretty well." He looked over his shoulder at the woods again. A faint layer of fog was rolling in. "Should we be moving on?"

She followed his glance, and hopped to her feet. "No, I need to get some stuff. Come this way." She hurried past him, and he followed her as she headed off down a trail behind the house. It seemed to lead straight into the swamp, but at the last moment, the path curved to the right so it went beside the mucky water. The trail was overgrown so thickly that he wound up pulling out his dagger and cutting a path for them. The farther they traveled, the quieter Jordyn became, and the darker the swamp became...except for the mist sliding over the surface of the water.

His hand on the hilt of his knife, he moved nearer to Jordyn. "Tell me how we kill Cicatrice, if he shows up. Beheading, fire, and a wooden stake?"

"No. Those won't kill him. They'll slow him down, but not finish him off." She shoved aside a huge branch, and suddenly they were in a clearing. He flashed his light around and saw an ancient wooden totem pole in the center of the clearing. Burn marks scarred the carvings, and the paint was old and faded. Bones lay in random designs around the base of it. Some of them were crumbling and gray, almost completely decomposed by the earth...but there was a small pile of them in a perfect pyramid, and the bones were gleaming white. Fresh and picked clean of all flesh. "Shit. Your grandmother didn't leave those, did she?"

"Those are new," Jordyn said, pointing to the pile of white bones. "Someone's been here." She whipped around, shining her light into the woods. "My grandmother died when I was ten. She was the last gifted magi in our family. I'm the only other one who can work this site."

"Apparently not." Tension slid down Eric's spine, and he dropped to his knee, shining his light on the earth. The ground was soft from the damp marsh, but there were no indentations. "No footprints," he said. "Do vampires leave footprints?"

"If they're walking, they do."

"And if they're...flying around like a bat?"

She laughed. "They don't turn into bats. That's such a

stereotype." She eased past Eric and into the clearing, giving the pyramid of bones a wide berth as she moved past it.

"So, the bats are a stereotype. They're all just vicious, blood-sucking monsters who will rip out your throat while their soulless bodies echo with the emptiness of their lack of humanity?"

She laughed again. "Something like that."

He grimaced. "I was joking." Well, he'd hoped he was. Apparently not.

He finally noticed the five-foot wide wooden shed that Jordyn was heading toward. It looked almost like a dilapidated outhouse, and an old, rusted padlock held it shut. A heavy spiritual energy surrounded it. There was a sense of warmth and safety, but it was intermingled with angry black jabs of pure evil. Something was inside that shed, something that was too damn close to being alive. "Jordyn, don't open that—"

Too late. With a few quick twists, Jordyn had already unlocked it and pulled the door open.

CHAPTER 7

"Wait!" Eric grabbed Jordyn's shoulder and yanked her back just as she opened the door.

She stumbled back as he jumped in front of her, his knife up. Thick energy clawed at her skin, and the hair lifted off the back of her neck. Eric was braced in the doorway, his body tense and ready.

There was a sudden screech, a howl so loud that Jordyn clapped her hands over her ears and went down on her knees. A black shadow burst out of the shed, streaking right at her. For a split second, she thought she saw a jagged, tormented face screaming as it raced toward her. Its incisors lengthened, and she scrambled back, fear tearing through her.

"No!" Eric shouted, and there was a sudden rush of wind. It tore through the clearing, grabbed the specter, and ripped the phantom away from her. It shrieked with agony as it was torn apart, its body dissolving into a thousand fragments.

The wind died down, and she saw Eric was down on his knee, one fist pointed at her, his other hand clamped around his forearm, as if he were supporting it. His face was a silvery gray, and shadows seemed to undulate over his skin. For a split second, she froze in terror, staring at him. "What are you?" she whispered.

Her voice seemed to jerk him back. He dropped his hands and stood up. Color flooded back into his face, and his eyes returned to their usual shade of brown. He strode over to her and crouched in front of her. "You okay?"

"Um, yeah." She touched her throat, half-expecting to feel that it had been torn apart by the specter that had come after her. It was fine, though. No damage, at least to her body. Her nerves, on the other hand, weren't doing so hot. "What was that?"

He brushed his hand through the air above her head, and her scalp tingled. "You're good. It didn't touch you." His face was grim. "What exactly was your grandmother into?"

"Why? What was it?" The bigger question was, what was *he*? For a split second, he'd seemed like a ghost himself, a creature from the beyond, hovering between the corporeal and a fate worse than death. "What just happened?"

He stood up and held out his hand to help her up. "Your grandmother trapped spirits," he said. "That was a bad one, and she'd trapped it between life and death. Being held in that place turned it into...something you won't want coming at you." He looked grim. "It used to be a form of torture reserved for those who deserved the most severe punishment, but the practice stopped many centuries ago when people learned it created a worse monster than they started with. It's not kind to do."

She stiffened. "My grandmother was a good person."

"Maybe she was, but I don't know many reasons that justify what she did to that spirit." He glanced over his shoulder at the shed. "It must have escaped its wards, but couldn't get out of the shed." He gestured with his fingers. "Come on. It's gone now. I'll check and see if there are any more."

She hesitated, almost afraid to take his hand, suddenly remembering that moment in the jungle when he'd said that he wasn't a man, not really. "What are you, Eric?"

His face was cold and hard. "You don't want to know, Jordyn. No one wants to know." He leaned over and grabbed her hand, hauling her to her feet.

His hand was warm and reassuring around hers, and she swallowed at the unexpected surge of comfort she felt from having her hand in his. "You're not human."

He pulled her toward him with a sudden jerk that knocked her off balance. She fell against him, and sucked in her breath at the feel of his hard body against hers. That same surge of desire cascaded through her, but this time, it was laced with the fear of the unknown, apprehension about the man behind the mask that she now knew he was wearing. Her fingers dug into his chest, and she wasn't sure if it was to push him away or bring him closer. "Eric—"

His fingers slid through the hair on the back of her head, gripping lightly. Anger shone in his eyes. "I don't give a shit what anyone thinks of me," he said softly, his tone edged with flint. "I really don't. But I just learned that I don't like it when you look at me like I'm a monster. Turns out, it matters what *you* think of me."

She swallowed. "I don't think you're a monster."

"That's the thing, Jordyn. I am one." Then he bent his head and kissed her.

It was more than a kiss. It was a sensual assault meant to throw her so off balance she couldn't even think straight. His mouth was demanding and hot, his tongue a sinful temptation, his breath a whispered seduction as it feathered through her.

It wasn't the kiss of a monster. It was the kiss of a man so sexual that his very essence as a male plunged right into her soul and wove desire through every inch of her body. She slid her hands up his arms, over his shoulders, and then locked them behind his neck, unable to do anything but respond to the fires that he had so ruthlessly stoked inside her.

A sensual growl sounded low in his chest, so deep that she felt it reverberate through her. He palmed her waist, his hands spread across her hips like he owned her body. Her skin felt like it was on fire, a blazing trail marking everywhere his hands touched. He gripped her butt, lifting her against him so her belly was crushed against his pelvis. She could feel his cock against her stomach, so hard that her body clenched in response.

God, yes, she wanted this man. This arrogant, beautiful, tormented man with secrets so terrible she'd seen them in his eyes when he'd driven off the specter. He was a man without a history or roots, a vagabond who had forged his way through life playing in cemeteries with a brother who could raise the dead.

He was every bit as dangerous as Walter, who had killed everyone who mattered to her. Eric was more, and worse, because she didn't understand him or even know what he was capable of. He was a man she should fear, a man she should shun, and yet all she wanted was to feel his hands on her body and lose herself in the sheer power of his presence.

"Jordyn," he whispered her name into the kiss as he grasped her thighs and lifted her up. Her legs went around his hips as he took two steps. Then her back was against a tree, and he was crushed against her, driving into her through their clothes as the kiss turned from hot to deadly.

She couldn't get enough of him. The fire burning through her was unlike anything she'd ever experienced. It was heat. It was lust. It was need. It was an insatiable craving for more, more, more, but she couldn't even articulate what it was that she needed from him.

He slipped his hand beneath the hem of her shirt, and palmed her bare back. She gasped as his fingers spread across her, a sensual caress of skin against skin. He locked one arm around her back, protecting her from the bark of the tree. He anchored her against him as he slid his hand over her ribs, tracing each bone as he moved his hand higher. He deepened the kiss, overwhelming her senses in a thousand different ways.

Then his hand closed over her breast. She gasped as desire rolled through her, a need so visceral she couldn't even breathe. He pinched her nipple, making her writhe as tendrils of wet heat coiled through her, like the flashes of lightning bisecting the sky on a hot summer night. She tugged at his shirt, frantic for more as she jerked it up, exposing his chest. His body was so hard and warm beneath her hands, and he sucked in his breath as she ran her hands over his muscular torso.

"God, that feels good," he whispered as he broke the kiss and began to trail his mouth hungrily down the side of her neck. "I want your hands all over every inch of my body."

The image of his naked body at her mercy leapt into her mind, and the sexual tension that had been gripping her so fiercely seemed to explode. "*Eric.*" She flung her arms around his neck and hauled him against her. The kiss was feral and dangerous, unleashing passion inside her that she didn't know existed.

He groaned again, a growl so deep and unearthly that it sent chills racing down her spine. Not a ripple of fear. It was more like pulsing, sensual anticipation of the wildness of the man in her arms, of what he could do to her if he stopped holding back.

Her nipples were aching with need, and her muscles convulsed every time he pinched them. Lightly at first. Then harder. Sensual pleasure edged with just enough pain to make her gasp. Then he shifted, moving his hands to her thighs. He began a slow, sensual caress as he slid his hands up her leg, raising her skirt higher and higher, baring her skin.

Her heart hammered in terrified anticipation as his hands closed around her buttocks, his finger sliding beneath the edge of her underwear. His thumb brushed over her clitoris ever so slightly, and she jumped, gasping in startled surprise at the sensations that ripped through her. Oh, God, what was she doing? She couldn't do this. Not with him. Not with anyone. "Eric, stop."

His hand stilled, his palm resting gently against the juncture of her thighs. He broke the kiss, but didn't move his head, so their foreheads were resting against each other, their noses still touching, their lips barely a breath apart. They were both breathing heavily, and she was trembling. "I'm not ready for this," she said, even as she tightened her grip on him, her hands entwined around his neck.

He let out his breath, and said nothing, his hands still on her body, hot and tempting against her flesh.

"Eric?"

"Give me a sec," he said, his voice so deep and raspy that chills shivered down her arms. "I have to pry my libido out of my brain. It takes a minute or two."

She almost laughed at his reply, the tension easing from her body. Eric might be part monster of some sort, and he might be a temptation that was far too dangerous to play with, but at the same time, he was still just Eric, the ridiculously charming man who made her laugh with his irreverence.

He finally lifted his head, and looked at her. His eyes were a turbulent swirl of emotions, and her belly immediately tightened at the realization that he hadn't been joking. His need for her was stark on his face, a desire so powerful that it made her want to melt into his arms right then and there and let him fulfill his every fantasy with her body.

"You're trouble," he commented.

"You're the one who's trouble."

His gaze went to her hair, which he oh-so-gently brushed off her face in the most tender of gestures. "No, sweetheart, I'm way past trouble on that spectrum. But you..." His attention settled on her face. "I'm going to have to make love to you," he said. "There's no other possibility."

She swallowed, her body suddenly awash with a tantalizing warmth. "No sex," she said. "We have to find Tristan—"

"I know we do. But my brother isn't the only thing I need to address." His face was dark, almost moody. "As it turns out, it appears that one of the things I need is you." There was such an edge to his voice that she shivered.

"Should I be afraid?"

"Yeah, probably." His gaze went to her mouth, and she instinctively licked her lips.

"Don't," she warned him. "Don't look at me like that."

He met her gaze again. "Can't help it." But even as he said it, he finally stepped back, lifting her away from the tree. He slowly, tantalizingly, lowered her to the ground, his hands sliding along her thighs and hips as he eased her down.

Her feet hit the ground, and her legs felt shaky and weak. She wanted to grip his arms, but instead she made herself release him. Instinctively, she folded her arms across her chest. "I don't want this to happen between us," she said.

"Are you so sure?" His eyes were burning hot, and she could see shadows swirling across them, just like she'd seen on the blade of his knife and on his skin, after he'd saved her from the ghost.

She swallowed. "Eric, I told you. I don't want this."

"Yeah, I know." He leaned forward, into her space. "But I do. One of us isn't going to get what we want."

His words hung in the air, a challenge so replete with sensuality and tension that she felt it prickle across her skin. What could she say to that? Because part of her wanted him so badly she could feel her need for him etched in every cell in her body, and she was sure he knew it. "I'm broken when it comes to relationships," she said. "My scars run too deep."

"I don't want a relationship. I just want you."

She frowned, her hands going to her hips. "You just want to have sex with me? Just satisfy your lust and then call it a day?"

He said nothing for the longest time, his eyes boring into hers so intently she felt as if he were stripping her raw. Then finally, he inclined his head ever so slightly. "Yeah, that's all I want."

Hurt twisted in her heart. "Well, that's not okay—"

"You said, if it was only sex between us, that would be fine. As I recall, your logic was that sex becomes a problem when it's more than just mindless rutting. Or is my memory flawed? Because I don't think it is."

She bit her lip as he threw her words back at her. Yes, of course, that was what she'd said, but she'd meant it from her perspective. If she wanted emotional connection, and he gave her only sex, it would break her. There was no way to lie to herself. Despite all her trauma over Walter, and her terror of becoming emotionally invested in another man, Eric was getting under her skin. Sex with him would put her over the limit. "Don't you know anything about women?"

He cocked an eyebrow. "You're asking a guy if he knows anything about women? Don't you know that to men, women are like this bottomless pit of mystery that we will never figure out, no matter how many centuries we live?"

She felt the inane urge to laugh again. "Stop it!" She smacked him in the chest. "Stop making me laugh! It's so annoying!" She glared at him as he opened his mouth again, no doubt to disarm her with more audacity. "Here's the deal on women. We equate sex with love, so if you and I have sex, it will make me emotionally attached to you, and I can't do that. Got it?" There. That was crystal clear. Even the most Neanderthal male couldn't fail to understand that logic.

He studied her. "What if I'm really bad?"

"Bad?" she echoed, trying to follow his thought processes. "What are you talking about?"

"What if I'm really bad at sex? What if I completely forget about foreplay, slobber too much when I kiss you, and have a really great orgasm before you're even in the game? Then, I could fall asleep while you're trying to talk to me, and roll away from you when you want to snuggle." His face brightened. "Oh, and I could even shout another woman's name while I climax. Or several women, even. I could just get a phone book and start going through names while I came. Would that work? That kind of sex wouldn't get to you, would it?" He grinned at her. "Want to try it that way?"

She stared at him. "Are you serious?"

His face was deadpan. "I'm always serious about sex, Jordyn. There's nothing more important in my life than having sex with women who make me so crazy that I can't even think when I'm around them, or hear their voice, or inhale that sweet, tantalizing fragrance that makes every muscle in my body clench the moment I smell it. And by women, I mean, of course, you. Your scent. Your voice. Your kiss. Your lips." He shrugged. "Yeah, pretty much, sex with you is all that matters, and I'll be completely willing to utterly suck at sex if that will make you happy. You in?" He held out his hand, his expression still completely serious.

Then, she saw the corner of his mouth twitch ever so slightly. She burst out laughing, and slapped his hand away. "Who are you kidding? Your ego is so huge that you'd never be able to make yourself bad at sex. What if I told people?" She eyed him. "You would promise me bad sex, and then completely break your promise and be totally amazing, wouldn't you? You'd probably give me seventeen orgasms in five minutes just from foreplay alone."

He pursed his lips. "Seventeen in five minutes? I admit, I'm great at oral sex, but seventeen in five minutes might be a challenge. Six minutes though, no problem." His eyes gleamed with sudden heat. "Is that a challenge? Because I'm up for it."

Her belly immediately clenched, and heat pooled between her legs as the image of Eric bringing her to climax repeatedly through oral sex flashed into her mind. Seriously. Really? Argh! No! Dammit. How had the conversation turned all the way back to making her want him again? "Just shut up." She shoved past him, ignoring his deep chuckle, and headed into the apparently haunted shed that held her grandmother's legacy. "We have vampires to deal with, remember? We don't have time for sex."

"Rumors say vampires are great at sex," Eric commented as he followed her across the clearing. "Seduction, passion, and that bloodlust thing. It's supposed to be pretty wild."

She glanced back over her shoulder at him. "Didn't you hear me tell you to be quiet?"

"Sure did." He grinned at her. "But I like pushing your buttons. You're sexy as hell when you put me in my place. I like it."

"Oh, for heaven's sake." She rolled her eyes at him, but couldn't keep the smile off her face as she approached the shed. She loved how he made her laugh, and his incessant comments about how much he wanted her felt good. He made her feel beautiful, funny, talented, and desirable, and she didn't have the willpower not to appreciate it. It had been a long time since anything had made her want to smile, and Eric seemed to have the knack for bringing her laughter when she needed it most.

She sighed. She was in trouble, wasn't she? Really deep trouble, and not just from vampires.

⊠⊠⊠⊠

Jordyn decided it was time to focus on the brother who didn't make her want to tear her clothes off and beg him to ravage her. Tristan needed her help, and heaven help her, so did her entire town if Cicatrice, or other vampires, had come back to reclaim her town.

Ignoring Eric as he shadowed her so closely that she could feel the heat of his body, Jordyn walked back over to her grandmother's shed and opened the door again. It had banged shut after the encounter with the spirit that her grandmother had apparently trapped.

Was Eric right? Had Oba been involved with something more than what she'd shared with Jordyn? After all their hundreds of hours together, Jordyn knew there were secrets her grandmother hadn't shared, secrets she'd planned to tell, but that had disappeared forever the day she died. "What didn't you tell me, Oba?" she whispered. "What do I need to know?"

There was no answer from the darkness, and Jordyn was suddenly viscerally aware of the absence of her grandmother's protective energy that had always cloaked her whenever she'd come. Instinctively, she looked over her shoulder at the clearing. The night was dark. The moon was casting eerie shadows across the swamp. Small pockets of fog hung suspended over the water. Not moving. Just waiting.

She had a sudden urge to retrieve her items and then leave the area as fast as she could. This wasn't the safe sanctuary it had once been. She thought of the fresh bones on the altar, and knew it was time to get her things and get out. "I'll just grab some stuff," she told Eric as she stepped up to the door. "It'll just be a second."

Then she turned and looked inside the room that she hadn't been in for more than a decade, the place where she had been protected by an old woman's magic and love long ago. Unexpected tears surged as her gaze fell upon the old, well-worn leather satchel that her grandmother had always, *always* had by her side, now sitting alone and forgotten on a dusty shelf.

Oba's bag of tricks, as she used to call it. It was slouched on the center shelf, packed and ready, as it always was. How well she remembered sitting out in the woods with her grandmother, watching avidly as the grizzled old lady explained every item in the bag, painstakingly making Jordyn repeat all the instructions back to her until she was certain that Jordyn knew every rule.

Her grandmother had been her respite, the only love she'd ever known growing up. She'd never once come to Jordyn's house, but she was always in the woods, always findable whenever Jordyn had needed her. Her cabin, the one she actually lived in and called home, was deep in the bayou, and Jordyn had seen it only one time, when she'd followed her grandmother one night. It had been a small cabin, simple but sturdy, and much homier than Jordyn's shanty had ever been. She'd knocked on the door, preparing to ask her grandmother if she could live with her.

That hadn't gone well. It was the only time she'd ever seen her grandmother angry, furious that Jordyn had come to the cabin. She'd never gone back, and they'd never spoken about it again.

The day that Jordyn had come to this clearing and found her grandmother sitting upright, her eyes open, and her hands clasped over her heart, it had taken her a full minute before she'd realized she was dead. Gone forever.

David had helped bury her, and they'd chosen a site deep in the swamp, as her grandmother had wished. Easing through the bayou on that old boat, with her grandmother's sightless eyes staring at her, had been a memory that had haunted her for years.

No one had known she'd died. To everyone else, she'd been nothing more than an old woman who had faded back into the earth that she'd thrived upon. Only Jordyn had mourned her. The rest of the world had continued on as it always had. Her father had never even acknowledged that her grandmother existed, and maybe he hadn't even known she did. Jordyn's mother had died when she was two, and her father had refused to discuss anything about her, leaving Jordyn to piece together what hidden elements of her past that she could. Even her grandmother had refused to talk much about Jordyn's mom, saying only that when the time was right, Jordyn would have the answers she sought.

But then Oba had died.

And now...Jordyn was back at the shed, crossing the threshold she'd never dared traverse before. She'd never opened the shed herself. She'd never trespassed on her grandmother's realm. But now, it was time. As she reached for the sack she could almost hear Oba hollering at her not to touch the bag. "It's my time now, Oba," she whispered as her fingers closed around the faded leather strap.

She lifted it, surprised by the weight of it. It was lighter than she remembered.

"What's in here?" Eric's voice was so close behind her that she jumped.

She spun around, startled to see him in the doorway, his shoulders filling up the narrow space as if he owned it. "I forgot you were there."

He cocked an eyebrow. "I give you my best kiss, and three minutes later, I'm invisible? Clearly, I'm going to have to up my game. I'm retracting my offer to give you bad sex. It would crush me forever if I wasn't your greatest fantasy come true." But even as he teased her, he was scanning the inside of the shed, rapidly assimilating every detail about the small space. "This looks like a shrine in here."

"It was my grandmother's office, in a way." Jordyn

shoved the bag at Eric. "Hold this for me."

He took the bag, but her fingers brushed against his as she handed it over. Electricity seemed to spark through her at the contact, and she jumped back. "Was that you? What did you do?"

"I didn't do anything." he said. "It just happens with you. I noticed it before." He studied her. "I should ask you what it is."

"It's not me." Was it? She didn't know. All she knew was that every time he touched her, her entire body hummed with awareness, even when they were ensconced in this tiny shed in the middle of the woods. She glared at him. "Stop touching me."

He grinned. "I don't think I can promise that. You're just so touchable."

She couldn't stop the sizzle of anticipation that tingled through her, and she quickly turned away, focusing on gathering some small burlap bags that were scattered on the shelves. She crouched and ran her hands over the wooden floor. She found the right board on her second pass. Excitement pulsed through her as she pressed her finger into the tiny indentation on the top right corner. She grinned at Eric as the board popped out. "I feel like a deviant little girl breaking into forbidden territory. I was never allowed to open this, but she showed me how in case I ever needed to."

Eric was standing in the doorway, watching the woods, shining his light into the clearing. He glanced at her, then into the hole in the floor. "What's in there?"

She reached inside, grimacing at the cobwebs wrapping around her fingers. Then she touched the leather-bound book that her grandmother had hidden away. She pulled it out and held it up. "This."

He shined his light over it. "There's no title. What is it?"

"Secrets." The secrets she'd never known. It was time. Jordyn stood up, clutching the precious book to her chest. "Let's go. We need to get out of the woods."

"You got what you need?" He stepped back just enough to let her pass by, and her shoulder brushed against his chest as she passed. She glanced up at him, but he was looking past her, still watching the woods.

She followed his glance and saw that a layer of fog was spreading across the swamp. The innocuous little pockets were coming alive, and that wasn't a good thing. "Yeah, time to go."

She led the way, and they were running by the time they reached the truck. Eric handed her the bag as he started the engine, and then he peeled out, the vehicle humming as he sped along the dirt road. "Go left," she said. "Back to town. We need to get away from the bayou tonight."

Eric did as she instructed, and she looked back over her shoulder, watching as her childhood faded from sight. Just as they rounded a corner, she thought she saw movement, and she caught her breath.

Jordyn waited for a long moment, watching behind them to see if anything emerged out of the darkness to follow them. She thought she saw a shadow streak across the road, and she jumped, gripping the headrest. "Please, no," she whispered.

She continued to watch the road, but nothing else appeared. Not even a rat scurried across the road in the moonlight. It was empty. She waited for several minutes, but she saw nothing else. With a sigh of relief, she turned back toward the front. She must have imagined it.

Eric glanced over at her. "You thought you saw a shadow move?"

She nodded. "I'm a little edgy. It was nothing."

"I don't think so."

She tensed as she looked at him. "Why not?"

"Because I saw it, too."

"You did?" She spun around in her seat, staring behind them again. Her heart was pounding. "What did you see? Was it a specter like the one that came out of the shed?"

"No." The tires hummed along as he picked up the pace. "It was the size of a man, moving faster than any human can move."

She stared at him. "Vampire?"

His fingers were tight on the wheel. "I don't know. I'm guessing that would be bad, if it was?"

"Yes, you could say that."

"Then let's hope it was a bunny rabbit."

She looked over her shoulder again, searching the road

behind them. She saw nothing but dark shadows and haunting mist, an ominous stillness. "Just in case it wasn't, I think you better drive faster."

He said nothing, but he hit the gas, and the truck leapt forward, its tires the only sound as they sped through the darkness. The trees were thick around them. The night was heavy. And she knew they weren't alone.

CHAPTER 8

Agonizing pain thundered through Tristan Hunter's skull.

He gripped his head, fighting against the searing agony. The invisible vice seemed to close tighter and tighter, unseen claws that could crush his head with ease. "Stop," he gasped, his voice hoarse from screaming as he hunched over.

His coffee cup lay on the floor, the pale brown liquid oozing across the wood, the china in shattered white fragments. The small safe house he'd discovered twelve months ago to protect him from Cicatrice was moldy and old, filled with anti-vampire paraphernalia that had stopped the ancient vampire from attacking him mentally...at first.

The protection had been lessening recently. Cicatrice's psychic attacks had become more and more violent and powerful. Tristan wasn't sure if Cicatrice was becoming stronger, if the protection was waning, or more ominously, if the anti-vampire wards were now affecting him and weakening him.

Cicatrice amped up the attack, and white light flashed through Tristan's mind. The master vampire flooded Tristan with images of haunted faces staring at death, bodies torn and bloodied, ripped apart by ruthless menace. Tristan knew he was seeing the victims that he was supposed to create, once he succumbed to the vampirism trying to take him.

"No!" The scream tore from his throat, a soundless shriek of agony that seemed to wrench his body in half as he fell to his knees.

His veins burned with acid, and his stomach felt like it was made of razor blades, sawing away at his intestines. He gasped and hunched over, fighting for each breath, struggling for control of his mind. The pain intensified in his brain, a brutal, vicious assault that was so relentless he wanted to rip off his own head to escape it.

You are not finished, Tristan.

The voice was like a sharp edged knife, and he flinched. *Get away from me, you piece of shit.*

You are mine.

Never! He shouted his denial, and then was blasted with pain so violent that he collapsed completely, screaming desperately. He squeezed his eyes shut, and flung himself sideways, rolling across the floor toward the fireplace. His back hit the stones that were covered in anti-vampire runes, and instantly, the pain crushing his mind lessened ever so slightly as the runes reacted to the part of Cicatrice that was trying to merge with him.

Tristan pressed his back tighter up against the carved stones, gasping for breath as cool relief flooded his body.

Your path is inevitable, Tristan Hunter. I cannot be denied. The voice scraped relentlessly through his mind.

Fuck you. Tristan dragged his hand above his head, and slammed his palm against the engraving on the top stone.

But this time, unlike every prior time, he didn't get a welcome relief as he pressed his palm to the ward. Pain sizzled through his hand and smoke rose from his charred flesh. Cold realization shot through him. He was losing his grip on his humanity and succumbing to the haunted beast within him. Once he became fully consumed by the vampire he was becoming, the wards would hurt him the way they did Cicatrice.

Soon his shelter would provide no relief. Soon, there would be no protection from Cicatrice at all. But right now, he was still going to claim his damned humanity. Grimly, he kept his hand on the powerful ward, refusing to succumb to the pain. His upper lip curled as he summoned the discipline not to break away from the rune meant to destroy what he was becoming.

He would not give up on his humanity that easily. If there was one sliver of it left that the ward could protect, he was going to give it that chance. So, even as his flesh burned and charred ash fell from his palm, he kept his hand pressed against the carved symbol, waiting for it to do its magic.

He fought to keep his grip on the carved stone. Cicatrice fought for control of his mind. Pain tore through him, and he felt like a thousand needles were plunged deep inside his brain, threading all the way through every cell in his head.

There are more to be resurrected. We are not finished!

Tristan reinforced his mental shields, but Cicatrice's grip on his mind was still tight. He could feel the pressure of the vampire as it tried to possess Tristan's will and force him to bend to his commands.

He didn't.

He just fucking hung in there, summoning the will to fight for another second. And then another. "Come on," he gritted out. "Come on!" By sheer force of will, Tristan twisted around, so he was facing the wall. His chest was pressed up against the carved stones, and the smell of his burning flesh was thick in the air. He scanned the wall, searching for another stone. He saw another, with a ward carved deep into the flesh of the rock.

With a roar, he hauled himself up and slammed his other hand down on it. The addition of the extra protection against his bare flesh sent shocks of agony ricocheting through him as the stone attacked him. Cicatrice howled with rage, and then he withdrew abruptly from Tristan's mind.

He was free.

Just for now, but free was free, a blessed relief.

Completely drained, Tristan released the rocks and slumped against the hearth, sprawled across the rocks as his mind became his own again, reclaimed by the carvings that protected the world from the darkest evil.

Jesus. And he'd thought resurrecting Jordyn had been a battle. Surviving an ancient vampire determined to possess him was…shit…he wasn't going to lie. It was a little tough.

With a low groan, he opened his eyes and gazed across the wooden floor that had become his sanctuary and his prison for the last twelve months. He'd stumbled across it when he was on the run from Cicatrice, and he'd been using it as his base ever since, always keeping it close enough to access if Cicatrice found him. Somehow, the magic in the house made it impossible for Cicatrice to track him, and whenever he walked in the door, the bloodlust in his own mind eased, and he could think like himself. Was it the runes? The bags of powder spread around? A magical protection woven into the boards? He didn't know what it was, but the haven was the only reason he hadn't succumbed to the lunatic's commands.

From what Tristan could gather, it was an old temple or shrine of sorts, created by a faction of extremists determined to rid the world of vampires. From each filthy, cracked window frame hung a cross. Lining the walls were racks with dozens and dozens of wooden stakes and the same number of bags of pale powder. Every inch of the exterior walls was covered in the same symbol that he'd just used against Cicatrice, the ancient symbol to protect against vampires. If he ever met any of the original creators, he'd have to tell them that the wards were pretty damned powerful.

Strength already beginning to return to his immortally-jacked-up body, Tristan shoved himself to a seated position. He wrapped his arms around his torso, unable to stop the shivering that had become an ever-present part of his existence. He could feel his ribs beneath his shirt, and his stomach churned from the coffee he'd been drinking in a pathetic attempt to cling to some remnant of humanity, before the attack by Cicatrice.

He stared grimly at the staked walls, dark knowledge settling deep inside him. He was out of time. The wards were becoming his enemy, and Cicatrice was becoming more ruthless by the day. The battle between them was coming, and Tristan had yet to figure out how the hell to defeat him.

Summoning the last remains of his energy, he stood up and trudged across the floor toward the wall. His legs were shaking, weakened by both the attack and the fact he hadn't eaten in weeks. No, not eaten. *Fed.*

Just the thought of feeding made hunger pulse through him, that dark and dangerous hunger that always started deep inside his soul and oozed through him like an unstoppable plague, becoming stronger and stronger until he lost the ability to control it.

But not yet. He had a few more hours until it took him. Cicatrice's attack had stolen precious time from him. Before the attack, he'd had at least another few days. Now? Hours.

At first, he'd been able to go for months between feedings. Human food had still tasted good. He'd believed he had it under control. He'd been arrogant enough to actually think that he would not end up like the others. He'd broken into a couple blood banks and left cash in exchange for the bags of blood he'd taken, and then had busted ass searching for the man who had set him up and commissioned the resurrection of Cicatrice. That man had answers. That man would know how to stop the monster he'd released.

He'd worked tirelessly, driving himself to exhaustion as he'd hunted for the man who had betrayed him and caused him to unleash such a terror onto the earth. But with each passing day, human food had become less palatable. The blood in the plastic bags had become less capable of diffusing the urge to hunt. The temple had provided less relief each time he walked inside. The bagged powder that had cleared his head so completely each time he sprinkled it on his skin had become less and less helpful. Night had become more energizing. Daytime had started to drain him. And the howling emptiness inside him had grown stronger and stronger.

Until the day he'd finally fed on a human being for the first time.

It had been beyond words. Horrifying. Intoxicating. And dangerous as hell, because the moment he'd tasted fresh blood, the warmth of its life-giving nourishment, he knew nothing else would ever suffice again.

He had crossed that line, and each time he fed, the hunger grew stronger. It was a need to kill his prey, not just feed on them.

Swearing, Tristan jerked his mind away from the thought, and the cravings it stirred up inside him. He had to focus. He had a mission, one that he had to accomplish before he became a monster that had to be hunted down and destroyed, just like Cicatrice.

Cicatrice.

He would never forget the moment he'd first seen

Cicatrice's face when he erupted from the ground with a scream of ungodly hunger that even now made his hair stand on end. Tristan would never forget that look on the vampire's face. Pure evil. Pure hunger. And unadulterated triumph.

He'd had only a split second to see his face before Cicatrice had attacked. The next thing Tristan knew, he'd woken up beneath two tons of dirt, his throat barely healed from being torn apart, and a hunger for human blood screaming through his veins.

Not that there was any point in dwelling over it. He was what he was, and he had to focus on the actions he could take now to stop what he'd begun.

He reached the south wall of the cabin and set his palms over the carvings on the wood. Smoke immediately began to pour from his palms, and the smell of burning flesh assaulted his nostrils. He jerked his hands back, leaving burned handprints on the wooden wall. The wooden ones had never really worked before, even to keep Cicatrice out.

Apparently, he was getting more simpatico with his vampire side, as he'd feared. Time was running out for him.

He stepped back as the howling emptiness within him grew stronger, a gaping void that had been a part of him since that moment he'd first awoken, buried a hundred feet beneath the earth.

Tristan sank back into the chair he'd been sitting on and pressed his forehead to his hands, his mind swiftly calculating all the facts to figure out his next move. His muscles were taut, adrenaline hammering through him. Hunger gnawed ruthlessly at him, but he didn't move. He held himself still by sheer force of will, refusing to surrender to the monster trying to control him. The void within him was like a wasteland of emptiness, an untenable hollow so strong that what was left of his humanity could barely withstand its pull.

His jeans were caked with mud and blood, and his feet were bare. His shirt hung in tatters from his gaunt frame, all that was left of who he'd been before Cicatrice had sprung from the grave. His breath was rasping in his lungs, and his muscles ached. He ran his tongue over his sharp teeth, and that same hunger surged through him again.

Slowly, Tristan raised his head and looked at the mirror hanging on the wall between two carvings. His reflection was barely visible now, but there was no mistaking the paleness of his flesh and the gaunt shadows of his cheeks. His eyes were a bottomless black, haunted and tormented. He pressed his lips shut, but he knew full well the power of his incisors. He knew what it felt like to sink them into human flesh and feel the rush of power that flooded him.

He hadn't killed yet, but he'd come close. Last time, he almost hadn't been able to stop himself. Last time, a woman had almost died. For some reason, he could feed only on women. Never men. Never scum-sucking bastards who deserved to serve themselves up as a snack to a depraved monster. If that's who he fed on, he might even be okay with it.

But it wasn't. Females only, and never the same one twice. It was as if he were hunting for the right one, the one that would truly fill the emptiness inside him. Shit. He needed answers about who he was and what he was becoming, but the only vampire he knew wanted to possess his mind and turn him into his minion, so he wasn't going to invite him out for a beer and some guy time.

A minion. A vampire wanted to make him a minion. Really? This was his life? Unreal.

But real. Yeah...he was really looking forward to getting together with Cicatrice. Maybe they'd exchange a few laughs over some bourbon, do the male bonding thing, and then try to crush each other. A thousand-year-old vampire against one that was less than a year old. Brawn versus brain. Or...something like that.

Grimly, Tristan eyed the largest stake on the wall, a long, wooden one covered with ancient engravings. It bled power, the kind of old-world power that hummed when he neared it. The other wooden stakes were just pieces of wood. Useless against him. He'd jabbed a few through his hand just to test them, and the hole had closed up within moments.

But the center stake was different. He'd tried to touch it twice, but he hadn't even been able to get close enough to grip it. The power emanating from it was intense, and incredibly dangerous.

Would it be enough to take down Cicatrice?

Slowly, he stood up and walked over to it. He studied it for a moment, inspecting the carvings on it. He picked up one of the small sacks placed around the corners of the room and dumped the powdered contents out onto the floor. He wrapped the burlap around his hand as protection, then grasped the stake. Sparks leapt into his hand, and he steeled himself against the pain as he took it down. This stake was special, he knew. This stake would do the job.

He turned it over in his hand, his body tensing as the ancient weapon hummed louder. The vibration was just the right pitch to set his teeth on edge, and he knew that was intentional. It was a vampire stake. One designed to kill monsters like him.

Testing it, he turned it so the end of the stake hovered above his chest, over his heart. He angled it so the tip pointed directly at his heart. Pain exploded through him instantly, and he gasped. The stake fell from his hand, landing with a clatter on the floor. He went down on his knees, his hand pressed over his chest as he fought to stay conscious.

It took several minutes before he recovered enough to drag himself away from the stake. With each yard he put between himself and the weapon, the humming became less agitated and urgent, and the pain diminished.

When he finally reached the far side of the temple, he sat down, using the wooden wall to prop himself up. He realized his hand was still over his chest. Curious, he pulled it away to inspect the damage. A black burn mark in the shape of the vampire ward was seared into his chest.

Oh, hell, that couldn't be good. He leaned over, grabbing a fistful of dirt from the pile he'd brought inside. He packed it over the wound, and then closed his eyes. The mark began to tingle, and a healing warmth formed under the dirt.

Yeah, the things he'd figured out about himself over the last year: drink blood, heal with dirt, and stay away from enchanted wooden stakes. Not exactly what he'd been hoping to learn when he'd embarked on his quest to find out what he was and where he came from.

As the dirt worked its magic, Tristan opened his eyes and studied the stake, which was still on the floor. It had marked him without even touching his flesh? What would it do if it were plunged into the heart of a vampire?

He had a good idea of the result. A part of him was tempted to shove the thing into his chest and not become the creature that was inexorably taking him over.

But that would be the easy out, the one that didn't take responsibility for the vampire making this town its hunting ground. And there was his brother to consider. If he used it on himself, Eric would die. But if he didn't use it, and he became like Cicatrice...how many would die because of him?

None. *None.* He was stronger than that. *He was stronger.* He had to find a way to stop Cicatrice, and himself. He knew it was time to confront Cicatrice. The longer he delayed, the tighter the grip his dark side would have on him.

It was time to become the hunter.

He dusted the dirt off his chest. The mark had faded only slightly. Shit. He didn't want to go beneath the earth to heal. If he were asleep underground, he would have no defense against Cicatrice.

It would have to wait.

He grabbed another of the gris-gris bags and dumped more powder out. Then he walked over to the stake and crouched next to it. It was humming again, and a faint, blood-red glow was emanating from it. He double-wrapped his hand in the first bag, and then picked up the stake. He dropped it into the second bag, and then tied it shut. The stake was still humming, and the bag was now glowing a faint red.

Shit. He was supposed to carry that around? It would burn his damned hip in a second.

He quickly inserted the bagged stake into the other bag, and tied that as well. The humming was much less, and the bag was barely red. It took two more bags before it was finally quiet. The floor of the shed was covered in the gray powder that he'd dumped out, and his jaw hurt from tensing against the humming, but it was secure.

He was ready for Cicatrice.

His heart thudding slowly in his chest, he stood up. His muscles were taut, his adrenaline jacked. It was time to face his maker—

A scent caught his attention.

He spun toward the door, moving with lightning quickness. He went utterly still, breathing deeply of the scent that drifted through the wood. Blood. Rich, tantalizing, and tempting. A woman. No, two of them. Outside.

A ravaging hunger and a burning lust tore through him, a need so instinctual and deep that it obliterated all thought from his mind. His incisors lengthened, and a savage need burned through him so intensely that it hurt. Their voices drifted through the closed door, faint, but easily discernible with his newly enhanced hearing. Their laughter drifted through the night, the giddy delight of youth.

Hell. They were practically children. No more than twenty at the most.

He closed his eyes, his muscles so taut that they were like rocks. He commanded his body to stay still. He would not prey on the innocent. Never. *Leave here now.* He instinctively pushed the thought toward them, reaching for their minds the way Cicatrice had done with him.

More laughter, and he heard their footsteps on the front porch as they dared each other to approach the haunted shack.

Hunger ate away at his self-control, and his stomach contracted with the need to feed. The scent of their blood filled his nostrils. The tangy, sweet smell of life. The void within him roared even louder, a howling wind of emptiness trying to drag what was left of his soul into it.

He stumbled backward, the bagged stake sliding from his fingers as he fought the primal instinct building inside him.

The doorknob rattled, and hunger roared through him.

No! He bellowed the command, thrusting all his mental energy at them. *Get away! Go home! Run!*

His words connected with their minds, and he felt their sudden fear. Their screams pulsated through him, an icy cold stab of terror that ignited an even greater need in him. A need to *hunt* the fleeing prey. To chase them.

No. He would not go. His body shaking with the effort of controlling his instinct to attack them, he held himself still as their feet pounded the earth and their screams faded into the distance. Their car roared to life, and then it was gone.

Dinner was gone.

But the need for them wasn't.

Their scent, their fear, and their flight had awakened a need in him that he could no longer control. Tristan knew he couldn't wait any longer, or he wouldn't be at liberty to choose. His need would make the choice for him. The next female he scented would be his. He had to make sure it was the right one.

With a low growl, he tore open the door of the tomb and stepped out into the night, leaving the stake behind.

It was time to feed. The hunt would have to come later.

CHAPTER 9

Something was tracking them.

Eric kept the truck speeding forward as he watched the road behind them in the rearview mirror. "What is it?" he asked. The tires hummed on the asphalt, but his preternatural senses were on high alert. The air had become heavy with threat, with the same taint of evil that he'd felt in the graveyard where he'd found Tristan's altar.

Another shadow flashed across the road behind them. It was too fast to discern, but it was definitely the size of a tall person, and walking upright.

Jordyn sucked in her breath as she twisted around in her seat, staring at the road. "I can't tell," she said. "It was too quick."

Eric flexed his hands on the steering wheel and reached out with his mind. The sudden noise was almost deafening. There were so many spirits in the air, swirling and raging. Screaming and howling. He tried to filter through them, but the cacophony was a violent mass of confused noise. "We must be near a burial ground."

"A burial ground?" She twisted around in her seat, scanning the woods. "No, not a burial ground. We're near the site of the great harvest."

"Harvest?" Something flashed across the road again, closer this time. It was gaining on them. "What kind of harvest?"

"Humans. It was back in the days when the vampires were active. Before they were destroyed."

"Well, hell." Had the bodies been left to rot and decay

in that very space? Their spirits trapped forever? Swearing, he tried to sift through them, searching for something that could help.

A shadow flashed past his window, and Jordyn gripped the seat. "It's there."

"I know—"

Suddenly, a man appeared in front of the truck. He slammed his hands down on the hood. Eric swore and hit the brakes. The truck skidded violently across the road as he fought to maintain control. He'd barely gotten it stopped when the man leapt up onto the hood of the truck and crouched there, like a panther about to attack.

Jordyn went still beside him. "Oh, God," she whispered. "This is really bad."

"You think?" The man's face was shockingly handsome, chiseled as if it were carved from stone. His hair was long and flowing around his shoulders, and his clothes were ancient, from many centuries ago. He was wearing black, fitted pants, a white ruffled shirt, and leather gloves, as if he'd been out driving his team of horses only moments ago. "I think Tristan's been at work. Is this Cicatrice?"

"No. Cicatrice has a scarred face."

"So, then, a lesser vampire. No problem. We got this." Energy swirled around Eric, the spirits disturbed by the vampire's presence. Eric thrust his mind outward into the night, searching for energy that would help him. Death. Destruction. Suffering. He brought the spirits together, holding them tightly in a metaphysical ball within him. It coiled through him, vibrating dangerously, seeking a foothold in his soul. "Don't get between me and him," he said softly to Jordyn. "No matter what."

She was already digging in her bag. "I have this stake that will kill him—"

The vampire's gaze went straight to Jordyn at her words, and his eyes glowed a bright red. She froze, her hand buried in her bag. "There's no stake in this bag," she whispered. "Someone stole it."

The vampire's attention was riveted on Jordyn, and the muscles in his neck were flexing. His eyes were glowing with an evil that crawled over Eric's skin like poison. The creature wasn't moving. He was poised on the hood of the truck as if he were waiting for them to run, so the game could begin.

Shit. He didn't like this. They were trapped in the truck, and he had no room to protect Jordyn. "How fast can they run?" he asked, as he moved his hand to his side and set his palm over his knife.

"Faster than we can drive," she said. "Faster than we can see."

"Then I guess we face him now." Pulling all the energy of the spirits closer, Eric suddenly flung open his truck door and vaulted out onto the road. "Hey!" he shouted. "Over here—"

The vampire moved fast. Too fast. He spun toward Eric and sprang off the truck, moving so quickly he was nothing more than a blurred shadow. He hit Eric in the chest before Eric even saw him, slamming him back into the ground so hard that the asphalt cracked beneath Eric's head. The vampire grabbed him and tore into Eric's neck with his teeth. Pain shot through Eric, and he slammed his hands onto the vampire's chest, exploding his magic into the vampire.

Green mist filled the night, and the vampire flew backward, careening through the air and skidding a hundred yards across the road. The moment it came to a halt, it bounded to its feet as quickly as Eric jumped up.

Neither male moved. They stood immobile, facing each other down with a hundred yards of cracked pavement between them, and dark, foggy woods on either side. Eric could feel the blood oozing down his neck, and he knew the bite was bad. He was bleeding too much. He had to end this battle, now, before the blood loss became too great.

He could sense the vampire's hunger, a craving so deep and so dark that he could feel it in his own gut. It was as if his entire body was screaming for salvation, and that Eric's blood would save him.

Eric had known that kind of hunger before, and he knew that the survival instinct would compel the vampire to do *anything* to save itself, including rip his throat out and gut Jordyn. *Shit.* He opened his mind to the vampire, traveling over the same pathways that he used to connect with the spirits. All he got from the creature was evil. Hunger. Survival. Base emotions that left no room for anything else, like a sense of basic human values. Son of a bitch.

They were in trouble.

Eric began to amass his powers again, calling them to him from everywhere. He took the magic from the night. He harvested the unknown. He controlled the ethereal. He summoned it all into his body, sifting through it with rapid speed to assess what he'd harnessed—

He heard the door of his truck open, and he swore, not daring to take his attention off the vampire as Jordyn eased out of the truck on the far side. "Jordyn, get back in the truck."

"No." Out of the corner of his eye, he saw her move to the front of the truck, her body illuminated by the headlights. She was pressed against the grill, keeping the vehicle between her and the vampire. "He's not going to stop until we're both dead."

"I'm not in the mood to die."

"Me either." She was holding a small turquoise bag with feathers tied to the cord around its neck.

The vampire's attention went to Jordyn. Eric felt the moment that it focused on her. The raging hunger turned into bloodlust. Sex. Feeding.

Possessiveness flooded Eric, jacking up his adrenaline. *She's mine, you piece of shit.* "Jordyn, you need to back up—"

He didn't get to finish his warning. The vampire launched itself at Jordyn. "No way, you bastard!" Eric leapt forward at the same time, and the two bodies crashed into each other in midair. The vampire was brutally strong, its claws raking across Eric's chest, tearing his flesh to shreds as it fought to get to Jordyn. "Back off," Eric shouted as he slammed his dagger into the vampire's torso.

The green blade flashed brightly and glittery gold flames erupted from its chest. The vampire screamed in agony, but then threw Eric aside with ridiculous ease, its strength insurmountable. It lunged for Jordyn, but she was gone. For a split second, it froze, its head turned as it scanned the night for her.

Eric used that moment to attack. He slammed his palms together, and power exploded from them. The burst of energy hit the vampire, throwing it against the side of truck. The metal collapsed like an accordion. The vehicle skidded across the road and into the ditch as the vampire tore itself out of the side of the truck. He shot toward Eric, moving so fast he was only a blur.

"Hold him still," Jordyn shouted from the edge of the woods, where she'd apparently gone when the vampire had targeted her.

"Hold him still? Are you fucking kidding?" But Eric held his power and didn't attack as the vampire launched itself at him. He let the vampire crash into him. The vampire's teeth sank into Eric's neck again, and this time, he didn't throw it off. He twisted his energy around the vampire, locking it against him, using the energy as invisible bonds. The vampire convulsed and screamed, trying to pull back enough to get its teeth out of his neck, but Eric held it tight against him, not letting it back off. His arm and a thousand pounds of magical force were locked around the back of the creature's head, holding its fangs into Eric's neck.

Because this was what he'd had planned when he woke up this morning. Find a clue about his brother, help a vampire rip his throat out, all in a good day's work.

"Perfect!" Jordyn raced over to them, putting herself right in the damned path of danger.

He was going to yell at her to back off, but he had no energy left to spare. He was too busy trying to hold a raging maniac in a bear hug, while keeping at least part of his neck still attached to his body.

Jordyn tore open the small bag she'd been holding and dumped it over the vampire, chanting words in a language he didn't recognize. Violet powder dumped over them both, and he gagged as it filled his mouth and burned his eyes, because he wasn't facing enough of a challenge at the moment, right?

"This is supposed to help him find his humanity," she shouted as she backed up.

The vampire's teeth sank deeper, and Eric swore. "It's not working!"

"It has to work! I used a huge amount!"

"Well, it's not!" He was out of time. He slammed his palms into the vampire's chest, and the explosion threw the vampire back again, ripping its teeth out of his neck, and taking too much of Eric's flesh with it.

Eric groaned and rolled onto his side, struggling to stand up as the blood poured from his neck. "Get in the truck," he gasped. "Get away. I'll keep it occupied as long as I can. Go!" He knew he couldn't defeat the vampire, but if Jordyn could get away, if he could give her time, then that was at least a heroic way to die, so yeah, that was good. He'd always had a bit of a hero complex, at least according to his brother.

Completely ignoring his command, Jordyn held up her hand, telling him not to move, which of course, he wasn't about to do. Moving required blood to be flowing to his extremities so they could function, and that wasn't really happening at the moment. "Wait a moment," she said.

"Because waiting for a vampire to get its strength back is such a good plan?" His legs gave out, and he went down on his knees. He bent his head, staring at the vampire as he began to summon more magic. The creature had been stunned by Eric's hit, but its fingers were twitching, so apparently, not quite dead.

He tried to watch the vampire, but the night was spinning, and he couldn't focus. "Get out of here," he ordered Jordyn, watching the vampire as it gathered what little strength it could assimilate.

Eric didn't have much left. One more assault, maybe, enough to give the vampire a small bruise before it finished the job.

The vampire rolled onto its side, and then to its hands and knees. It raised its head to look at Jordyn and Eric. Blood cascaded down its face and over the front of its shirt.

"That's my blood," Eric gritted out. "You're wasting it."

The vampire's gaze went to Eric, but it didn't stand. It was still on its hands and knees.

"Look at his eyes," Jordyn whispered.

Eric noticed then that the vampire's eyes were no longer red. They were dark, hidden in the shadows of the night.

"It worked. The shock of your blow was enough to break the hold of the vampire and let the powder work. He's fighting for his humanity now." She took a step, as if she were planning to march over there and give the vampire a high five.

Eric grabbed her ankle. "I don't think so."

She didn't fight him, but she put her hand on his shoulder. "You have to leave," she told the vampire. "The powder won't last long. You have to do it on your own. You have to fight it. Make the right choice now. Remember that you were once human, and you still have that inside you. Leave before you kill another innocent. *Leave.*"

The vampire stared at her, and this time, Eric saw that hard, sculpted face contort, as if he were in great suffering. He saw the humanity in that creature, just for a split second. Tentatively, he opened his mind to the vampire, and this time, woven among the bloodlust and the evil was something else. A thin, barely-there tendril of light, spreading out like the most fragile of filaments through the darkness "Son of a bitch," he whispered. "You're right." But even as Eric spoke, the dark red of bloodlust began to creep down the silvery filaments, eating away at that brief glimpse of humanity.

Eric reached out with his mind, pushing barriers at the vampire, shoving metaphysical obstacles in the path of the evil, trying to help the vampire break his ties to his prey.

The dark eyes met his, and Eric felt a sudden howl of anguish roll through his mind, a wail of human suffering so great that it was almost unfathomable. Then the vampire leapt to his feet, whirled around, and sprinted into the woods, disappearing in a whisper of movement.

"Oh, my God," Jordyn whispered. "It worked. We did it."

"Yeah, I'm a badass." The words slurred as Eric slumped onto the road. "I think I'm part vampire. I need blood." He thought it was a joke, but when Jordyn sucked in her breath, it occurred to him that he wasn't sure exactly how vampires were made. Something about being bitten and drained, right? 'Cause he'd been bitten, and he was pretty low on pints.

Nah.

He wasn't the vampire type.

An IV bag would do just fine.

He felt Jordyn's arms wrap around him as he fell. "Eric," she commanded, her voice distant through the haze of his mind. "We need to get to the truck. Your legs work, so use them."

"Bossy chick," he slurred, as he tried to make his legs

function. Weirdly, they didn't feel like they were attached to his body. "Totally hot."

"I'm not bossy. You're bossy. I'm just a nice, sweet girl." She threw his arm over her shoulder and put her arm around his waist. "Now get up and get to the truck. We need to get you some help or you're going to die."

He cracked his eyes open enough to see the truck. It was half in the ditch and at least twenty feet away. He stared at it numbly, having difficulty focusing on it. "That's too far to walk. Drive it over here to pick me up." Yeah, that sounded good. "I'm just going to sit down here." He started to sit down, but Jordyn wouldn't let him.

"That powder won't last long," she snapped. "He'll be back. So get your butt into the damned truck so I can tell everyone what a hero you were fighting the vampire."

"I'm a hero. Everyone knows it. You don't need to tell them." He let his head flop to the side and closed his eyes as his face wound up in her hair. The strands tickled his nose and he sighed. "You smell good," he slurred. "Like a really hot, sexy woman who wants me and kicks vampire ass. Let's have sex." He wasn't sure he'd actually said it out loud. His body was so heavy, and cold. He was really cold. It took too much effort to talk. Or think. Or breathe—

Jordyn's breath was warm against his neck. "If you get your cute little butt to that truck," she said softly, "I promise I'll have sex with you."

He let that thought roll around in his head for a long moment, struggling to process it and figure out what it meant, but his head felt thick. "Sex?"

"God, you lose half your blood supply, and you become a complete idiot. I didn't realize you were such a wimp," she complained as she continued to drag him along.

"I'm not a wimp." He tried to stand up again, and his legs just didn't seem to care. He didn't like being called a wimp, but was disproving it really worth the effort of walking? No, no, not really. He was pretty sure it wasn't.

"Damn, you're incredibly difficult. You know that, right? Challenging your manliness doesn't get you going, so let's go back to the sex thing. You know what sex is, right? Making love. Orgasms. Me naked. You naked. But only if you get in the truck, you big oaf. If you die, you'll never have a chance to have sex with me, and I'm really good at it, so you'll be majorly missing out."

Naked. Jordyn naked. An image flashed into his mind of her breasts. Perky nipples. Rounded hips leading down to... What was left of his blood shot straight to his groin, and he was suddenly a hell of a lot more conscious than he had been a moment before. "Okay." He closed his eyes and concentrated really hard. One step. Then another. Then one more. "Yeah, check this out. I'm awesome." He kept his face in Jordyn's hair, his eyes closed as he let her direct him. Then, finally, weirdly, he was in the truck. He sank into the leather seat, slumping down as Jordyn climbed in beside him.

Yeah, he did it. He was the man. "Naked," he mumbled. "You promised."

"I know. Later."

"Okay." Later sounded good. Right now, he just needed to sleep. He closed his eyes as the truck roared to life, but he was still cold. So cold. "Jordyn."

"Just hang in there," she said. "We'll get you help soon."

"Where's your hand?"

"What?" The truck lurched forward, and he slid lower on the seat, unable to hold himself up.

"Your hand." His eyelids were too heavy to keep open, and the coldness was crawling down his limbs. "I want it."

"Why?" But even as she asked, he felt her hand on his. He immediately slid his fingers between hers, entangling them together.

"Warm," he slurred. "Nice."

The smile was still on his face as he faded into unconsciousness.

⁂

"Still alive?" David raced up to the truck as she slammed on the brakes in his front yard.

"I think so. God, I hope so." She was trembling as David opened the passenger door.

He whistled softly as he took in Eric slumped almost on

the floor of the vehicle, literally covered in blood. "Damn," he said. "I knew this was coming. Let's go."

She grabbed Eric under the shoulders, but he didn't respond as she angled him toward the door. She helped David get him upright, and then David squatted down and hauled Eric across his shoulders. He stood up easily, not even flinching at the effort of lifting a well-muscled man. She frowned as she grabbed her bag and hurried after him.

When they were kids, David had been about as strong as she was. A nerd with a heart of gold. And now he was slinging Eric over his shoulders as if he weighed nothing?

"I can feel his heart thudding against my back," David said as he broke into a jog. "He's still alive."

"Oh, thank God." All thoughts of David's strength fled as she raced across the yard after them. She followed them through the front door, just barely getting indoors in time to see David disappear down the basement stairs. She ran after them, her feet thudding on the steps as she went down into the dimly lit space.

Dammit. She didn't like basements. The old familiar fears crept over her, and she instinctively looked around as she hurried down the steps. The cement walls were cracked, and the small windows were so covered in grime that they were completely opaque. The only lights were a few barren light bulbs jammed into sockets in the ceiling. "This is where you work now? Seriously?"

"Don't judge," David said mildly. "I'm always full of surprises." He kicked open a broken wooden door at the back of the basement, and strode inside.

Glancing over her shoulder to make sure nothing was following her, she hurried after them, then grinned with relief as she walked into the room and saw David setting Eric down on a hospital bed. The room was pristine and immaculate. There were gleaming white cabinets, a glistening stainless steel sink, and a beautiful wooden worktable that was laden with an assortment of herbs and plants, along with several pots of dirt. On the wall above the table were shelves filled with hundreds of small glass bottles filled with assorted powders and liquids. "Wow, you have even more than you used to."

"A lot of shit's been going down here lately," he grunted as he unpeeled Eric from around his neck. "I've been busy."

Eric groaned and suddenly grabbed David, his fingers digging into his throat. David grimaced and grabbed Eric's wrist. "Get your boyfriend off me, because he's in no shape for me to hurt him right now."

Jordyn hurried across the room and grasped Eric's arm. "Eric! Stop it! He's trying to help you!"

Eric muttered something that sounded like her name and naked, and then he collapsed again, apparently unconscious.

"Good." David sprinted over to the table, and swept up a pile of herbs. "I'm glad you called on your way. The heads up gave me time to get ready." He hurried over to the bed, and started packing the plants into Eric's wound, muttering words that Jordyn recognized from her childhood.

"You're not going to stitch him up?"

"Not for this," David said. "That's not what's going to save his life. This is." He held his hands over Eric's neck, and closed his eyes, his lips moving in a silent chant.

Jordyn scooted closer and leaned her head next to David's, joining him in his chant, repeating the words she'd heard him say so many times when they were kids. For a long moment, nothing happened. "David?"

"I know. Keep it up." His voice was calm, but she sensed the urgency beneath his mellow demeanor as he grabbed another pile of herbs from the table. "This might kill him," he said. "I didn't want to have to use it."

Jordyn tensed. "I don't want him to die."

"Death is better than his fate if I don't get this managed." He rubbed the dried plants between his palms, and the crumbled remains fell into the gaping wound on Eric's neck. He started chanting again, this time words she didn't know. As he did it, smoke began to rise from Eric's neck.

Jordyn became alarmed at the idea of Eric's skin catching fire. "Um, David? Is that supposed to happen?"

He ignored her, and his chant became even faster, building speed as he sprinkled more herbs onto Eric's ravaged throat. Then, she saw a spark on Eric's neck. Then another, then suddenly a, black flame erupted from his flesh. She jumped back, her heart thundering as the flames stretched up higher and higher, pure black fire. "David?"

David didn't move, his hands now consumed by the fire, as he continued to chant.

Eric shifted and groaned, and David jerked his finger toward Eric, without breaking the rhythm of his chant. "Manage him," he snapped.

"I got it." She lunged for Eric, scooted onto the bed next to him, and then pulled his upper body onto her lap. "Don't move," she ordered him. "Stay still." She couldn't imagine how much it must hurt to have flames eating away at his flesh. He twisted again, trying to get away even in his unconscious state. She bent her head so that her mouth was next to his ear. "Eric," she whispered. "Think about me naked. Think about making love. Think about—" She glanced toward David, embarrassed to be caught in dirty talk, but his eyes were closed, and he was clearly in the throes of his healing magic.

She returned her attention to Eric, resting her palm on his forehead. He was still groaning and moving, trying to get away from the flames.

"Hold him still," David shouted. "He can't move!" The flames were stretching almost three feet in the air, a raging violent purple and black. His entire neck and throat were engulfed. The scent of burning flesh seared her nose. His skin was shriveling into a charred wasteland.

Bile churned in her stomach, and for a split second, she was tempted to shove David back and make him stop. But David was the one man in this world who she truly trusted. If he betrayed her, she would have nothing left to rely on. "David?"

He didn't answer, his face contorted with focus as flames enveloped his hands.

Eric shouted suddenly, jerking her attention back to him. She looked down at his face, and as she did, his eyes opened. For a split second, she saw full awareness in his brown eyes, then he smiled. "You promised," he said, his voice gritty.

"I know." Heat flushed her body, knowing exactly what he was talking about. She hadn't *really* intended to get naked with him. She'd just wanted to penetrate his mind and get him mobile. Of course, now wasn't the time to tell him that.

Pain flashed across his face, and he grimaced, twisting back against the bed. "Son of a bitch," he muttered. "I'm going to beat your friend up when this is over. He's having way too much fun with it."

And that's when she knew it was going to be okay. Eric wasn't fighting David. He trusted him, and he was already more conscious. Relief eased the tension in her muscles, and she managed a smile as Eric's grip on her hand tightened. Then there was the sound of a small explosion from the region of his injury. His entire body went rigid, and he swore under his breath.

Jordyn gripped his hand, and then noticed that the black flames were now intermixed with streaks of orange. She suddenly realized what David was doing. It was the same thing he'd done as a kid when they'd found all the dying ants that had been poisoned. He'd hit them with the fire, using it to burn off the poison that was trying to consume him. "The orange is good," she told Eric. "It means the evil is being cleansed. When the flames are all orange, there's nothing evil left."

"Evil is such a melodramatic word," he gritted out. "That piece of shit bit me. Let's call it cooties."

Jordyn almost laughed, and she heard David snort. "You're fighting death," she pointed out. "Focus."

"I am focused." His eyes were closed again, his body stiff. "Trust me, I'm focused." She heard the steely edge to his voice, and saw the sheer hardness of his muscles, every single one of them tensed to the limit, and she knew he was telling the truth.

The orange bits vanished from the fire, and suddenly it was full of purple and brown streaks.

David swore. "He needs to relax," he shouted. "He's too tense. I can't break him free if he doesn't let me in."

Jordyn bent over him. "Eric—"

"I heard him." His jaw was rigid. "A little fucking difficult to relax right now."

"You have to," David snapped. "Now!"

Eric opened his eyes. "Kiss me."

"What? Now?"

"Yeah. Please." There was a desperate edge to his voice, and her heart tightened. "I need a distraction. A big one. *Now.*"

"Dear God, Eric. You're insatiable. Really?"

He didn't answer. His eyes rolled back in his head, and his back arched as a he sucked in his breath.

"Kiss him, Jordyn! It's a guy thing! Just do it!" David shouted.

"Okay, fine!" As she spoke, she leaned forward until her mouth was hovering over his, but she felt so foolish, about to kiss a guy who was on fire. Then she looked at him more closely. His lips were pressed tightly together, his cheeks were sunken, and gray circles haunted beneath his eyes. His face was pale, almost as pale as the vampire's had been. She realized he was dying, truly *dying*, and the last thing he'd asked for was her kiss.

Her heart tightened and tears filled her eyes. "I'm here," she whispered, before she lowered her head and pressed her lips to his.

CHAPTER 10

Jordyn's kiss was like an anchor, dragging Eric back from the darkness trying to suck him down. The moment her lips touched his, his entire being surged toward her, desperate for her touch. Instinctively, he slid his hand through her hair and palmed the back of her head, trapping her against him, while he used his right arm to create a shield between the flames and her face. The fire was scorching his skin, but he barely felt it. The sheer power of her kiss dominated his senses so much that she stripped away everything from his consciousness...everything except her.

He'd made a smart remark about evil, but he'd been completely lying with his cavalier attitude. He knew damn well what he was facing. He could feel the evil coursing through every cell in his body, streaking through him like a poison, trying to take hold and claim him. David's fire was having a party, incinerating healthy cells and poisoned ones alike, burning through Eric's living flesh to eat up the poison before it could claim him. David's rhythmic chants were so loud in his head that his brain was screaming in pain. Everything hurt like hell, but he could tell the evil was winning, eating away at his life force with insurmountable speed.

He was losing the battle.

"Eric?" Jordyn touched his face, drawing his attention away from the battle raging in his body, and back to her.

He blinked, staring blankly into her eyes for a split second, while he tried to process what she was asking. His gaze slid to her mouth, and he realized he'd stopped kissing her. As redemptive as her kiss was, it hadn't been sufficient to distract him from the agony screaming through his body.

"He's got to relax," David shouted. "Now!"

Jordyn tensed beside him, and Eric realized he was rigid, his entire body screaming with suffering. *Shit.* He'd never experienced anything like the sheer power of the two forces battling within him, and he knew the good guy was losing. "I need light," he gritted out. "Yours." He didn't mean light. He meant her spirit. Something good. He didn't even know what he was trying to say. He just needed *her* to ground him.

"I'm not light," she muttered, but even as she protested, she kissed him again.

This time, he focused his entire being on the kiss, doing everything he could to shut out the agonizing pain in his neck, and the smell of burning flesh. He concentrated on the softness of her lips against his, a caress so innocently seductive that it was surreal. He was accustomed to bruising, passionate kisses that were about lust and uncontained need. He wasn't used to a kiss that was so gentle and soft that it made his entire body go utterly still in anticipation, vibrating with the need for what came next.

She kissed him again, her lips lightly nibbling against his. It might be a soft kiss, but it wasn't chaste, not one bit. Her kiss was a tentative exploration of sensation, and warmth. It was a kiss that promised a slow, hot night of sensual loving in the humidity of a southern bayou. He could almost envision the golden glow of moonlight over her bare flesh. He could almost taste the trickle of sweat between her breasts as he ran his fingers across her collarbones. He could almost feel the heavy thickness of the air wrapping them in a blanket of damp heat as he slid slowly inside her.

The frenzied energy of his body slowed down, attuning itself to the slow seduction of her kiss and the images in his mind of a lovemaking so erotic that it would take hours. He went still, his heart moving in a slow, languorous rhythm as it succumbed to the soft, persuasive kisses of her seduction.

His fingers relaxing in her hair, he became aware of the silkiness of the strands tangled around his fingers. He was a visual guy, all about what he was seeing, but with his eyes closed, he suddenly became viscerally aware of how she felt. Her hair was so smooth, tendrils of pure tactile decadence. The faintest fragrance of something light and summery teased him, as if she'd woven fresh flowers into her soul. And her mouth...his cock tightened when she lightly ran her tongue over his lips, a wet, hot whisper of all that could be between them. She made a small noise in the back of her throat, a sound that made his own body react.

With a low groan, he pulled her tighter, deepening the kiss. His need for more was insatiable, but it wasn't just a craving for sex. It was for *her*. For her kiss. For her touch. For the sounds of desire that slipped from her lips as he deepened the kiss. This was so much more than the lustful attraction that had been building between them since the first moment he'd seen her. This was exponentially more powerful, and infinitely more personal. It was not about a kiss between a man and a woman. It was a kiss between him and *this* woman.

"Jordyn," he whispered, needing to say her name, to hear proof that it was Jordyn who was in his arms, that it was Jordyn who tasted of sun-warmed beaches and ocean breezes. Her mouth parted for him, and he slid his tongue past her teeth. She accepted him completely, tangling her tongue against his, a searing hot invitation that rocked him to his core. Her breast was pressed against his arm, a curvaceous temptation that was incredible. He lost track of the fire, of the chanting, and of the pain, until all that remained was Jordyn.

It was simply a kiss. Not sex. No bare flesh. No screaming throes of passion. And yet it seemed to consume him, swallowing up his entire existence until all he could feel was her. He wanted more, but at the same time, the kiss was so exquisite that it was sheer perfection itself.

"Done." David's voice was filled with relief, and his interjection broke through the veil of protection that Jordyn's kiss had given him.

Jordyn pulled back, and for a split second, they simply stared at each other. Her blue eyes were wide, her lips flushed from the kiss. Then her gaze went to his neck, and she paled. "Oh, God."

The moment she said it, the pain came surging back

over him. He sucked in his breath, startled by how vicious it was. His throat felt like it had been torn out, and his flesh burned like it was still on fire. But more than that was the sense of weakness and numbness stealing over his body, sucking the very life from his bones. Son of a bitch. He was suddenly flooded with the images of the vampire attack, of Cicatrice, of Tristan out there somewhere. It was night. It was dark. Who knew when the next one would come? Who would protect Jordyn? He had to be ready. He had to be prepared to fight, to save her, to protect her.

Instinct took over, and he tried to sit up, but David was suddenly beside Jordyn, his beefy arm across Eric's chest as he pushed him back down. "No," David said. "Don't move. Just lie there."

Eric gritted his jaw, pausing for a moment as sudden weakness flooded his body. "Back off," he gritted out. "I'm getting up." There was no way he was going to lie in bed when vampires were out hunting, and Jordyn was unprotected.

"Eric!" Jordyn bent over him, cutting off his view of David. "The fire's gone," she said urgently. "Your skin isn't black anymore. You're okay, but you still need to heal. Just a few hours, and then you'll be good—"

"I'll heal on my feet." He shoved David's arm off him and rolled off the bed, forcing his limbs to obey him, despite the weakness pervading them. He somehow managed to land on his feet, but as he stood up, the room suddenly spun violently. He had time only to decide he needed to call some magic to help him out, and then blackness consumed him and he hit the floor, unconscious.

⊠⊠⊠⊠

"Shouldn't he be awake by now?" Jordyn paced restlessly by Eric's bed, skittishly tracking the movement of the setting sun. The pink, purple, and orange sky was magnificent as it stretched over the trees, the streaky clouds reflecting the sun. Normally, she would have sat down on David's back deck and basked in the beauty of nature and the fact she was alive to see yet another sunset. Tonight was different. Tonight the sunset meant darkness was coming. Another night where the sun went down and the not-so-mythical creatures came to life. Another night when the vampire that had attacked them was still at large, another chance for Cicatrice to do terrible things, and another night for Tristan to do what? Become a vampire? Resurrect more monsters? Another night to face with Eric still hovering between life and death.

"Yeah, he should." David was bent over the bed, checking on Eric. He'd been in every hour since he'd moved Eric upstairs, never letting more than sixty minutes go by without checking on him. Ever. "The wound is healed, and his blood appears to be untainted. I don't know. I thought he'd be out for only a couple hours." He straightened up, beads of sweat on his temples. "He was badly injured, though. Maybe there was something else I should have done. I've never had someone that torn up, but still be alive."

Jordyn's heart pounded as she stared at David. "Something else? What do you mean?"

David ran his hand through his auburn hair, tousling what was already a mess. "I don't know, Jordyn. I honestly didn't think I'd save his life. I thought he'd die. I've never seen anyone heal that kind of injury before." He nodded at Eric. "There's not even a scar. He's clearly not entirely human, and I don't know if that changes how I should have treated him."

Jordyn inspected Eric's neck, as she'd done so many times over the last two days. At first, his neck had looked horrible, with a huge, blackened crater where his throat was supposed to be. But hour by hour it had begun to heal, so gradually at first that she'd thought she was imagining it. But now? David was right. "It's completely healed." She sat down next to Eric and traced her finger over where the injury had been. The flesh was soft and warm. Flawless. Even his whiskers had grown back, getting long after almost two days of not shaving. "He hasn't moved," she said.

David frowned at her. "What do you mean?"

"He's been in this exact position since you brought him up here," she said. "He hasn't made a sound, or even blinked. I haven't even seen him swallow. The only way I even know he's alive is because I can feel his pulse." She pressed her fingers to his neck, then frowned. She couldn't feel anything. "Eric?" She shifted her fingers, and still felt nothing. Her heart started to hammer, and then she felt a single, slow, thump of a heartbeat. And then, one more. It was slow, so very slow, but still alive. "Okay, yes, see? His heart's still beating." She looked at David. "But barely."

Frowning, David set his fingers on Eric's neck, feeling for a pulse. He didn't move for several minutes, his face becoming more and more grim as he stood there.

"David? What's wrong?"

For a long moment, David stared at her, then he looked back at Eric, his face unreadable.

Jordyn stiffened. "Talk to me."

He removed his hand from Eric's neck and walked to the window. He set his hands on the window frame, staring out at the swamp. "It's been forty-four hours since he was bitten," he observed.

Jordyn glanced at her watch. "Yes, just about." It was almost eight o'clock, and they'd been attacked shortly after midnight.

David didn't turn around. "The stories tell of a forty-eight hour turnaround time."

She sank down on the mattress next to Eric. "Turnaround time for what?"

"Do you really need to ask me that?"

Jordyn suddenly froze, her fingers tangled in Eric's hair. "You think he's been turned into a..." The words died in her throat. "No. It's impossible. He never died. He wasn't drained of blood."

David spun toward her. "What do we really know about vampires?" he asked. "All we know are ancient stories. They're supposed to be long gone, not running around town ripping people's throats out. I've had over a dozen people in here in the last month who are feeling weird. They have no memory of what happened, and no bite marks that you can see with the naked eye, but they're there. I can find them. Vampires have returned, Jordyn, and we don't know enough about them."

Jordyn bit her lip, her gaze involuntarily sliding past David to the woods behind his cabin. "That's what you wanted to talk to me about at the bar?"

"Yeah. People are getting bitten, and these are just the

ones that come to me. What about the ones I don't know about? Three people have been reported as missing, but we both know that it's not unheard of for men to go into the swamp for days at a time, so there may be even more victims that we don't know about, the people who haven't been gone long enough to be considered missing."

Jordyn thought of the woman Eric had heard scream in the woods. "Of course there are vampires, or at least one," she said. "I saw him. I'm not denying that, but what does that have to do with Eric? He's not a vampire. He's been in his bed in the sunlight for the last two days and hasn't burned to a crisp, right?"

"Yeah, but how do we know that matters? All we know are ancient stories from people like your grandmother. Everyone who fought them before is dead. Everyone who knows how to stop them is gone. Everyone who knows their secrets has taken them to the grave." He spread his hands wide in a gesture of helplessness. "We don't know enough about them, Jordyn."

Jordyn's fingers stilled in Eric's hair. "He's not a vampire," she said softly.

"And what if he is?"

David's question hung in the air, a looming threat of danger. She looked down at Eric, who was so utterly still and silent. His skin looked somewhat ashen, but that could have to do with blood loss and the fact he'd almost died. "He won't hurt me."

"Are you willing to risk your life on that one? How well do you know him?"

"I—" She bit her lip, fighting the urge to ease off the bed and put some distance between them.

"We need to get him downstairs. I have a room we can put him in. It should hold him."

She frowned. "A room? What kind of a room?"

"It's a room that I built for myself to keep the bad guys out. It should keep him in okay, at least until we know."

Jordyn hesitated. "Lock him up?"

"You want your neck to look like his?"

"Of course I don't." She glanced down at Eric, remembering what his kiss had been like before he'd passed out. Not his arrogant, domineering kisses that had nearly melted her boots in the jungle, though those had certainly been pretty much amazing. No, she thought of the kiss when he'd been dying. There had been emotion in that kiss. Not just sex. Need. Tenderness. Appreciation. Connection. Was that the kiss of a man on his way to becoming a monster? She shook her head. "No, he's not a vampire. He's okay."

David walked back over to her and crouched in front of her. "You remember Caleb and Susan Hart?"

She frowned. "Of course I do. They got married right after we graduated. How many kids do they have now?"

"Ten, but ten months ago, Caleb went crazy. He bit Susan in the neck and killed her. Drained her blood. Left her dead in the living room."

Jordyn went ice cold. "He loved her. Dearly. He'd give his life for her, a thousand times over."

David shrugged. "He murdered her. The cops say he went crazy. I saw her body, and the fang marks were obvious. He went vampire, and he killed her. He's gone missing, and no one can find him."

"Oh, God." Jordyn thought back to the vampire who had attacked Eric. It hadn't been Caleb. "So, there are more out there. More than just one."

"Of course there are. We were fools to think they were ever gone. They've probably been living among us this whole time, but something has upset the balance and now they're hunting again." He jerked his chin at Eric. "I don't care how much you like this guy. You barely know him. If he's a vampire, you're not safe, and I care about you too much to risk your life. I don't *ever* want to see you on the floor the way Susan was." Something cracked in his voice. "You let me put him in the room, or I'll lock you up and then stake him before he wakes up."

"What? No!" She instinctively moved between Eric and David. "What's wrong with you? You don't even know if he's a vampire! You can't stake him just in case!"

"I will." David's eyes were dark and anguished, and suddenly she remembered that night in tenth grade, when she and David had been sitting on the swings behind the school, watching the other students go into the gym all dressed up for the Homecoming Dance. Caleb and Susan had gone in together, and David had broken down right then, confessing that he was deeply in love with Susan, and that she had been the first person he'd ever made love with.

Sadness coursed through her. "You still love her," she said quietly. "You've loved her all these years."

David's jaw tightened. "She's dead. It doesn't matter."

"Yes, it does." She walked over to him and set her hand on his arm. "I'm so sorry, David. I can't imagine what it must have felt like to walk in there and see her like that."

His eyes were blazing. "If I'd fought for her back then, maybe she wouldn't have married Caleb, and she'd still be alive. Do you know that one night a couple years ago, she was in my bar with her girlfriends? They'd all had a little too much to drink on their girl's night out, and after they left, she hung out with me. Do you know what she told me? She told me that she'd always loved me. That she made Caleb wait for until she married him, because she kept hoping that I'd come forward. I didn't do it, she married someone she didn't love, and now she's *dead*."

Jordyn's throat tightened for his anguish. David wasn't the type of man who ever talked about his emotions. *Ever.* For him to speak now meant that the weight was too unbearable for him to suppress. She shook her head. "You can't blame yourself, David. She was just as capable of reaching out to you. It's not your fault. You respected her choice. It's not your style to try to break up a relationship. You waited, and if she'd broken up with him, you would have asked her out then. It's not your fault."

"She's dead, and she wouldn't be if I'd done something about it. Those are facts." His voice was bitter and angry, harsher than she'd ever heard from him. "So, I'm not sitting back again and letting people get killed because I didn't act. Eric goes into my vault, or I kill him. End of story. Which is it?"

Jordyn stared at him, and she realized he meant every word. Where was the geeky, nice guy she'd been best friends with? David was different. Stronger. More muscular. More powerful. Harder. Bitter. "He's not a vampire. He doesn't need to be locked up."

David shrugged. "I don't really care. Caleb wasn't a vampire either, until he was. So, decide. Now. Death or imprisonment." He fingered a cord around his neck, and she suddenly noticed that the pendant on the end of it was in the shape of a miniature stake, covered in the same carvings as the stake that she'd expected to find in her grandmother's bag. "What is that?"

His fingers tightened around it. "Protection."

"You carry your own stake around with you?"

"I do." He jerked his chin toward Eric. "So, make your choice."

She knew then that David would kill Eric in his sleep without hesitation if she gave him a reason. He was that certain that Eric could have gone vampire. Slowly, she looked over at Eric. He looked dead. Pale. Sunken cheeks. His flesh was utter perfection. What if David was right? What if Eric had turned? What would he be like when he awoke? "Okay," she said softly. "Lock him up."

※※※

Locking Eric up was a huge mistake.

Jordyn was certain of it the moment David had slammed the steel door shut, and for the last six hours, she'd become increasingly restless.

She set her hands on the door to David's safe room, pressing her ear to the door, listening. "Eric," she called out. "Are you awake?"

There was still no response.

In one minute, it would be forty-eight hours since he'd passed out. The forty-eight hour deadline since he'd been bitten had already passed, and he was still unconscious. David was now thinking that maybe the clock started ticking when he actually died, which, for their purposes, could have happened when he collapsed after David had treated him.

Less than fifty seconds to go.

"Eric!" She banged her fist on the door, frustrated that she couldn't see past it. There were cameras inside to let the occupants see out into the main house, but David hadn't rigged it the other way, failing to predict that he might have to take a potential vampire prisoner.

She had no idea what was happening to Eric, and it was starting to scare her. What if he was dying? What if he needed help? "Eric!" She hit the door again, and then her phone alarm went off.

She jumped, startled by the noise. She grabbed her phone out of her pocket and turned it off, staring at the door. The timer had gone off. It had been forty-eight hours.

David appeared in the doorway. He was disheveled and pale, having spent most of the night in his lab, feverishly working on putting together more powders, in case he got another vampire victim into his practice. "Any sounds?"

She shook her head. "This is ridiculous, David. I need to check on him."

David held up his hand as he walked across the room. He pressed his ear to the door, and rapped lightly with his fingers. "Eric," he called out. "You awake?"

Jordyn folded her arms over her chest. "Isn't the door solid steel? How would we hear him anyway?"

"It's not soundproof." David braced his hands against the door, suddenly looking exhausted. "I don't know what to tell you. I don't know what to do. He could be sitting in there, silently waiting. They're brilliant predators."

She swallowed, thinking of the attack that had taken Eric down. "I know." After a moment, she walked over to her grandmother's bag and pulled out a tin of the powder she'd used on the vampire who had attacked Eric. "Let me go in there. If he attacks, I'll use this."

David shook his head. "That only works if they're still trying to hold onto their humanity. It doesn't work for those who embrace the depravity. You don't know what he'll choose. The power of bloodlust is intoxicating."

Jordyn cocked her head to study David, surprised by the vehemence of his voice. "How do you know?"

He looked away from her. "I know." His phone rang suddenly, making them both jump. He turned away as he answered it. He listened, then hung up. "I need to go check on someone. I'll be back by dawn. We'll open it then. If he's a vampire, he'll at least be weakened by the daytime. I hope. Who the hell knows how much sun affects them anyway?" He shoved his car keys in his pocket and headed toward the stairs that rose up out of the basement.

"Wait!" She held out her hand. "Give me the keys. Just in case something happens, and I need to let him out."

David glanced at the steel door, and then at her. "No," he said. "I'm sorry, but I see how you look at him. I don't want you to risk your life because you like this guy. We'll deal with him when I get back, I promise." Then, he turned and sprinted up the stairs, ignoring her shout of protest.

Jordyn raced up after him, but by the time she reached the front door, his truck was already pulling out of the driveway. "David!"

Gravel sprayed from his back wheels, and then he was gone, nothing more than red taillights. She growled in frustration, and immediately called him on her phone.

He didn't answer.

"Dammit, David!" She slammed her finger onto the off button, and shoved the phone back in her pocket. Now she remembered why she'd moved away from this town. It was too hard to find her own path when she was surrounded by people who still thought of her as a young girl who needed to be protected and coddled.

She didn't need protection from Eric. He wasn't a monster, and he wasn't a vampire. What she needed was his help. It had been two days since they'd been back, and she'd made no progress toward finding Tristan, because she'd been focused on Eric.

It was time for him to give up on his beauty sleep. They had work to do. Where to start to find Tristan? Go to assorted graveyards around the town and look for evidence that he'd been raising the dead? Or—

A shadow crept across the edge of David's overgrown lawn.

She stiffened, whipping around to stare at the woods. It was dark now, in the deep of night, the hour when sunlight was nothing more than a distant memory and a vague promise. She held her breath, frantically searching the woods as she eased back toward the front door.

Nothing moved, but the hair on the back of her neck

prickled, and her skin crawled, as if invisible fingers were sliding over her flesh. Was it true that vampires couldn't enter a house uninvited? She tried to remember what her grandmother had said, and she had a distinct memory of Oba saying that the night was never safe, no matter where you were.

The sensation of being touched intensified, and she suddenly felt a warmth on the side of her neck, as if someone were breathing on her. She jumped sideways, instinctively slapping at her throat.

Nothing was there.

But she knew she'd felt it.

Something had come for her. Or someone.

She whirled around and darted into the house. She slammed the door and locked it, then raced through the first floor, shutting all the windows as she frantically dialed David. "Come back," she shouted into his voicemail. "Something's outside the house!"

She raced upstairs and shut those windows, her heart pounding with fear. What would glass do to stop a vampire? Nothing. *Nothing.* No wonder her grandmother had had heavy wooden shutters on the *inside* of her house.

Something banged against the glass of the window she was closing, and she jumped back, stumbling over the bed Eric had been sleeping in. For a split second, she froze, gaping at the window as she waited for a vampire to burst through to the sound of shattering glass. It was so dark outside, and the light in the room was bright, making it impossible for her to see if anything was there.

A slow, creepy scratching sound drifted through the room, as if razor-sharp claws were being dragged across the window. "Oh, God." She bolted for the stairs, racing toward the basement. What fools they'd been to be so focused on Eric being the threat. Instead of saving him, they'd cut her off from the one man who could help save her.

She thundered down the stairs and hammered on the door to his cell. "Eric!" she shouted in a stage whisper, afraid to draw attention to the basement. "Wake up!"

There was no response.

Frantic, she leaned her back against his door, scanning

the basement. The stairs opened right up to the first floor, giving her no place to hide. David's lab was behind the decrepit wooden door that wouldn't stop even a toddler. She had no stake, and no weapons. All she had was the powder she'd been saving for Eric.

Reluctantly, she grabbed her grandmother's bag and pulled out the pouch containing the last of the powder. If she used it on a vampire coming to kill her, it might do nothing, and she'd have nothing left for Eric if he were a vampire.

Despite what David had said, she knew Eric, and she had no doubt that if he'd somehow gone vampire, he'd be fighting it every step of the way. The powder would help him.

Dammit, she wished she had a gun.

She had nothing except a half-empty bag of powder. And what if it wasn't a vampire? What if it was something else? She needed *something* to defend herself with. David must have something hidden away. He was sort of paranoid now, and he'd never set up his office without making sure he had a way to defend himself.

She raced into his lab and looked around. Shelves of powder. Some traditional medical supplies. No, no, no.

Then she saw a steel cabinet in the corner. *Yes.* She ran over to it and grabbed the handle. Locked. Frustration roared through her, and she slammed her palm against the metal in frustration. What now?

Then, above her, somewhere in the house, a window shattered.

CHAPTER 11

She was here.

Tristan paused on the second story windowsill, perched on the frame with ease as the glass shattered from the blow of his fist. His fingers dug into the wood, and the entire room was bathed in a red tinge from his vision. He inhaled again, and her scent wrapped around him, deepening the hunger raging through him. It was familiar, but he couldn't place it. All he knew was that she was here, and he was going to claim her on every level.

His incisors lengthened, and his fingernails elongated. Desire and lust roared through him, a need so loud it was almost deafening.

He'd been hunting her for the last two days. Drawn to her scent. Needing her flesh. Her blood. Her body.

And now, he'd found her.

The urgency that had been driving him heightened, and he leapt soundlessly to the floor. His jeans were in tatters, and his body was gaunt with the need to feed. Once he'd scented her, no other would suffice. It was *her.*

Hunger gnawed at him, eating away at his flesh and his sanity, getting stronger and stronger, until all he could do was stalk her.

When he'd seen her standing on the front porch, his entire body had clenched. Need had roared through him so violently that he'd almost screamed with the glory of it.

He'd started to attack. He'd moved swiftly to the edge of

the woods, his body lean and primed for the hunt, and yet, when he'd seen her standing there, he'd stopped. He'd been riveted by the moonlight on her face, by the way her blond hair seemed to glow in the darkness. Her lips had been pure temptation, and her neck had been an elegant line of beauty.

She was his. He knew it. And yet...he hadn't moved to take her.

He'd just stayed where he was, at the edge of the shadows, mesmerized by her. Her scent had drifted across the night to him, a rich fullness that had made his body taut with need. He would have her. She would save him. Bloodlust had roared through him, and yet, when she'd turned her head and looked right at him, something had stayed him from attacking.

He hadn't moved until she'd disappeared from sight, breaking the hold she'd had on him.

The bloodlust had roared back, and he'd charged across the lawn and leaped up to the second floor window just as she'd slammed the window shut.

He'd held onto the frame, his face pressed up against the glass as she'd stumbled back, falling. She'd stared at him again, so intensely that he'd felt his entire being go still, and the howling emptiness inside him had quieted for one brief moment.

He'd wanted to touch her. He'd dragged one fingernail across the glass, tracing it right across her lips.

Then she'd run, racing out of the room, prey in flight.

And now...now it was time.

Tristan straightened up, striding to the door of the bedroom. He was almost there when another scent caught his attention. A familiar one. He stopped and spun around, searching the room for the source of the scent. It was a man. A man he knew had slept here. Memories nudged at his mind, but he couldn't quite remember.

"Eric. Wake up!" Her voice drifted up from downstairs, sweeping through his body and igniting his need to feed. With a low hiss, Tristan spun around and sprinted for the door, the scent of the man forgotten, obliterated by his need for *her*.

✵

When Jordyn heard the sound of the window shattering,

her heart plummeted in terror. It was inside the house! She raced over to the door of Eric's prison and pounded with her fist on the steel. "Eric! Wake up!"

Again, no response.

Frustration roared through her, and she heard footsteps gliding down the stairs from the first floor. Movement so swift and quiet, that she knew it was preternatural.

Something was coming for her.

"Eric!" She hit the door once more in frustration, then spun away, her heart thundering through her as she frantically scanned the basement for something she could use to defend herself. There was nothing in the foyer except an old carpet. *Nothing.*

She ran back into David's lab, skidding on the smooth floor as she whipped around the corner. He must have something in here! Desperation galvanizing her, she grabbed every cabinet door and yanked it open. She shoved her hands across the shelves, knocking things off as she searched for some hidden weapon behind the bags, bottles, and vials of powder, feathers, and other supplies. Bottles crashed to the floor, the glass tinkling as it shattered, and feathers flew up into the air, drifting down with a serenity that drove her mad with impatience.

She yanked open drawers. She searched cupboards. She even broke a pair of scissors trying to pry open the locked metal cabinets against the back wall. Nothing worked.

Then she heard footsteps on the basement stairs.

She was out of time. The only place to hide was the safe room that David had locked her out of. Damn him!

Everything went still out in the basement foyer, as if her assailant was pausing to assess the layout.

She grabbed the pair of scissors and tucked herself into the sliver of space between the locked metal cabinet and the wall. The gap was only about six inches wide, and she could barely fit. She was trapped, but at least three sides of her were protected. She went still, holding her breath as she waited. Her heart was hammering so loudly she could barely think, and she took a deep breath, trying to slow her pulse. Whatever was out there would track her heartbeat with ease. She had to slow it down. Again, another deep breath, as she fought for control that she couldn't attain.

For the longest time, there was only silence.

Had he left? Had she somehow been spared? She whispered a little prayer to the God that she had long ago stopped believing in, her fingers tight around the handle of the scissors. They weren't a wooden stake, but maybe a direct blow to the heart would give her enough time to make it to Eric's truck that was still sitting in the driveway.

She leaned her head back against the metal and closed her eyes, listening carefully, straining to hear the smallest sound that would warn her before he attacked.

There was a small creak, and she caught her breath. It was the sound of the lab door opening. He was inside the lab now.

The air became colder. A dank, penetrating chill settled directly into her bones.

She shrank further back into her sanctuary beside the metal cabinet, her fingers tight around the handle of her scissors.

She waited.

Then suddenly, the cabinet she was hiding behind was ripped away from the wall and flung across the room. It crashed into the opposite wall, tearing David's shelves apart with a horrifying screech of metal. The contents went flying into the air, filling it with so much powder it was as if a sandstorm had swept into the room.

Standing in the middle of the whirling tornado was the man who had resurrected her eight times. Jordyn was so shocked, she forgot to be afraid. His jeans were shredded over his emaciated thighs, no longer packed with muscle and sinew as they once had been. His shirt was gone, and his chest was streaked with blood and dirt. His ribs were protruding from his chest like a skeleton that had been barely covered with the flesh of a human being. His eyes were sunken and glittering with a faint red tinge. His feet were bare and filthy, and his cheeks were caved-in hollows in his face. Her heart stuttered in horror at his condition. "Tristan?" She barely even recognized him, he was so far gone.

His body visibly flinched when she spoke, then he began to inch closer, like a predator stalking its prey.

She realized his face was devoid of human expression. None of the good humor and smiles that had once been a part of his personality. He was pure predator, and he was coming for her.

"Tristan. It's me, Jordyn. I'm your friend." There was no way Tristan would hurt her. He had practically given up his soul to save her life.

But he kept advancing, the slow inexorable approach of death. His fingernails were curved into claws, and his eyes began to glow an even brighter red. "Tristan! Stop it! Back off!" She edged to her right, toward the storage cabinet that was now on its side, dented and twisted from Tristan hurling it across the room. The lock had broken from the impact, leaving the door ajar. What did David have in there? Would it save her?

Tristan kept watching her, his gaze riveted on her as she inched to the side. She kept talking to him, trying to bring him back from the monster that had him in its grip. "I know you're in there, Tristan. You don't want to hurt me. I know you don't." She reached the cabinet and nudged the door open with her foot, trying to peek inside without alarming Tristan.

"No."

She jumped, startled by his voice. It was rough and ragged, as if he'd been screaming for days. She looked at him sharply, her heart breaking for the torment in his voice. "Tristan—"

"You are *mine*." His lips curled, revealing gleaming white fangs, and then he sprang at her with lightning fast speed.

She yelped and dove to the right, but he was on her before she even hit the floor.

※※※

Eric awoke with a start, adrenaline screaming through him. He instantly realized he was trapped. Something was holding him down. Something that hurt his skin, like a thousand razor blades bleeding acid into his flesh.

Menace was thick in the air, and the atmosphere was heavy with the scent of evil. He didn't move. He didn't even open his eyes. He just snapped into full consciousness, his instincts warning of immense danger. He reached out with his mind, sending his power in all directions to summon spirits to assist him. Magic came fast and furious, humming through him with violent strength. With a roar of fury, he thrust it outward and exploded the chains off him.

The metal links slammed into the walls, clattering to the floor. He rolled off the metal table, and landed on his feet. Every muscle in his body hurt. His head was pounding, and he was so hungry his insides felt like they were twisted into a ball of barbed wire.

He looked around, quickly assessing his environment. He was in a small room that contained nothing other than the metal table that he'd been chained to, and a long table of computer monitors. Where the hell was he? The sensation of darkness and doom grew heavier, as if the air itself was tainted with malevolence. He spun around, searching, trying to remember what had happened.

His neck was sore, and he brushed his fingers over it instinctively. The moment that he touched his flesh, the memories of it all came flashing back. The attack. Jordyn bringing him to her friend. The fire incinerating his flesh. The kiss. *The kiss.* "Jordyn!"

He whirled around, searching again, this time for her. He was in a small, enclosed room with steel walls, including the door. He sprinted for the door, and tried the handle, but it was locked.

Trapped.

He spun around, swiftly assessing his prison. There was a row of computer screens on a table against one wall, and there were what looked like grainy security videos on them. He leapt across the room and slammed his hands down on the table as he stared at the screens. The lab was in shambles, and a man was leaping across the room, sailing through the air like a predator. "Tristan!" Eric shouted his name, and his brother stopped, swinging around to face the camera.

Eric swore at the sight of his brother's face. His cheeks were sunken, and ashen. His eyes were haunted, almost glowing with anguish. He was so thin, his coiled muscles straining against his flesh, his clothes hanging in tatters from his beleaguered frame. He rested his fingers on the screen. "Tristan," he whispered. "What happened to you?"

Movement behind Tristan caught his attention, and Eric's gaze shot to the far wall. For an instant, he couldn't make out what had moved, and then he saw Jordyn crawling across the carnage toward David's upended storage cabinet. Blood was pouring down her temple, and her shirt was torn. He went cold. "Jordyn!" He bellowed her name, and she looked at the wall to her right, not at the camera.

She lunged for the wall, and he heard a thud behind him. He spun around as she banged on the wall. "Eric! Help me!"

He looked back and forth between the pounding and the camera, and he realized his makeshift prison was adjacent to the lab. "Jordyn!"

There was a guttural growl from the other room, and Eric saw Tristan turn away from the camera, back toward Jordyn.

She dove for David's upended cabinet and yanked open the door. She frantically started digging through it as Tristan faced her. "Eric!" Her scream ripped through the wall. "He's a vampire! Get out here and help me!"

"A vampire?" Eric went cold when he saw Tristan coil his body, as if preparing to launch himself at Jordyn. His fingers were curved in a clawed grip. "Tristan!" He bellowed at his brother. "Cut the crap! Back off!"

Slowly, Tristan turned his head to look back at the camera. He lifted his upper lip in a snarl, and Eric saw his teeth. They were pointed and gleaming white. He gripped the desk in shock. "Holy shit," he whispered.

Then Tristan slammed his fist toward the camera. It went black, and Eric lost sight of the lab.

"Eric!" Jordyn screamed again, and there was a low growl from the lab, and then a crash.

"Tristan! Stop it!" Eric whirled toward the door and sucked in every sliver of energy, spirit, and magic in the room. He inhaled it into every pore of his body, until his skin almost burst. Then he faced the steel door. "Say goodbye," he muttered, and then thrust all his energy against the door. His power exploded with a crushing roar and slammed into the door, then ricocheted back at him, hurling him against the far wall.

He crashed into the table of computer monitors, and fragments of glass pierced his flesh as he fell to the ground. He leapt to his feet, staggering in pain as he reached behind him and yanked a shard of glass out of his back.

The door wasn't even dented. Son of a bitch. David had reinforced the door with something magical.

There was another scream, and another crash. "Eric!"

Sweat poured down his temples as Eric swung around, searching the room for some weakness in the structure. Nothing. He was in a sealed steel vessel. "Tristan!" he shouted. "Back off!" He summoned more magic, and hammered at the door again.

Again, it rebounded at him and flung him against the far wall. He groaned as he hit the ground, but he was already calling back the magic and spirits the moment he landed. "Come on!" He barely managed to pull himself to his knees as he heard another scream and another crash. He thrust another round of power at the door, and it once again bounced back.

His head hit the steel wall, and for a split second, blackness fluttered through his mind. Crap. He didn't have time to knock himself out. Jordyn needed him! Battling dizziness, he made it to his knees, bracing himself on his hands as he studied the door. He hadn't even scratched it. Son of a bitch. Jordyn was dying out there, and he couldn't even save her?

Fuck that.

He sprang to his feet and braced his legs. He bowed his head and spread his fingers wide down by his hips. He closed his eyes, and then reached way inside him. Energy spun through him, searing through his cells. He took it deeper and deeper into him. He felt the darkness of Tristan's spirit. The evil that stank in the swamp. He reached out across every inch of space, and he drew upon every spirit in the air. The evil. The darkness. The raw, pure power of hate. He drank it all into him, and he didn't block it.

His mind began to spin with images of the hell he had once lived. Death. Destruction. Carnage. Evil. *Pure evil.* His skin shifted, becoming translucent, revealing the swirling miasmas of energy beneath the surface. For a moment, he hesitated, knowing all too well the cost of going any further.

"Eric!" Jordyn's scream ripped through him, and he

made his choice.

He dropped his shields, and he let the spirits consume him.

⌘

"Tristan!" Jordyn stumbled as she backed away from Tristan, holding the last stake she'd found in David's cabinet. She'd managed to grab four stakes from the broken cabinet, and she'd already used three of them. Only one left, and Tristan was still standing. Blood was trickling down her neck, and she felt dizzy. "You don't need to do this, Tristan," she said, trying desperately to reach him. "You don't have to be a victim! You're not a monster!"

He was down on one knee, one hand braced on the floor while he gripped the stake that she'd shoved into his heart when he'd bitten her. His pale fingers tightened on the wood, and he yanked it out.

She grimaced as he flinched, and then he looked up at her, still kneeling on the ground. His blond hair was tousled and dirty. His eyes were glowing red, and his face was the cold, lethal visage of a predator. "You're mine," he said. His voice had been rough and ragged when he'd first shown up, but after biting her three times, it was silky smooth, rolling over her like a dangerous seduction.

Chills raced down her arms as she held up the stake. "Don't do it," she warned.

"The stakes can't kill me," he said as he rose to his feet, moving with the languid grace of a predator. Three times he'd bitten her, and each time she'd staked him, taking advantage of the moment when he first tasted her blood and was sucked into the bloodlust. Each time, the blow had knocked him down, but each time, he'd gotten back up before she could get past him to the door. "You're mine, Jordyn. We both know it." He held out his hand to her, his eyes still red with a dangerously feral gleam. "Come with me."

Sensual compulsion slid through her, and she felt a silky touch glide across her cheek, as if he'd caressed her with his mind. To her shock, desire licked through her belly, desire that was his, not hers. Dear God, was this the power of the vampire?

That he could incite lust in his victims even if they were repulsed by him? Not that she was *repulsed* exactly, but sexual attraction was simply not a part of her relationship with him. "You're like my brother," she gasped, moving back against the wall. Where was Eric? She'd heard several explosions from the safe room, but he hadn't come out.

Her heart had leapt with hope when she'd heard him shout her name, and she'd hurled herself at the wall desperately... but he hadn't emerged. There'd been some booms that had shaken the entire house, but the steel cell he was in had held him captive. Damn David for locking him in there. Seriously. She was going to stab David with Eric's knife if he dared come home.

Eric had shouted at Tristan a moment ago, but now it was quiet. She didn't dare yell for him again, not with Tristan oozing toward her like a well-oiled lothario bent on seduction. "Tristan—"

She felt an invisible caress on her breast, and she sucked in her breath. "Hey!" She batted at her chest. In that split second distraction, he moved, exploding so quickly toward her that she had no time to react.

He leapt across the room, knocked the stake out of her hand, and pinned her up against the wall, in a single, effortless move.

Her heart hammering violently, she went still, afraid to put him over the edge. "Tristan," she urged. "You're my friend. You don't have to be like this."

She thought she saw regret flicker in his eyes. "Oh, but I do, my darling. I do." Then his fingers slid through her hair in a caress so seductive that her legs started to tremble. His mind wove through hers, making her belly tighten with lust.

"Damn you," she whispered. "I don't want this!" She moved slightly, and then slammed her knee into his crotch.

Tristan grunted, but instead of collapsing in pain, he tightened his grip on her hair and yanked her head backward, exposing her neck. "I'm dying without you," he said. "I'm *dying.*"

She stared up at him, her heart tightening at the anguish in his voice. For a split second, she saw the handsome, carefree visage of the man she'd once known, the man who was her friend. His face was steeped in torment, and she felt his pain so viscerally that her muscles clenched in empathy. She realized he spoke the truth, that he *was* dying. Her eyes filled with tears as she set her hand on his face, her fingers prickling from his whiskers. Of course she wanted to save him. She owed him everything. "Not this way, Tristan. You don't want this. I don't want this. *Not this way.*" She'd give him her blood if that would save his life, but not with her pinned up against the wall. Over coffee maybe, trading jokes. "Tristan, I'll help you, but not as your prey."

"Not my prey. My lover," he whispered, his voice gliding silkily across her flesh, and making her thighs clench. "*You do want this.*"

Did she? She sort of felt like she did. But no, those weren't her thoughts. Tristan was in her head, twisting her emotions. "No—" Sudden warmth fluttered through her body, a soul-deep longing, and then he sank his teeth into her neck.

Desire rolled over her, the most intense craving she'd ever felt in her life. A raw, uncontrollable need for sex, intimacy, for the feel of naked flesh beneath her hands. She gasped, her entire body shaking as Tristan drank from her. "No," she gasped, gripping his shoulders. "I don't want this." But she did. She wanted to save him. She wanted him to drink from her. She craved his body, his kiss, his touch. Her entire being screamed for more...but it was Eric's face in her mind. Not Tristan's. *Eric's.*

She twisted, confused, both wanting to lose herself in Tristan's spell, and craving Eric at the same time. Their bodies and faces merged in her mind, until they became one, two parts of a whole, twins of the same spirit and soul. What was happening? She shook her head, trying to clear it, but, her need for both brothers, for Eric, for Tristan, for whatever she could have continued to mount, raging in its ruthless intensity.

Her mind struggled to resurface, but her body began to weaken as he took more blood from her. She sagged in his arms, collapsing against his body. His chest was harder and more muscled than when he'd first arrived, and his flesh was warm now, pulsing with life and strength. She didn't want him, she knew she didn't, but at the same time, she couldn't separate him from Eric in her mind, in her body. It just felt too good to be where she was, and the heat flowing through her from where his teeth were locked into her flesh felt so amazing.

But it was Tristan feasting on her, not Eric. She wanted to save Tristan, but not by feeding the monster trying to take him, and she definitely didn't want to get naked with him. She didn't want Tristan. She didn't want to have sex with him. She didn't want him stirring up lust in her.

She wanted his brother.

"Eric?" She managed to say his name, but her words were slurred, and her legs suddenly gave out.

Tristan swept her up in his arms before she fell, cradling her against his chest as he continued to drink from her. Her head fell back against his shoulder, and her body became too heavy to move. Her eyes closed, and a languid weight settled across her soul. *Eric.*

No, not Eric. Tristan's voice filled her mind. *You belong to me, not him. Me.*

Tristan's thoughts were weaving through hers, tangling with her own, trying to take over. She hadn't remembered how beautiful his voice was, gliding through her like the most deliberate and sensual caress. It felt so good...too good... *No. I'm not yours. Let me go.* She knew she was in danger. She knew she had to get away, and yet her body didn't feel like hers. She couldn't fight. She could barely think.

His teeth slid out of her neck, and he licked the wound once, cleansing the pain before it began, but the desire didn't lessen. His mind was tightly woven around her, sending waves of longing crashing through her as he tucked her more tightly against his chest.

She felt him turn, and she managed to get her eyes open enough to see he was heading toward the stairs, moving so swiftly that she could barely even process. He was taking her away. Where? Why? To seduce her and feed on her? Crap! No! She tried to move, to struggle, but her muscles wouldn't obey. *Eric!*

She felt a sudden rush of dark energy, rolling over her skin. It was pure, undiluted evil, so intense that a scream welled up in her soul. Then, Eric's voice brushed over her mind. *Duck.*

Chapter 12

The urgency in Eric's voice was enough to jerk Jordyn free of the haze coating her mind. Duck? *Duck?*

Desperate energy rolled through her, and she collapsed her body, slipped right out of Tristan's unsuspecting arms. She hadn't even hit the floor when there was a deafening shriek, as if a thousand souls were being tortured in hell. A dark cloud exploded past her and smashed into Tristan's chest. The force of the blow flung him across the basement, spinning him in a violent whirlwind.

The dark mist was filled with thousands of screaming, translucent faces torqued in suffering so horrible she couldn't even fathom it. They reached out with their arms, trying to grab Tristan. Jordyn stumbled backward, gasping in shock as she watched the macabre display before her.

Tristan bellowed with fury and attacked the cloud, moving with lightning speed. Incredibly, he seemed to be able to make contact with the screaming faces. Each one dissolved the moment he made contact, shrieking with a wail of eternal torment as it disintegrated. Cuts and bruises appeared on Tristan's skin as they attacked, damaging him as quickly as he was wiping them out. His body was lithe and well-muscled now, no longer as gaunt as it had been before he'd fed on her, but it was clear that he was still over-matched by Eric's assault. He glanced toward Eric's prison cell with a look of pure anguish. "You fool, Eric! What have you done?"

He gave one more lethal swipe through the storm

of spirits, then he whirled around and sprinted up the stairs, moving with almost incomprehensible preternatural speed and grace. The screaming mass of specters streaked after him, still attacking him as they all disappeared up the stairs. She heard a window shatter, and then the shrieks faded, as they chased Tristan into the night.

Exhausted, she turned toward the door to the steel room, expecting to see Eric standing there, tossing her one of his arrogant grins, ready to request sex as his due for saving her.

But the door was still closed.

The lock was shattered into a thousand pieces, strewn across the floor, and there was a hole in the steel door the size of a man's fist. Through the hole, she could see nothing but darkness. She leaned back against the wall, sinking onto the top step with fatigue. "Eric?"

"Don't come in." His voice was raspy, laced with such deadliness that she froze.

The edge in his voice made her skin prickle with alarm. "What's wrong?" She grabbed the stair railing and pulled herself to her feet. Her legs were shaking, and she swayed.

"Get in my car and leave," he commanded, without any of his customary flirtation. "Go anywhere. Just don't stay."

"I can't leave." The room was spinning, and her mind was still fuzzy. The lust was still pulsing through her, residual from Tristan. She braced her palm against the wall, trying to keep her balance. "If I drive right now, I'll crash and die. Your brother took too much blood from me."

There was a dark silence from the room. "He fed on you?"

She touched her neck, and her skin tingled where he'd bitten her. "You could say that." She leaned her forehead against the wall, fighting to stay vertical. "Thanks for saving me."

Again silence.

"Eric?"

"You need to leave."

His voice was taut, as if he were in extreme pain. Foreboding crept down her spine, and she turned her head toward the room. "Are you okay?"

Again silence.

"Eric?" She levered herself off the wall, and stumbled across the floor toward the door. Dizziness overtook her as she reached the door, and she fell against it with a loud thud. Utterly drained by the trek across the room, she slid down the door to the floor. Wearily, she rested her head against the steel. "What's going on?" She noticed a trail of black mist oozing out from the hole in the door. It looked almost like droplets of black rain, moving horizontally.

She stared at it, mesmerized, as she watched the steady stream pass by her head. It seemed to be glittering, almost as if it were alive. Curious, she lifted her hand to touch it—

"Don't." Eric's low voice froze her, but it didn't sound like it was coming only from the room anymore. It seemed to be all around her, as if he were in stereo.

Adrenaline pulsed through her, galvanizing her. She sat up. "Talk to me, Eric." The mist was continuing to stream out the hole in the door, but now it was gathering several feet away, spinning in a centrifuge of blackness. "Tell me what's going on."

"Get the fuck out of here."

There was no mistaking the pain in his voice. Something was very wrong. "Eric!" The black mist was pouring out of the hole in a stream almost six inches in diameter. "Is that you? Are you disintegrating or something?" Her heart began to hammer in fear. She needed Eric. Without him, Tristan would have kidnapped her and engaged in an untold number of nefarious activities with her. She couldn't do this without Eric! "What's going on?"

Using the doorknob to support herself, she leveraged herself to her feet, and tried to open the door.

"Don't open that!"

"You don't get to tell me what to do!" She yanked on the door. At first, it didn't move, and then it moved a tiny bit. "I'm coming! Hang in there!" She braced one foot on the wall and gripped the doorknob, throwing all her weight into it. "What did you do? Melt it shut? Couldn't you just have opened it?"

"Jordyn." His voice brushed over her, so thick with evil and danger that she froze. "You do not want me to get out of here, and you do not want to see what I am. Get out of here. *Now.*"

"Oh...so that's it." She sighed with aggravation. "You've turned into that 'I'm not human, I'm a scary monster' guy, and you don't want me to see you?" She planted her foot back on the wall and resumed her assault on the stuck door. He'd broken the lock, so now it was up to her. "Well, I have news for you, big guy. I've been through rogue Calydons and two vampire attacks, as well as my dad's drinking, so whatever it is you've turned into is fine with me. The fact you're talking and worried about my safety tells me there's enough Eric left that I'm safe. So, for heaven's sake, get over yourself and stop trying to do the independent guy thing. Seriously—" As she spoke, the door finally gave way. It flew open, and she went sailing backward, tumbling through the cloud of mist that was assembling.

The moment the particles touched her skin, she felt as if her flesh had just been torn from her body. She screamed in agony and crashed into the stairs, twisting and convulsing from the assault. The pain invaded her mind and body, creating images in her head of scenes of torture and death. She saw people's faces screaming in anguish. She felt their horror. She smelled the scent of rotting flesh and dead. "Get it away from me!" She rolled across the floor, away from the mist, crashing into upended chairs as she tried to escape.

By the time she hit the wall, she was out of its range, and the attack ended, leaving her with a blessed respite. For a moment, she lay shivering on the floor, her arms wrapped around herself as she tried to get warm. She was so cold that she felt like every last bit of life had been stripped from her, leaving her body behind to slowly freeze to death. Her teeth were chattering, and her belly was shaking so violently that her muscles were cramping. Dear God, was that from Eric? Was that what he was? Maybe he was right. Maybe she should leave—

A creak sounded from the safe room.

Jordyn spun around, scrambling to her feet as the floor creaked again, as if something of immense mass was walking across it. "Eric?"

She glanced at the stairs, and saw that the funnel of dark mist was gathering in front of it. There was no way to get up the steps without passing through it again, which she suspected wasn't top on her list of smart activities. She glanced toward the safe room again. The stream of mist was thicker now, moving even more quickly. Where was it coming from? "Eric? How do I stop it?"

Again, no answer.

Frantic, she looked at the stairs and the mist again, and realized it was closer to her than it had been a moment ago. She studied it for a moment, evaluating it. It was moving quickly enough that she could monitor its progress. With rising concern, she realized it was heading right for her, getting larger at every moment. There was no way she could get past it. "Oh, come on!" She'd been dined on enough tonight already! "Enough!"

On one side was Eric. On the other was the shimmering cloud of hell. Not a difficult choice. The mist wasn't human. Eric was close enough. She was throwing her lot in with him!

Summoning strength she was pretty sure she didn't have, she ducked past it and raced across the floor toward the safe room. She slipped in through the open door and ran into Eric's prison.

She stopped just inside the doorway, straining to see into the darkness. "Eric!" At first she couldn't see anything, but her eyes quickly adjusted. She was soon able to discern him in the corner. The moment she saw him, horror rippled through her, and her fists clenched. "Oh, God. *Eric.*"

He had backed into the far corner, his hands back by his hips. His fingers had dug holes in the steel, and he was gripping the wall, as if to hold himself back from attacking her. His head was down, but he was watching her intently, his gaze boring into her, like a predator about to launch himself at her. His muscles were strung so tight that they were straining against his jeans and tee shirt. His skin was no longer flesh, but an undulating mass of shadows and darkness, streaking across his face. His eyes were glittering black diamonds. He didn't look like a man. He looked like a creature from the beyond, a very terrifying, and dangerous beyond.

She froze. "Eric?"

He shook his head once. "Leave." His voice was strained and rough.

"What's wrong with you?"

"I had to save you." The shadows lengthened across his

flesh, until he appeared to be almost transparent, as if he were the doorway to a bottomless chasm of hell that resided in his body. "I can't hold it off. You have to get out. I'll destroy you."

She glanced behind her, and she saw the mist was getting bigger. Her gaze followed the stream of mist back into the room, and she realized it was coming from Eric. Every surface of his body was dissolving, turning into the particles that were reforming by the stairs. "What's happening to you?"

He bowed his head, and she saw the muscles in his forearms tighten as he dug his fingers into the wall even deeper. The steel creaked in protest as it bowed beneath his strength. "Get out, Jordyn. *Now.* Run for your life." He raised his head and met her gaze. "You can't save both of us, so save yourself. I need to die knowing that you're safe."

She heard the truth of his words, and something in her heart seemed to come alive for the first time in so long. Walter had endangered everyone who mattered to her in order to bond with her, but Eric had sacrificed himself to save her. Was this really going to be his reward? To die? "How do I save you?"

"You can't."

"Tell me what you did." She walked toward him, carefully avoiding the stream of poison coming off him. "You summoned magic right? Dark spirits? And now they have you in their grasp?"

His eyes met hers, and she saw their haunted depths. "Jordyn," he said desperately. "I did this to save you, not kill you. I can't stop myself if you stay. You have to get out of here."

"No." Her hands trembled with fear as she approached him. "Tristan saved my life. If you die, he dies."

"He's a monster—"

"I know he is, but he's Tristan." She'd spoken so cavalierly about killing him before, but now that she'd seen his face and heard his voice? Never. The Tristan she knew was buried in there somewhere, and she was going to save him. And she was going to save Eric as well. She owed both brothers, and she wasn't going to let them die. There was no one to fight for them except her. "Tell me what to do!"

"Nothing! There's nothing! Stop being so damned stubborn!"

"Hey!" She grabbed the front of his shirt, careful not to touch his shadowy flesh, just in case that did the same thing as the mist. "You don't get to boss me around! You're a spirit guy, yeah, I get it. Don't you remember when we were in the jungle? You weren't the only one who saw that ghost? I did too, remember? You said you were simpatico with spirits, and I said I was too, and then you said we should bond over sex, and I punched you? Remember?"

He stared at her. "Why are you talking? You're supposed to be leaving!"

"I'm saving you!" God, men were so thick sometimes! "I can do the spirit thing, too! My grandmother had some special talents, and I've got it too. I don't know how to use it all that well, because she died before she taught me, but I'm not afraid of spirits or the dead."

Eric gritted his teeth, and his face contorted with pain. "Jordyn, don't do this. You're worth more than this—"

"Listen to me, Eric." She leaned into him. "You don't get to tell me what I'm worth, so shut up and tell me how to save you, or I'm going to start making up things, and that will probably get us both killed. So, either you tell me what to do, or you can just go live with the repercussions of your refusal to give me hints, so my head blew up and it's your fault." She noticed that his body was fragmenting with alarming speed, and she tightened her grip on his shirt. "Tell me, Eric, you damn fool. Just tell me!'"

He was disintegrating so quickly, she knew that even if he gave her information she could work with, it might be too late already.

❑❑❑❑

His control was slipping. Eric knew he had only moments left in his corporeal form before he was gone completely. He couldn't believe Jordyn was still standing in front of him, gripping his shirt like a crazed lunatic. He'd done everything he could think of to make her leave, and she was still there.

A memory long suppressed flashed through his mind, an image of the girl he'd once loved. Fifteen years old with wispy blond hair, and those radiant blue eyes. His first love. True love.

The only female he'd ever dared to love. He saw her reaching for him, then screaming when her hand began to dissolve into the same deadly mist that he was becoming.

He bellowed his rage and shut the memory out of his mind. His body was shaking now with the effort of containing the monster he was becoming. "Jordyn, I can't stop this. Jesus. Don't stand there and let me kill you."

The blasted woman moved even closer, her eyes blazing. "If you don't want to kill me, then don't. It's your choice. If you die, then Tristan dies, and the only two men left on this earth that have stood by me will be dead, and I will be crushed." Pain suddenly flashed across her face. "I can't lose someone else," she whispered. "I can't. Don't die without at least trying."

The anguish in her voice plunged deep into his soul, knifing through the darkness eating away at him. He felt her loneliness strike him, and he recalled the depth of her grief after she'd killed her soul mate. He knew suddenly, without a doubt, that he could not afford to die on her. "You might die, too."

She nodded. "I know. I've died eight times. I'm used to it." She managed a grim smile. "Tristan is flush with my blood. I bet he comes back to save me if I die again. So, let's try it."

"He might not."

Her smile faded. "I know. I'm okay with it. *Tell me what to do*."

He swore, every instinct inside him rebelling against endangering her. "I don't know if it will work."

She pounded her fist on his chest. "Shut up and tell me! Your face is almost gone, for heaven's sake!"

Her desperation broke down the last of his resistance. How could he not try for her? Walter and her dad had never tried. She deserved someone's best effort, and he was all she had left. "Okay." He steadied himself, energy surging through him as he fought to give them more time. "Give me your spirit."

She blinked. "Forever?"

"No." Pain wrenched through him, and he closed his eyes. His muscles were shaking now, and he could feel his arms beginning to dissolve. Once he became fully incorporeal, there would be no recovery. "Now!"

She didn't hesitate. She threw her arms around him and

slammed her body against his.

He gasped as her body sank into his, merging with what was left of his. His soul wrapped around hers, enfolding her literally within his body. The cold that had been assaulting him parted for the warmth of her soul as it flooded him.

Despite the pain he knew she had to be feeling, she locked her arms even more tightly around his neck. "This is what you live with?" she gasped, her voice tight with empathy.

"Yes." He bowed his head, pressing his face against hers. Her skin was soft and warm, living flesh that pulsed with a life strongly grounded in the physical world. He immediately summoned what little of himself he had left and wrapped her in it, shielding her body and spirit metaphysically even as she sank deeper into him.

The evil, tainted spirits searing through his body lunged for her, and she sucked in her breath as they attacked her, trying to possess her as well. She screamed, and he tried to shove her away from him. "It's not worth it—"

"Shut up!" She leaned into him, sinking into his body, which had become nothing more than a translucent mist holding the form of living flesh. "I'm not leaving, so shut up and help me!" She screamed again, twisting in his arms as the dark spirits attacked.

Son of a bitch. What had he done to her? It was too late to stop it. He could only fight for survival on the path he'd already let her take. He pried his fingers out of the steel wall and wrapped his arms around her. The moment he let go of the wall, he began to slide across the floor toward the swirling mist that was growing by the stairs. His boots had no traction, and together they were dragged toward the spirits trying to take physical form.

They were out of time to regret actions taken. It was about survival now. "You have to ground yourself," he said. "You have to shut them out."

She tightened her grip on him. "Yeah, sure, no problem. And I would do that, how?"

They were almost to the door of the safe room now. "Weave a metaphysical shield around your mind and soul. Don't let it in." He touched her mind, showing her how to do it.

"Right, of course."

He felt a sudden surge as she called energy to her. He was shocked by the strength of what she summoned, and he felt the tug of distant spirits responding to her. She hadn't been exaggerating her skills. She did have a spiritual affinity. Unlike him, however, the ones she called were beneficent ones, not the dark magic he called. But even as he thought it, her contact with them slid away.

"No!" He merged his mind with hers, guiding her down the thin tendrils that she'd woven with the spirits. Together, they raced toward help. Jordyn reached out for assistance while he fought to maintain the last shreds of his own protections against the spirits sucking them toward their death.

Spirits whirled through them, good and evil, fighting for supremacy. She clung to him, and their minds, souls, and bodies merged, as they battled to retain control of their souls. The evil was violent and enraged, hammering at her, trying to pry her out of his arms and body. But she didn't release him, and he kept himself anchored around her as they slid closer and closer to their doom.

"We need more," she shouted, her voice strained. "It's too strong. What in God's name did you summon?"

"Everything I could reach." The mist behind her was almost the size of a man, and it was less than six inches away. Cold began to eat through him, a vicious, life-sucking cold draining the last of their souls.

"Eric!" She screamed, her body bowing in pain as the cold hit her.

Son of a bitch! What the hell else was there to do? Their body temperatures were plummeting with the cold onslaught of death. They needed heat...heat! He grabbed the back of her hair and tugged her head back so she was looking at him. He had no time to explain. He just bent his head and kissed her, pouring in every bit of pent up sexual tension he had in his soul, unleashing all the burning lust he could harness into that kiss.

He had to set them both on fire, right now.

CHAPTER 13

Eric's kiss was more than a kiss.

It was a sensual assault that plunged right into Jordyn's soul and ignited the desire that had been building inside her since she'd met him, stoking into flames the lust that Tristan had stirred so ruthlessly. The kiss was instant combustion between two souls who had been denying their attraction for so long.

The moment the desire exploded through her, Jordyn felt the icy chill lessen its grip on her. She threw herself into the kiss, pouring weeks of suppressed passion into it. The heat radiated between them, and she heard the howl of outrage from the darkness as it fought to hold onto them.

It attacked viciously, ripping at her flesh and her soul, flooding her mind with images of torture and death. Her body shaking violently, she focused all her energy on the sensation of Eric's mouth on hers. His lips were tantalizingly soft, and his arms were strong and muscular where he held her against him. His very being was wrapped around her, holding her tight as she sank against him, into him, sliding through his fading flesh until they were entwined on every level.

As he kissed her, warmth flooded her, beginning in her belly as desire pulsated through her. She felt the soothing protection of the spirits she'd called as they wrapped around her and Eric, cocooning them against the howling rage of the spirits that Eric had summoned.

She felt the emptiness of his soul, and the pain that haunted him. There was so much suffering and death in Eric, beyond what any living creature could endure. She experienced the lethal side of his being, a bottomless chasm laced with the ruthless rage and destruction that had given life to the evil now trying to claim him. There was so much darkness within him, so much agony, that she wanted to cry for what he lived with. But as the tears started to form, the coldness returned with a vengeance, and she realized that the negative emotions fed it.

Eric deepened the kiss, a frantic, desperate kiss that she returned with equal force. The malevolent spirits screeched in protest, a battle raging for supremacy. She reached out with her mind, connecting with Eric's spirit. It was fragmented and torn, fluttering in an invisible wind, barely intact. Her heart broke for the state he was in, and she understood why he was so vulnerable to the spirits he had summoned.

She opened her heart to her memories of her soul mate and her grandmother, and let love fill her. She felt the warmth of that love spread through her, and she shared it with Eric, bathing them both in the glow of the positive energy. She called to the spirits that had answered her request, and they encircled her and Eric, casting them in a protective net. As powerful as the positive energy was, however, it shrank under the sheer force of the evil trying to consume them. She felt Eric's spirit shudder, and his shoulders began to fade beneath her fingers. "Eric!"

He locked his hand behind her head and kissed her more deeply, bending her back from the sheer force of the kiss. Passion exploded through her, and suddenly, she didn't care about the spirits battling for their souls, or the vampires or anything. She just wanted *him*.

Jordyn. His breathless gasp plunged straight into her mind. *It's not working. Leave!* He shoved her backward, and she landed on her butt as Eric's body began to disintegrate, sucked into the ever-enlarging funnel cloud.

"Damn you!" She leapt to her feet and lunged at him. She hit him so hard he flew backward. They crashed into the wall, and he slid to the floor as she fell on top of him, her knees on either side of his hips. She grabbed his head and kissed him before he had a chance to move, sinking down over his pelvis.

He swore and grabbed her hips to shove her off him, but she kissed him again, sliding her hand beneath his tattered shirt. His skin was cold, like the damp ocean wind on a frigid winter day, and he shuddered as she spread her palm over his flesh, spreading warmth into his body. She gave him no time to stop her, preying on his ridiculous overabundance of testosterone with tantalizing kisses over his chest.

His cock was hard against the seam of her jeans, and he groaned. She could feel them sliding across the ground, being dragged back into the miasma of doom. The spirits were screaming at her, hammering in her mind, but she didn't care. This was Eric, who had thrown himself into this hell to save her from Tristan, and she owed him.

But it wasn't about whether she owed him. It was simply about *him*.

As they kissed, her knees scraped across the floor as they were dragged. The kiss became more and more frantic, two souls fighting to bring themselves together, but the vortex had caught them both, and they had no anchor to keep them out. All they had were the spirits she had summoned, but the most they could do was keep her sane. They couldn't stop the slide.

Dammit!

Eric turned his head and looked past her. His skin was a swirling mass of shifting shadows, his eyes bottomless pits of torment. Feral determination flashed in his eyes, as if he'd just thought of a solution. Then it was gone, chased away by grim resolution, and he shook his head. He swore, and grabbed her hips. "Get off!"

She tightened her thighs around him. "What did you just think of? I know you thought of something!" Her foot hit the funnel cloud, and she gasped in pain.

"It's not worth it! Get off!" He tried to push her off, but then his foot hit the mist, and his eyes were completely black, glistening with such evil that she sucked in her breath. She saw the moment he changed from Eric to the monster he'd been trying not to be.

She'd been here before, when the man she'd trusted had gone crazy, and she'd killed him. Screw that. She wasn't going to do it again. This time, she was going to fight for him. "If you die, I die. Do you want that guilt on your shoulders? What did you just think of that we could do?" She slammed her fist into his chest. "Tell me!"

His gaze flicked to her neck, right where Tristan had bitten her, and sudden desire plunged through her. "Bite me? You want to bite me? Are you a vampire?"

He closed his eyes, his entire body shaking violently as his feet began to dissolve, swept into the growing mist. "No."

Screw it. Vampire or not, she wasn't ready to die today. She shoved her wrist in front of his mouth. "Do it."

"No!"

"Do it!"

He opened his eyes, and she saw absolute guilt in them, and she realized he'd let himself die before he'd ever do whatever it was going to take to save himself. "I'm not doing that to you, Jordyn. I'm not worth it."

"Screw you!" She grabbed his face and kissed him. For a split second, he fought the kiss, but the sex-crazed hunk of burning love was completely unable to resist her charm. With a roar, he grabbed her face and kissed her, hard, ruthlessly, with everything he had. He poured his soul into the kiss, flooding her with desire and lust, and something so dark and evil that it ate away at her soul.

Her leg was in the mist now, and she called more of the warm spirits to her, encasing them both in a protective circle that kept out the worst of the pain, enabling her to think clearly enough to function. She slipped her tongue inside his mouth and ran it over his teeth.

They were sharp. Pointed.

For a split second, fear ripped through her. What in heaven's name was he? Then his body convulsed, and the screams of the dead surged through her protections, and she knew she had no more time. "Guess what, Eric? Tonight, it's about what I want, not what you want. My choice, big guy, not yours."

She slipped her tongue between his teeth, and then she smashed the heel of her palm into the bottom of his jaw, slamming his teeth together and piercing her tongue with his fangs.

※※※

Jordyn's blood tasted like the nectar of life, and it

thundered through Eric like the gods themselves had just given him a second chance to live. With a roar of passion so intense that it stripped all control from him, Eric cupped her face and drank of her offering, mixing the salvation with a kiss so deep that he felt he would never be able to reclaim himself, and he didn't want to.

No longer was it about doing the right thing or being the hero, or being willing to die to spare her from what he was. It was all about Jordyn now. It was about the burning need for her that had been eating away at him since the first moment he'd seen her in the jungle, pointing that damned gun at him. She'd broken the wall he'd erected between them, and now there was no turning back. He poured himself into the kiss, and his body fed upon her life force, thrusting it through him. Energy ignited in his cells, and he shoved it at the darkness trying to consume them.

Flashes of light and dark exploded off him, showering them both in a cascade of sparks so bright and so dark it felt like he was alternating between heaven and hell, which he probably was. Jordyn returned his kisses with equal passion, until their lips and tongues were a tangle of raw sex and pulsating need.

With each kiss and drop of her blood, strength flooded him, not just his body, but his mind and soul as well. It became about surviving, about saving her. It was no longer about protecting her from what he was, because she'd broken that seal. There was no halfway now, not anymore.

She screamed suddenly, and he looked past her. They were in the mist from the waist down now, and his lower legs were almost gone. Now that she'd connected with him, it was preying on her as well, and he saw her skin starting to flake off into thousands of fragments.

Fuck that. No one messed with his woman.

Without hesitation now, he swept her hair back off her neck and kissed her throat. She gasped, and he felt the desire roaring through her, even though they were both being consumed by a force so dark and deadly that it was almost unstoppable. *Almost.* He swept his tongue over her skin, calling her blood to the surface. He could taste the mark of his brother, where Tristan had left his brand behind. Heat poured through her flesh as she screamed again. "If you're going to do something, do it now, Eric! Don't be so damn slow!"

Lust exploded through him, and he gripped her hair more tightly. "Forgive me, Jordyn." Then he sank his fangs into her neck, and took the lifeblood that would save them both.

⊠⊠⊠

Ecstasy flooded Jordyn as Eric bit her. Her entire body clenched with need so strong she felt like it would tear her apart. Heat flooded her, and the cold that had been attacking her so violently screamed with outrage.

Let me in, Jordyn. Open your mind to me, and anchor yourself to your spirit guides. I'll connect to them using the bridge you establish.

She did as he instructed, lowering her mental shields. She was immediately overwhelmed with the magnitude of his being. She could feel the corded strength of his body, the agony of his soul, and the strength of his will as he fought to hold them together. The skin on her legs burned, fighting the disintegration.

Connect with the spirits!

Trying to ignore the desire and cold warring for supremacy inside her, Jordyn reached out with her mind to the spirits she'd brought in to save them. She opened her heart to them, embracing the benevolent warmth of their female energy. Mothers. Daughters. Grandmothers. Infants. All those who had died and offered their energy back to the earth to heal and endure for future generations. They wrapped their feminine strength around her, protecting her against the doom trying to obliterate her defenses.

Jordyn realized suddenly that the darkness trying to take her was pure male energy. All of the spirits were masculine. She was Eric's anchor, not only because of her goodness, but because she was a woman, the complement to his maleness. Eric touched her mind, sliding down the pathway she was holding with her spirit guardians.

They recoiled from his dangerous male aura and tried to sever the connection, but Jordyn didn't allow them to retreat. She held the connection between Eric and the females, allowing him to wrap the tendrils of his soul around them, one by one, until he was so connected with them that they couldn't break away. For a moment, she and Eric were held in suspended animation, the maleficent forces battling with those protecting them.

Eric's arms tightened around her. *Stay with me, Jordyn. Hang on.*

She nodded, concentrating on the feel of his body against hers, his teeth still deep in her neck as he drank from her, connecting them on a metaphysical level. His skin was as cold as hers, but there was a strength emanating from him that she clung to. She could feel her blood singing through his veins, giving her access to his every thought, every emotion, and every need.

She felt his anger. His guilt. Deep, deep loss. The strongest sensation, however, was his need for her. His desire flowed through her, and she clung to him, sliding her hands beneath his shirt to feel his skin. His groan of desire saturated her mind, and his cock pressed against the junction of her thighs, where she was still straddling him. A carnal craving burned through her, so acute she wanted to scream.

It was different from when Tristan had bitten her and infected her with his lust. This time, the passion was emanating from her as well as Eric. Together, they were a raging combination of heat so penetrating that it was shattering the last bit of her self-control.

With a low groan of capitulation, he flipped her beneath him. She landed on her back, and then gasped as he slipped his hand beneath her shirt and cupped her breast. "God, yes." She arched her back, her body aching for more as his finger brushed over her nipple. Need raced through her, battling the cold still screaming at them.

Eric's fangs slid from her skin in a tantalizing seduction that made her entire body clench with need. He met her gaze, and she saw the battle raging in his eyes. "We need more connection," he said. "My bond with your guides isn't strong enough yet."

She didn't need to ask. She knew what he was talking about. "Make love to me."

The moment the words were out of her mouth, the most incredible sense of rightness poured through her, as if this was the moment she'd been hurtling toward for her entire life.

Eric's face darkened, and he framed her face. "I will not betray you," he said urgently. "I swear it."

She nodded, the pain in her head so great she could barely think. "I believe you."

He swept her up in a fierce kiss even as his hands went to her jeans. She tried to help him, but her fingers were so cold she couldn't grasp the button. He fumbled, but eventually succeeded. It took precious seconds, but then her jeans were gone, and so were his.

He slid between her thighs, his cock pressing against her entrance. He met her gaze, and behind him was a towering inferno of doom. A face was starting to take shape in it, and she realized it was Eric's face. "Dear God," she whispered. "Is that you?"

"It's my true self." And then, he caught her mouth in a kiss and sheathed himself inside her in one swift move.

Her entire body clenched in response to his invasion, a burst of need and passion so extreme she felt her soul fragment. She wanted every part of him to be hers on every level. He moved inside her, slowly at first, then faster, even while he continued to kiss her, devastating kisses that drained her of all thought. She felt his soul wrap around hers, gripping so tightly she almost couldn't breathe, but it was a beautiful, amazing sensation.

She was being pulled in all directions: the ruthless pull of frigid evil against the warmth of her guardians, her own ardent longing, Eric's passion, and her crushing need for him. She felt her grip on the benevolent spirits beginning to falter, but Eric's immense strength surged through her. He reinforced the bond, calling upon centuries of discipline to lock their protectors to them and keep them from breaking away.

Her spirit guardians shrieked in protest, trying to escape from the darkness, but Eric held on, using his physical connection with Jordyn to bridge his gap with them. As they retreated, Eric kept them connected, forcing them to take Eric and Jordyn with them. As she and Eric were pulled away from the darkness, he continued to kiss her, his hips driving in a relentless rhythm that sent shards of desire knifing through her. Her nipples burned for his touch, aching for more, and her body was trembling with hunger for him.

The lovemaking grew more demanding. His thrusts became deeper and faster. His kisses became even more passionate, but she still needed more. She clung to him, kissing him back just as fiercely while her hips bucked and twisted, unable to hold still beneath his lovemaking. The howling coldness raged in protest, but it was in the distance now, growing fainter and fainter, until finally, it was gone.

The moment it vanished, she and Eric released their guardian spirits, so there was nothing left but the two of them. Eric became her world, his kisses, his body, his mind, and his seduction.

She held onto his shoulders, gasping as she felt his legs solidifying against hers. Suddenly, there was no more coldness, just burning hot flesh. They were fully corporeal, and alive. Sensation cascaded through her newly awakened body, and desire coiled more and more tightly between them.

It unleashed with sudden fierceness, catapulting her into ecstasy as the orgasm erupted through her. She convulsed beneath Eric, and then he shouted her name, driving even deeper into her as he stiffened, his body going rigid as his climax took him. Together, they clung to each other, barely holding on as the orgasm elevated them both, drawing them over the precipice, and hurling them ruthlessly into the beautiful beyond.

CHAPTER 14

Jordyn didn't want to ever move again.

The floor of the basement was hard and cold, and a piece of metal was digging into her back, but she didn't care. All she could focus on was the feel of Eric's body wrapped around hers. His leg was draped over her hip, and he'd pulled her against him, cradling her against his chest and sliding his arm under her head for a pillow.

He was playing with her hair, an instinctive, tiny movement that was intimate and tender.

She closed her eyes, basking in the feel of his warmth and strength. It had been so long since she'd been intimate with a man, and her time with Walter had been besieged with the fear of what was to come. Of course, the worst had still come despite all the time she'd spent worrying about it, but she'd survived, older, wiser, and carrying enough battle scars to toughen her up.

She'd learned her lesson. Now, with Eric, the worst would come whether she worried about it or not, so it simply wasn't worth getting all neurotic and upset about. If he was going to kill her, well, then, he could go ahead and try. If Tristan was going to try to make her his personal sex toy/blood donor, well, then, she'd deal with it. But right now, neither Hunter twin was actively endangering her life, so she just wanted to be in this moment, to appreciate what it felt like to be protected by a man who had pretty much just sacrificed his soul to save her.

Seriously, that was incredibly romantic, even for a woman who had long ago given up on romance as a practical emotion. He made her want to be soft again, and that felt good.

He traced his finger over her neck, and her body trembled with sudden lust as he touched the place where both he and Tristan had bitten her. She opened her eyes to find him studying her, his dark eyes unfathomable. His skin was normal again, devoid of the dangerous shadows that had nearly taken him.

Wearily, she touched his jaw, tracing her finger over his whiskers. "You're back."

"Yeah." He caught her hand in his and pressed his lips to her fingertips. "Thank you."

She smiled, idly watching him feather kisses on the tips of her fingers, one by one. "You're welcome. You're a little difficult to save, you know. Too stubborn and possessed, for starters."

"I'm not stubborn. I just didn't want you to risk yourself."

Her smile faded. "I figured that out. Do you want to tell me what that was all about?"

He kept kissing her fingers. "Not really."

She lightly punched his chest. "You lost the right to shut me out when you turned into some sort of ghostly specter thing and then bit me."

He sighed and finally raised his head from her hand. For a moment, he said nothing as he gently tucked her hair behind her ears, his dark eyes searching her face. All his little gestures were so intimate and tender, nothing like the arrogant sex-maniac he had always presented himself as. Was the true Eric finally allowing himself to be seen? "I don't know exactly what I am," he finally said, still smoothing her hair back instead of looking at her, almost like a little boy who was too shy to make eye contact.

Her heart tightened for this vulnerable side of him that he'd never shown her before. "Because you don't know your past?"

He nodded, then finally dropped his hand and looked at her. "There's something inside me that's pure evil," he said simply. "I've always been able to draw power from spirits, but the only ones that I can hear are the ones that are evil and dangerous.

I bond with them, but it's always a battle not to let them take me. They give me power only if I let them in." He shrugged, and began tracing designs on her chest, just above her heart. Her shirt was still on, but that didn't keep her body from tingling in response to his touch. "In order to get through that steel door and take down Tristan, I had to go deep."

She snuggled more intimately against him. "Has that happened before?"

"Once." He splayed his fingers across her chest, as if he were palming her heart. "When we were teens, Tristan and I were messing around with some friends. We were showing off. Tristan resurrected my girlfriend's dog, and she thought he was so amazing. I got pissed that she was into him, instead of me. I wanted to impress her. I wanted to put on a big show, so I summoned as much magic as I could. Unfortunately, we were near a graveyard that had been used as an ancient burial ground for people accused of being demons." He suddenly released her, sliding his arm out from under her shoulders. He sat up, bracing his arms over his bent knees as he stared across the room. "They owned me," he said. "Completely."

"Demons?" Oh, God, she could only imagine. Jordyn sat up, shivering at the loss of contact with him. She glanced around the room, and saw that a deep crevice had been burned across the floor where the funnel cloud had been. Furniture was broken and upended. It looked like a battle had occurred here, which, of course, it had. "What happened?"

"I killed her." His shoulders were hunched. "I killed all our friends, except Tristan."

Jordyn stared at him, her heart breaking for what he must have endured. "Oh, Eric—"

"Tristan killed me to break the spirits' hold on me, and then he resurrected me. The resurrection was complicated, because I'd been claimed by the spirits. He had to give me a piece of his soul in order to save me, connecting us irrevocably. Part of his life force is in me, so if I die, he dies. Conversely, if he dies, then the light that's sustaining me dies with him, and I have nothing left."

Jordyn's heart tightened at the sacrifice. What would it feel like to be loved so deeply by someone that he would give his very life for her? She thought of Tristan, who had done that for his brother, and of Eric, who lived with the realization of his brother's sacrifice every day of his life. "Tristan is not a fool," she said quietly. "He would never have given you part of his life force if you didn't deserve it. You know that, don't you?"

"Nothing is worth his life, the damned fool," he muttered, shaking his head. "He got me back to the living world again, but those spirits are still in me. I'll never be free. I'm their chance to go corporeal in this world, and they'll never stop fighting." He managed a grim smile. "They're where my magic comes from. If it's easy magic, I'm in control, for the most part. But when I need something stronger, things change." He held out his hands, showing her his scarred knuckles. "See? Monster. Told you I wasn't human. I wasn't before that night when we were teens, but now? Shoot me now, babe, because I'm your worst nightmare." He gestured at the burned out crevice. "That's only the tip of the iceberg, sweetheart."

"So, you're a demon?" She studied him carefully. Demon? She shook her head. That didn't feel right. Even when he'd been almost taken, his humanity had still been present. "What about when you bit me? Demons don't have breakfast at people's arteries, do they?"

"No." He looked over at her. "I'm not a demon. They were accused of being demons, but they weren't demons. Not entirely."

Her heart tightened, and then she knew. "They were vampires? The spirits that claimed you were vampires, weren't they?"

"Yeah."

She sat up. "So you're a *vampire? A demon vampire?*" Because being the soul mate of a rogue Calydon wasn't enough, right? She had to complicate her life by getting off the celibacy train with a demon vampire.

"Not exactly, but kinda." He shook his head and ran his hand through his hair. "I don't know what the fuck I am, Jordyn. I don't know what I'm capable of. I don't know anything." He looked over at her. "All I know is that I've never bitten anyone until you, and I've never wanted to. But when that thing was taking us, I knew that's what I had to do." He ran his fingers over his teeth, which were flat and human again. "I've been changing since I've been here. The darkness is getting stronger. I don't know what's going to happen." He looked at her neck. "I *bit* you. What the fuck was that? I *bit* you?"

He shoved himself to his feet and strode across the room. He braced his hands on the wall and let his head drop toward the floor.

Slowly, Jordyn stood up. She was still shaky, but her balance was better now. Her neck was aching, but in a good way, like she'd just downed a gallon of the richest chocolate fudge ever. Instinctively, she ran her fingers over her neck again, drawn to the spot where the brothers had bitten her. "Eric? Why didn't you want me to connect with you? Why didn't you want to bite me?"

He didn't answer, but his body was rigid with tension.

"Eric?" She walked over to him and put her hand on his back. His muscles jumped beneath her touch and he spun around, stepping away from her.

"Why didn't I want to bite you? Maybe because it's psychotic and insane?"

She almost smiled at his reply. "If you're a vampire, like Tristan, it's not psychotic and insane. It's part of survival. Yes, maybe a little barbaric, and terrifying under certain circumstances, but it's actually sort of sexy, in a weird sort of way." She thought back to the vampire that had attacked him and grimaced. "I mean, not when you got your throat ripped out. That wasn't sexy. I just meant when you did it to me." Great. Now she sounded like a vampire groupie? "I mean, I knew you needed to do it to survive, so it was okay. Because I knew you weren't going to kill me." Yikes. What in heaven's name was she rambling about? "Nevermind. So, yeah, how are you feeling?"

His eyes darkened as he looked at her. "Sexy? You thought it was *sexy* when I bit you?"

She felt her cheeks heat up. Of course he'd focused on that one word. He might be part demon-vampire-spirit assassin dude, but he was also Eric, who was always very pleased when the topic of conversation turned to sex. She cleared her throat, and walked over to retrieve her jeans, which had landed near the stairs. "Well, I guess. Didn't you?" Had she been the only one to have her body turn into a boiling cauldron of pure sex when his teeth sank into her flesh? Fully mortified now, she grabbed her underwear and pants, and yanked them on, not looking at him.

He said nothing, and she felt his gaze on her, drifting over her nakedness with the same heat that he'd sent in her direction so many times in the past. This time, however, it felt different, because the sexual tension had been shattered, sliced through with the mind-blowing sex that was still making her legs tremble.

She glared at him. "Can we talk about something else? It was one moment of weakness. So, I thought it was kind of sexy when you bit me. That doesn't mean that I suddenly think *you're* sexy or that I want a repeat of that little lovemaking session. That was to save us both, nothing else. Right? Right. Of course, right? Men," she muttered under her breath as she finished zipping her pants. "They overdramatize everything."

Slowly, he shook his head once. "You thought it was sexy."

The rough edge to his voice made prickles slide down her spine, and her gaze snapped to his. His eyes were blazing, and his gaze was suddenly so hot she felt her skin began to burn.

She froze, staring at him. "Did you?"

He nodded slowly. "Yeah. I did. It was hot as hell."

The tension between them thickened, until her belly began to throb.

"You want to do it again?" he asked.

She swallowed. "No. I don't."

He smiled, a predatory smile that had all the attitude of the man who'd chased her through the jungle to save her from being incinerated by a madman. "You're not a very good liar."

She lifted her chin and set her hands on her hips, ignoring the trembling of her belly. "You're not a vampire, Eric," she said, redirecting the conversation. "We both know that. You've been running around during the day since we met, and this is the first time you've ever wanted to bite someone, right? So it was just because you were in so deep to those spirits that have some vampire background—"

"I was bitten two days ago, and then I got daggers for teeth, bit you, and fed off your blood." His expression had become grim and serious. "So, yeah, makes a guy think, doesn't it?"

His words settled around them, and she stopped, staring at him. His eyes were dark and brooding. "You don't think you're an actual vampire now? I mean, you can't be. You're standing here sane, right? Vampires aren't sane. Just look at Tristan."

He took a deep breath and ran his hand through his hair. "Tristan," he said softly, his pain evident in his voice. "The poor bastard."

Her heart softened at his evident anguish, and she nodded. "I know," she said. "He was my friend, too."

His gaze studied her. "You okay? What did he do to you?"

Instinctively, she touched her neck, and Eric's gaze followed her movement. His eyes narrowed. "He bit you exactly where I did?"

"Yes. He was dying. I could tell. He needed to feed." She turned away, suddenly embarrassed by how she'd responded to Tristan's bite. Yes, she'd been thinking of Eric, but there'd been no doubt about the sexual nature of her response to him, even as she'd been trying to get him to stop. She picked up one of the upturned chairs and righted it. "I could see he was present, but the vampire side of him was dominant." She bit her lip as she lifted another chair. "He wanted to kidnap me. He said I was his." She glanced over at Eric. "I was kind of scared," she admitted softly. "I couldn't stop him. You saved me. Thank you."

Eric was quiet, and she glanced over at him. He had a strange expression on his face, one that she couldn't quite interpret. Guilt? Horror? Shock? "Eric? Did you hear me?"

Slowly, he turned and grabbed his own jeans. He yanked them on, his muscles flexing as he did so. Was it her imagination, or was he more chiseled than he had been before? Once his jeans were on, he turned to face her, his hands fisting by his sides. "I'm not the good guy, Jordyn. Don't thank me." He ran his hand through his hair again, in a gesture she was beginning to recognize as indicative of his tension. "We both bit you? How fucked up is that?" He shook his head. "Don't thank me, Jordyn. I'm your worst nightmare. We both are, apparently."

She frowned at his refusal to acknowledge that he'd

saved her life. "You went simpatico with some really bad spirits to save me. I think that makes you a good guy."

"No. Just as Tristan is, well, he's not right in the head anymore, I'm also messed up. I'm a monster, worse than he is. If I go over that line, there's no more of me left. Just the predator."

Jordyn bit her lip, thinking of how it felt to have that mist touching her. The unbearable cold, sucking life from her body. There had been nothing of Eric in that nightmare, even though it had been created and built by the very flesh from his body. So, yes, he did have the big, scary, bad guy thing going on, but at the same time, he was Eric. After seeing the love of her life go completely insane and turn into a rogue predator with no mercy, nothing could really scare her anymore, especially not a guy who'd managed to stay completely sane while his body was disintegrating into the funnel cloud of hell.

"Yes, I admit that your woo-woo side is sort of daunting." She gave a slight shrug. "But it didn't get us, so it's okay."

"Is it?" he challenged. "You really think so?"

She frowned. "Well, we're both standing here, so yes, I think we're okay at the moment."

"Well, we're not. Those spirits are all over my soul, eating away at it. What do you think's going to happen to you now? Didn't you feel how they came after you?" He walked over to her and caught her arm, pulling her close to him. "Your blood burns in my veins now. Our souls are interconnected. We're linked on so many levels." His voice softened. "Your goodness saved me, but now the poison that haunts me is a part of you." He ran his finger over her jaw so softly that her throat tightened.

He spoke of terrible things, and yet his touch was mesmerizingly tender. "I feel the same as I did before," she said stubbornly. "I'm not tainted."

"You are. They'll hunt you now, through me. Because of what we just did, you're in my world, my hellish, dangerous, shitty world. Didn't you see your skin start to flake after I bit you?" He closed his eyes and dropped his hand. "You need to go," he said softly. "Get as far away from me as you can. It's your only chance."

"Leave? After all we've been through to save Tristan? My whole town is in danger now, as well." Jordyn shook her head.

"No. I'm not leaving. If you're right, it's too late for me to escape you anyway." She raised her chin. "I'm not afraid."

He opened his eyes. "But I am. I'm afraid I can't protect you from myself."

Jordyn's heart thudded at his words. Walter had shown her that a man could kill those people closest to him, people he loved. She'd seen it, and she still lived with the bloodstains on her soul.

And now, here she stood before a man who had the same capacity, and he'd already lived that hell once. He'd already killed those he loved. He'd already had to die to stop himself. And now it was getting worse...and he'd brought her into it. Was she naïve in believing she was safe from his inner beast? "You saved me," she said firmly, her mind rebelling at the comparison to Walter. This was Eric. He was different. He wasn't compelled by some horrific destiny that could not be stopped. He lived in a world of choice, where sheer force of will was a power unto itself. "You came back from the edge. It doesn't own you."

"This time I triumphed over it. I didn't the other time, and people died. People I loved died." He gently clasped her shoulders. "You didn't run away from Walter, Jordyn. You stayed by his side, and he betrayed you. Don't make the same mistake again and trust the wrong man. I'm the same as he is, only worse."

"Worse?" She raised her chin. "How are you worse?"

"Because there's no *sheva* bond holding us together and forcing me to protect you." His thumbs traced small circles on the front of her shoulders as he continued to hold her, a gesture of affection and intimacy that belied his attempts to push her away. "Walter killed everyone, but not you. He'd never have physically harmed you because your bond with him protected you. I'm not like that. I killed the woman I loved. There's nothing to protect you from me. So, yeah, worse."

She swallowed. "Your willpower protects me."

He swore under his breath and released her. "Hell, Jordyn, I'm not the good guy. Don't you get it? You believed in the wrong guy before, and you paid the price. Do you really want to take that risk again?"

Jordyn thought of her daughter, of her family, of her

friends. She remembered the horror of watching the man she'd loved rip them apart as if they were made of rags. She'd believed in Walter so completely. She'd believed in her love for him, and his love for her, and so many had died because she'd been wrong. She looked at Eric, tears brimming in her eyes. "Eric—"

He set his fingers over her lips. "Don't say it," he said. "Just let it go. Let us go. Pack your bags, go back to your life, and let me save Tristan. Now that I've located him, I'll be able to find him more easily."

A part of her wanted to do as he suggested. The part of her still bleeding from what had happened with Walter wanted to flee, just as Tristan had told her to do when she'd still had the chance. And here she was, with another Hunter male giving her the same advice she'd ignored from Tristan. Once again, she had the chance to run before bringing hell down upon her and everyone she loved.

Except, there was no one left who she loved. Everyone was already dead.

She'd been running ever since Walter's death, frantically trying to save other women from the men in their lives, living in fear of what could go wrong. But the moment she'd met Eric, something had awakened inside her, something that had been dead for so long. Eric and Tristan had fought for each other against all odds and obstacles, and they'd shared that with her, each of them risking themselves in order to give her another chance at life. Was she going to waste that opportunity and go back to Boston to her shelter, which was being competently run by her stand-in? Or was she going to use that gift to make sure Eric and Tristan didn't pay the ultimate price for helping her? Who else would help them if she left? Eric would have crossed that line tonight if she hadn't been there for him. Tristan had been close to death before he'd fed from her.

They needed her, and no one else could help them, just as how she'd needed them both and they'd stood by her.

She knew there was no choice to be made. She lifted her chin, and faced Eric. "I'm not leaving until we're finished here. We came to help Tristan, and my town." She met his gaze, and didn't say the last words, the ones reverberating so deeply in her heart. Yes, she'd come here to save Tristan, and then expanded that to include her town when she'd realized vampires had returned, but it had become more.

She also wanted to save Eric, not just from the darkness that flowed so freely within him, but also from the guilt that haunted him so deeply. She knew what it was like to have the past wrapped so tightly around her throat that it was impossible to breathe, but being with Eric had loosened that noose ever so slightly. Eric was choking that same way, and he had no one else to stand by him.

Eric grimaced. "Jordyn—"

She marched over to him and glared up at him. "Shut up." She knew she had to stay, but she was barely brave enough to make that choice. She needed him to support her, not talk her out of it.

He blinked. "What?"

"You don't get to tell me what to do. No one does. I have nothing left to lose, except the lives of two brothers who taught me what it was like to believe in someone again. So, no, I'm not leaving. I'm not scared of what you might become. So—"

"Dammit, Jordyn!" Eric grabbed her shoulders, his fingers digging in. "Don't you get it? *I killed her.* Her name was Jane McPherson. She had curly blond hair, dimples, blue eyes, and the most infectious laugh in the world. She fucking lit up my life, and she accepted me as I was. She didn't give a shit about what I attracted into my soul. She was the only good thing I'd ever experienced in my life, other than my brother. I fucking worshipped her, and I killed her."

Her throat tightened at the anguish in his voice, and the depths of his self-hate. "Eric—"

"She was screaming at me to stop while I was killing everyone else. She and Tristan were shouting at me, screaming their heads off. I turned around and walked over to her. I grabbed her around the neck. I can still see her blue eyes the moment she realized I was going to kill her." His voice broke. "Jesus, Jordyn. Her eyes filled with tears as she grabbed my wrist. I can still feel her fingers digging uselessly into my flesh, or what was left of it. She looked me right in the eye and said, 'but I loved you.' And then I killed her. She literally disintegrated in my hand, turning to dust. I heard her scream of horror as her soul was sucked into the hell that lives within me. I still hear her screaming. Every fucking minute of every day, I hear her scream." His fingers tightened. "So don't tell me you're going to stay, Jordyn. Don't fucking do it."

He shoved her away from him and turned his back, striding into David's lab, hurling items aside as if he were searching for something. His back muscles flexed as he lifted the upended cabinet as if it were made of feathers.

She sank down onto the bottom stair, hugging herself as she watched him bulldoze through the lab. She'd felt every bit of his agony when he'd been talking about Jane. It was so obvious that he'd loved her, the kind of deep, uncluttered love that only teenagers can have, and yet he'd stared into her eyes and killed her.

Eric had killed the woman he'd loved in cold blood.

Tears filled her eyes, and she wrapped her arms around herself, hugging tightly, but unable to stop the shivering. He was just like Walter, only worse, because he'd killed the woman he'd loved. "Were you drinking?" she asked. "When you killed Jane and the others?"

He looked back at her, and she saw his eyes were bloodshot. "No."

No. A simple answer that put full responsibility onto his own shoulders. Walter, at least, had been drunk when he'd completed the bond, and then been taken by it.

Eric tossed a chair against the wall, where it thudded with a clatter. "But even if I had been completely intoxicated, it's not an excuse. Walter was an unworthy bastard who betrayed you. The fact that he got drunk shouldn't have changed a fucking thing. He owed you his life, and he stole it from you. Just like Jane and me. There's no excuse in the world sufficient to justify a man who fails the woman he loves." His words were bitter and hard. "Walter didn't love you, Jordyn. I don't care about that damned *sheva* bond. It's crap, if you ask me. If it was that strong, if he'd loved you that much, he couldn't have done anything that would have hurt you. Let him go. He's not worth all that you've already given him. Just fucking let us all go. We're not worth it." He walked over to the door and kicked it shut.

The door slammed closed, making a loud crack like a

gunshot, and instinct made her jump, terror leaping through her at the sound…but it was nothing. She sank back onto the step.

No. It wasn't nothing. It was everything. Eric had just shut her out.

Jordyn hugged herself as she sat on the stairs, trying to hold her emotions together. She bowed her head, resting her forehead on her knees as she listened to Eric muttering to himself as he rifled through the carnage of the lab. She felt his pain. His suffering was so extreme it was eating away at the very air they breathed.

Would he really kill her?

He might. She had to acknowledge that. He really, and truly, might kill her.

CHAPTER 15

Jordyn let out her breath as she touched the mark on her neck, facing the somewhat less-than-rosy reality that she might be completely wrong to believe in Eric. She had to acknowledge the truth that either brother might kill her. Not because they weren't in awe of how fantastic she was, but because of that parasitic demonic aura that was so fond of clinging to the men she cared about.

In addition, no matter how much of a Pollyanna she wanted to be, after seeing the twins in action, she couldn't deny the fact that they might kill others besides her, turning innocents into a midnight snack, much like Walter had done, but with their own creative spin.

And, finally, they might even lay waste to the entire community of Parrish Creek. Although it wasn't the most idyllic town on the planet, it was her home, her world, and the place where her roots had first sunk into the earth.

So, a potential trifecta for the Hunter men, unless they were the men she wanted them to be.

What if she was wrong? Would saving them cause more harm, both to herself, to the community in general, and even to them? Were they actually the men she was meant to stop when she'd made her vow to protect women from the bad men they loved? Or was she supposed to expand her shelter of protection to include them and protect them from themselves?

An invisible band tightening around her chest, she surveyed the carnage of the basement. There was blood spattered across the floor. Hers? The floor was burned, and the air was thick with the stench of death and decay. Smoke still leaked from the ragged hole Eric had blown through the steel door. So much damage in so little time.

She watched the smoke spiral into the air, dissipating harmlessly from sight. The shadows still present in the mist were almost the same as those that had been undulating beneath Eric's skin, a thousand cursed spirits threatening to overtake him.

If she hadn't been here to stop Eric, what would he have become? She bit her lip, unable to deny that he'd been awfully close to the edge. Would he have been able to regain control without her? She didn't think he would have. If not, how many would he have hurt? If she hadn't fed Tristan, who would he have killed to find sustenance? How strong was their will in comparison to the monsters trying to take them?

She bowed her head as the enormity of the situation pressed down upon her. She wasn't sure either brother would have been able to hold their inner monster at bay without her help. If they had any chance, they needed her. But what if she helped them, and they wound up crossing that terrible line anyway, a line they never would have crossed if she'd been brave enough to kill them before they acted? How could she endure what she'd been through with Walter?

Walter. The name that used to spread love through her entire soul now sent a cold ripple of fear and doubt. Was he really as bad a man as Eric said? Was he really not worth all the love she'd poured into him? Should he really have been able to stop himself from destroying everyone, and killing their daughter? Was the *sheva* destiny not an excuse? He'd told her he'd loved her a thousand times, and she'd believed him. Yet, he'd still turned on her.

Eric had said he'd loved Jane, and yet, his love hadn't been strong enough to defeat the spirits that had taken him—

A loud crash sounded from the lab, making her jump. "Eric? Is everything okay?"

He didn't answer, and the door was still closed, cutting him off from her. After all they'd just endured together, that was his choice? To drive a wedge between them in a denial of the bond they'd just created between them?

She pressed her face to her hands, her head throbbing with all the anguish cascading through her. After a childhood of being betrayed by her father, no matter how much she'd tried to love him, she'd poured everything she had into Walter...and had it all meant nothing? Was she so wrong about it all? Was she so stupidly desperate for love that she was completely blind? Her heart felt like it was cracking open, and bleeding all over what was left of hope, love, and life. What did love even mean? What were the bounds? Had Walter and Eric not really loved her and Jane? Or did love mean nothing in the long run?

She didn't even know what to think or believe in anymore.

Eric suddenly yanked the door open. His eyes were blazing with emotions. "You've given your life for others too many times," he said. "Start living for yourself. Tristan didn't save you to die for us. He saved you because he wanted you to live. Just go."

Tears spilled down her cheeks, and she shook her head silently, too overwhelmed to speak.

For a moment, Eric said nothing. His face was stoic, but his dark eyes were swirling with emotion. He looked so human in that moment, a man staggering under the weight of what he was. That was why she believed in him, because he was more than the spirits trying to bind him. His hands were bunched in fists, and his skin was still ashen and flaking, barely recovered from what had happened. "I don't know what to do," she said quietly, unable to keep her voice from breaking. "I don't know what to think."

Eric ran his hand through his hair, muttered something under his breath, and then walked across the room toward her. She said nothing as he approached, too drained to even lift her head from her hands. How different from when he'd approached her in the bar, with so much electricity and anticipation crackling between them. Now? Just a feeling of overwhelming loss and emptiness.

Without a word, he knelt before her, two steps below where she was sitting. For a moment, he didn't move, and her vision blurred with the tears she couldn't stop. He was so strong and handsome, his eyes a turbulent swirl of torment.

"I'm sorry," he whispered.

She held out her arms, and he came to her, pressing his face against her belly. She wrapped her arms around his head, holding him close as she rested her cheek on his hair, unable to stop the flood of tears. He encircled her waist with his arms, pulling her close until he was between her knees.

The sobs wracked her body, tears that she'd held at bay for so long. Tears for that truth that her choices had led to her daughter dying at the hands of the man she'd loved. "I failed my daughter," she whispered. "I didn't protect her. I don't know who to believe in or what to do. I just can't keep failing."

Eric lifted his head. "He killed her. Not you. You loved. It's not your fault. You aren't the one who screwed up."

"Yes, I did! My love was a mistake!" She covered her face with her hands, fighting back the tears. Her love had been a mistake. A failure. The stupid choice of a desperate girl who wanted only to be loved. "I tried. God, I tried. Was he really the horrible man you said he was? And if he was, how did I keep loving him? Why did I believe in him? Why didn't I see what would happen? Why didn't I run with Laura while I still could?"

"It's not your fault." Eric pulled her into his arms, and pressed a kiss to her forehead as she cried. "I'm sorry," he said. "I shouldn't have said all that. I'm just so fucking terrified of hurting you. What if I kill you?" His body began to tremble where he held her. "What if I wipe out the only good thing that has happened to me since that night from hell? What if I destroy the one light that has been able to suppress the darkness that consumes me?"

She opened her eyes and looked up at him. His face was haunted, as haunted as it had been when it had become nothing but shadows, only this time it was his living, human face that was crumbling with anguish. She touched his cheeks, and he set his hand over hers, holding her against him. "You feel so good," he said, his voice raw. "Like you're this angel sent to give me a second chance." His fingers tightened on her. "I'm so fucking terrified that I'm going to kill you. Hell, just knowing I made you cry makes something inside me fracture." He ran his fingers through her hair, a touch far too tender for a man like him. "You're this bold, courageous fire that lights up the world for a thousand miles, and I'm extinguishing it. I can't do that to you, Jordyn. I want to uplift you and bring light into your life in a way I've never done before, not drag you into the hell that I live in."

His words were raw with emotion, cut ragged by the depth of his torment. Her heart ached for his pain. She understood it, because she felt the same way, as if her love could destroy. "I know you're afraid of hurting me." This empathetic soul was the Eric she'd sensed, beneath all his macho arrogance, a man whose soul had been shattered so long ago.

His fear was so thick she could feel it pressing in on her, an invisible weight trying to squeeze the air from her lungs. It was a fear that Walter never had. He had accepted that it might happen, but never allowed himself to feel the horror of it in his bones. Eric wasn't running away from the possibility of hurting her. He was facing it, and that made him different from Walter. She lifted her face to his, looking at him steadily, even though her heart felt like it was bleeding from a thousand different places.

"And I understand you might hurt me." God, to say the words aloud was devastating. *I understand that the man I am falling for might kill me, just like before.*

A shudder went through his muscular frame, and he closed his eyes, his grip tightening on her. "So, you'll leave?"

Tears were streaming down her face so thickly that she could taste the salt from them. "What if I leave, and then Tristan kills the entire town without me there for him to feed on? What if I leave, and you lose control and kill someone because I'm not there to help you back from the edge again? What if you find yourself standing there, above a score of your victims, knowing that you pushed away your one chance to win? You can't do it without me, can you?" She knew the answer was no. Eric needed her. Tristan needed her. *They both needed her.* Energy surged through her at the knowledge that she could make a difference. Just like she could make a difference at her shelter in Boston, she could make a difference with these two men. With Eric and Tristan, however, it was personal, and that made it impossible to walk away.

He opened his eyes, staring at her. "You want me to put you at risk so I can save others?"

She shrugged, resolve beginning to pulse through her, shoving aside the fear and doubt. "If I leave, then we're all giving up. Walter gave up, and he killed everyone. I don't want to be like him. I won't be like him. I'll fight the battle to the end." As she said it, she knew it was true. Walter had surrendered to his need to bind them. He'd used the alcohol as an excuse, but he'd done it. He'd stopped fighting. She wouldn't do that. Yes, she wouldn't be dumb enough to fall in love again and risk emotions that could blur her vision, but she wasn't going to walk away when she owed people her life. She wasn't that weak. She hadn't survived eight deaths just to be a wimp and stop fighting.

Eric ran his hand through his hair. "I can't make that trade, Jordyn. I can't risk your life to save other people."

She managed a small smile. "I appreciate the sentiment," she said honestly. "But if you feel that way, then don't kill me."

He cocked an eyebrow at her. "Just like that?"

"Just like that."

"Ah, my optimistic sweetheart." He brushed his finger across her jaw, sending sparks cascading through her. "You know I can't promise that—"

She sat up, turning toward him, fresh resolution pounding through her. "I think you can." She couldn't quite keep the challenge out of her voice, but it felt good to feel that conviction again. This was Eric, not Walter. They were different, and she knew it.

His eyes narrowed, and he dropped his hand. "Jordyn—"

"You give your life for your brother, and he does the same for you. Both of you are honorable, courageous men who stand by those you love." She touched his face, her fingers prickled by his whiskers. "Walter never promised he wouldn't go rogue. He would never say it. He always warned me it might happen, and I chose not to believe it. Did you ever promise Jane you wouldn't kill her?"

He blinked. "What kind of question is that? Of course not. It was kind of implicit, you know? When you love someone, there's an underlying assumption that you won't disintegrate them. I didn't think it was something that I needed to preempt by a promise."

"Well, there you go. You're older and wiser, and now

you know." She stood up and faced him, challenging him. "You told me in the jungle that you would never lie to me. Ever. Well, then, if you promise you won't kill me, then you have to stand by it."

His forehead furrowed, as if he thought her logic was inane. "A promise can be broken. You want me to pinkie swear that I'll never kill you in order to assure your safety? It doesn't work that way."

"I'd believe in you." The moment she said it, she knew she did. It didn't matter what had happened when he was a teenager, or what he was capable of. Eric was not Walter. He could do it. She'd seen Eric take on the vampire, and she knew how hard he'd battled to save them both from the cloud-o-doom. "I'll accept your promise. Promise me you won't kill me."

He swore. "I can't—"

"Promise me!" Even as she made the demand, she saw the doubt in his eyes, and felt the depths of his self-recrimination.

"No." He shook his head, his jaw flexing with stubbornness. "I won't lie to you, Jordyn. I might be a murderer and a whole lot of other unpleasant shit, but I can at least be the guy who stands by his promises, so yeah, I'm not going to promise that you can hang with me and walk away unscathed. I know what I'm capable of."

She sighed. Yes, she understood his trauma from the past, but she also knew who he was now. He'd been a teenager before. He was a man now, in every sense of the word. "Giving validity to your possible shortcomings isn't always a positive character trait. You know that, don't you?"

He cocked an eyebrow at her. "You're giving me therapy? Really? Do I look like a guy who wants his character traits mapped out?"

"No. You look like a guy who thinks it's heroic to wallow in the fact that he happens to be possessed by any number of malevolent, deadly spirits who like to prey on assorted living creatures. It's not heroic."

He narrowed his eyes. "I'm not trying to be heroic. I just don't want you to sit around knitting on my lap when you should be shooting me in the head. Personally, I think it's kind of commendable to warn people that you might kill them *before* you actually do it, so yeah, I think I'm taking the high road here."

"Well, I don't knit, so you don't need to worry about it. Seriously. Do I look like a knitter? Besides, if I were on your lap, the last thing I'd be doing is knitting, because your wandering hands just don't keep to themselves, do they?" She grinned when his eyes darkened, and his arms tightened instinctively around her waist. See? All it took was a little sensual undertone, and she'd pried his attention off his deadly nature. Men. So easy to manipulate.

"So, here's the deal." She stood up, extricating herself from his lap before he could put her accusation into action... ah...too late. "Stop it." She slapped at his hand as it slid over her hips, as if he were reluctant to let her go. She had to admit, the feminine side of her loved the fact that he couldn't quite let her go even when he was demanding she walk away, but at the same time, he was distracting her from her rant. Sometimes, rants were important. Damn him for being so tempting. "The only one you're lying to is yourself." She set her hands on her hips. "I'm staying, because I'm not done here. Not with you, not with Tristan, and not with this town. If you don't like me being near you, then you can be the one to leave."

He glowered at her, all the sexual heat gone from his gaze. "I'm not abandoning my brother—"

"Of course you're not. Then you have a choice to make. Commit yourself to being the man you wish you'd been when you were a teenager, or just give up, like Walter did." She brushed past him and headed up the stairs. "Come find me when you decide." Before he could protest, she spun around and strode up the stairs, ready for him to call her back, or protest, or do some equally irritating Eric-type move.

He didn't follow her, and she made it all the way to the top of the stairs and slammed the basement door shut before he'd even moved.

She leaned back against the door, resting her head against the wood, proud of herself for standing up to him. See? She wasn't going to give up so easily.

Then she noticed that the picture window in the living room was completely shattered. Glass was all over the windowsill and the yard outside. Tristan must have leapt right through it when he was escaping Eric's assault. The memories of what had happened settled down upon her, stripping her of the momentary feeling of triumph. Fear rippled through her. How long until Tristan came back? And what about Cicatrice? She stiffened, adrenaline surging though her body as she looked out the kitchen window, looking for Tristan's face peering in at her, and then noticed the first orange streaking across the sky.

Dawn had come. Tristan and the other vampires would have to go below ground.

She and Eric had time. The respite was too brief, but it gave them time to at least breathe.

With sudden exhaustion, she slithered down the door to the floor, too weary to stand. The last exchange with Eric had drained her of her final reserves of energy. Now the weight of the last two days settled in on her. Two days of desperately awaiting Eric's return to consciousness, and then donating too much blood to each brother, and then nearly being disintegrated. A full weekend by any standards.

There was no noise from the basement, and she knew that Eric hadn't moved either. She decided to take that as a good sign, that he'd absorbed her words of wisdom and beauty, and was contemplating ways to swear his undying oath that he would never kill her.

She stared at the sky, watching it come alive with beautiful pinks and oranges. What would happen when night returned? Would she die at Eric's hands?

She might.

Until he believed that he could stop himself, he wouldn't be able to. She knew Tristan would be coming for her. Her blood had strengthened him, and he would have a day of sleep. He'd be strong and ready, and on the hunt.

The bite wound on her neck tingled, and she rubbed it. The skin was warm beneath her touch, as if the blood was thundering beneath the surface. Tristan was stalking her, of that she had no doubt. Without Eric's intervention, would she be buried in the earth somewhere right now, on her way to becoming Tristan's concubine and blood donor?

She hadn't been able to stop him by herself, and

that didn't even count the vampire that had attacked Eric, or Cicatrice, who was still out there. It had taken both of them to defeat Tristan and the other vampire. Alone, they both would have died. Against Cicatrice, they would need even more than what they'd been able to summon thus far. She knew Eric wasn't going to abandon Tristan, and neither was she, but going solo, they had no chance. They had to fight together, and they had only today to figure it out, because tonight would bring Tristan back.

"Eric," she called out.

He didn't answer.

"We need each other for this. We can't do it alone."

There was silence.

"We can work together without having sex, you know. We could just be partners. Keep an emotional distance so you don't fall madly in love with me and get all tangled up in emotions, like you did with Jane." And of course, so she didn't get so caught up in him that she couldn't see the truth for what it was.

More silence.

She sighed and let her head thud back against the door. "I'm kind of a badass, you know. I did kill my own soul mate. I will be happy to promise to kill you in the event it becomes necessary, if that will make you feel secure enough to work with me."

Again no reply.

She sighed. "Men," she muttered. "Too damned heroic to even be a hero."

A creak drifted up from the basement, and then she heard footsteps heavy on the stairs. He was coming.

CHAPTER 16

The doorknob turned, and Jordyn felt Eric push against the door.

The door didn't open, because she was still leaning against it.

There was a thud, as if he'd let his head drop against the wood. "Jordyn."

"What?" She tensed, ready for some melodramatic angst, or a he-man declaration that she had to leave, or a heartfelt promise that she'd showed him the light, and he was now willing to swear on his life that he would never kill her.

"Move."

She almost laughed. So typical Eric. They'd both bared their souls, and his response was a one-word command. *Move.* She folded her arms over her chest and settled more comfortably against the door. "No."

His sigh prickled over her skin like a warm breeze. "Move your hot little ass, or I'm going to come through this door and move you myself."

She did smile then. Leave it to Eric to turn it to sex. "Did you know that there's a word in the English language that many people consider it polite to use when making a request?"

His sigh was a little more forceful this time. *"Please* move your hot little ass or I will be *pleased* to come through this door and move you myself. You may think that a ban on sex is a great solution to the fact I might kill you, but I think they're completely unrelated. I'm shallow enough to admit that if I get my hands on you again, I'm not going to exercise a lot of self-control. It was that good, and I'm a little bit on edge. Another round of sex would work for me right now. So, move. Please. Now."

That spot on her neck tingled with sudden heat. She grinned and scrambled to the side, using the kitchen cabinet as a backrest instead. The door swung open slowly, and Eric met her gaze. He was standing on the third step, so he was almost at eye level with her.

His eyes were turbulent, and his face was tense. "You are a stubborn, difficult, pain in the ass," he said.

She folded her arms over her chest, her body humming at the intensity of his gaze. This was no longer the defeated Eric from downstairs. He had become the warrior again, a brazen, heated mass of testosterone ready to go to battle. "So?"

"So, you're also right." He leaned against the wall of the stairwell, and folded his arms over his chest, studying her. His muscles were completely relaxed, but there was a readiness humming from him.

She could almost feel the energy leaping off of him and sizzling through the air. "I was right about which part?"

"That I can't do this alone." He ran his hand through his hair, which made it spike even more in a disheveled, sexy mess. "I have to save Tristan," he said simply, "and I need your help."

Disappointment sagged in her belly. Of course, it was all about Tristan, but a part of her wanted it to be more. The woman in her wanted him to acknowledge *her* and the connection intensifying between them. Dammit. She shouldn't have let him make love to her. Now she wanted it to be more. She wanted him to look at her and see the heart that was lying in broken fragments inside her body, in desperate need of being glued back together.

He didn't. He saw only sex.

Of course he did. He'd told her from the beginning that that's how he saw the world. So, yes, it was a timely reminder that nakedness and orgasms meant nothing more than nakedness and orgasms.

She lifted her chin, and gave him a haughty look. "Fine. Great. I love being right." She grabbed the edge of the counter, and pulled herself to her feet, keeping her voice brisk. "So, what now? Where do we go from here? He'll be back tonight." She noticed her grandmother's bag on the dining room table, half open, with most of the contents untouched. She'd been so consumed with Eric's state that she hadn't taken time to go through it in detail. Once she'd realized the stake wasn't inside, it had felt like a dead end. But maybe she'd been wrong. Maybe there was more. "I should check her book. I haven't had a chance to do that yet." She started to walk toward it. "Maybe you could grab us some breakfast, and I'll see if maybe she knew more about vampires than she told me—"

Eric moved with alarming speed, grabbed her arm, and pulled her to a stop. "I wasn't finished."

"Wow, relax, a little. I wasn't going anywhere," she said, startled by his quick move. How had he moved so quickly? "I was just going to look at the book—" Her words died when she saw the blazing intensity of his gaze, and suddenly, her skin felt hot. "You had an idea about Tristan?" Even as she asked the words, she had a feeling that his twin was not on his mind at that moment. The heat in his gaze was too searing for him to be thinking about his brother.

"What I was going to say," he said softly, "was that I'm staying in town not only because of my brother, but also because I'm not done with you."

She swallowed, trying not to notice the sudden pounding of her heart. "Oh? What does that mean?"

"A lot of things." His gaze swept over her face. "It means that I dragged you into my hell, so it's my responsibility to keep you safe. Pushing you away clearly won't work, because you're too damned stubborn to back off, so I'm keeping you close." His fingers tightened on her arm, and he drew her closer against him, until her breasts were against his chest.

Her heart felt like it was going to pound right out of her chest, and heat coiled in her belly. He was so dominant and strong, as if he were wrapping her in this great cloak of power... and sex. There was simply no way for her to be this close to him and to have his hands on her body, and not respond physically.

His eyes were blazing as his grip tightened around her waist, anchoring her so tightly against him that she had to crane her neck to look at him. "I swear on the soul of Jane McPherson that *I will not let you die.*"

His words were suspended in the silence between them, and she felt tears threaten again. She wasn't sure if it was for the promise, or the fact that he'd decided to believe in himself enough to make the promise. She couldn't even imagine what it had taken for him to say those words. It was a tremendous moment for him, and for her. Eric had a lot of flaws, but staying true to his word wasn't one of them. His promise was real. It mattered. It made her believe. She nodded, unable to come up with the words to reflect his oath. So, she simply nodded. "Okay. I accept that promise—"

He slapped his knife into her hand. The blade was almost transparent, but there were hundreds of shadows shifting in the green-tinted blade, as if it were a portal into an unknown world of spirits and specters. "This will kill me. Take it."

She stared at the knife in surprise. "You want me to kill you?" *That* was his promise? Not that *he* wouldn't kill her, but that he'd arm her so that she could carve out his heart if he tried to kill her? Because that really wasn't high on her list of romantic moments she aspired to.

"I want you to have the ability to kill me if necessary." He closed her fingers around the handle, his eyes dark. "You were able to kill your soul mate when he went rogue even though you loved him, so I know you can do it to me if necessary." His gaze met her in a challenge. "I know you don't love me, so it should be easy for you."

She swallowed, her entire soul rebelling against the feel of his knife in her hand. She wanted to hurl it away and watch the blade plunge deep into the kitchen wall. "Easy?" she repeated in disbelief. "You think it would be *easy* for me to kill you?"

For a split second, he hesitated. Doubt flickered through his dark eyes, along with something else. Hope? A yearning? A longing? It was gone before she could fully identify it, but she felt as if she'd glimpsed something deep inside him, the true Eric that he kept hidden.

"Don't waste emotional energy on me," he said. "This is the *only* thing that will work on me for sure." His grip was tight around hers. "Promise me that you'll kill me if it is necessary to save your life."

"Oh, no, no, no. I'm not doing this." Yes, she'd killed Walter, but it had traumatized her so badly that she'd then killed herself eight times. "If I kill you, Tristan dies." And a part of her own soul would die as well, because that was just the kind of soft-hearted wuss that she was. It was impossible to kill someone without having it knot up inside her chest and eat away at her until she was nothing but a shriveled ball of guilt and misery, and the truth was, she liked Eric, which would make it a thousand times worse. She liked him a great deal, in fact. Yes, he had all sorts of flaws, but her connection to him was strong. She admired his loyalty to his brother. The way he'd risked everything to save her spoke of a man she could afford to trust. He made her feel safe, sexy, and appreciated, despite all of her own flaws and baggage. She didn't want to kill him.

Again, emotion flickered across Eric's face. "You don't want to kill me because it would inadvertently kill Tristan?" There was an edge to his voice that slithered across her skin. "That's why?"

She raised her chin. "Of course I don't want to inadvertently kill Tristan." She wasn't going to say anymore. She really wasn't. But the moment she spoke, she saw Eric's face harden, and she felt him withdraw. "God, you dumb man!" She grabbed his jaw. "What do you think my answer is? I never had sex with Tristan. I never even kissed him. I don't kiss men anymore. I don't have sex with them. I don't get involved. I haven't kissed a man since Walter, and I haven't even wanted to. So, don't pull some macho male crap on me. You know damn well that I don't want to kill you either, and to do so would break my already shattered heart, so don't force me to make that choice. Got it?"

Eric stared at her, and then his hand wrapped around hers and he slowly removed her hand from his jaw. "I am not dumb." His voice caressed her flesh like an invisible silk ribbon trailing over her skin.

She swallowed, her entire body humming as his thumb swirled circles across her palm. "So, you did that on purpose, to make me feel bad for you so that I'd blurt out some asinine confession about how I feel about you?"

"No, I didn't do that on purpose." His thumb slid over the underside of her wrist. "But I liked your outburst. I like it when you try to put me in my place."

She pressed her lips together, unable to muster up the mental fortitude to make herself pull away from him. "Let go of me."

"No." He traced the letter E on her skin, as if he were marking her.

Chills ran down her spine, and her blood seemed to hum through her, racing toward that spot he was touching.

"Yes, Jordyn, I know that Tristan will die if you kill me. And if we wind up having to kill Tristan to stop him, then I die. It's the cost of our brotherhood. I accept it, and so does he. Sometimes, death is the right choice. Make me the promise, Jordyn. It's non-negotiable. I will not kill anyone else, end of story...especially you." The way he said *especially you* feathered across her soul like a sensual, unspoken promise.

Jordyn bit her lip as fear of what he might do warred with the instinct to melt into him and succumb to his seduction. She had to face the fact that Eric still didn't believe he could stop himself from killing her, or anyone else for that matter. Was he right? Was she the one who was wrong? Because, she had to be honest, he was the one inside his head, not her.

"Promise me." His voice was low and rough. "Promise me that no matter what happens between us, no matter how much you succumb to my irresistible and impressive charm, that you will *never* lose sight of the fact that you may someday need to sink that blade into my heart."

Making that promise was an acknowledgment that she'd once again aligned herself with a man who could destroy everything, and betray all her belief in him. She didn't want to do that. She wanted to be right that there was someone in this world worth trusting. But as she looked into his eyes, she saw the shadows swirling. Dark, lethal shadows. "Eric—"

He pressed a kiss to the spot on her wrist that he'd been caressing. "Make the promise, or you go home."

She didn't have to look at his broad shoulders or the stubborn set to his jaw to know that he was perfectly capable of following through on his threat. "Damn you for being built like a house."

A small smile quirked the corner of his mouth. "Is that a promise?"

"You seduce me and make me promise to kill you in the same breath? You make me crazy, Eric." She sighed, jerked her wrist away from his annoying kisses, and accepted the knife from him. His expression was inscrutable as she shoved the knife through her belt loop. "Fine. I promise to showcase my amazing man-killing skills if you turn out to be less than the man that I think you are. And if you keep being so annoying, then I might even enjoy it. Satisfied?"

He nodded, and his entire body seemed to relax. "Yeah, I am. Because I know you can do it. I know you *will* do it."

She rolled her eyes, feeling deflated. "Yay, me. I'm capable of murdering the men I care about. I should put that in my online dating profile—"

"*No.*" He caught her arm just as she was turning back toward the dining room. "No online dating profile. Just me."

His claim of possession on her was evident in every line of his suddenly taut body, and in the intensity of his voice. Desire rushed through her, tumbling in all directions like a wild river, crashing through every obstacle in its path.

She stiffened, even as her heart jumped. Yes, she didn't want anything from him, but to have the man who'd just made love to her declare she was off limits to anyone else was a really nice feeling, even if it came on the heels of an order to murder him if necessary...not that he was going to get her. She couldn't let herself fall any further. She already felt like she could barely breathe around him, and his knife felt as if it were burning through her jeans. "We have to focus on Tristan," she said. "We must have a plan by the time the sun sets."

"I know." He pulled her closer, his eyes glittering with intensity. "But a plan isn't the only thing I need right now."

Oh...there was no mistaking what he meant. She pushed against his chest, trying to get some space. "I already told you. I'm not getting naked with you again. I'm not good at casual, and anything deeper just doesn't fit with you, with this entire situation, or with me."

"I know it doesn't fit." He skimmed his finger along her

jaw. "Sometimes, that just doesn't matter." His gaze went to her mouth. "There's something about you that gets to me, Jordyn. You're inside me, like this light that won't let the parts of me die that have been fading for so long." His arm wrapped around her lower back, and he pulled her close. "I wasn't hungry until I met you, and now it's like a thousand years of deprivation have come roaring back into me, and the only thing that will take the edge off is you."

Something inside her softened at the truthfulness of his words. She'd felt his emptiness, and she knew he was telling her the truth. It wasn't flirtation or arrogance, just a stark honesty and a baring of his soul.

The intensity of her response to his words was terrifying. She felt so naked and exposed, her emotions dangling dangerously in a wind that could rip her apart. The depth of her grief after Walter's betrayal was almost insurmountable, an abyss so deep that it had almost sucked her away forever. She couldn't go there again, not for Eric, not for anyone. Trepidation made her hands tremble. "Don't start with me, Eric. I can't do this with you."

A slow grin spread over his face, as if he knew exactly how much he was affecting her. "I think you can."

"Stop it!" She poked her finger into his chest, irritated by his disarming smile and the arrogant gleam she saw in his eyes. "Just because you think you can be charming, and you gave me a spectacular orgasm doesn't mean that you are allowed to try to woo me with some suave approach. I'm immune, thank you very much." Total lie, but if she lied enough times, it would become real, right? "I want to deal with the vampire situation, which is kind of pressing at the moment, not deal with this." She smacked his hand away as he reached for her. "I mean it. You're just not that charming." But he was. Utterly charming. How could she possibly think he was charming when he was made of shadows and demon spirits, and couldn't promise not to kill her? But she did. She loved the way he craved her. She loved how he challenged her on every level. And she resonated with the depth of torment that permeated every cell of his body, and the strength of his being that had kept his dark side in check for so long.

"Jordyn." His voice slid like a silken caress over her flesh, and suddenly she was reminded of what it had felt like when Tristan had spoken to her, only Eric's voice was even more alluring, playing over her flesh like fingers dancing across her soul, sliding with the utmost temptation across every inch of her flesh.

She swallowed, torn between covering her ears and engaging in random chants so she couldn't hear him, or capitulating completely to him and bounding into his arms begging for him to make her his. She tried to settle for a dignified response, and simply glared at him. "Don't speak. Seriously. Don't."

"I need you." His gaze went to her mouth, and her neck began to pulse where he'd bitten her. As if sensing her response, his gaze slid from her lips to that same spot that was tingling, and his eyes darkened to pitch black, and she felt a pulse of hunger from him.

Did he want only sex? Or did he also want more, like her soul? Because, despite his claims to the contrary, the sheer intensity of the energy rolling off him felt like it was far more than a superficial seduction that would be easy for her to resist. It was a deep, instinctual craving that gripped her ruthlessly, awakening an answering response in her.

Oh, God, was that a vampire thing, or an Eric thing? Not that it mattered. He was so utterly compelling that she loved every second of his attempted seduction, and the game they seemed to be playing. Oh, Lordy. She was in deep, wasn't she?

Heat simmered in his eyes, and a deeper longing raked across her flesh. She took a step back, chills prickling down her arms. For a split second, she thought she saw a shadow flicker beneath the skin on his cheek. "Do you feel okay?"

"Not sure. I feel a little hungry." He quirked his brow. "Are you offering me a light snack?"

"What?" Her hand instinctively went to her neck. "Do you want one?" Oh, God, had she really just asked that? She hadn't meant to. Damn him for getting past her shields. Was she really so easy? Apparently, yes.

He didn't answer aloud but she felt his voice brush

through her mind. *Jordyn. You have no idea what I want to do to you. Sinking my teeth into your flesh is just the beginning.*

Oh...wow. "You're talking in my head."

It appears that I am. Strange. His eyes blazed. *Intimate.*

Yes, she had to agree with that one. She met his gaze, her heart thundering. "You're different than you were. You know, since that vampire bit you."

"Yes, and no. You're just beginning to see me for what I am. But the fantasies in my head? Yeah, they're different now." He ran his thumb over her neck, and she sucked in her breath as all her blood seemed to race to that spot. "I can't sever the tie between us. I know I should, but I don't want to. I loved every single moment of making love to you, and, I'll be honest, biting you was unbelievably hot." His voice lowered. "You're under my skin, Jordyn, deeper than I want, deeper than I need, and deeper than I ever thought of going with a woman."

Her heart hammered violently at his words. "I'll try to be less adorable."

He laughed softly. "Won't help. I like it when you boss me around. I like a lot of the shit you do. All I want is quick and casual, as I told you when I first met you. But one night isn't going to be enough with you. Not even close, no matter how dangerous it is to both of us." He lowered his voice, sliding his fingers over the handle of the knife she'd tucked into her jeans, reminding them both that she had the power to stop him. "I fought it, but I'm in now, and I'm not pulling back."

She shook her head, not wanting to hear those kinds of words from him, because they felt too good. There was too much at stake to risk making choices based on affection and, heaven forbid, love, and if he kept saying things like that, she was going to plummet straight off the proverbial cliff into his lethal arms. "No, Eric. I can't do this with you. I told you, I can't get emotionally involved. Sex complicates things for me. Love blinded me before, and I'm not doing it again. So, let's keep it that way. We had sex one time, to save our lives. That's it, okay?" She saw the denial in his eyes, and wanted to hit him with frustration. "Don't say it," she warned. "I don't want to hear it."

Eric didn't release her. Instead, he leaned closer, until his lips were brushing against her ear. "I want more."

She shoved at his chest. "Get off me. Go take a moment of privacy in the corner and deal with yourself that way."

"Won't work. It's not just the orgasm that I'm craving. I want *you*." Eric's eyes were turbulent, swirling with shadows that held a new significance now that she'd seen what he could become. "I don't like it. I don't want to want you. It's dangerous. To you. To me. To Tristan. I want to keep you at a distance, and protect you from afar. And yet..." His finger traced a circle around the mark in her neck. "It's going to happen again. Sex. Intimacy. *Biting*."

Her pulse hammered in her neck, but she pulled out his knife and angled it against his neck, so the tip was pointing under his jawbone. He went still, his eyes blazing.

"Don't touch me," she said. "Don't even fantasize about me. Do you understand?"

For a long moment, he didn't answer, and her heart started hammering. She could see from his relentless stare that he understood perfectly, and it didn't matter. "You'll have to kill me to make me stop fantasizing about you," he said, his deep voice playing over her flesh like invisible fingers. "Use the knife, Jordyn." As he spoke, he palmed her hips, pulling her against him.

Her belly hit his, and heat seared through her. He waited, his thumbs tracing small circles on her hips.

Then, slowly, ever so slowly, she let the knife fall to her side. Dammit. She wasn't going to kill him for wanting her, and they both knew it.

He grinned, triumph gleaming in his eyes as he lowered his head to kiss her, moving ever so slowly, and giving her plenty of time to stop him.

She didn't want to do this. Kissing him to stay alive could be excused. If she kissed him now, there was no way she could claim it was for any reason other than she wanted to. His life wasn't at stake. Hers was perfectly intact at the moment. No demon was hunting them. If she succumbed to his maddeningly endearing charms, he would know that it had simply been because of him, and even worse, *she* would know it was simply because of him.

"I don't date men." Her fingers tightened around the knife. She had to stop him. She had to. Why did the damned knife feel so heavy to lift? It felt like it weighed a thousand pounds. It was doing her no good down by her hip, but she couldn't bring it up. It was as if her arm had gone numb.

"I know you don't." He brushed his lips over hers. "I don't either."

"Ha. Funny man." She clenched her fist tighter around his knife, but couldn't quite manage to do anything other than press the flat of it across her thigh. "I don't have sex with them either."

"I know. I don't either." He kissed the other corner of her mouth.

She had to bite her lip to keep from smiling at his infuriating response. "Stop it."

"The kisses? You don't like them?" He trailed sensual kisses along her jawbone.

"Of course I like them. You know I do. Don't pretend to be an idiot. We both know that you're perfectly capable of feeling my emotions now that we did that blood bond thing." She folded her arms over her chest, fighting against the ardor stirring inside of her.

"You mean, when I bit you? That blood bond thing?" He swept his tongue across the spot where he'd bitten her, and desire whipped through her body so fast that she had to grip his arms to keep from falling.

She let out a completely embarrassing squeak before she could stop herself. "Yes, the biting thing." She gripped his arms. "Don't you dare kiss me, Eric. Just don't."

He grinned at her, his mouth barely a whisper from hers. *Are you so sure about that?*

"Yes." She could feel his breath across her lips. His hands were drawing sensual circles on her hips. He smelled of outdoors and fresh earth, along with something more potent and dangerous.

Kiss me, Jordyn. Kiss me.

The unbridled hunger in his voice cut through her, and she sucked in her breath as an answering need rocked through her. She snapped her gaze to his, and she saw in his face that he needed her as badly as she wanted him. They were in it together, way over both their heads.

He met her gaze without flinching, and the air thickened between them until it was wound so tight that one breath would shatter it.

"Jordyn."

She swallowed. "What?"

"Now."

They both moved at the same time, coming together in a kiss that grabbed them both mercilessly and hurled them into an abyss of need and unrelenting hunger, from which there was no way out.

CHAPTER 17

The moment Jordyn's body sank against him and her arms wrapped around his neck, Eric knew he was lost. He was hers. Forever. No matter what the cost. With a low growl of possession, he locked his arms around her, trapping her against him as he kissed her.

He wanted to finesse her. He had too much pride to fumble. He needed to give her a long, slow seduction that brought her to release a thousand times before he even thought about taking care of himself. That's what he wanted, and yet, with the taste of her lips, every last bit of the control he prided himself on vanished, consumed by a need for her so great that he could perceive nothing except the woman in his arms.

He swept her up against him, and nearly staggered when she wrapped her legs around his hips, kissing him back every bit as fiercely as he was kissing her. The last time they'd made love, he'd been more than half-insane, and barely aware of what was going on.

Now, he was aware of every nuance of her body, of her kiss, of her scent, and of her own need for him. Her femininity swirled around him, mixing with his own roaring hunger, igniting it even further. He dragged them away from the kitchen, and leapt up the stairs to the second floor without breaking the kiss. He caught her scent at the door to the first bedroom and knew this room was where she'd been sleeping.

No floor this time, honey. Not for you. He reached the bed and lowered her on it, sinking down with her.

I don't allow men in my bed. Her voice was a seductive whisper in his mind as she reached for his shirt, dragging it out of his jeans.

Ah, my sweetheart, it's too late for that. He grabbed her ankles and upended her onto the tangled sheets that revealed a restless sleep for his woman.

She landed on her elbows, her eyes hooded with a sultry sensuality that made his entire body tighten. "Except you," she said, her gaze steady. "You're allowed."

Her voice was light and teasing, but he felt the enormity of her words. She was choosing him, inviting him into an inner sanctum where she'd never thought to allow a man again.

He jerked off his shirt and kicked off his boots before sinking down on the mattress, propping himself above her, his entire body suspended over hers, almost touching everywhere, but actually touching nowhere. "I won't betray you," he said. "I swear it."

Her face softened, and she nodded. "I know."

She knew. How in the world had a woman who had endured so much granted him such faith? She knew what he was, but he could see the complete acceptance in the softness of her body and the desire in her eyes. She wanted *him.*

She held up her arms to him. "Come to me, Eric. I want you to be with me."

His chest contracted at her words, but he tried to shake it off with humor. "What man could ignore that invitation?" He lowered himself ever so slowly, inch by inch, until her nipples brushed his chest. He trapped her breasts against him, and then his hips sank onto hers. Hunger reverberated through him as he felt her body yield to him. All his senses were on overload at the feel of her body against his. So feminine, and yet so strong. A woman who could bring him to his knees a thousand different ways. *Jordyn.*

He tunneled his fingers through her hair and swept her mouth up in a kiss so hot that fire seemed to leap between them. She wrapped her arms around his neck, holding him close, as if she would never let him go. He held onto the kiss, deepening it, pouring all his hunger into it as he slipped his hands beneath her shirt and palmed the soft skin of her belly. Her muscles clenched, and he felt a rush of desire pour over him. Her desire, not his, and yet every bit as intense as what was rushing through him.

Suddenly, he couldn't take it slow anymore. He couldn't seduce. "The clothes have to go," he said, rolling off her. He pulled her up, yanking her shirt over her head as she grinned at him, humor dancing in her eyes.

"Do you remember when we were in the jungle? You said you'd never beg for sex?"

"It was a lie." He grabbed her hips and tugged her jeans off, tumbling her back on the bed as he did so. "You have me wrapped so tightly around your little finger that I'd get down and kiss each of those sexy as hell toes of yours until you agreed." He swept his fingers under the edges of her lace underwear. "Black." He pressed a kiss to the tiny pearl stitched in the front of it. "You wear black lace."

Jordyn sucked in her breath, her hands tangling in his hair. "You didn't notice that before?"

"I didn't notice anything before, but I am now." He dropped to his belly, sliding down until he could cup her buttocks in his palms. He pressed another kiss to the pearl, his gaze raking hungrily across her body. Her breasts were held tightly by a white sports bra that was in stark contrast to her lace underwear. The sight of that spandex was like a punch to his gut, and his cock got even harder.

"You like the sports bra?" Jordyn had propped herself on her elbows again, and she was watching him intently, as if she was systematically extracting every single emotion he was feeling.

"Yeah. I do." He crawled back up her body, trailing kisses across her flesh as he went, until he reached the elastic band circling her ribs. He spanned her ribcage with his hands, and lightly bit her nipple through the spandex.

She let out a small gasp, her blue gazed fixed on him. "It's a sports bra, Eric. Not lace."

"Yeah, I noticed." He bit her other nipple, and satisfaction hummed through him as he watched the peaks tighten beneath the spandex. "It's hot as hell, because that's so you." He hooked his finger around the neckline of her bra and tugged it down, pressing a kiss to the soft flesh. "You're sexy, but you're also tough. You're a warrior all the way through, but you're also a woman." He pulled it further down, exposing more of her breast. "You run through the damn jungle to save a friend. You can't do that in a lace bra, and I love that about you." He cupped her breast in his palm, watching her eyes darken in response. "You're spandex and lace. You've got major attitude, but you can be the biggest pile of emotional goo a woman could be. You're brave. You're scared. You're everything." He took her nipple into his mouth, sweeping his tongue over the hot peak.

Jordyn gasped and arched her back, gripping the sheets. "Goo? You called me goo? I take offense to that on behalf of women everywhere. Just because I cried, it doesn't mean—"

He bit her nipple, and she yelped, twisting beneath him.

"Don't distract me, Eric," she gasped. "I'm trying to berate you."

"I'm listening. Go ahead." He pulled down the other side of her bra, and ran his teeth over that nipple.

Jordyn moved again, and her fingers dug into the sheets. "This is completely unfair, you cretin. Let me at least finish."

He rolled off her and grabbed her hand. Before she could protest, he pulled her to her feet, and then hoisted the sports bra over her head. Her breasts spilled free, and she grabbed the front of his jeans, unfastening them and shoving them down his hips. His boxers went with them, and he kicked them aside.

The look on her face drew him to a complete stop. Her gaze was raking over him, unabashed thirst for him so stark on her face that his entire soul burned in response. He reached for her, and she held up her hand, her gaze jerking to his. "Wait."

He stopped where he was, letting her look at him, watching the pathway of her gaze as it traveled across his chest, down his abdomen, to the pulsing erection between his thighs. His skin was burning with the urge to take her, but he didn't move even an inch, giving her the time she needed.

She looked back at him, wonder on her face. "It's been so long for me," she said.

"I know." He didn't want her thinking about the last man she'd been with. He wanted her with him, and only him. He lightly clasped her wrist and raised her palm to his chest. "It's me, Jordyn. No one else."

She spread her fingers across his pecs, her palm searing hot against his flesh. His muscles rippled with the compulsion to close the distance between them, but he stood stock still, allowing her to touch him.

Her face was soft with wonder as she ran her hand across his chest and down across his torso. His abs tightened involuntarily as her whisper-soft touch fluttered across his skin. "I don't think I've ever been touched that softly before," he said.

Her blue eyes flicked to his. "Is it okay?"

He nodded slowly. "More than okay, honey. Far more than okay."

The corner of her mouth lifted in a small smile, and his heart quickened. It was incredible the power he felt knowing he could make her smile. It made him feel like he was the king of the whole damn world.

Jordyn moved closer and ran her hand over his bare hip. Hunger began to build inside him, a thundering need that pounded through his veins, but still, he didn't move. Her fingers traced a path across his buttocks, and then traced his spine upwards. She was so close that her breasts were almost brushing his chest, but not quite. He stared down at her, watching the play of emotions across her face. "This is excruciating torture for me," he commented. "To have you so close, and not touch you."

She glanced up at him again, her hand pausing halfway up his spine. "Thank you," she said. "I like it this way."

"What way?" Hunger was so loud in his head he could barely hear her. It sounded as though thunder was booming through his entire soul, a black, bottomless reverberation that was more than just sound. It was like the pounding of a massive drum deep inside him. He wanted more than her body. He wanted to consume every part of her, to entwine their souls so tightly together that he would never get free.

"Slow." She leaned forward and pressed a kiss to his right nipple. Electricity leapt through him, and he palmed her hips, dragging her against him.

Jordyn slapped at his hands and twisted out of his reach, a grin sparkling in her eyes. "No, I want to be in charge." She held up her hand to him, palm out. "Stay."

Sweat trickled down his temple, the only indication of

how hard he was fighting not to claim her, when every instinct he possessed was commanding him to make her his. His gaze went to her mouth, and then drifted down to her neck. He could smell her blood swirling through her veins like a hot spring of life, and his incisors began to lengthen. He opened his mind to her, and let her feel his longing for her.

Her eyes widened, and she sucked in her breath. Her nipples hardened instantly, and he focused on them. He envisioned sweeping them into his mouth, twirling his tongue across their peaks, and sucking on them.

Her hand went to her breast, and she took a step back. "How are you doing that?"

His gaze snapped to hers. "You can feel that?"

"It's like you're kissing my breast, but you're not. It was the same way with Tristan—"

"Tristan? You felt Tristan kissing your breast?" White-hot possessiveness exploded in his mind like a flash of lightning, and he closed the space between them, dragging her into his arms. "Not Tristan. *Me.*" Without waiting for a response, he bent his head and kissed her, unleashing all his hunger into her.

A small noise of satisfaction escaped from Jordyn, and her hands went around his neck as she melted into him, kissing him back just as fiercely. He cupped her buttocks, lifting her belly against his throbbing cock, never letting up on his single-minded assault on her senses. She lifted her legs, wrapping them around his hips.

His head was pounding with hunger now, so overwhelming he could feel nothing but the woman in his arms. Nothing else mattered but her. He lifted her, and his cock pressed against the lace of her underwear. She twisted restlessly in his arms, and he knew she was ready for him. He wanted her. He needed her. But not yet.

Not yet.

He let her inch down his body in a tantalizing assault to his senses. The moment her feet touched the ground, he dropped to his knees in front of her. He palmed her hips as he licked his way across her belly, lower and lower, to the waistband of her underwear. He bit that white pearl as he smoothed his palms down her thighs, and wrapped his fingers around them.

Jordyn grabbed his shoulders, leaning on him for balance. He could feel her desire thick in the air, every bit as strong as his.

He pressed a kiss to the inside of her left thigh as he lifted her leg and draped her thigh over his shoulder.

"Eric. Seriously? I'm going to fall down. My legs are shaking." Her fingernails were digging into his shoulders, and her toes were curled into the carpet, trying to keep her balance.

I've got you, honey. Just lean on me. He wrapped his right arm around her leg, using his strength to support her while he kissed his way up her inner thigh, closer and closer to that black lace.

"You're in my mind," she said, her voice breathless.

I am. I feel your soul. You hide nothing from me. He caught the edge of her underwear with his index finger and dragged it aside as he pressed a kiss to her damp folds. Her essence flooded him, a searing mixture of sweetness and temptation. Possessiveness roared through him, and he parted her folds, plunging deep with his tongue, taking her as his own, making her his.

Her standing leg started to tremble, and he wrapped his arm more tightly around it, infusing her with his strength. He could feel every nuance of her emotions. Her attraction to him that was so staggering she didn't even understand it. He could feel the softness of soul, her complete openness to him. She wasn't afraid of him, and she wasn't shielding herself from him. She was pure goodness, far beyond anything he ever thought would be a part of his life.

She was his, and he would protect her with everything he had. The scent of her blood racing through her was beckoning to him, tempting him, demanding that he take what she had to offer. Not the neck. Tristan had bitten her neck. It had to be intimate, personal, where no other man had ever gone or would ever go. He needed to make her his, only his, forever his.

He rubbed his thumb over her inner thigh, over the humming blood beneath her skin.

Yes. Jordyn's voice whispered through his mind, a sensual play across his thoughts. *I want it. You're mine, Eric. Mine.*

The palpable need driving her words plunged into him,

shredding the last of his control. He slipped his fingers inside her at the same time that he sank his teeth into her inner thigh. She screamed his name, her body tightening around his fingers, as the orgasm swept over her. She clung to him, her body shaking as her blood flowed through him, seeking out every last recess of his soul, bringing light and life into the darkness that beat at him so savagely.

The blood raged within him, driving his lust to a frenzied peak. He eased his teeth from her body, licking away the drops of blood to seal it, then stood, lifting her with him. In two steps, they were beside the bed.

He lowered her gently to the mattress, and this time, she didn't let go of him, pulling him with her. He met her gaze, and saw in her eyes a warmth and softness that made his heart tighten. *Make love to me, Eric. Not sex. Make love to me.*

Her request felt like a sudden jab through his chest. He didn't make love. He didn't even know how. What was he doing? He couldn't—

It's okay, Eric. Whatever you have, is okay. Her fingers went through his hair, forcing him to look at her. *We need this. We both do.*

He fought to hold himself back, exerting every last bit of his strength to hold back the tide rushing through him. "I don't want to betray you, Jordyn. I can't do that to you. You're too special."

She didn't answer. She just fisted his hair and dragged his head down to hers. The kiss she gave him set him on fire. The feel of her tongue against his, her mouth demanding more, and the desire she poured into the kiss. She took him hostage, shredding the last of his control, igniting that which he'd been trying to hold back, until there was nothing but them.

She wrapped her legs around his hips, drawing him into her. His cock brushed against her entrance, and he felt her damp wetness calling to him. He pulled back, searching her face. She smiled at him, that same smile he'd cherished since the first time she'd gifted him with it. This was his Jordyn, the woman who was brave enough to go after a fire god to save her friend. A warrior. A survivor. A passionate woman who wanted *him.*

The hard shield that had been protecting his heart for

so long suddenly cracked, and into that fissure slipped Jordyn, enveloping him in a warmth he'd never experienced in his life. "Jordyn." He whispered her name, and slid inside her.

She gasped and tilted her head back, gripping his shoulders, but never breaking eye contact with him. Her sheathe was tight and hot around his cock, as if her body was fighting to hold onto him and never let him go.

He thrust deeper, unable to take his gaze off her face as their bodies came together. He tangled his fingers through her hair, relishing the feel of the silken strands against his roughened hands even as he bound them tighter and tighter with every slow thrust of his hips.

Jordyn's fingers began to dig into his shoulders. "How did I end up being the one to do the begging?" she asked.

"I'm that good." He smiled at her comment, relaxing as the woman he knew so well showed herself. He kissed her, a kiss meant to show affection, which turned carnal the moment he tasted her. The kiss became about more than need, more than sex, more than hunger. It became about the woman in his arms, and his urge to belong to her.

He'd never belonged anywhere. He'd spent his life as a vagrant on the run from himself. It was a life that was exactly as he'd wanted it to be…until now. Until Jordyn. Until this moment. *I'm yours.* He sent the words into her mind, unable to articulate them aloud, accentuating them with a driving thrust that sent flashes of heat sparking through him.

He felt her smile, and braced himself, waiting for her return declaration, for the one that would bind them forever. *I know you are, Eric. You've been mine from the beginning.*

There was pleased satisfaction in her voice, and a hint of humor.

He thrust again, pulling back enough to look into her face. "Say it," he said. "Say you're mine."

She smiled. "No."

He thrust again. "Say it, sweetheart. You know you are."

She gripped his shoulders, her fingernails pricking his skin. "No. I belong to no man. I won't. I can't."

He withdrew slowly, so slowly that he felt his own gut clench from the sensation of her body sliding along his cock.

The orgasm swirled at the edges of his control, trying to claim him, but he fought to hold it off. He needed to hear the words from her. He needed to know he wasn't alone. The urge to be anchored to her was so strong it was almost a compulsion. He felt like he was dangling in the unknown, circling desperately, searching for a place to land. *Jordyn.* He poured his urgency into his words, and thrust again.

She gasped his name and arched beneath him as she climaxed. The wildness of her orgasm rushed through him and ignited his own, and he shouted her name as the spiral exploded through him. He sank his teeth into her neck, and the orgasm went over the top, an explosion of fire and salvation that tore them both from their bodies and flung them into a world of color and beauty, fireworks exploding through them in a culmination that he knew had changed his soul forever.

CHAPTER 18

"I can't believe you refused to tell me you were mine." Eric's face was buried in her neck, his lips feathering soft kisses over the place he'd bitten. "I feel very vulnerable. You should declare yourself now."

She giggled, running her fingers down his muscular back. After the orgasm, he'd collapsed on top of her, pinning her to the bed. She had to admit, she loved the feeling of his body covering every inch of hers. She felt safe and protected, shielded from the world. And she felt deliciously cherished. There was just something about his post-coital kisses that made her heart tighten. They were tender and affectionate, not about sex. It was perfect. "You're fine," she teased. "You didn't want me to actually declare myself to be yours for all eternity. You're all about being footloose and fancy free."

He kissed her neck one more time, then raised his head to look at her. She stopped, startled by the emotion roiling in his eyes. "What's wrong?"

"There are a few things I haven't told you about me."

Her heart began to pound. "Like what?"

"The incident with Jane MacPherson happened over three hundred years ago."

She stared at him. "What? You're over three hundred years old?" How was that possible? She'd thought he was like her, human enough that he carried a regular lifespan. But even as she thought it, she realized she'd always known. The darkness he carried within him was ancient, entrenched in his soul. There was a heaviness to his soul that took more than several decades to form.

"Tristan and I stopped aging when we were in our early thirties." His eyes were dark, but she could see those shadows roiling around beneath them, always lurking. "We've spent our entire existence trying to find out where we come from. We move around, never staying in one place. People notice if you don't age. We can't find any record of our past, or of others like us."

She felt the weight of his words, the burden of being without a history or an identity. "You mean, with an affinity for spirits?"

Eric nodded. "Yes, as well as other things." He traced a symbol on her breast that she didn't recognize, but her skin tingled, as if it were significant. "But for the last couple hundred years, things have been changing. The hold of the darkness has grown stronger. Tristan has become more and more drawn to those long dead. Something has us in its grip, and we don't know what it is."

"Like what?" Chills crept down her spine.

"An ancient magic. An old evil." He cupped her breast, his palm warm and protective. "Since I've come to Parrish Creek, it's been worse. It's coming for me. Whatever it was that we first saw that night of Jane's death, it's coming to claim me." He pressed a kiss to her nipple, not a kiss of seduction, but a kiss of ownership and possession, a quiet statement that her breasts were part of his domain.

She should feel threatened by his clear expression of his claim on her, but she didn't. It felt right and good. Shouldn't she be scared with what he was telling her? She supposed that any woman who had a marginally functioning brain would realize it was time to get out, but all she wanted was to wrap her arms around him and protect him. Walter had always been too strong, too dominating, too consumed with his own destiny. He'd never allowed her close. He'd never let her in like Eric was doing. It was a first for her, and it made her realize how much she had missed out on. It was a gift to be so connected with another person, a man, with Eric.

Something had happened when he'd bitten her while

they'd been making love this time. She'd felt a part of herself merge with him. She didn't know exactly what had happened, but it was different now. They were intertwined on a metaphysical level, and it felt good, as if it was how it was supposed to be.

He searched her face and she tensed at his expression, knowing before he spoke that it was going to be bad. "Jane MacPherson isn't the only woman I killed."

Her fingers stilled in his hair. "There's another?"

"Yes."

"Really?" She stared at him, her mouth suddenly dry. "What happened?"

"After Jane, I stayed away from women. I refused to take any chances that it would happen again. But then I met another woman. One night, in an alley. I didn't even see her face, but the moment I passed by her, she called to me. I don't even know what happened. Just one minute, she was a stranger that had passed by me, and the next moment, I had her pinned up against the wall, buried inside her like we were rabbits." His eyes were blazing. "The moment we both came, something came alive inside me, and took her. She disintegrated while I was still inside her."

Jordyn stared at him. "You're serious?"

"Yeah." His gaze bore into her. "I don't know what I am, Jordyn. I don't know if you make me safer, or if you're being set up to be my final victim."

"Wait a sec." She suddenly wanted to push him off her. "You disintegrate women when you have sex with them? And you had sex with me?" She pushed at his chest. "Get off."

"Listen to me." He caught her hands, his eyes blazing as he sank more heavily onto her. "The way I respond to you is not the same as how that woman affected me. With you, it's different. But if you recall, I did everything in my power to make you leave earlier, and you wouldn't. Making love actually kept us both from disintegrating, and that's a fact. I would *never* have risked you."

She heard the grim focus in his voice, and felt the desolation of his soul, and she knew he was telling her the truth. She felt the weight of his words, the burden he carried. "How many times did that happen? How many people have you disintegrated?"

"Just those two times. I've been very careful around women ever since. I don't get close, and I bail at the first signs that things are headed in that direction." He met her gaze. "Until you." His fingers tightened in her hair. "You're under my skin, Jordyn, and that scares the living daylights out of me. I am very, very afraid of the monster within me."

A wave of anguish washed over him, so thick she could almost taste it. "What do you want from me?"

He said nothing for a long moment, his gaze going to her hair as he combed out the tangles. His touch was so gentle, a move that was incredibly sexy because of the fact he wasn't actually trying to seduce her. "I feel as if you're my anchor," he said quietly. "If I can somehow lock my soul around yours forever, I'll be free."

She felt the truth of his words, and her heart tightened. Where was the arrogant playboy she'd met in the jungle? She bit her lip, unable to keep the tears from her voice. "Eric, I can't bind myself to you. I can't trap myself with a man again. I—"

"I know." He kissed away her objections. "I admit, I'm a really great guy. If you killed yourself eight times after losing Walter, it would probably take you about a hundred resurrections to get over me. That's a lot to ask of you."

She managed a small laugh. "A hundred? That's a lot of deaths."

"I know. I'm pretty fantastic." His smile faded as he tucked her hair behind her ear. "It was wrong for me to ask that of you. You should kick me in the ass and tell me to take a hike."

"You have a very nice butt. I'd never kick you in it." The instinct to commit herself to him was so strong, she could hear the words shouting in her mind. But how could she do it? How could she cross that line? Emotionally, she'd barely survived sex with him. How could she make herself even more vulnerable to him? "How else can I help you?"

His thumb flicked over her neck, and awareness leapt through her. "This helps."

"Biting me?" She put her hand over his, pressing his palm into her neck. "What are you really, Eric? Don't tell me you don't know. You know something. Vampire? Is that why you're so old? What else could you be?"

He met her gaze, and she saw grim reality in them. "Many creatures feed on the blood of others, or can connect telepathically with others, not just vampires."

"But?" She heard the hesitation in his voice.

"The one trait that makes vampires unique is that they don't possess a soul," he said quietly. "Instead of their eternal spirit, they have simply a gaping emptiness howling within them. Without their soul, their humanity erodes away, little by little, until there is nothing left but the predator within. The transformation to vampire means the complete loss of one's soul. For some, the predator wins instantly. Others fight it, enduring for centuries as they tread along that razor-thin line, searching for salvation from the nightmare that haunts them."

Jordyn nodded. "My grandmother alluded to that." But Oba's words hadn't been so weighted with anguish and suffering that Jordyn felt pain to the deepest recesses of her soul. "Do you have a soul, Eric?"

He stared at her, then shook his head once. "Not really."

Her heart seemed to freeze in her chest. "The night Jane died? Is that when it happened?"

He nodded. "Boys play with fire too often, and they get burned."

"So, you've been a vampire all along?" She didn't understand.

He shook his head. "Being linked to Tristan gave me an anchor. He held it at bay. We worked together, building shields, trying to anchor ourselves to life and humanity. Until I met you, I never bit anyone, or even had fangs, but it's been there inside me, pushing me in that direction."

He opened his mind to her, and she was cast into the shadows of his memories. She saw a skinny, underfed, filthy teenage boy huddled in a grimy alley, curled into a ball. His body was shaking violently, droplets of blood seeping through the pores of his flesh. Tempestuous gray clouds swirled around him, diving at him, forming into spikes that tore at his skin. She heard the whispers of evil temptation whirling around him, ancient spirits calling to him, their voices whispering one on top of the other, trying to entice the boy. The boy's head was down, his forehead pressed upon his skinny knees, his thin arms hugging his legs to him.

The noise grew louder, whispers cajoling him to let them in. She felt the boy's hunger gnawing at his belly, hunger not for food, but for blood. She saw the images they placed in his mind, those of a winged creature of the night, streaking against a black sky, hunting for prey. She watched the creature swoop down, claws extended, to a small figure below. It was too far for her to make out clearly, and then as it got closer, she saw it was a young woman running through a cornfield. Her brown hair streamed behind her, and her breath was rasping in her chest as she pushed herself. She looked over her shoulder at the creature flying at her, her face stark with terror.

The creature grew closer, and the thirst for her blood became stronger, until it was almost there—

"Eric!" Another boy grabbed the huddled youth, shattering the image of the girl and the bird. Like the young man, Jordyn was ripped from the illusion and jerked back into the reality of Eric's memory. The spirits swirled violently around the newcomer, trying to shake him loose. She recognized Tristan immediately. He wasn't nearly as thin as Eric, but he was just as filthy, two brothers on the run together.

Tristan grabbed Eric around the shoulders. "Come on! I found a place!"

Eric stumbled to his feet, letting Tristan drag him upward. As he stood, she caught her first glimpse of his face. His cheeks were sunken, and his face was gray, as if he were already dead. His eyes were empty, a bottomless abyss of suffering. "I have to feed, Tris. I can feel it."

"No, you don't." Tristan threw Eric's arm over his shoulder and began to drag him down the alley. "I found a graveyard. A woman is buried there who was a healer. Her spirit is still strong. I can bring it up. She'll help."

"No." Eric jerked his arm off Tristan, and then fell. "Don't resurrect anyone. It will take you too close to the edge. You don't want to be like me."

"I won't. Come on!" Tristan grabbed him. "We're in this together, Eric. I won't resurrect her. I'll just bring up part of her energy, okay?"

"Swear?" Eric stumbled again, all his weight heavy on his brother.

"Blood swear." The two boys disappeared out of sight around the ramshackle building, but Jordyn could hear their bare feet shuffling as they hurried away from the whispers that were still calling to them.

Eric pulled out of her mind, and she was suddenly back in the present, with tears trickling down her cheeks. There he was in front of her, the boy from his memories, now a man. His cheekbones were strong and defined, his body rippling with muscle, but she could see in there that same gaping wound in his soul that had been there before. "Eric." She put her hand on his face, almost surprised to feel his skin was warm.

He pressed a kiss to her palm. "Tristan's gone vampire," he said. "He can't anchor me, and I can't anchor him. We're both lost. I started hearing the whispers again a year ago, and my guess is that's when Tristan became a vampire." He met her gaze. "I've concluded he anchored himself to you to protect us. He was succumbing to the whispers as well, even before he was bitten. He needed an anchor for both of us. He always knew how to find something to save us, a spirit that was strong enough to hold us a little longer, until we drained its supply of good. He must have chosen you to save us."

She shook her head, unable to pull away from him when all she wanted to do was cradle him in her arms and take away the suffering he'd endured for so many centuries. "How could I possibly save you?"

He brought her hand to his lips, tracing a kiss over each knuckle. "It's not your job. I love my brother, but he was a bastard for tying you to us. He's never anchored us to a living person before. He's always chosen spirits of the dead with a strong benevolent presence. I don't know why he selected you." His eyes were haunted. "I would never have brought you into this hell, and I'll find a way to free you from him. Got it?" Contrary to his words, however, he didn't release her hand. He just kept pressing kisses to it. "I'm sorry, honey. I'm sorry beyond words that you were brought into this nightmare, and I'm sorry that you're my salvation. I didn't realize it until a few minutes ago, when I felt how badly I needed you to be mine." He shook his head. "I wasn't joking about that, and that's when I realized what had happened. But your role is finished, and I'm releasing you—"

She put her hand over his lips, silencing him. "Shut up."

His eyebrows shot up. "Shut up? You only say that when I'm trying to get you in bed, not when I'm setting you free."

"Hello? Did you hear me tell you to shut up?" She shook her head when he tried to talk. "Eric, you're one of the most idiotic men I've ever met. Do you really think there is a chance I would abandon you?" Her heart softened at the look of surprise on his face. "How can I possibly abandon you to the life you've endured for so long?" She put her hand on his chest, over his heart. She felt the steady thump. "Your soul was stripped from you three hundred years ago, and yet you bleed with emotions so vivid they almost tear both of us apart. Your need for me breaks my soul, because I feel the same way for you. I won't leave you, Eric. I want to help you reclaim your soul." She couldn't quite say she wanted to be his anchor. Being forever bound to a man again was beyond what she could accept. But she would give him everything else she could.

"I can't reclaim my soul," he said. "It's gone. Believe me, we've spent three hundred years researching it. All I can do is hold on as long as I can." He slipped his fingers beneath her chin and feathered a kiss across her lips. "Every moment with you gives me more time. Every kiss heals one of the millions of fragments in my soul. Every drop of your blood assuages the hunger burning through me. You give me time, Jordyn. Time to find Tristan, to stop Cicatrice, and to inhale your scent one more time."

Tears threatened at his words. "How can you be so romantic?"

"I'm not romantic. You know that. I just like breathing you in." He pulled back. "But when I'm out of time, you must do what you promised."

She knew what he was talking about. "Kill you."

He nodded. "It's no longer simply about defending myself against the spirits. Now we know that at some point, I'm going to become a true predator, like the vampire that haunt the legends of this town, because I'm extremely powerful. Are you with me?"

She bit her lip, but she nodded. "Don't make me do it, or I'll hate you forever."

He grinned and kissed the tip of her nose. "It would break my heart to have you hate me, so I'll do my best to stay on the right side of sane." He touched her neck and sighed. "Now, it's time to make some vampire plans, don't you think? We need to bring Tristan back and kill the bad vampire."

She caught his wrist as he rolled off her. "Eric."

He paused and looked back at her. "Yeah?"

"Do you truly believe you're going to turn?"

For a long moment, he said nothing. Then he leaned forward until his face was inches from hers. "I swear on my life that I will do everything in my power to protect you from having to kill me. I will fight it with every last breath of my body, because if I succumb, I lose you forever, and that's not acceptable." He kissed her once, hard, and then turned away. "Time to get dressed, Jordyn. Sunset doesn't wait."

She sat up, hugging her knees to her chest as she watched Eric get dressed. His muscles were rippling, and power seemed to radiate from his nude body. He moved with swift grace and ease, with the stealthy lines of a predator, even when he was engaging in the simple act of getting dressed. She thought of how he'd suffered, of what he and Tristan had endured together. "If I said that I was yours, would that save you?"

He glanced over at her, his hands stilling on his boot. Electricity leapt between them, and the air in the room became so dense she could feel it coating her flesh. "It would take more than that," he said. "It would take a merging of our souls that would be so complete that we'd never be complete again, unless we were together. It would be like what I have with Tristan, but far more."

Heat rippled over her skin. "How do you know?"

"Because I met one vampire who'd done it."

"Did he have a soul?"

"His woman's soul had expanded and given itself to him, recovering the lost fragments of his. It wasn't complete, but it was enough."

The room was silent and tense. "Do you want that?

With me? To be a part of me forever?" She could barely breathe her chest was so tight. What he described was similar to the *sheva* bond, but it was so much more. Giving up a part of her soul to him? It was terrifying, but at the same time, it felt right beyond words, as if this was the place she was supposed to be, that this moment, with Eric, was what all the paths in her life had been leading toward.

A fire of longing flared in his eyes. "You would do that?"

No. Yes. "I...I don't know."

"There was one more aspect to it." His gaze was heated, burning through her.

"What?"

"Love."

She stared at him. "Love? Well, of course there had to be love. You don't do that with someone you don't love, with someone who isn't the very air you breathe every minute of every day."

His eyes darkened. "Honey, I can't even comprehend that kind of love, let alone offer it to you. Love has to go both ways, and I have no idea how to go there."

His words made her heart freeze, and all the thoughts and emotions that had been pounding through her congealed into a solid lump of pain. She realized, too late, much, much too late, that she'd fallen for him. Did she love him? She didn't want to. Oh, God, she didn't want to. Love brought so much pain and terrible decisions. "Okay," she whispered. "That's fine."

He walked across the room to her, and leaned on the bed so his hands were flanking her hips. "But I'll tell you one thing, Jordyn. If there was any chance that I could be that guy and feel that emotion, you're the woman I'd do that for. No one else. Just you." He pressed a hard, fierce kiss to her mouth that tore at her heart.

Before she could respond, he broke the kiss, and walked out the door.

Eric leaned on the kitchen counter, his fingers digging into the Formica as he listened to the sounds of Jordyn getting dressed in her room. The urge to haul ass back up the stairs and take her up on the offer she'd almost made was so strong that he didn't dare take even a step away from the counter, fearing it would lead him right back into her room.

He hadn't meant to revisit his memories, and he sure as hell hadn't meant to drag Jordyn into them. It had just happened, an automatic pull toward the past, toward the unending taint that had become increasingly virulent in his mind. There was no way he was going to trap Jordyn in his downward spiral, no matter how tempting it was for both of them.

But, he had to admit, the moment when she'd looked at him, and he'd realized she was actually thinking about it… damn. It had been the best moment of his life to have her look at him like that. It was enough to make a man want to be more than he was capable of being. How the hell had Tristan been amoral enough to trap her the way he had?

But hell, he'd almost been willing to do it back there, himself. He'd never do it, but the thought of being bound to her filled him with relentless need. She was a light in the darkness that had beat at him for so long. She was his anchor, not because of Tristan, but because she was funny, irreverent, brave, and vulnerable. She was able to see through all the shit he dished out. She made him feel alive, like a human being, in a way that he could barely remember feeling. He was used to being the monster, and more recently, too damn close to being a vampire.

Vampire? Really? He ran his tongue over his teeth, but they were flat again. Did they emerge only for Jordyn? Grimly, he stared out the window at the yard, contemplating exactly how deep he might drag Jordyn if he took her with him. The grass was patched and worn, as if David never bothered to notice he had a lawn, let alone take care of it. Just beyond the tired lawn were the thick woods of the swamp. The edges of the woods were lit by the rising sun, but ten feet inward was untouched by the light, a haven for vampires that was protected from the sun by trees too thick to penetrate.

He could see the path his brother had taken as he'd fled from the house. His footprints were invisible to everyone, except to him. It was easy for Eric to discern the traces of energy Tristan had left behind. He stirred, moving closer to the window. Would he be able to track him? Could he find him before he even awoke?

Adrenaline raced through him. Yes, he could do it—

He noticed a ray of sunlight drifting across the countertop toward him and stopped inching toward the door. He watched it for a long moment. Sun had never bothered him before. Had that changed? He slowly slid his hand across the counter toward it, his index finger extended. He paused with the tip of his finger at the edge of the sunlight, then moved his hand into the sun.

Pain exploded through him, and he jerked his hand back. His skin was blistered and red. He let out a breath, then flicked his finger at the wound. Green mist swirled from his hand and wrapped around his injury like a glove. Green light glowed, then sank into his flesh, leaving behind no trace of the burn.

It was as if it had never happened...but he knew it had. There was no way to deny it anymore. The inner vampire he'd been denying for three hundred years had finally begun its inexorable creep of possession.

What next? Would he eventually have to go to ground during daylight hours, buried deep in the earth like a monster while Jordyn thrived and flourished in the sunshine, on the surface of the earth? How the hell could he ask her to merge with him, to bind herself forever to a man who was trapped in the shell of the dead?

He wouldn't ask her.

Not that it would work anyway. Love was something he had no concept of. There wasn't a forever for him. There was only a never.

He swept a protective coating of green mist around his hand, and then slid his finger into the sunlight again. The heat prickled, but the protection he'd woven kept his skin from burning. He held it there, counting the seconds as the temperature rose and his skin began to hurt. The blisters started at forty-two seconds. Swearing, he jerked his hand back. He could protect himself from the sun for less than a minute?

Grimly, he looked out at the world of daylight he'd taken for granted for three hundred years. No longer. He fisted his hand and began to call more magic to him, needing to see how well he could protect himself from the sun. Could he shield himself long enough to search for Tristan?

"Eric?" Jordyn's voice broke through his reverie, and he spun around, startled that he hadn't sensed her coming.

She was on the bottom step, wearing a pair of faded jeans he hadn't seen before, and a hot pink tank top that reminded him of the one she'd been wearing in the jungle the day they'd met. Her hair was in a ponytail, her feet were bare, and she had no makeup on. She was pure earth and nature, simply a woman.

And she was beautiful.

His gut clenched, but he didn't move toward her. How was it possible for him to need another human being this badly? "You okay?" he asked, his voice gruffer than he'd intended.

She nodded, her gaze searching his. "We need some stakes."

His own heart seemed to burn at her comment, and he instinctively channeled energy toward his chest to protect it. "Really? Stakes work?"

She shook her head. "Ordinary ones don't do much. They must be engraved with certain runes. I'm going to go look through my grandmother's book and see if I can find the right design. If you can get us the wood, then I'll work on the designs." Her gaze flicked toward the broken picture window. "I don't want to kill Tristan," she said softly. "I'm hoping my grandmother's book has another way."

He narrowed his eyes. "What exactly is in your grandmother's book?"

"I don't know." She shrugged. "She never let me read it." She glanced at the fridge, and a sudden yearning flashed across her face. "Is there any food? I'm starving."

He noticed then how drained she looked. What kind of a bastard was he? After all she'd been through, she needed sleep and food to heal, not endure a lovemaking session that was so passionate that it had pretty much flatlined him as well.

She frowned. "Eric? Did you hear me? About the food?"

He nodded silently, not trusting himself to speak. All he wanted to do was drop to his knees at her feet and declare himself to her, to pledge his oath to protect her for all eternity, to ensure her incredible spirit would be forever safe from creatures like him. "I'll find something for you to eat," he finally said.

"Okay, thanks." She hesitated, as if she were going to

say something else, then she shook her head and walked into the dining room where her grandmother's book lay on the table.

Eric slumped against the counter and closed his eyes. How the hell was he going to be around her without throwing her over his shoulder, vaulting up the stairs, and losing himself in her until the rest of the world ceased to exist? His attraction to her was so strong that—

His eyes snapped open with sudden realization. His response to Jordyn was the same as his response to Jane and the other woman. It hadn't started that way with Jordyn, but something had changed. His entire soul burned for her on every level of his being. Stunned, he backed away from the dining room where she was pulling out a chair. He could see her bending over the book as she opened the front cover. He saw the delicate curve of her neck, the tilt of her nose, the soft waves of her ponytail as it curled around her neck. The world disappeared until it was only her, until his entire body howled with the need to go to her.

"Shit." He stumbled backward toward the door. He needed to get out. He couldn't do this to her. He reached the backdoor, and put his hand on the knob. He could feel the heat from the sun burning his back. Would he even make it to the woods? Could he get that far?

He pulled the door open, and his skin began to sear. He tried to weave a protective spell over his body, but he couldn't keep his focus long enough to do it. Shit! He would die if he left the house. He could tell he'd never make it to the woods. But if he stayed...would he kill her? Would he disintegrate her? Where was the knife? Did she still have it? He saw it then on the floor by the dishwasher, right where he'd swept her up in his arms before they'd made love.

"Jordyn," he rasped out. "Get the knife. *Now.*"

CHAPTER 19

At his sharp command, Jordyn looked up quickly. Her eyes widened, and then she leapt up, her face etched with concern. "Eric. What's wrong?"

"Get my knife." He jerked his chin at it, gritting his teeth against the pain in his back. "Just get it now."

She ran over and picked it up. "What's happening to you?"

"You. It's you. It's the same. Like it was with Jane." How could this be happening? He had been so sure it was different with her. But he could feel the haunting, relentless drive to possess her. It was so much more than sex. It was a pulsating attraction that came from somewhere so deep inside him that he couldn't even source it. It was beyond him, beyond who he was, beyond anything he could control.

Realization flooded her face, and she paled. "It can't be. It has to be different."

"I need you." Three simple words, but he poured all his feeling into them, showing her the depths of his need for her.

Her cheeks flushed, and a smile erupted on her face. "Wow. No one has ever needed me like that before."

He blinked at her cheerful demeanor. "What?"

She shrugged. "It's kind of intoxicating." She held out her arm. "Goosebumps, see?"

Why the hell was she standing there, watching him like he was some fascinating science experiment? "Get the knife ready, Jordyn."

She made a face. "No. No knife. Not today."

Hell. What was wrong with her? "Don't you get it? I'm about to disintegrate you. That's not a healthy kind of wanting."

"Yes, it is." She lowered the knife and walked over to him. "It's different, Eric." She placed her hand on his cheek, her touch cool and soothing against his hot skin.

He closed his eyes, his body stiffening. "Babe, you gotta back off. Really."

"Babe? I'm not a babe." She lightly smacked her palm against his cheek. "My name is Jordyn, you arrogant male, and you are not about to turn me into a billion screaming particles of suffering and torment."

He opened his eyes to find her grinning at him, her eyes sparkling. "What in the hell is wrong with you?"

"Lots of stuff," she said cheerfully. "A lot more than you know. I have a lot of baggage, even for a woman. But—" She poked his chest. "—*you* are not one of my problems right now. Don't you recognize what you're doing?"

He wrapped his hand around her index finger and pointed it away from him. "I'm trying to save your life. Most women would find that an admirable quality in a guy, instead of trying to talk him out of it."

"It would be admirable, but that's not what you're doing." She wrapped her hand around his, her fingers a warm temptation. "What you're doing is projecting your fears about the past onto the present, even though the situation is different. You need to evaluate the present and see this moment only for what it is."

He couldn't stop the slow grin from curving his mouth. "Therapy again?" Why did he find it so damn cute when she tried to heal his damaged psyche? "It's like you actually believe that you can save me."

"Don't be ridiculous. Only you can save yourself. All I can do is point your stubborn head in the right direction, and kick you. The rest is up to you." She raised her brows. "Seriously, Eric, I can see it in your eyes. You're nowhere near that state of being about to disintegrate me. I've seen you do that, and you're not there right now." She beamed at him. "You're just finally acknowledging to yourself that I'm really fantastic, and you can't resist my charms. You burn for me desperately, and it scares you, because you're a stereotypical guy who wants to be an emotional island. It's not deadly. It's just called goddess worship."

He laughed, his tension easing away at her lighthearted demeanor. He realized she was right. His skin wasn't shadowy, and the voices weren't deafening. He just liked her? That's what this was? Weird. He had no experience with feeling this way at all. "Goddess worship? Is that what I'm doing? You're the goddess?"

"In your eyes, yes. Others might call it love, but since we both know you aren't capable, we'll just call it goddess worship. You've realized how great I am, and it's making you panic." She patted his cheek. "So, stop being so melodramatic. Go get some wood, and come back here, okay? We kind of need to focus." Her smile faded. "Tonight's the night, Eric. I don't know what's going to happen."

His amusement faded, and he flipped his hand over so he was holding hers. "We need more information about Cicatrice. We need to know what we're facing." Love? Had she really just used the L word and himself in the same sentence? The woman never listened to him.

She nodded, tightening her fingers in his. "My grandmother knew a lot about him. I'm going to look him up in her book as well." She glanced at the clock over the kitchen sink. "The sun will set in fourteen hours."

Eric's gaze flicked involuntarily to the trees. "It's possible," he said, "that we may not be so safe. Maybe neither Cicatrice nor Tristan have to sleep during the day."

Sudden alarm flashed across her face. "You mean, like you."

He shrugged. "I'm wide awake, and the sun's out."

She looked past him at the yard, her brow furrowed in concentration. "Does the sun affect you?"

He nodded, unwilling to hide anything from her. "It burns me now."

"Wow." She rubbed her chin, contemplating the information, but apparently not remotely fazed by his confession. "So, maybe the sun is like a moat around this house? Protection until sunset, even if they're awake?"

"Hopefully." He sighed. "It also traps me inside, though, like a monster in a cage." It made him impotent, and he didn't like that.

She wrinkled her nose at him. "You're not a monster. I'm getting really tired of you saying that." She poked him lightly in the chest, and he grabbed her hand, trapping her palm against him. "You, my dear Eric, are just a guy with some issues. Everyone has issues, right? So, you're sort of a vampire. Big deal, right? There are worse things, like being an insufferable adulterer, for example. What woman wants that in a man?"

He grinned, unable to contain his amusement at her perspective. "A bloodthirsty vampire is preferable to a guy who sleeps around?"

She rolled her eyes. "You even have to ask? Men, they just don't get women." She stood on her tiptoes, her eyes turning sultry. "Do you have any idea how sexy it is when you bare those fangs at me?" She pressed a kiss to his throat, and a rush of sudden lust roared through him. "Or when you bite me?" She kissed the corner of his mouth, and he went utterly still, poised in delicious anticipation.

Her lips feathered over his in a heated promise. "Or when you—"

A car horn blared outside, and she jumped, smashing her forehead into his teeth. He grunted, and she grimaced, pressing her fingers to her head. "Sorry, I just—"

"Jordyn!" David shouted, his voice hoarse and rasping. "Help me!"

Eric turned in time to see David's truck come to a stop by the back door. The hood of the truck was smashed, as if he'd driven straight into a tree, and the windshield was shattered, a thousand fractures barely holding together.

The entire right side of the truck was dented and covered in dark red smears of...blood.

※※※※

Eric and Jordyn moved at the same moment, sprinting for the door. He yanked it open and she ran through just as David kicked open his door. Adrenaline galvanized Eric, and his magic swathed him in a protective barrier as he sprinted out into the sunlight. David fell out of the truck, landing on his hands and knees. His clothes were covered in blood, and there was a ten-inch gash on his forearm.

"David!" She lunged for him, but Eric was there first, catching him as he collapsed. David's skin was ice cold, and his eyes were bloodshot.

David grabbed the front of Eric's shirt, his fingers a vice grip too strong for someone who'd lost as much blood as was on his clothes. The coppery smell of the blood was penetrating, and Eric knew it was fresh. He experienced a brief moment of relief that the smell didn't make him want to pull out a napkin and start dining on anyone, and then David twisted in his arms, trying to get away. "Get away from me," David ordered, reacting as if Eric were a threat.

"Stay still," Eric ordered. "Tell me what happened."

David stared at him for a moment, his eyes moving rapidly over Eric as if assessing him in great detail. Apparently satisfied, he nodded. "You can help."

"Help with what?" Eric didn't even move as Jordyn ran up beside him, bumping his arm. Her contact distracted him for a split second, and he felt the sun burning his arm. Swearing, he reinforced his shields, the urgency of the situation feeding him enough strength to keep the sun at bay.

"Get the woman out of the back," David gasped as he tried to throw Eric backward. "I'll get Richard. You get her! Bring her inside! We have to hurry!"

"Who?" Eric looked over his shoulder at the truck, not letting go of David until he knew whose blood was on him. Just because Jordyn trusted him didn't mean he was going to jump on that bandwagon. He lowered his mental shields ever so slightly, allowing David's energy to roll over him. Fear. Desperation. Anguish. There was no doubt that something bad had happened, and that David was reeling. "What's going on?"

"They're going to die," David gasped. "We have less than five minutes!" He shoved at Eric again. "Hurry. She's in the back of the truck."

She's in the back of the truck? A *woman's* blood was all over David? Protectiveness surged through Eric, and he threw David into Jordyn's arms. "Take him!"

Jordyn caught him as Eric shoved the driver's seat forward to get to the back of the cab. A man in his early twenties was tied up in the back seat. His eyes were closed, and his skin was pale, deathly pale. Instinctively, Eric's gaze went to his neck, and he saw two tiny pinpricks. He grabbed the man and lifted him out. "What happened to him?"

"Last night's dinner for a vampire." David took the man from Eric, staggering briefly under the weight before regaining his balance. "I'll take him. You get the girl."

Jordyn threw the man's arm over her shoulder and began to help David drag him back toward the house as Eric sprinted around to the back of the truck. He tried to wrench the tailgate open, but the metal was completely smashed, making it impossible to open. Swearing, he shaded his eyes to peer through the tinted glass. With only the first rays of dawn penetrating the smoky glass, he could see nothing but a motionless lump inside.

It could be anything.

He looked over at Jordyn, who was almost trapped beneath the unconscious man's arm. She was gripping his waist, her feet braced as she supported him. Blood was already streaked across her face and arms, and *this* time, the sight of blood on her did make things stir inside him. Shit. He was completely insane. When this was over, he was going to have to rip out his teeth or something, because wanting to sink his teeth into her was just not his style. "Get back," he said. "I don't know what's in here."

David swayed, his face pale. "It's Skye," he mumbled. "Get her. She's dying."

Jordyn's face paled. "*Skye*? Skylar Morgan?"

When David nodded, she started to run toward Eric. David stumbled, unable to support the injured man himself. Jordyn grabbed him again, gesturing frantically to Eric. "Get her, Eric. Just get her!"

"Get inside," Eric ordered. "Now."

David nodded. "To my lab. We need to get there. Hurry." He pointed a finger at Eric. "Hurry."

While Jordyn and David dragged the man toward the front door, Eric fisted his hand, drawing energy into it. He closed his eyes for a split second, and then slammed his fist into the window. The glass shattered before his fist made contact with it, his power preceding his own flesh. He jerked his hand back and peered inside.

Sprawled across the back of the truck was a young woman. Her neck was bloodied, and her dark hair was matted. Her face was ash-gray and her eyes were closed. She'd slid across the truck bed, and was torqued against the sidewall, her limp body at the mercy of external forces. Urgency pulsed through Eric. Had his brother done this? Was this Tristan's carnage? *Tell me you didn't touch her, Tristan, or I'll have to kill you.*

There was no answer from Tristan, but his scent wasn't on the woman. It was another man, a creature haunted by darkness and evil, his stench permeating the woman's clothes, and even her flesh. Vampire, and not the kind you wanted to invite to a sleepover.

Eric immediately reached for her. He was just sliding his arms beneath her shoulders when he noticed her necklace. It was a silver charm in the shape of a panther racing across a blazing sun. He went still, shocked by it. He'd seen that symbol only once before, around the neck of the girl he'd murdered so long ago. Suddenly, it wasn't a stranger with a broken body before him. It was another Jane, the girl from so long ago, that had never stopped haunting him. It was her body that lay sprawled in front of him—

"Eric!" Jordyn's shout jerked him out of his stupor. He plunged his arms through the broken window and scooped her up. Despite her pallid appearance, her body was heavy with the weight of the living, and he could feel her spirit was still clinging to her physical form.

Alive, but barely—

Even as he thought it, he sensed her spirit detach and begin to leave. Swearing, he pulled her tight against him and flooded her with magic. It wove through her, instantly binding her spirit to her physical body. It hovered in abeyance, struggling to leave, but contained by his magic. *Stay,* he commanded. *Give her time.*

For a moment, it continued to fight, and then it sank slowly back into her. Her body jerked, and he felt her reject her own spirit, trying to expel it from a physical body that was already crossing that threshold into a wasteland that couldn't support it.

Come on, he said urgently. He summoned more magic and thrust it into her. The wound in her throat stopped bleeding, and he got her heart pumping again, a steady, fragile pulse of life that would hold for several minutes at least, giving her time. He wasn't a healer, but he could glue things together in a rudimentary way. Not to save, but to buy time.

Satisfied she would survive long enough for David to work on her, Eric swung around and headed into the house, where Jordyn and David had disappeared only moments before. He jogged across the yard, his body rigid at the idea of leaving Jordyn alone with David, who was still covered in blood.

Careful not to jar Skye, he leapt up the steps. He was just stepping inside when his instincts tingled with sudden warning. He stopped instantly and spun around, searching the shadowy trees that surrounded the property. Although the sun lit up the trunks near the edge, deeper within the swamp was still dark, dark enough for a vampire to walk without being burned, if he wasn't forced into daytime sleep.

Something moved off to his right, and Eric stared at it for a long moment, waiting for it to move again.

It didn't, but he knew they were being watched.

Tristan? Cicatrice? Or someone else? Something else?

He flicked his finger and sent a puff of energy in that direction. It drifted through the air, and pinged softly against the tree, dissipating easily...except for one spot that was heavy and thick with an energy his magic didn't penetrate.

He stiffened and turned to face the woods, staring at that spot.

As he watched, he saw a flash of two red pinpricks of light. Eyes? And then, a low growl, the same one he'd heard before. Cicatrice?

Between them, the sun cast its morning rays across the grass, a chasm that a vampire could not cross. Or could it? How much did they even know about vampires? He was standing out in the sunshine right now, with just a slight sunburn to show for it.

"Eric!" Jordyn's voice rang out from the house, but he didn't move.

He kept watching, and he knew he was being hunted. "Tristan," he said, his voice echoing across the space between them. "Show yourself."

He waited, but nothing moved. He couldn't get a feel for the nature of the presence in the woods. He wanted to think that if it were Tristan, he would know, but he wasn't sure. It could be his brother, or something worse, not that his brother was good news at the moment anyway.

"Eric!" Jordyn shouted again. "Bring Skye down! Come on!"

He tightened his grip around the woman in his arms, battling against the instinct to head into those woods and face down whatever was hunting them. He didn't like turning his back on danger, not when his woman was counting on him. But Skylar was dying, too, and Jordyn was upset about it. He pulled Skye closer against his chest, pulsing his magic gently into her, keeping her heart thudding steadily in her chest. "I'll be ready for you," he said aloud, making his voice carry across the air into the darkest regions of the shadows. "You won't hurt anyone else."

Again, the growl, but this time, it was louder, and more menacing.

Eric focused on the black spot of energy, summoning magic into his fist. He reached out into the swamp, opening his mind. Spirits came rushing to him, desperate for a chance to parasite off the living. He channeled it all into his fist until his skin glowed. Then he opened his palm and thrust it outward. The magic exploded from his hand in a fierce burst, and it crashed into the blank spot. There was a howl of pain, and the scent of something burning filled the air. The leaves rattled, and then there was silence.

Eric sent out another ping of magic, this time, there were no blank spots. Whatever it was had retreated, for now. He held no illusions the he'd done permanent damage. It would be back, soon. Instinctively, he took a step toward the woods, wanting to track it while it was hurt—

"Eric! Come on!" Jordyn sounded frantic now, jerking his attention back to the present. He became aware of his own flesh beginning to burn. His skin started to sear from the sun, his protections no longer able to hold it off. Swearing, he stepped back over the threshold into the shadows of the house, propped Skylar against his chest, and then pressed his palms together, calling even more magic. It flowed through him like a green mist, swirling out. He turned his palms outward and released the magic. It flowed into the walls of the house and up toward the roof, coating the structure in a faint, green glow.

It would protect them a few hours...if they were lucky... and if he'd gotten it right.

He felt as if red eyes were tracking his every movement as he turned and raced into the house, Skye still cradled in his arms.

※※※

When Eric reached David's destroyed lab, he found Jordyn frantically tying down the guy who'd been almost dead when they'd arrived. He was conscious now, and struggling to get free. She was working with practiced efficiency, her body rigid with tension as she carefully stayed clear of his hands and feet. The man was battling hard, but his expression was blank, as if his mind had been utterly wiped out. What was going on?

"Contain him!" David yelled at Jordyn while he rifled through the debris on the floor for supplies. "We can't let him go."

"Eric!" Jordyn shouted when she saw him approach. "Help me! Hold him down!"

Swearing, Eric raced across the floor, shifting the woman into Jordyn's arms just as the guy flung Jordyn off him and leapt off the table. "Hey!" Eric shoved him back down, and then found himself back on his ass as the guy threw him backwards.

"Skye!" Jordyn's anguished cry distracted him as he leapt up. He glanced over as Jordyn lowered Skye to the ground, cradling her as if she were someone that mattered to her.

The man rushed Eric with an unearthly howl.

"Stand down!" Eric strong-armed the guy, throwing him back against the wall so hard it cracked under the force of the impact. "Do I hurt him or contain him?" He shot the question at David, even while he divided his attention between Skye and the man he was trying to contain, attempting to prioritize the situation.

"Contain." David flung aside a steel filing cabinet, and then grabbed a glass vial from the floor. "Richard's a good guy. He's one of us."

"Us? What's an us?" Richard launched himself at Eric again, and this time Eric slammed his fists into his chest, again throwing him backward. This time, he followed his hit with magic, thrusting it at Richard. A dozen glowing green chains shot out of his palms and slapped themselves around Richard, pinning him against the wall.

He strained against them, and Eric went down on his knees, using all his might to hold the chains in place. His body strained as he fought to maintain the shields around his mind, while still accessing his magic. The man wasn't entirely human. He was far too strong for that. "What is he?"

"Be careful, Eric," Jordyn warned as she wrapped a torn blanket over Skye. "Your skin is getting shadowy."

He ground his jaw, focusing intently on holding his magic in control. "You're so nurturing. I love that about you."

She snorted. "I'm not nurturing, trust me."

"No? Sounds to me like you're falling madly in love with me, actually," he gritted out. "Don't chicks always worry about the guys they love?" Richard's eyes met his, and Eric realized his expression wasn't blank at all. Raging fury was brimming in his eyes, which were glittering with gold.

"Oh, for heaven's sake," Jordyn said. "Stop with the sex stuff."

"No. We got interrupted. David owes me a kiss."

"I'm not going to kiss you," David shouted. "You're too damned hairy for me. Jordyn, where the hell is the blue vial? What the fuck did you guys do to this place anyway?"

"We had a piñata party," Eric gritted out, as he increased his pull on his magic to hold Richard still. "The man was strong, unnaturally strong. "Things got out of hand." He watched Jordyn run across the room and drop to her knees beside David, both of them frantically scrabbling through the rubble. "Kind of like how they're about to get out of hand now, if anyone is curious." He noticed Skye's spirit starting to weaken, and he pulled some of his energy off Richard and sent it into Skye, trying to prop her up until David could get to her.

The drain on him was immense, and he grimly called up more magic. His skin began to ripple with more shadows, and he felt them sliding through his body, searching for a handhold.

"Got it!" Jordyn held up a two-inch bottle, and David snatched it from her hand.

He grabbed an empty flask from the wreckage and set it down beside the blue vial as he started to mix up the ingredients of several different bottles, much like he'd done with Eric. Jordyn navigated her way across the rubble and back to Skye. She glanced at Eric, and concern flickered across her face. "How close are you?"

"Still time, but I appreciate the concern." A small explosion jerked his attention back to David, who was now leaning over a three-foot tall pillar of blue flame that was wrapping around his face and weaving its way through his skin. "What the hell are you?"

"I'm a bartender," David said.

"Yeah, and I'm a ballet dancer. Fuck that." Richard moved again, and Eric slammed more power at him. The green chains glowed brighter, shoving the man more securely against the wall. "You want to tell us what's really going on here?"

"Vampire attack. Richard and Skye were trying to take him down. By the time I got there, things were not going well. We got him, though. That bloodsucker isn't going to come back from what I did to him." David picked up the crystal bowl that the fire was pouring from. "Almost ready. Jordyn?"

She was hunched over Skye, her hands on either side of the woman's face while she chanted. Magic danced over his skin, and he knew that she was calling upon her own spirit guides to help. Skye's life force was still weakening, though. She had minutes, maybe seconds left. "David," he said. "Get over to Skye. She needs help."

"No, Richard first. He's almost gone."

Richard's eyes were fixed on his, his entire body still straining against the chains Eric was holding him with. Eric felt the darkness of his spirit pals creep around the edges of his mind, searching for an opening. Swearing, he raised his shields further, and Richard got his hand free, taking advantage of Eric's distraction.

Shit! He shoved more magic at Richard, pushing him back against the wall, and then the darkness coiled around his head more. He could feel it leaching into his mind, forcing tiny cracks in his shields. "I can't hold him much longer," Eric announced to anyone who cared.

"Don't let him go!" David limped past him, and then stumbled. He fell to his knees, and Eric saw then that his jeans were torn and bloodied as well. His face was pale, and his breath was rasping in his chest.

"David?" Jordyn didn't take her hands off the woman. "What's wrong with you?"

"Nothing." David tried to stand, and fell again. Without breaking his hold on Richard, Eric grabbed his arm, hauled him to his feet, and practically threw him at Richard.

He went down on his knees beside Richard, who was still straining against the bonds. "Lower him down to me," he ordered Eric.

"Lower him? This isn't as easy as I'm making it look, you know." Gritting his teeth, Eric moved the chains, dragging Richard toward the floor. Richard started to fight with renewed vigor, twisting and battling against the bonds. Eric felt his grip on him start to weaken. He called up more magic, and it hit him hard, rushing through him like a high. Shit. He was too vulnerable after the last close call. His shields were too weak. "I can't hold him much longer—"

"You can do it," Jordyn interrupted. "You're just afraid of what you are. Believe in yourself."

"Believe in myself? Really?" He glared at her as he worked on Richard. "Inspirational Hail Marys are a little overly optimistic in this situation, even coming from you," he said. "Besides, I'm not afraid. I'm just smart about the risks, and I think it's polite of me to warn every one present that I might devour them shortly."

"You're afraid!"

God. Did the woman have no sense of boundaries? "Don't call me afraid. I'm not afraid. I'm irritated!"

She shook her head at him. "You'll never get over your fear until you face it. Maybe this is your moment. Face your fear and then master your domain."

"I have no interest in mastering my domain," he choked out, still concentrating on Richard. "At least, not when you're around to take care of things."

She gaped at him. "Sex? Really? Now?"

"It's a good distraction," he muttered. "You know how guys think about baseball to keep from getting off too early? Well, it works the other way, too. I think about you naked to keep from exploding into some sort of demon-vampire mixed breed of doom and destruction."

"A little lower," David ordered. "I can't reach him."

Eric slammed Richard to the ground, and the man grunted with pain as he hit the floor, but it knocked the wind out of him enough to tame his struggles for a moment. David immediately bent over him, dumping powder on him.

The air in the room thickened, and Eric glanced up at the ceiling as a sudden crack echoed through the room. The ceiling had split, a six-foot long crack in the plaster eating its way across the length of the room.

Jordyn looked up, and she bit her lip.

David's chants grew louder, and Richard's struggles increased. Eric gritted his teeth, focusing all his energy into holding him. Dark shadows began to streak through his mind, like teeth digging into his brain. There was another crack, and the wall split.

Jordyn looked over at him. "Is that you?"

"Might be me. Maybe Richard. I'm not sure. There's a lot of energy being tossed around right now." He felt a shift in Richard's energy. It suddenly became much darker, and the green chains wrapped around him began to drip with a black coating. For a split second, he wondered if Richard was a vampire as well. No, not vampire. Something else. Something really bad. Suddenly, his ability to hold Richard took on new urgency. Whatever he was, it wasn't good. No wonder David had tied him up before putting him in his truck.

He jerked his attention off the cracking plaster and focused on Richard. He quieted his mind and thrust more energy at him. Hairline cracks appeared in his chains, and the green began to fade as Richard's power grew. The man's eyes shifted to a lethal shade of gold.

"We're losing him," David shouted. "Come on!" He slammed his hand down onto Richard's chest, and the other man coughed as smoke poured out of David's palms and into his body.

"Eric!"

He looked over at Jordyn, whose face was pale. "What?"

"Your face." She looked down at Skye, and then back at Eric. "You're slipping again.'"

"I'm aware of that, thanks." He knew damn well that there were shadows solidifying beneath his skin again. Hard to miss them, really.

Her face was pinched with worry. "Let go of Richard. You can't hold him."

He glanced back at Richard, who was thrashing under David's ministrations. "I'm not thinking that's a good idea right now, honey—"

"But—"

A sudden keening wail scraped through the air, and Eric jerked his gaze back to Richard just as the man's head went back in a convulsion of agony. His back arched as if he were being stabbed between the shoulder blades.

"No, no, no!" David shouted. "Come on—"

Richard suddenly went limp, collapsing on the floor, his life force spilling out of his body. Eric swore as he watched the mist gather above his heart, and then spin out through the wall. It didn't take being simpatico with spirits to know what had just happened.

Richard had just been killed by a vampire.

CHAPTER 20

Jordyn felt the entire room creak and groan, and the walls seemed to bend inward toward them from the sheer weight of the oppressive doom. She blinked back the sudden tears as Richard's death closed in around them. She didn't even know him, but the raw vulnerability of his life, and all of those she cared about, seemed to swell inside her. His death leached through her body, as if it were trying to contaminate the very air around it and drag them all with it. She felt the weight of the death tearing at her, and tears filled her eyes, that same anguish that had made her kill herself before, after so many she'd loved had been ripped from her grasp so ruthlessly.

Stay with me, Jordyn. Eric's voice brushed through her mind, surrounding her like a warm embrace of strength. *Think of how great of a lover I am, and how you can't wait for me to make love to you again. If you get suicidal, you'll never get another orgasm from me again.* She felt his lips brush across hers, but it wasn't a kiss of lust and sex. It was tenderness and sensuality, encircling her heart and easing the tight grip of anguish.

She managed a small smile, and took a deep breath, her lungs suddenly working again. His metaphysical caress was wrapped tightly around her, giving her a precious buffer from the negative emotions swirling through her. As she regained control of her emotions, she realized the air was thick with a taint that crept across her flesh, and tried to grip her soul. What in heaven's name was that? "Away!" She flung out her hands, and it backed off, seeping away and into the cement walls.

As it departed, Eric released Richard, and then fell to his hands and knees. His fingers dug into the floor, and his head was bowed with exhaustion from the battle he'd just waged. Even his muscles were shaking visibly. Richard's lifeless body collapsed without Eric's support, and then Skye's body convulsed violently.

Both men whirled toward her, and Jordyn bent over her, frantically trying to infuse her own energy into Skye. But her friend's back arched, and her mouth opened in a cry of anguish. David lunged at her, skidding to a stop beside her as he launched into muttered chants in a language she didn't understand, but that she recognized.

Eric leapt across the room, landing beside Jordyn in a crouch. He pressed his shoulder against hers and set his hands over hers. She felt the press of his energy swirl into her. Dark, terrible images flashed in her mind, and she instinctively recoiled.

"I know I'm bad shit, but you need to stay with me," he said. "We need to do this together. She's trying to die."

"Okay." She didn't hesitate. She simply closed her eyes and leaned against Eric, focusing on the feel of his body against hers, using his physical presence to ground her from her panic about losing Skye. She dropped her mental shields, and he swept into her mind, a vibrant, masculine force. His energy was violent and terrible, and she could hear the screams of souls that had been tormented echoing through him.

She didn't shy away. She just opened herself to him, wrapping herself around him. Their spirits connected, and she felt the moment his darkness sensed her. Everything came racing toward her in a frenetic, rabid assault—

No! Eric's roar of denial echoed through her as he slammed up his shields between them. She was instantly cut off from his darkness, and she swayed, as if he'd taken away part of her foundation.

She could feel the iron grip of his control as he wove his energy around her again. This time, he was more careful, keeping his energy tightly contained, so that only hints of it spilled through her as he entwined their magic. Holding onto her beneficent energy, he guided her through the metaphysical web and into Skye's body. Together, they held onto Skye's spirit, feeding it enough of their own energy to sustain it while David frantically worked on her physical being.

Another keening wail echoed from Skye, and her body convulsed again. Her pain shot through Jordyn, and she gasped, struggling not to pull away. Eric put his arm around her shoulders, pulling her against him as they held onto Skye ruthlessly, refusing to let her go. The energy Eric was pouring into Skye was incredible, and Jordyn was stunned by the sheer force of what he could channel. It was a thousand times more than what she could do, exponentially more powerful. But his was pure evil, a raw, unstoppable hunger that burned through him like an insatiable lust for blood, death, and domination.

For the first time, she truly understood what a danger Eric presented, because that dark side of him wasn't him at all. It was something else, a parasitic soul living within him, trying to take over him at every opportunity. It wasn't as if Eric could simply choose to embrace his good side. It was whether Eric had the strength to hold off the enemy from within, that was, quite clearly, not the type of boy that a girl would bring home to her mother, or even to her drunken, abusive father.

Fear rippled through her, a deep, real fear of the reality of what he was.

Skye's body shuddered again, and smoke exploded from her neck. It raged in black and orange, spinning wildly around them as if they were in the middle of a raging forest fire. The air was rancid with the stench of burnt flesh, and Jordyn felt Skye's soul try to escape again.

Eric thrust his magic into her, and Jordyn clenched her teeth, joining up with Eric. For a terrifying moment, everything was held in abeyance: Skye's body fighting David's treatment, her soul trying to leave, and Eric's shadowy self pulsating through her. Eric's darker side was getting stronger and stronger, and she could feel it starting to leach into her. She opened her mind and reached out with her own powers, seeking help from the benevolent spirits that surrounded them. They came to her, spirits of women and children long since departed from this world, and poured their love into her. She thrust it into Eric, wrapping him in the shield of her own magic, trying to give him room to work on Skylar.

He glanced at her, and she saw his face was almost pure

shadows. *A few more seconds.* His voice was strained in her mind. *Then I can't pull back.*

Jordyn glanced at David. "You have to do it now!"

David looked up, and his eyes flicked to Eric's face. He swore under his breath, and then grabbed a small pile of herbs to his right. He glanced at Jordyn, and she saw a flash of pain in his eyes. Then he tossed the herbs into the fire.

The explosion threw them all back. Eric crashed into the wall beside Richard, and Jordyn landed beside him, saved from serious head injury when Eric caught her just before impact. She slammed into his chest, and he grunted as his arms wrapped round her. David hit the ceiling, and then crashed down beside them.

Then, just as suddenly as they'd appeared, the flames disappeared, leaving behind a caked layer of ash across everything. Skye was laying on her back, covered in black filth, her eyes closed and her body still.

Jordyn coughed, trying to clear the ash from her lungs.

"You okay?" Eric asked.

"Yes." She rolled over to look at him and gasped when she saw his face looked almost like a bottomless pit of poisonous mist. His skin was undulating, and his face was sunken. "Eric?"

He shook his head and closed his eyes, letting his head rest against the wall. "Check Skylar. I'm fine."

She touched his arm. "Eric—"

"Check her!" He opened his eyes. "I'm fine." His eyes bore into hers, and she felt the depths of his struggle. He was barely holding onto the edge, and her heart ached for him.

You're not in this alone, Eric.

For a long moment, he didn't move, then he nodded once, and closed his eyes again. The air around him grew empty, and she knew he was building his shields again, waging that internal battle he'd fought so many times in his life.

She glanced over at Skylar, and new worry rippled through her. Skye was motionless, her skin ashen, her cheeks almost as sunken as Eric's. "Skye?" Jordyn scrambled to her feet. Was she dead? Her mouth dry with terror, she raced across the floor and fell to her knees beside her. Skye's face was caked, and Jordyn used her sleeve to wipe her eyes clear of the soot. "Hey, sweetie, it's me. Jordyn."

For an agonizing moment, nothing happened, and then Skye's eyes opened. They were just as radiantly green as they'd been so many years ago when they were kids. For a long moment she stared at Jordyn without speaking.

"Skye? Talk to me."

Skye's green eyes flicked to the men, and then back to Jordyn. "That was fun, don't you think?"

Relief rushed through Jordyn, and she sat back on her heels. The same old Skye, despite the fact it had been so long since they'd seen each other. "Super fun. Another thing off your bucket list, right?"

Skylar grinned then, even as she winced with pain. "I have a distinct memory that having my throat ripped out by a vampire might even have been number one. I can't believe it took this long." She grimaced. "I'm such an underachiever, you know?"

"Never, and your dad's a bastard for even putting those words in your mouth."

Skye laughed softly. "Your dad's the bigger bastard."

"I know, but he's dead."

Skye managed a faint smile. "Mine too. We should celebrate, don't you think?"

"Definitely."

"Tired. Need to sleep." Sky's smile faded. "We need to kick some ass," she muttered. "It's time. David's a badass now," she whispered. "Did you notice?" Her body shuddered. "I missed you, Jordyn. You're the only one who got me," she said, her voice fading as her muscles went limp. Jordyn opened her mind to search for her spirit, but she couldn't sense anything, which could mean either her soul was back in her body, or it had already left. Jordyn's only skill was with spirits that were no longer bound to their corporeal form, but which were still in the vicinity.

She looked frantically at Eric, who was looking at her with a strange expression on her face that she couldn't decipher. "Is she dead?"

David knelt beside her and set his palm on Skylar's neck, where she'd been bitten. His fingers were blackened, covered in soot and burns as he cupped her injury. "It's clean," he said, his voice rough and ragged. "I got it all. I just don't know if it was too late."

"She's okay," Eric said quietly. "Her soul is staying put. She's healing now."

Tears filled Jordyn's eyes at his words, and she bowed her head in exhaustion. *Skylar was going to be okay.*

She grabbed a half-burned blanket and tucked it around Skye as David slumped beside her. His wounds were still bleeding profusely, the blood mixed with ash and soot from the explosion. Eric was sitting with his back propped against the wall. His forearms were draped over his knees, and his face was swirling with shadows. His cheeks were sunken, and he looked like a man who had spent an eternity in a dungeon of hell.

Beside Eric lay Richard, his body sprawled in the indignity of death. She didn't know Richard, but he looked as if he'd been in his late twenties, and he was heavily muscled, a man who wouldn't lose very many battles.

David let out a muffled groan as he reached for another jar of powder, which he dusted over the wound in his forearm. As she watched, she saw the bleeding stop and the ends of the gash began to heal, so quickly she could actually see it happen. She glanced at Eric, who was watching David closely. No powder could make a person heal that quickly. It was David who was healing himself.

Eric held out his hand to her in silent invitation. She brushed her fingers over Skye's forehead, and then stood up. Her legs were trembling, but she managed to get to Eric without falling. The moment his hand wrapped around hers, she felt the depths of his struggle to contain the spirits swirling through him. His sheer strength filled her, and at the same time, she felt how dangerously close to the edge he was.

I need to touch you. His voice was warm and intimate in her mind. Not flirty. Not seductive. Just a statement of fact.

Of course. She sank down next to him, as he wrapped his arm around her shoulders, tucking him against her. His chest was warm and hard, a solid foundation that felt safe and good.

He pressed a kiss to her temple, but his lips were cold. She glanced at him, concern pulsing through her. *Are you okay?*

I'm not going to disintegrate anyone right now, if that's what you mean. If I were, I wouldn't have let you come close to me. He closed his eyes as he rested his head against the wall, but she could feel the trembling of his body. His hand rested on her hip, over his knife, which was tucked in her belt loop.

Jordyn sagged against him, too exhausted to battle with him. Eric pulled her tightly against him, but it wasn't simply intimacy. There was a tautness to his muscles, a warrior ready to react.

"David." He spoke aloud, but didn't bother to open his eyes. She could feel his energy pulsing through the room, however, and she sensed that he was aware of every nuance of David's actions, even though he didn't appear to be watching. "I think it's time that we all sat down and had a conversation. You know more than you've let on. You were out fighting vampires last night, and it's really quite rude not to invite your guests to join you when you do fun stuff like that."

David raised his head to look at Eric, and then he looked at her. His eyes were bloodshot, and his face was pale. "Is he a vampire?" he asked Jordyn, ignoring Eric.

There was an edge to his voice that made the hair on her arms prickle. Without flinching, she met David's gaze. She'd never lied to David in her life, but suddenly, the truth wouldn't come. "No, he isn't." Was he? She didn't know, but if she had to guess, it was more likely a yes than a no, though he clearly wasn't like Tristan. No red eyes to be seen.

Eric's arm tightened around her. "Do not ignore me, David." Eric opened his eyes to look at David. His eyes had become almost black. "I asked you a question."

David met his gaze, and there was a sudden tension in the basement. "You broke my lab. No one can get out of that room."

"I can."

"Which means you're not human." David's hand went to his throat, to the necklace with the miniature stake.

Jordyn studied it, recalling how it had reminded her of the runes engraved on her grandmother's stake. Was it the same one? Had he somehow copied the markings?

"No. Not human," Eric agreed conversationally. "And

your lab wouldn't be broken if you hadn't locked me up where I couldn't fight the vampire that broke in. Jordyn almost died because I couldn't get to her, and I find it unconscionable that you would leave her here without protection of any kind." His voice was laced with a deadly threat.

David stiffened. "I had to go. She can handle herself."

"Yes, she can, but everyone has limits." Eric's voice was smooth and lethal, and his message was clear. "What the fuck is going on, David? You know more than you've been telling, and it's time to talk."

David tensed, and he grabbed the upended shelving to pull himself to his feet. The moment he did so, Eric stood as well, moving with speed far beyond what he should be capable of, given the level of exhaustion he was facing. As he rose, he grabbed Jordyn's arm and set her just behind him, enough that he could protect her. The moment he put himself in front of her, she saw David tense, possessiveness flashing across his face, even though he was so weak that he was actually swaying.

Something was stirring between the two men, and she realized she had to step in. They had no time for a battle.

"Okay, okay." She held up her hands. "Richard's dead, Skye almost died, and I want to know what's going on." She looked at David. "I don't know what's up with you," she said softly, "but we're on the same side. We always have been." She could feel the tension radiating from Eric, and she knew he was ready to launch himself at David, but to his credit, he didn't try to stop her from stepping between the two men. His fingers wrapped loosely around her wrist, but she didn't lie to herself that it was all lovey-dovey. He was prepared to pull her out of the way if things escalated.

It was sweet, really, that Eric wanted to protect her, even though it was clearly not so endearing to David. "What happened to Skye, David? And why didn't you tell me she was back in town?"

"What happened to my lab while I was gone? I want details," he asked instead.

She sighed. "A vampire is hunting me," she said, declining to mention it was Tristan. "He found me. Eric saved me."

David's face paled. "Cicatrice? He's hunting you again?"

"Again? *Again?*" Eric's fingers tightened around her wrist. "Cicatrice is *hunting Jordyn?* Since *when?*"

She sighed. "Since I was a baby."

"What?" Eric looked like he was going to explode. "He's been dead for four hundred years. How old are you?"

"Twenty-six, but he's been hunting me from the grave." She ran her hand through her hair, too exhausted to think. She needed to get out of the basement, and focus. "Eric, you look less like you're going to pass out, so you carry Skylar upstairs to David's room. David, you can figure out what to do with Richard. I'm going to go make coffee." She pointed at the men as she began to pick her away across the wreckage of the lab. "I expect the two of you to join me, but you have to leave the posturing behind. I don't have the energy for men being men right now. I just don't. A battle is coming for us tonight, and we need to be prepared."

Neither man moved, as if each was waiting for the other to stand down, but as she reached the stairs, Eric walked over to Skylar and picked her up. He tucked her against his chest, cradling her head against his shoulder. His energy was still tainted, and shadows were still shifting beneath his skin. He turned toward David. "We need your help," he said simply.

He didn't waste any more words on the man who had been her friend since childhood. He just turned and followed her up the stairs. *Jordyn.*

She glanced over her shoulder as she reached the top of the steps. Her heart skipped a beat when she saw the shadows circulating beneath his skin. *You're not okay, are you?*

I'm stable, he said. *I like that you're worried about me. You like me, don't you?*

The weariness in his voice kept her from being annoyed. Instead, she shrugged. *You're growing on me.*

He grinned, shifting Skye to free his left hand. *It's because I'm such a great lover. I knew I could win you over if I could only get you naked.* He caught Jordyn's wrist and pulled her against him. She was too tired to resist, and let him fold her against him in a long embrace. Skylar's hair tickled her shoulder as she melted into him. She wrapped her arms around his waist and buried her face in his neck. His body was strong and warm, and it felt good, so good, to be wrapped up against him.

You feel good. His voice was rough and intimate as he brushed over her mind.

So do you. She lifted her face to his, and he was ready, capturing her mouth in a kiss that seemed to go right to her heart. His mouth tasted as wonderful as it always did, but this time, there was something more in his kiss. A tenderness. A softness. A realness that was so much more than a kiss by a flirtatious playboy who wanted to bed her. It was the kiss of a man who was already deeply connected to her, on so many levels.

Skye shifted in her sleep, and Jordyn broke the kiss. Eric was studying her, his eyes unfathomable. "How do you take your coffee?" she asked.

"Straight up," he said.

She grinned. "I figured." She pushed back from him. "I'll have it ready—"

His fingers tightened around her wrist, halting her retreat. *I don't trust David, honey. I want you to be careful around him.*

Her smile faded. *He's been my friend forever. He'd never betray me.*

Promise me you'll be careful.

He didn't say anything more, but she heard the whisper of a name in his mind, one that he didn't intend to share with her, but that he was thinking about. Walter. She'd trusted blindly before, and lost. She bit her lip, her heart suddenly heavy. Would David betray her as well? Denial pulsed through her, but at the same time, she knew that David was hiding things from her. He wasn't the boy she'd left ten years ago, and she wasn't sure exactly who he had become. *I'll be careful,* she said, unable to keep the sadness out of her voice.

I'm sorry, honey. I don't want to be right. He pressed a kiss to the back of her hand, his eyes shadowed with secrets that she'd just begun to decipher. "I'm going to put Skye in David's room. You okay for a moment?"

Involuntarily, she glanced toward the broken picture window in the living room. The sun was streaming through it now, a bright golden blessing upon the day. Even the trees at the edge of the swamp were lighter, but night still held the deeper woods in its grip. "Yes, I'll be fine. Take care of her."

Eric nodded, and she felt him push energy toward her. It seemed to wrap around her like a protective cocoon, prickly but secure. *It's not much protection, but it will give you a couple extra seconds to react if he comes after you.*

Her throat tightened as he turned away. His movement was slow and labored, as if it was taking all his strength simply to maintain a straight line as he walked down the hall with Skye, and yet he'd still given her what little protection he could summon, just in case he was right about David.

She took a deep breath as she headed into the kitchen. Eric could say all he wanted about how he was the bad guy, but he was her rock on so many levels. She'd always liked him, despite his arrogance, but now, it was more. She ran her hand down her arm, and felt the prickle of magic that he'd enshrouded her with, offering her the last of his resources.

As she turned to get the coffee out of the freezer, the dagger on her hip caught on a drawer handle. She looked down at the glittery green blade, glowing as if Eric had fueled it with his own magic. Was it really possible she might have to use it on him?

No.

She wouldn't do that again. She *wouldn't.* Biting her lower lip, she grabbed the coffee, even as the grim reality hovered in front of her, refusing to be denied. If she had to kill Eric, it would be even worse than when she'd killed Walter. She'd been with Walter because the *sheva* bond had tied them together. She was falling for Eric all on her own. What she and Eric had was a thousand times more powerful than anything she'd felt with Walter because it was fueled solely by her heart and his...which meant that the crash would be so much more devastating.

With a sigh, she walked over to the sink to fill the coffee pot. As it filled, she surveyed the woods. Something moved, and she jerked her gaze to the right, trying to see what she'd missed. For a split second, she thought she saw glowing red eyes, and chills ran down her spine. She went still, the water pounding onto the metal sink, as she watched the woods.

She'd seen eyes like that in her sleep before.

Red eyes.

Looking for her.

Hunting her.

Eyes that weren't real. Eyes that were alive only in her dreams...eyes that her grandmother had said were almost as powerful in her mind as they were in real life.

Slowly, her hand unsteady, she shut off the water. The steady drip, drip, drip pinged on the stainless steel sink, like the droplets of blood she used to dream about. She quieted her mind, using the same tools that her grandmother had so painstakingly taught her.

Jordyn. Cicatrice's razor-edged voice was a whisper through her mind, the cold brush of menace.

"No!" She slammed up her mental shields, and stepped back from the window, pressing her hands to her temples. Her hands were shaking, as she stared at the woods. Had that been Cicatrice? Or her imagination haunting her, as it had so many times?

If it wasn't her imagination, if he really had found her...

"Jordyn? You okay?"

She whirled around to see Eric running down the stairs, his shoulders so broad they almost took up the entire stairwell. Relief flooded her at the sight of him, despite his shadowy skin and sunken cheeks. "We have nine hours until sunset," she said, trying to keep her voice steady.

Eric looked past her as he walked up, studying the woods. She felt a push of energy as he sent something out past her. For a moment, he said nothing, then he nodded. "There's nothing out there right now." He looked down at her. "You're safe."

Relief rushed through her so that she had to lean against the counter to keep her balance. "For now."

"For now." He raised his brows at her. "I heard him in your mind," he said quietly. "I felt his presence. You didn't imagine it. He's alive, and he's found you."

CHAPTER 21

"We need stakes." David appeared in the doorway of the basement stairs. He was still covered in blood, but the gash on his arm was healed, and his eyes were brighter and less sunken. He was grasping a bloodied towel that he was using to wipe off the last of the dirt, ash, and blood from his hands. "A lot of them."

Jordyn and Eric broke apart, turning to face him. She couldn't help but glance over her shoulder again at the woods, and Eric moved closer to her.

"Stakes don't work," she said. "It only slows them down."

"Ordinary stakes, yes, but not the special ones." He walked across the kitchen, pulled a stake from the folds of the towel, and put it down on the counter. "This works. If we duplicate the runes onto other stakes, they'll work almost as well."

It was her grandmother's stake. Jordyn's heart jumped and she grabbed it, turning it over in her hands. She remembered every detail of it, and this was definitely it. She looked at David. "Where did you get this?"

"I've had it for a while," he said, reaching for it.

She pulled back, not letting him take it. As if reading her mind, Eric slipped it out of her hand, ostensibly to look at it as he walked away from David, taking the stake out of his reach. She thought she smelled something burning, and she glanced quickly at Eric. His face was composed, but there was a faint tendril of smoke rising from his fingers. A vampire stake?

David sniffed the air, and she spoke quickly to distract him. "You stole that from my grandmother," she said. "It's hers, but it was gone when I went to find it."

David's gaze jumped to hers. "I didn't steal it. It's my job."

"Your job? Really?" She folded her arms over her chest. "What job is that? I'm guessing that's not part of your bartender duties."

"I'm a NightHunter."

She blinked. The word sounded vaguely familiar, but she couldn't place it. "What are you talking about?"

"NightHunters. The ancient guild your grandmother was a part of. She was the last active one left that we know of. When she died, there was a void. You left town, so I took over. I'm resurrecting it." He rolled up his sleeve, and she saw a symbol carved on his bicep that she recognized.

It was the shape of the pendant that her grandmother used to wear around her neck. A double crescent moon bisected by a triangle. "The moon, and the three promises: life, love, and peace," she said softly.

"It's the symbol of protection from the creatures of the night," he explained. "We're the secret guardians of the innocent. We're the last line of defense."

Eric was leaning against the counter, twirling the stake in his fingers. The smoking of his skin seemed to have stopped, and she could see a faint layer of fluorescent green on his fingertips, as if he'd created a shield to protect himself. "And what exactly do you all do?"

David walked across the room to the cabinet above the stove and pulled it open. "We hunt them, and kill them." There were no plates on the shelves, just dozens and dozens of wooden stakes, all of them carved with the same markings as her grandmother's stake. He picked one up. "These work pretty well," he said, wiping the towel over it almost reverently, as if to wipe imaginary taint off a priceless item. "You hit the vampire anywhere with them, and it slows them down long enough to get one in the heart." he tossed one at Jordyn, but didn't take his attention off the one in Eric's hands. "With these ancient symbols, there's usually no need for beheading. It works on its own most of the time, but if you need to behead one, these engraved stakes make the vampire so incapacitated that it's easy to finish them off. I always decapitate just to be sure, though. Can't risk being wrong, you know."

Jordyn gripped the stake in her hand. The wood was smoothly polished, and the tip was razor sharp. It looked like a lethal weapon designed to destroy, and she hated holding it in her hands. "I don't think my grandmother was a killer," she said. "She wasn't like that."

Her grandmother had taught her to honor life and cherish spirits. Oba was the one who had taught her to commune with the spirits and to allow them to bring positive energy into her. She'd believed in the benevolence of the female spirit, and that women could make a difference in the world. She wasn't an advocate of *killing*.

"Your grandmother was a NightHunter," he said. "Read her book. You'll see."

She stared at him as a feeling of violation crawled over her. "You read her book? That was private."

"I needed to know if there was any information in it." He shrugged. "There's nothing of value, so I left it there." He looked over at Eric. "Tonight we hunt Cicatrice. You in?"

Eric balanced the stake on his palm, watching it steadily. His gaze slid to David, silently assessing.

David stared at him for a long moment, then looked away, unable to hold his gaze. "Cicatrice will come for her tonight," he said. "He knows where she is."

There was something in his tone that put Jordyn on alert. "How do you know that?"

Eric had stopped twirling the stake, and was watching David carefully as well.

David glanced between them. "I heard you saying that he was talking in your head again, right? So, yeah, that's my guess." He glanced past them. "I'll go harvest some more wood. We'll need more tonight. I'll be back in a couple hours." He moved past them to his truck, now moving with lithe grace, despite the fact that he'd barely been able to walk only an hour before.

Neither Jordyn nor Eric moved to stop him, and they

were silent as he started his battered truck and drove it away.

As his engine faded into the distance, Jordyn felt her heart tighten. She glanced at Eric. "Last night, in his battle with the vampire, he let it slip where I was." It wasn't a question. She knew it in her heart. "He did it on purpose. Whatever vampire he fought, he didn't kill it. He let it go." Was that why that man Richard was dead? And why Skye had gotten hurt? Because David had exposed them to set his trap?

No. No, that wasn't right. David wasn't like that. But the denial rang empty within her. Maybe he was like that.

But Eric nodded. "He set you up to trap Cicatrice. I can't say I approve of his method." His voice was lethal.

Jordyn bit her lip, refusing to dwell. She wasn't here to rediscover a lost childhood friendship with the one person she'd trusted. She was in town because she owed Tristan, and now, she also wanted to protect her town. Stopping Cicatrice was the only way to do it. "Well, I guess we might as well take advantage, right? I mean, Cicatrice is who we want." But she couldn't suppress the ripple of fear. Her grandmother had warned her over and over again how dangerous Cicatrice was, not just to the world, but to her, specifically.

Eric tossed the stake on the counter. It rattled on the Formica, and then slid off and clattered to the floor. "There is *never* a reason to use you as bait," he said. "Ever." He held out his hand, and she saw angry burn marks crisscrossing his flesh, as if someone had laid a hot poker across his palm repeatedly.

She held out her own hand, which hadn't been affected at all by the stake.

"David doesn't see in shades of gray," he said softly. "He sees only in black and white."

She looked at him, understanding what he was saying. "He'd kill you, even though you're perfectly sane. And Tristan."

"With great pleasure." Eric closed his hand, and she felt him push energy across it. His hand glowed green, and this time, when he opened his palm, it was almost healed.

Almost, but there were still a few faint lines across it, as if even he couldn't quite take away the damage of the stake. He met her gaze. "Tonight, the enemy won't simply be Cicatrice. It will also be David. He knows there is something going on with me, and he will work to take advantage of it."

Jordyn brushed her hair back from her face. "The woman he loved was killed by a vampire," she said. "I understand where his hostility comes from."

Eric shook his head. "Hostility is dangerous. A good warrior never lets personal vendettas drive him."

Jordyn bit her lip. "I know." She knew Eric was right, but at the same time, she understood what it felt like to be coping with extreme emotions. "I think his heart is in the right place," she said softly. "Plus, he's a good fighter, apparently," she said. "We'll need his help to stop Cicatrice. As an ancient vampire, he's ridiculously powerful. David will know how to stop him."

"David is a bull in a china shop," Eric said. He walked over to the dining room table and picked up her grandmother's book. "I was in your grandmother's shed. I felt the strength of her power, the finesse with which she'd woven her protections. She had skills far beyond what David possesses. Find out what she knew, and find out quickly."

She took the book, her fingers brushing against his. "That spirit that was trapped in her shed? The one that you said was cruelly trapped? Was that her magic?"

He met her gaze. "It wasn't David's," he said, answering the question she hadn't asked. "He's not talented enough to do it. It was hers."

Jordyn's heart sank. "So, maybe she had a good reason."

He nodded at the book. "Figure out what it was. And fast."

⌘⌘⌘

Eric paused in the doorway of David's bedroom to check on Skye. She was still in deep healing mode, but her spirit was settled. He couldn't sense danger from her, and her energy seemed balanced, unlike David's.

Satisfied that Skye was neither a threat, nor in danger of dying, he turned away and strode down the stairs to where Jordyn was hunched over the book. She'd been reading for two hours straight while Eric had searched every corner of the house, seeking information about David and vampires.

He'd found out what he wanted to know when he'd

discovered the room hidden behind the safe room that he'd destroyed. It had been a cache of vampire hunting paraphernalia, along with extensive runes carved on all the walls. It had smelled of stale blood that had turned Eric's stomach. Bad things had been in that room, but he hadn't been able to identify the specifics.

Grimly, he walked into the dining room and sat down across from Jordyn. Her hair had long ago fallen out of her ponytail, and it was curling in tangled tendrils around her neck. She looked exhausted, and he was filled with the urge to pick her up and carry her away from all this hell. She awoke in him feelings of protectiveness that he hadn't felt in a very long time, perhaps ever.

She made him want to be the man she thought he was. Just sitting there near her eased some of the torment in his soul, and it softened the voices screaming inside his head. The shadows that he hadn't managed to settle after the festivities in the basement eased back, giving him room to breathe, simply because he was near her.

He tipped his chair forward, giving him enough reach to pick up a tangle of her hair and run his thumb over the ends.

She looked up, a startled expression on her face. She saw him, and then she relaxed. "Oh, it's you. I didn't hear you come in."

"How is it that your hair is so soft? I didn't know it was possible." He continued to slide his fingers along the strands.

Jordyn smiled. "It's called conditioner."

"It's good." He bent his head, breathing in the scent. "It smells like lavender," he said. "With a touch of peach."

She raised her eyebrows in surprise. "How on earth did you discern those scents? But yes, that's what it is, at least according to the bottle."

"We spent a lot of time in graveyards as kids. People leave flowers there. It always seemed incongruous, the beautiful flowers and all the hell that I called up. I used the flowers as an anchor, to remind myself that not everything in the world was like me." He idly watched the sunlight sparkle across the strands. "I haven't thought of flowers in a long time."

She put her hand over his. "Flowers are good," she said

softly.

"Yeah, I know they are." He released her hair to enfold her hand in his. "Thanks for reminding me."

"You're welcome to sniff my hair anytime."

"Yeah? Be careful what you offer." He wanted to smile, which indicated just how good it felt to be near her. He never thought he'd be the guy who wanted to smile when he had no time to do so. "Tell me about Skye. You seemed to know each other." He knew they had to get to business. He had to tell her what he'd found, and he needed to know if she'd come up with anything. But for a minute, for a brief respite, he wanted to simply focus on her and to settle his soul. When he'd watched Jordyn and Skye talk to each other, the tangible bond between the women had been so beautiful that he'd wanted to walk over to them and breathe it in. He had that kind of bond with Tristan, but he'd never witnessed it between anyone else. It shouldn't surprise him that Jordyn was capable of that kind of connection, but it had still stunned him to be shown, yet again, what an incredible woman she was.

Genuine affection flashed across Jordyn's face. "Skye was a few years younger than I was," she said as she leaned back in her chair, apparently feeling the same need to be in the moment and step away from the gritty reality engulfing them. "Her dad was an extremely famous singer, but he was a terrible person. He had tons of drugs in his house, and an endless stream of groupies that came through there. Skye used to sneak out and hang out with me. I felt protective of her, especially since I knew what it was like to have a terrible father."

Eric smiled at the tenderness in Jordyn's voice. "Always the one with the heart that's open to others," he said. "I'm sure she appreciated it more than you know."

Jordyn picked up his hand and traced the burn marks on his palm. "I liked helping her. It made me feel good to try to bring some brightness into the world. My grandmother was nice to her as well. David even took her under his wing. It was a team effort. She was such a spunky kid, and I didn't want her father to destroy her."

He was mesmerized watching her fingers stroke his palm. "I'm pretty sure no one has touched me like that in my entire life," he commented.

She glanced at him. "Like what?"

"Softly. Absently. As if touching me is the most natural thing in the world for you, so much that you don't even think about it. It just happens."

Her fingers stilled, and he instantly regretted bringing it up. He knew damn well that she didn't want anything between them, and the last thing he wanted to do was scare her off. "She ended up moving away?" he asked, trying to draw her attention back to Skye.

Jordyn nodded, and began to trace the lines on his palm again. "Her dad sometimes took her on tour with him, and the last time they went, they never came back. His mansion just sat there empty. I never heard from her again, so when my grandmother died, I left. I always wondered what happened to her." She smiled. "I'm so glad she's okay, well, relatively speaking."

"She seems to still have her spunk," he agreed, wanting to draw out the conversation. He liked seeing the sparkle in her eyes. It made her face light up, which, in turn, made his gut clench with need, but he had the discipline not to launch himself at her. Right now, just sitting there with her felt like a treasured moment in time that he had to remember in perfect detail, because he'd never have another moment like this again.

"Do you think she's a NightHunter as well?" Jordyn asked, her face becoming troubled.

"I think David's trying to recruit her, yes." Grimly, he accepted the inevitable intrusion of reality. He grabbed a leather-bound folder that he'd set on the table, and he handed it to her. "He's not the only NightHunter," he said. "He's found others." He flipped open the cover and showed her a list of names, and the vampires they'd killed. He pointed to a man named Richard LaSalle. "I'm guessing that's our friend from downstairs," he said. "He'd killed seventeen vampires, but you can see from the notes that he'd been bitten badly eleven times."

Jordyn leaned forward to read, her hair falling across her face like a shield, cutting her off from him. He didn't like it, so he tucked her hair behind her ear, pulling it back from her face. "David wrote that he thinks Richard is turning." She looked at him. "You think he is the one who attacked Richard last night?

Not a vampire?"

"I don't know." He thought back to the moment when David had been treating Richard. "I'd assumed he was trying to save him. It certainly felt that way."

Jordyn met his gaze, refusing to shy away from the truth, no matter how bad it might be. "What if he wasn't? What if David brought him back here to kill him?"

Eric thought back to Richard. There was no doubt the man had been crazed and deadly. He whistled softly and draped his arm across the back of her chair, instinctively using his body to shield her. "David kills his own teammates? He should die for that."

"No." Jordyn sat up, shoving the file away from her. "We don't know he's killed his own people. I'm not judging him." The turmoil of her emotions pressed at him. Doubt, mixed with sadness and love. "He was trying to save him. I could tell."

"I agree." And he did. David had definitely been trying to save Richard…but had he been trying to save his life, or save him from a fate worse than hell? Maybe David had concluded that Richard had become vampire, and he'd pulled the plug on the guy. Or maybe he'd really been trying to save his life all the way until the last moment. For Jordyn's sake, he wanted David to be the good guy, he really did.

Eric watched the play of emotions across Jordyn's face, and allowed them to filter over him. She didn't try to suppress her love for David, a deep, penetrating emotion of warmth that made dangerous energy ripple over him.

She looked sharply at him, apparently sensing the thunderous jealousy suddenly crashing through him. "What's wrong?"

"Nothing." There was no way on this earth he was going to admit he was jealous of that bastard, because he wasn't. Yeah, it grated at him that she got all soft-looking when she thought of David, and he wanted her to have that expression for *him*, but he was cool with it, right? Yeah, right. "What did you find out from the book?" he said gruffly.

"Oh, well." She sat back in her chair. "My grandmother was a NightHunter. David was correct."

Eric nodded. "Not surprising." He'd figured as much.

"I'm guessing that spirit trapped in the shed was a vampire."

She nodded. "Yes. It was a vampire, but my grandmother trapped it instead of killing it because she was trying to figure out how to bring it back to sanity. She died before she could finish her project. Her goal was to find a way to make all vampires sane, but she didn't have much success. She apparently was the one who invented that powder I used to help that one vampire, but she never was able to make the effects last long. "

A small smile played across Eric's face. "Exactly what you would do as well," he observed. "A NightHunter who wanted to save what she was born to kill."

Jordyn nodded. "She did kill over a hundred, though." She sighed. "David's right about vampires in general. They've slaughtered so many innocents. My grandmother met only one vampire who was able to hold onto his humanity for the duration," Her gaze was troubled as it settled on his face. "There are hardly any like you," she said. "Except for that one vampire, even those who start off sane eventually all cross that line."

He shrugged. "I'm a special guy. We both knew that already, right?"

"It's not a joke, Eric." She touched his hand, her fingers brushing across his palm as if reassuring herself that he was really okay.

He squeezed her hand. "I know, honey. It's habit to diffuse the heavy shit with humor. Keeps me sane."

"Humor is the secret, then?" She managed a smile. "Then you should be all set."

"Without a doubt." He nodded at the book, not wanting to get to the point of having to make promises he couldn't keep. "What else is in there?"

She pulled back from him, focusing on the book again. "The first half is mostly the meeting notes for the guild. They were just getting started, so there isn't any new information on killing vampires in that part, just mostly the runes and beheading. I'm guessing David flipped through that section, and didn't bother to read the rest."

Eric sat up, his instincts firing up. "The rest?" He chuckled. "I knew the man was a thug. Of course he'd miss the real value in it. What did he overlook?"

"A lot." She flipped back several pages. "Look here. See this date?"

He leaned over her shoulder, enjoying the opportunity to inhale her scent again. "1595? Your grandmother wrote a journal entry in 1595?" He frowned, reading it again. "Mistake?"

"No." She sat back, and looked at him. "As it turns out, my grandmother was more than four hundred years old. She apparently led the team that was hunting Cicatrice back then. She tracked him to his mansion, which, ironically, is the same house that Skye grew up in four hundred years later. My grandmother went there intending to kill him, but instead, they fell in love."

He blinked. "What?"

"Roses, hearts, shooting stars, the whole nine yards. From mortal enemy to true passion and the kind of love that transcends everything else." She flipped to another page. "He even wrote her poems. See?"

The words were somewhat blurred and faded with age, but there was no doubt that there was something about roses, kisses, endless moonlight, and blood. "Damn."

"Yes, exactly." She closed the book. "An accomplished NightHunter and a master vampire, mortal enemies, fell madly in love. They exchanged blood enough times that she became immortal. So, true love forever, right?"

He raised his brows. "No?"

"No. He was still a deadly killer, and he couldn't contain himself, even for her. One night, after he'd been sane for over a hundred years and had fed only from her, something set him off. She didn't write what it was, and I don't know if she knew. He slipped out and went hunting. He found a farmhouse, and he lost control. He killed the farmer and his wife, and was just heading for the children when my grandmother showed up."

He didn't need to ask. He knew enough about the strength of the women in Jordyn's family. "She killed him."

"Yes, she did." There was no pride in Jordyn's voice, just sadness, because she knew exactly what it was like to have the man she'd trusted betray her. "He stayed true to his nature, and she did what she had to do."

He touched her arm. "I'm sorry, Jordyn."

"There's more." She put her hand over his, but her fingers were cold. "For all those four hundred years when he was in the grave, he kept his spirit alive by feeding on hers. That's why she was so old when I knew her, because he had literally drained the life force from her until she died, taking away the immortality he'd granted her." Anger flooded her voice, and she set her hands on her hips. "Is that love? No. But he did it anyway, and when he sensed that she was dying, he tried to latch onto me."

Eric stared at her, grim realization settling in him. "So, Cicatrice wants you as a replacement for the woman he loved?"

"Her blood runs strong in me. We have the same magic. To him, I'm almost as good." She sagged against the seat, folding her arms across her chest, as if to ward off the memories. "That's why my grandmother spent so much time teaching me how to fend him off. She used to make me sleep out in the swamp by her side, and she would teach me how to weave safeguards against him that held even when I was asleep."

Eric leaned back in his seat, running his hand through his hair. Son of a bitch. A master vampire had been preparing to harvest Jordyn for decades, and now he was back, ready to finally make her his? Shit.

"My grandmother was so scared of him," Jordyn said. "But now I realize she was afraid for me, not for herself." She met Eric's gaze. "She was terrified I would suffer the same fate as she had." She gestured to the book. "Even after all that, even on the last day before she died, she wrote that she still loved him." She laughed bitterly. "It's the curse of the Leahy women," she said. "Love the wrong man until they destroy you. Four hundred years with him, and she could never get free." She pointed her finger at him. "That's why I can't love you, Eric. Do you get it? Seriously? Because loving the wrong man is a terrible, terrible curse that makes you sacrifice those you love."

"Jordyn." He wrapped her index finger in his hand and turned it away. "I do understand," he said softly. "I would never, ever ask you to make a choice that would hurt you."

"You don't want me to love you?" She searched his face, her gaze desperate and vulnerable.

As she asked the question, he thought again of what it had felt like to feel her love for David and Skye, and he knew he'd be lying if he said he didn't want her to include him in that circle of love. He wanted it. He absolutely wanted it.

Jordyn's brow furrowed, and her face paled. She went still, so still that he could hear the rustle of leaves in the trees outside, and the ripple of something swimming through the swamp. "Eric? You don't want me to love you, do you?"

What the hell was he going to do? Tell her that his entire soul literally burned for her to fall in love with him, a cursed killer she might have to murder at any moment? He was a man who was steeped in death and demons, and now, apparently was on his way to becoming the same kind of vile creature that had trapped and killed her own grandmother, if he wasn't already there.

He wouldn't do that to her. Ever.

So he met her gaze, and he lied to the woman he'd promised he would never, ever lie to. "No, Jordyn. I don't want you to love me." He cut himself off, unable to utter even one more syllable of untruth to her, knowing that if he kept talking, he wasn't going to be able to be the guy she deserved and put her safety before his own needs. He'd probably go down on his knees like some sap and offer what was left of his soul if she would, for one blessed second, bestow upon him that love that she gave so freely to everyone else. No, not simply that kind of love. He wanted that one and only love, the kind of love that a woman gave only once in a lifetime. He wanted more than the love she'd given Walter. He wanted it *all.*

"Oh." Disappointment flickered across her face.

Disappointment. She was *disappointed* that he didn't want her to love him. Suddenly, his chest seemed to tighten, and he couldn't breathe. Did that mean she wanted him to say yes? That she was already falling for him the same way that he'd tumbled so completely under her spell?

He sat back, removing his arm from the back of her chair. "Sorry." He was sorry. He was sorry as hell on a thousand different levels. He was far sorrier than that damned, inadequate word could ever begin to express, no matter how many times he uttered it.

She stared at him for the longest time, as if she was reaching inside him and wrapping her hands around his very soul. "I am, too," she said.

He wanted to ask what she was sorry for. For falling in love with him? For wanting him to give a different answer? For the fact that she knew damn well how he felt, and she pitied him for loving a woman who would never love him back? What the hell was she sorry for?

She waited, as if she'd offered that opening for him. He knew in that moment, that all he had to do was ask what she was sorry about, and she would tell him the truth, even if it meant telling him that she loved him and wanted him as much as he craved her.

He could ask, and she would tell him, and then what? It would be that much harder for him to keep his distance.

He could ask, and he would know what it was like to be loved by the one woman who had truly touched his heart.

He could ask.

He didn't.

◆◆◆

Tristan awoke abruptly, his mind shocked into full consciousness by the sudden awareness of danger. He instantly went on alert, reaching out with his mind to check his surroundings. He was deep beneath the earth, his body shrouded in the rich, damp soil beneath the swamp, where he'd been forced to go after the attack by his brother.

Never before had the spirits been able to penetrate his flesh like that, but it had been like a thousand teeth ripping apart his skin, burrowing straight through him toward his heart. He'd barely made it into the soil before he'd passed out, plunging through the depths of the rancid swamp to try to hide his trail.

It was still daylight. He could feel the lethargy in his limbs. He should be asleep now, but his mind was crystal clear, devoid of any of the heaviness that customarily assaulted him when the sun was high. His body hummed with energy as the earth worked to heal his wounds, and yet his instincts were on edge, sensing a threat so deadly that it had broken through his deep sleep.

He reached out with his mind, sending tendrils in all directions through the earth. The rich soil spoke to him, assuring him that there were no threats coming toward him. The ground was rich and healing, pouring life into him.

He shifted his focus upwards, and instantly caught the stench of pure evil, and the urgent pulse of a hunter. He slammed his shields up, cutting himself off and swathing himself in the silence of a tomb.

Cicatrice was hunting him, and he was nearby.

Tristan lay still, unable to move and defend himself due to the heavy beat of the sunshine. Adrenaline rushed through him, along with the need to open his mind and track the hunter, to follow his every move as he swept back and forth above the swamp, searching for Tristan.

He didn't succumb to the urge. If he opened his mind, Cicatrice would be able to sense him as easily as Tristan had been able to locate him. He didn't have the physical strength to defeat the master vampire right now. His only chance was to eliminate his trail, and wait until nightfall returned his strength to him.

He would fight him this night. Jordyn's blood had restored his depleted body and brought clarity to his mind. The hunger still beat within him, the predator that he kept barely leashed, but he was more now. Jordyn had given that to him.

Jordyn. He had a sudden memory of feeding on her, of her stabbing him with a stake. More flashes of memory came back to his mind. He recalled the surge of lust for her. Shit. *Lust?* What the hell had he done to her?

Loathing rushed through him, hatred for what he had become. Tonight, Cicatrice would die, and then he would find the bastard who tricked him into resurrecting the vampire. And then...shit...would he kill himself? And doom Eric?

Frustration roared through Tristan, and he wanted to strike out in fury, but his muscles were like lead. This was what he had become? A half-dead creature who preyed upon the woman he was supposed to protect? And Eric... Sudden grief seized him, a deep, penetrating sadness for the brother he would have to destroy. *I'm so fucking sorry, my brother.*

Tristan. Eric's startled voice flooded his mind, and Tristan froze in shock.

Eric? He reached out tentatively, unwilling to risk Cicatrice finding him. But the urge to connect with Eric was too strong. For a year, he'd kept his brother out, unwilling to drag him into his hell, but the attack by Eric's phantoms had broken down his shields, reestablishing the presence of Eric inside his mind. Shit, it felt good to hear from him. Energy hummed through him, a lightness he hadn't felt in over a year. *You almost killed me, you bastard.*

You were munching on my woman. Can't have that. She's mine, by the way. I love you, but you can't have her. Glad to hear you're coherent and sane, though. Always a nice trait in a vampire brother.

Yours? Tristan was shocked by the revelation. Jordyn was too sweet and wholesome for either of the Hunter twins. *Fuck that, Eric. She's not your type. She's too damn nice for you. You have to leave her alone.*

I know that, bro. I'm not going to take her, but she's mine. Why the hell did you bind her to us? She deserves more. Eric's voice was hard.

Guilt rushed over Tristan, the same guilt that had haunted him when he did it. Guilt, but no regret. He would make the same choice again. *It had to be done.* He offered no explanation. There wasn't time. *Cicatrice is hunting me. I need to cut off communication soon.*

Where are you? I'll come save your ass.

No. I'm dangerous. Stay away. He hesitated. *How's Jordyn? Did I hurt her?* Shit. He knew he had. His brother wasn't good enough for her, and neither was he. *Take her and get out of town, Eric. Make her leave.*

Eric's impatience flooded him. *We're not leaving without you. Where are you? We need to get to you before Cicatrice does—*

A hand shot through the dirt, and Tristan had no time to react before claws sank into his heart. Instinct galvanized him, and he grabbed the bony wrist, breaking it as he yanked it from him, thrusting energy at his assailant. The earth parted above him, and the swampy water poured down on top of him.

Tristan gasped and rolled to his side, desperation igniting his lethargic body into action.

Claws sank into his back, right through his ribs. Fury roared through him and he spun around, slashing as he did. His claws raked across flesh, but before he could fully turn to face

his assailant, a searing pain tore through his head, and then there was nothing.

CHAPTER 22

"Tristan!" Searing pain shot through Eric, and he gripped his chest. Burning agony tore through his heart and he went down on his knees, staggering under the onslaught of pain.

"Eric?" Jordyn knelt beside him, her face stark with worry. "What's wrong?"

"Tristan." He grunted as pain ripped through his back, and he felt like his ribs were breaking. "Something's happening to him." The pain was unreal, coursing through him so savagely it felt as though it was tearing his flesh from his body. He gritted his teeth, his fingers digging into the floor as evil flooded him, the same evil he'd felt in Jordyn's mind and outside David's house, an energy he now recognized as belonging to Cicatrice. *Tristan. What's going on?*

There was no reply from his brother, and then, the pain was gone...and so was Tristan. The connection between the brothers had been severed.

"Tristan!" *Tristan!* Eric lurched to his feet, sending out mental energy in all directions, but he couldn't find his brother again. All he felt was the insidious invasion of Cicatrice in his mind and body. He whirled around, summoning magic even as he turned, but there was nothing there. No threat. Nothing to defend against. Just Jordyn, staring at him from her knees.

"What happened?" she asked.

"Cicatrice. I felt him." Eric moved toward the window and inspected the woods, carefully sending out pulses of energy in all directions. There were no empty spots, and he could identify everything. "He's not out there." Swearing, he turned back toward her. "He has Tristan." Urgency coursed through him. "We need to find him. Now."

Jordyn didn't move. She was still on her knees, staring at him with an ashen face. "Eric—"

"Cicatrice was fully functional. I felt his energy. He's not slowed down by the daylight." Refusing to acknowledge the residual pain still drifting through him from Cicatrice's attack on Tristan, Eric strode across the dining room to the kitchen. He grabbed the stake that he'd tossed on the floor. It seared his palm before he remembered to block it, and he cursed as the scent of burning flesh streamed through the air. "We have to locate him. Now."

"Eric!" Jordyn stood up, her hands on her hips.

This time, the urgency of her tone broke through his tension, and he spun around to face her. "What?"

"Look at your chest."

He looked down. Blood was oozing through his tee shirt in five long lines. He yanked up his shirt. The skin on his chest had been torn open. The flesh was already turning black, and he knew it was poisoned.

"Your back as well." Jordyn pulled his shirt up, and he felt her fingers brush over the jagged wound on his back. Pain shot through him, and he became aware of a sharp ache every time he breathed. "He broke my ribs."

"He?" Jordyn's face was pale. "Who?"

"Cicatrice." He braced his hands on the counter and summoned magic, sending healing light through his body. "He attacked Tristan, and I was wounded through our connection. Shit. That's powerful to be able to manifest physical injury in me from a distance."

Jordyn bit her lip. "It's not healing."

He gritted his jaw. "I know." The taint was thick and noxious, just like what had happened to him when the vampire had bitten him, only much worse. It was beyond what he could heal with his magic. It needed more than he could give. He glanced outside at the ground. He could smell how rich it was, almost as if it were calling to him.

Jordyn followed his glance. "Dirt? You want dirt?"

"I'm fine." He didn't have time to go to underground to heal. His brother was dying. He could feel it. His lungs felt heavy, and he coughed. "We need to find him now."

Jordyn didn't move. She was just staring at him. "You're dying, aren't you? He's killing both of you right now, isn't he?"

"He's trying, but we're stubborn bastards." Steeling himself against the pain, he walked across the kitchen and yanked open the cabinet of stakes. "I'm going to try to open my connection with Tristan, and find him."

"You don't need to do that," she said quietly. "I know where he is."

He looked over at her. She looked like the fierce warrior he'd met in the jungle. Her feet were spread, her hands were on her hips, and her jaw was jutted out. She looked absolutely beautiful, pure fire and passion, and he knew then that he was hopelessly lost for her. He might not be willing to trap her in his life, but he'd never abandon her. He would follow her for the rest of his existence, protecting her from afar, making sure no one ever laid a finger on her again.

Her face softened, and she smiled. "No one has ever looked at me like that," she said softly.

Eric turned away. "Like what?" he asked gruffly.

"Like you'd never, ever betray me." Her voice was soft, full of surprised wonder. "Like you would sacrifice your very soul to keep me safe."

He grimaced and turned back to her. He strode over to her, grabbed her wrist, and tugged her against him. Her body thudded against his, and her breasts were full against his chest. An ancient hunger howled through him. He didn't give into it, though. He just rode it out, allowing it to pulsate through him as he pulled her even more tightly against him. "I swear on what's left of my tattered, blackened soul that you will never be alone in this life again. Do you understand? I will protect you from any threat, at any cost."

She nodded once, her eyes brimming with emotions. "You're awfully bossy and domineering."

He grinned. "Of course I am. I'm kind of an asshole. You know that."

"I do." She stood on her tiptoes and kissed him.

He went still as the need for her ripped through him. His fangs lengthened, and his entire body clenched. His body went rigid, and his arm locked around her back. "Don't play with fire," he gritted out.

She pulled back. "You need the fire right now, Eric. It's the only way we're going to win." There was no fear in her eyes. Just steady determination and commitment. "Cicatrice has a connection to me through my grandmother," she said. "Just like how you and Tristan have one. He's going to try to use that against both of us."

Eric's arm tightened around her lower back. "No." He immediately reached out with his mind to hers, wrapping a protective shield of his magic around her mind, leaving access only for him. "He can't touch you."

"The only way this will work is if you don't shut me out," she said. "We have to be stronger than he is, and the only way we can do that is together."

He tightened his grip on her, every instinct shouting at him to leave town with her and get her away from this battle, but he knew he couldn't do it. Cicatrice would eventually find her no matter where she went, and if he allowed Cicatrice to kill Tristan, and consequently himself, then she would have no one left to protect her. The only solution was to go to war, which meant allowing her to be on the front lines. If he left her behind, she'd be without protection, and that was unacceptable.

"Together," he agreed. His wounds throbbed with pain, but he ignored it. "You said you know where he is. Where is he?" But even as he asked it, he realized he knew. "His mansion. Skye's house."

She cocked her head. "It's the place where he met my grandmother. It's the place where it all began and ended for him. He has to be there."

"Then let's go." For a brief moment, neither of them stepped away. Her blue eyes were clear and focused, but shadows still fluttered in them, the weight of so much loss and betrayal in her life. He wove his fingers through her hair and kissed her.

It wasn't a chaste kiss. He poured every word he didn't dare speak into the kiss, a deep, penetrating assault. She didn't shy away from it. She just flung her arms around his neck and kissed him back, two desperate souls trying to hang onto their last moment, knowing that what was looming could tear them apart forever.

His cock was rock hard, and his fangs were burning with need, but he broke the kiss and stepped back. "You ready?"

"Ready." She hesitated. "I should leave a note for David."

He ground his jaw. "No. We do it without him. He's trouble."

More shadows flickered over her face, and he grimaced. "You know him best," he said reluctantly, knowing they didn't have time to argue. "Your call."

For a long moment, she didn't move, and he could feel her emotions warring within her. How many times had she been burned by trusting the wrong person? She looked at Eric. "We need him." She turned away and jotted a note for David, telling him they had gone to the mansion.

She left it on the counter as she grabbed an armful of stakes, and then held out her hand for her grandmother's stake.

He gave it to her.

"We don't have any more of that powder that will allow a vampire to regain his sanity," she said. "This is all we have." She swept his car keys off the counter, and then walked out the door toward his truck.

For a long moment, Eric didn't move. He just stared at the piece of paper on the counter. If David was on their side, they needed him. If he wasn't, they'd be fucked if he showed up. He was their wild card.

Was Jordyn right about him?

Every instinct he had was telling him that David was bad news, and yet, Jordyn clearly felt the opposite. Did he trust Jordyn's instincts or not? Her life depended on him making the right call.

He glanced out the window as Jordyn started the engine to his truck. She looked so tiny in the cab. Her ponytail made her look so young and innocent. This was the woman Cicatrice was planning to claim? And Eric was all that was standing in his way?

No way was he entrusting her life to some crazed self-proclaimed NightHunter. David was not going to be a part of this. Swearing, he reached for the note and grabbed it. He crushed it in his hand and was just about to shove it in his pocket, when he noticed a picture taped to the fridge. The tape was old and yellowing, and the picture was faded, but there was no doubt that it was an image of a young Jordyn, with her arms around a thin, teenaged David. Jordyn had a bruise on her cheek, but she was laughing. David's arm was around her, and he was smiling too, but his gaze was on that bruise, and there was a lethal fire in his eyes, the same one Eric had seen when he'd been talking about vampires.

David had never been innocent, even back then, but Jordyn was included in his sphere of protection. If David came to the mansion, he was most likely going to kill Eric and Tristan, because he'd realize pretty damn quickly that they were vampires, but Eric knew in his gut that the man would never hurt Jordyn. What if Eric failed her? What if he got killed or went over the line with the shadows? What if he lost his shit, and there was no one to step in and help her? David would help her. David, who would kill him and Tristan, would also defend Jordyn to the death.

Which did he value more, his life and Tristan's, or Jordyn's?

Silently, Eric unfolded the note and smoothed it out. He walked over to the open front door, held it up, and then jammed one of the stakes through the note, pinning it to the door where David would never miss it.

He'd made his choice.

❈

"Tell me about Cicatrice." Eric was sitting forward in the passenger seat, a stake in each hand. His gaze was intent on the woods, carefully and methodically scanning every inch as Jordyn drove.

She could see that his skin was glowing a faint green, as if he'd wrapped a protective coating around his flesh to protect him from the sun. He was wearing sunglasses, and the dark lenses hid his face, making him look even more dangerous than he already did. His muscles were taut, and energy was humming off him. Shadows were shifting beneath his skin, but they were in the background, not claiming him. He looked every bit the predator, and she had to admit she was glad to have him along.

"Tell me about how he's been hunting you your whole life," Eric pressed, still not taking his gaze off the woods.

She turned the car down a dirt road that would take them toward Skye's old house, the same path she'd ridden so many times on her bike. "The first time I heard him in my mind, I was five years old. He was whispering my name in my sleep, calling to me. I could see a long, dark tunnel, with something at the end of it. I wanted to see what it was, so I started walking toward it." She still remembered how the air had become colder and colder the further she walked, and the silence had grown in thickness until it hurt her ears, and yet, she'd kept going. "I couldn't stop. I had to know what was at the end of the tunnel. I had to know who was calling my name. I had almost reached the end of the passageway when my grandmother woke me up."

Eric turned his head toward her, but his eyes were hidden behind the smoky lenses. "Had she struggled to awaken you?"

Jordyn was surprised by his observation, and she nodded. "She said she'd been screaming at me for two hours. I was in very deep. Cicatrice had a strong hold on me." She shivered, recalling how ashen her grandmother's face had been, true fear visible in her eyes. "She'd actually climbed in my bedroom window to find me. She said she'd felt my distress and come to me."

Eric rubbed his jaw. "Maybe she felt Cicatrice. She was connected to him." As he spoke, she felt the push of his energy in her mind. It wasn't even intentional, just an automatic brush to connect with her and check on her. The bond between them was very strong already. Why wouldn't her grandmother's and Cicatrice's been even more powerful, after such time together?

For a brief moment, she wondered what it would be like to be so closely connected to a man that his love still touched her even through death. Would that have helped the aftermath of killing Walter, if she'd still been connected to his spirit? Or would it have been an unbearable hell to have his demon-infested mind filling hers?

I'd never do that to you.

She glanced at him, and her heart tightened at the grim

look on Eric's face. "With the right guy, it would be beautiful and romantic to be connected for all eternity." The words slipped out unintentionally, but when she said it, she knew it was true. As much as she'd been betrayed by men, she hadn't given up hope. "With the wrong one, hell, though."

Eric said nothing, but his expression was moody. "Cicatrice," he reminded her. "What happened after that night? Did he keep coming after you?"

"Yes." She turned right, the truck tires churning up the gravel road as they got closer to their destination. She wondered if David would find them in time to help. "My grandmother came to me every night after that. She'd sit on the end of my bed, sneaking in so quietly that my dad never heard her. She spent hours helping me weave protections in my mind, and she gave me a necklace with runes on it to wear at bedtime." She touched her neck, recalling the pendant she hadn't thought of for so long. "I lost it a long time ago." Huh. She was sort of wishing she hadn't now. "He came for me every night for a year, and she would merge her mind with mine and help fight him off. He enjoyed it. I could tell that he loved her involvement. It was a game to him, and he fed off it."

She bit her lip, a sudden thought occurring to her. "If I'd been stronger, she wouldn't have had to exert so much energy protecting me. Maybe then he wouldn't have been able to drain her life force so quickly."

"No." Eric was adamant. "Don't do that to yourself. You were a child, and your grandmother made her own choices. He would have taken her anyway, but at least she got to save you. That's what she would have wanted, right? And she did it, didn't she?"

She nodded, her chest suddenly aching for the woman who had guided her through so much. "She loved him, you know. Even though he was draining her, she loved him and didn't want to stop him from reaching for her. She wanted to hold him alive as long as possible, but not at the cost of me. She gave herself to him, but wouldn't let him take me. He was a murderer, but she didn't care. She just saw him as a vampire following his instincts, and she knew he was more than simply a monster." As she spoke, she looked over at Eric.

His face was shadows, and he was staring out the windshield again, his attention riveted on the woods around them. He was, in part, a monster, just as Walter had been, and yet, he was also a good man. A great man, actually. One who made her laugh, who kept her safe, and whose loyalty to both his brother and her would never cease. He was the worst of what a man could be, but at the same time, he was the pinnacle of what every man would aspire to.

Her grandmother had fought for Cicatrice, but she'd failed to redeem him. But even in that last entry in her journal, when she knew she was dying, she'd held no regret, because love was never a mistake. Oba had believed that it was worth the sacrifice of her life to try to save the man she loved.

"Jordyn?" Eric nudged her. "Finish the story."

She swallowed, and nodded. "After a year, I finally developed the skills to keep him out better. He came less often, but when he did, it was unexpected. He'd come after me while I was napping in the afternoon sun, or dozing off during class, or the nights when I was so tired I didn't have shields."

Eric turned to face her, and shoved his sunglasses up so he could see her more clearly. His eyes were pitch black and fermenting with lethal danger. "What did he do to you?"

She bit her lip, surprised that Eric knew there was more to the story than what she'd told him. Or maybe she shouldn't be surprised that he'd looked past the surface to the truth she'd tried to hide. She liked that about Eric, that he never let her put up walls between them.

"Stop the truck," he commanded.

She hit the brakes, and the truck stilled, the engine idling in the silent woods. Sunlight was filtering through the trees, but dusk was still several hours away. "What?"

He turned to face her, weaving the stake rapidly between his long fingers. "What did he do to you?" His voice was lethal, like ice.

She'd hidden it her entire life, but suddenly, she didn't want to hide anymore. She wanted Eric to know.

She pulled the collar of her shirt down, revealing the top of her left breast. She carefully unwove the magical illusions that she'd held there for so long. It took a moment, because she was so used to holding it. And then, finally, it was gone, revealing a carving above her breast exactly like the one David had shown them, the symbol of the NightHunters. The scar was deep and precise, the skin still blackened and angry. That same sense of violation slithered down her spine as it had each time she'd woken up and seen another mark. It began to burn again, just like it had when he'd done it. "It took him two years to complete it." Two years of hell in which every night was a terror, and she fought not to sleep. "After my grandmother died, he came after me really aggressively."

Eric swore under his breath, and he placed his palm over the marking. His skin was warm, and his touch seemed to ease some of the pain. "You hid this from me when we made love. How did I not sense it?"

"I hide it from myself." She wanted him to understand. "He claimed me, Eric, just the way Walter did, and Tristan. He can still reach me through this mark. I've tried everything to get it out of me, but it's there, forever, linking us. It's like a stain on my body. I hate it."

Eric bent his head and pressed a kiss to the angry scar. His kiss was so gentle that tears sprang to her eyes. She leaned her head down, resting her cheek against his hair as he trailed soft kisses over every line. Her skin tingled and hummed, and she felt as if blood were rushing to that part of her body for the first time in years. "What are you doing?"

"Offering you what I can." His voice was rough but tender, and he set his hand on her hip as he pulled back.

She looked down and saw the scars were glowing with a faint green aura. As she watched, the verdant light sank into the dark, soiled flesh. When it faded, she realized the scars were smoother, and less dark. She brushed her finger over them, and they were no longer ice cold like they'd always been. They were warm, as if they were no longer dead tissue rotting away in her chest, but were beginning to repair. She looked at Eric, and saw that his face was more shadowed than it had been, with streaks of black sliding down his throat. "You took it into your body?"

"Yeah. He was in spirit form when he did it, so it falls within my particular skill set." He ran his hand down her hair, his fingers tangling in the tendrils. "Better?"

She stared at him, her throat tightening. "But you can't risk that. You're so close to the edge. You can't add to the darkness that you're already battling."

He shrugged. "It's my gift to you, Jordyn. Freedom from all the bastards who have tried to trap you." He trailed his fingers over her forehead. "Did you ever get inside his head? Did you learn any weaknesses he has?"

She shook her head. "I didn't break his hold on me until I moved to Boston. It was far enough away, I guess, and I was really pissed about the marking. I fought him off, and I hadn't heard from him since. Until today."

"Well, I don't like him messing with my woman, so he's going to get his ass kicked today." He tugged lightly on her hair. "I might not be a NightHunter, but I have skills." His gaze went to her eyes, and his face softened. "And I have motivation," he said softly, just as he leaned forward to kiss her.

His kiss was pure beauty. His lips were so soft and tender against hers, a caress that went right to her heart. She could feel his hunger for her coursing through him, urging him to take her body and blood, and yet his kiss was undemanding and his teeth never came near her lips, let alone her body. She could feel his iron-willed restraint, battling his need for her with every fiber of his being. His protectiveness wrapped around her like a fierce shield, drawing her tightly against him as his spirit enfolded her. She felt the intensity of his drive to protect her, but there was something else, something deeper. She sensed a vulnerability in his shields, a crack through which she had filtered, breaking through the walls he'd held around himself for so long.

Her heart jumped, and she pulled back, staring into his eyes, shocked at the depth of his feelings for her. "You love me?"

A muscle ticked in his cheek, and his hand tightened in her hair. The silence stretched between them, thick and rich, and she knew then that he did.

And she also knew he would never admit it, not even to himself, which made her own heart swell with empathy. She pressed a kiss to his palm. "You're an arrogant, emotionally reserved loner," she said softly. "You make me laugh. You make me want to live again. So, it doesn't matter what you feel. I will always love you for all that you are to me." Before he could respond to the words she'd never thought she would utter again, she leaned forward and kissed him.

She expected him to reject her, to throw up walls between them, but he didn't. He wrapped his hand around the back of her head, hauled her against him, and kissed her like his life depended on it. The kiss wasn't tender or sweet. It was a desperate joining of two souls, struggling toward a light that neither of them had believed in. She threw her arms around his neck and kissed him back, offering him everything she had. She poured a lifetime of anguish into the kiss, and a lifetime of love that had burned her. She gave it all to him, and with each kiss, he held her more tightly and kissed her more deeply, until their souls were so entwined that his darkness and her lightness were blurred together as a single unit.

His hunger roared through him, and desire flushed through her, an answering need that was far deeper than simple lust. It was a primal bond that came from deep within her, from a place beyond her soul. *Eric.*

He broke the kiss, wrenching his lips from hers. For a moment, neither of them moved, and the only sound in the truck was the sound of their heavy breathing. Eric rested his forehead against hers, one hand still in her hair, and his other arm around her waist, not releasing her. "I can't do this to you," he said. "This isn't your world."

"I make my own choices. I thought we established that from the beginning." She closed her eyes, breathing in his scent, a mixture of earth, danger, and wildness.

"Don't love me," he said, his lips brushing against hers as he spoke.

She lifted her head to look at him, startled by the anguish in his eyes. She felt the depth of his guilt for those he'd killed, and for the fact that he'd drawn her into his world. Her heart tightened, and she knew that this man was the one she'd been waiting for. "It's too late for that," she said. "It's too late for both of us. We can't just disengage. We can only hold on with everything we have."

"It's not too late." He stroked his hand through her hair. "It's never too late to walk away—"

"Shut up." She pressed her finger to his lips. "Walter

never truly committed to what was between us. He held back, knowing that he was going to snap. If you hold back, you're endangering us the same way. Don't you understand that the only way for us to win is to let this happen between us? If my grandmother's love for Cicatrice was so strong it could bind them across death for almost four hundred years, then we can be so tightly connected that Cicatrice can't break us apart. We have to do it. Don't you get it?"

His hand stilled. "Cicatrice used your grandmother's love to kill her and assault her granddaughter." He gently extricated her hands from around his neck. "Love can be the greatest betrayal of all, Jordyn. We both know that." He reached behind him and produced his dagger. "It clouds the mind and muddies the vision." Her heart fell as he put it into her hand. "I have a feeling you'll need this, sweetheart."

Frustration roared through her. "Dammit, no! Stop it, Eric! I'm so tired of this—"

His face suddenly paled, and he grunted, his hand going to his chest. She stared at him in horror as a thin trickle of dark blood spread across the front of his tee shirt.

"Oh, God." She jerked his shirt up, and she saw claw marks across his chest, right over his heart. Just as Cicatrice had done to her in her sleep. "He's coming after you."

"He's killing Tristan." Eric grabbed the stakes off the floor of the truck, bracing his forearms on his thighs as another shudder wracked his body. "Get driving, sweetheart. Time's up."

Jordyn jammed the truck into gear, and hit the gas. The vehicle leapt forward, fishtailing across the dirt as she sped down road. "He knows we're coming," she said, her heart thundering as the truck hurtled toward the mansion. "He's luring us into a trap."

"Yeah, I know." Sweat was trickling down Eric's brow, and she felt the shift in energy as he called his magic to protect him. "But he doesn't know exactly how pissed I am that he's hurting my brother and hunting my woman."

Her fingers tightened around the steering wheel, anger rolling through her. Cicatrice had hurt too many people she loved. She was tired of running, not just from him, but from Walter, from her past, and from everything. No more running.

It was time to fight.

She looked over at Eric, and he nodded his agreement. "Together," she said.

"Together," he agreed.

Silently, he set down one stake and held out his hand. She took one hand off the steering wheel and clasped his. An unspoken promise of more than either of them could put into words.

Minutes later, after breaking the speed limit and watching the bloodstain on Eric's shirt get bigger, Jordyn finally slowed the truck, coasting to a stop at the entrance of the long, dirt driveway. The bushes were overgrown, creeping across the abandoned driveway as if they'd decided it was their job to keep trespassers out.

Through the trees, she glimpsed the mansion that Skye had lived in, the one Oba had lived in with Cicatrice. It was silent and dark, a mausoleum of terrible things that Skye had experienced there. A dark, lethal curtain seemed to coat it, and she shivered. "I can feel him."

"Me, too." Eric glanced at the sun, and she saw that it was lower in the sky, but still strong. "If we die, I'll find you in the afterlife. You won't be alone. I swear it."

Her throat tightened. "I know you will." It wasn't a declaration of love exactly, but it was enough to make her want to cry. "But just so you know, I'm not going to sit around waiting for you. I'll find you first."

He grinned. "That's my girl."

She smiled back, and then she hit the gas and headed up the driveway.

CHAPTER 23

Eric felt the brush of evil as Jordyn navigated the winding driveway. It was thick and heavy, like tainted blood blanketing the air. The overgrown trees blocked most of the sun, and he pulled some of his magic away from protecting him from the sun. He redirected it outward, sending tentacles into the surrounding area. His energy bounced off the trees, and a few small animals, but there were no dead spots that would indicate a vampire. "I can't locate him."

He didn't like not knowing where the threat was coming from, and he instinctively moved closer to Jordyn, using his body to shield her as she drove. He had two stakes in his left hand, but he kept his right hand free to use for magic. A ball of energy began to form in his right palm, and he reached out, calling to the spirits of the dead. They surged to him, delighted at the opportunity to latch onto him. He summoned them from everywhere, accepting them all, sweeping them into him, and assembling their power.

"I can feel what you're doing." Jordyn didn't even look at him as she guided the truck past the potholes. "Don't push it too far. If you implode, you can't help Tristan. Or me." She reached out with her mind to offer him some of her more positive spirits, but he kept his shields strong between them.

"I can't worry about protecting you from myself," he said. "I need to make sure you're secure against all threats so I can focus. Let me shield you."

She glanced at him. "I don't want you to die," she said

softly.

Something tightened in his chest. "I know, honey. I'll do my best—" Pain suddenly ricocheted through his chest, and his ribs cracked. He bent over, gasping for air, as Jordyn's door was ripped open.

A streak of black smoke whipped into the cab, wrapped around Jordyn, and dragged her out of the truck. She yelped and grabbed onto the steering wheel, trying to anchor herself. "Eric!"

"Hey!" Eric lunged for her, but her fingers slipped off just as he reached for her wrist, and she disappeared out of the car.

"Jordyn!" He dove across the seat and shot out of the truck. He hit the air and instinctively dissolved into a mist. He had a split second "what the hell" moment when he turned into particles, and then embraced it and streaked across the expansive, overgrown yard in pursuit of the black smoke wrapped around Jordyn. Cicatrice was entwined around Jordyn, almost completely obscuring her from Eric's view as he dragged her back toward the towering mansion. She was struggling to get free, but the mist was over her mouth and eyes, silencing her.

"Let her go!" He kept a tight grip on his magic, bearing down on the older vampire with surreal speed. He urged his hand to take shape out of the mist, and then he fisted the glowing ball of light he'd been channeling before the attack. He summoned all his energy, coiling it tighter and tighter as Cicatrice began to pull away, outpacing Eric. *Shield yourself, Jordyn.* He gave her a split second of warning, and then unleashed his magic at the master vampire. The magic exploded from him and tore after Cicatrice.

Eric's magic hit Cicatrice with violent force, and there was a massive boom that threw Eric backward. He lost his mist form and slammed into a tree as Cicatrice's black mist dissolved in a thousand particles. Jordyn began to fall, tumbling from thirty feet in the air.

"Jordyn!" Eric lunged to his feet and raced across the ground, trying to get to her—

The master vampire suddenly took the shape of a man, and the shadowy figure streaked across the sky. He scooped up Jordyn before Eric could get to her, and shot back into the sky, sweeping her away from him.

"She's my mate, and you can't bond with her as long as I'm alive," Eric shouted, his hands fisted by his sides.

Cicatrice looked back over his shoulder, his booming laugh scraping across Eric's flesh. His face was pale, and his cheeks were sunken, but his eyes were a deep black of power. A black duster hung from his broad shoulders, a sharp contrast to his starched white shirt. For a split second, the two vampires stared at each other, and then Cicatrice whirled around and charged directly at him, Jordyn tucked under his arm. She twisted, and he glimpsed her grandmother's stake in her hand. She still had it! That was his woman, all right.

"Come and get me!" Eric leapt into the air and launched himself at Cicatrice. As Eric streaked toward him, his fingers curved into claws, and he felt his fangs lengthen. His vision shifted into a blood-red hue, and the hunger to take a life raged through him. His upper lip curled in a snarl, and his entire focus went onto the creature hurtling toward him.

In his left hand, Eric held a stake, but his right was empty of everything but his own power. He braced himself, preparing for a collision. "Now!" he shouted to Jordyn. They crashed into each other, and the impact sent them both tumbling through the air.

Cicatrice's hand slammed into Eric's chest, and he felt the claws clamp around heart. Swearing, he gripped Cicatrice's wrist, holding the vampire's hand in his chest so he couldn't rip out his heart. At the same time, he shoved his own stake straight into Cicatrice's heart.

For a moment, they stared at each other, and then the stake was sucked out of Eric's hand and went right through the other vampire's chest and burst out the other side. The stake tumbled to the ground as Cicatrice healed the wound instantly.

Shit. The ordinary stake had done *nothing* to the vampire. They needed her grandmother's stake.

"And now you die." Cicatrice twisted Eric's heart, and he gasped, tightening his grip on Cicatrice's arm, trying to immobilize the vampire so he couldn't rip his heart out. At the same time, Eric tried to jam his own hand into Cicatrice's chest, but his claws couldn't penetrate the older vampire's skin. Eric hit him again, and again, fighting to distract him while Jordyn twisted around, trying to get the right angle.

Pain ripped through his chest, and he felt his body weakening as Cicatrice tightened his grip on Eric's heart. *Jordyn?*

I got it. She twisted around, and he saw her arm arcing up from beneath to slam her grandmother's stake into the master vampire's chest. The stake was glowing red now, and all the runes carved on it were dark black, standing out against the red. It looked alive, and he knew with sudden certainty that it would work, even on a master vampire.

He released his grip on Cicatrice's wrist and grabbed the vampire's throat, tearing through the soft flesh. Cicatrice's free hand went up to stop him, exposing his chest so Jordyn could stake him. Eric felt his own heart being pried from his chest just as Jordyn slammed the stake upward toward Cicatrice's heart—

The master vampire lunged violently to the left, throwing Eric off balance. Jordyn shouted a warning, and then Eric felt her stake sink into his stomach. There was a flash of blinding pain, and suddenly his mind seemed to shatter into a thousand fragments. His entire body went numb, and he fell, catapulting out of the sky.

Above him, Cicatrice grinned down at him, and Jordyn hung in his arms, staring down at Eric with a look of absolute horror on her face. Numbly, Eric touched his belly, and his fingers closed around the stake that was buried in his gut. Son of a bitch. Cicatrice had made Jordyn stab him instead. *Fuck.* His hand burned the moment he touched it, but he grabbed it anyway. His arm went numb, and he tore it out of his body, flinging it aside.

It clattered to the ground, landing point-down in the earth just as he crashed beside it.

The impact jarred every bone in his body, and he lay there, unable to move as the sun poured over his unprotected flesh. Smoke rose in tendrils from his body, as Cicatrice spun around and flew back toward the second floor of the mansion, Jordyn still in his arms.

"No." Eric managed a gasp, and tried to summon magic...but there was nothing. His body was empty of power. The spirits had abandoned him, as there was no life left in his dying body for them to prey upon. He tried to roll over, and he managed to get himself on his side. With agonizing slowness, he began to drag himself toward the mansion, inch by inch, ignoring the burning of his flesh, and the blackened smoke emanating from his stomach wound. His blood mixed with the dirt, leaving a dark, muddy trail behind him, but he didn't stop.

He would never stop.

He would get to her.

He would not fail.

Eric. Tristan's gravelly voice brushed through his mind.

Cicatrice has her. Eric dragged himself another six inches, but the pain in his body was excruciating. His muscles were beginning to burn up inside his flesh, and his organs were searing hot, moments from bursting into flames. He didn't even know if it was from the sun or the stake, or some combination. *You have to stop him.*

Tristan's pain cut through him before his brother rebuilt the shields between them, but it was enough to let Eric know that his brother was in the same condition he was in.

Can't move. Tristan shared an image with Eric, and Eric saw his brother staked down on the roof deck of the mansion. Cicatrice had driven a rune-carved stake through each limb, with three more of them forming a triangle in his belly. Tristan's skin was blackened, and smoke was rising from his body. Contaminated, open wounds oozed across his torso, as if Cicatrice had clawed him for pure pleasure before staking him. His brother's chest was barely moving, his breath stuttering through the broken ribs that Eric had suffered with him.

Son of a bitch. Fresh urgency roused Eric, and he surged forward another two feet toward the mansion that was still a hundred yards away. *You gotta do better than that, bro. How are you going to save the girl?*

Just so you know, Tristan wheezed, *if you die, I don't think I can resurrect you right now. Feeling a little under the weather. Chicken pox, maybe. I never did have that as a kid, you know.*

Eric managed to lift his head to inspect the distance to the roof. The mansion was three stories high, and it looked like an impossible feat to get up there. *You're such a pansy. You get hit with a few stakes, and then you're too weak to withstand the sun? Did I teach you nothing about survival?* He rolled over, too exhausted to move, as he stared up at the roof, reaching out to try to find his brother, willing every last bit of energy into his fading body. *I'm not going to make it to the mansion, bro.*

I know you're not. You got stabbed by the one stake that can kill you. What the hell kind of plan is that? Tristan's energy surged toward him, and Eric suddenly pinpointed the location of his brother. He thrust his life force toward Tristan, and the brothers met in midair, their energy combining to hold them together.

What now? Tristan gritted out, the effort of sustaining the connection ruthlessly draining his last reserves.

I'll come up there. Eric's mind was almost non-functioning, the pain was so great. He could barely think, barely hold onto his mind, and he shoved himself to his hands and knees, rocking back and forth as he tried to keep his balance. The numbness pervading his body was devastating, and he felt his entire system shutting down.

Leap up here? That's your plan? This is the worst idea you've ever had. It will never work. Even as he said it, Eric felt Tristan summon what little strength he had left. Both brothers locked more tightly upon each other, and the invisible cord between them became stronger.

You have a shitty attitude, little brother. Go! Eric thrust all his remaining energy into his body and leapt straight up into the air, latching onto the metaphysical link between them, dragging himself closer inch by inch.

Tristan held the connection, and Eric raced along it, using the bond they'd built over so many years. He was almost at the top of the mansion, and then he was over the roofline. He could see Tristan staked out on the roof, his skin burning with violent flames. The moment he made visual contact, the connection between the brothers surged. It latched onto Eric and jerked him forward, dragging him violently across the battered roof toward Tristan.

His brother turned his head, his eyes mere slits. They made eye contact, and Eric felt fresh energy rush through him. He collided with his brother, and the impact tore the stakes from the roof, ripping Tristan free. Eric grabbed his brother and let the momentum carry them toward the shadows from the massive chimney.

They crashed into the brick and collapsed in the small shaded area. For a long moment, neither brother moved. The flames had stopped, but Eric could feel his flesh melting from his body, and his heart was shriveling inside him. He turned his head, and saw Tristan lying beside him with his eyes closed. His body was covered in far more wounds than Eric had realized, and his chest was barely moving. *Tristan.*

His brother opened his eyes a crack, turning his head just enough to look at Eric. "I missed you, bro."

"You're a dumb shit to cut me off like you did." Eric closed his eyes, unable to keep them open. "Jordyn's down there," he muttered. "We have to get her."

"I know." But Tristan didn't move either.

Swearing, Eric turned his head. He realized suddenly that Tristan's soul was beginning to detach from his physical body. Summoning energy, he lunged toward his brother. His fingers brushed Tristan's arm, and he wrapped his hand around his brother's wrist. The physical contact unleashed the combined energy of the brothers. He tightened his grip on Tristan and opened his shields. Their spirits rushed toward each other, two halves of one whole, trying to repair the broken bodies enough that each had to only sustain half a life.

Tristan rolled onto his side, facing him as the energy erupted between them, feeding and repairing—

A stake suddenly slammed into Tristan's back. His eyes widened, and blood trickled out of his mouth as his chest burst into flames. The end of the stake protruded from his heart, and then was jerked backward. Eric's body convulsed, twisting in agony as it fought to withstand the attack that had hurt him through his connection with Tristan. A boot shoved at Tristan's shoulder, rolling him to the side, and then someone squatted in front of Eric.

The sun backlit him, and Eric couldn't see his face, but he recognized the build. "David," he gasped. "That was the wrong, fucking vampire, you fool."

David leaned forward, his face hard. "It's never the wrong vampire, Eric." In his hand was Jordyn's grandmother's stake, and the blade was glowing. The bastard had swiped it from the ground where Eric had dropped it. David's hand was clothed in a heavy work glove. For a long moment, Eric stared at the glove, trying to process it. He recalled the towel that David had been holding in the kitchen when he'd been handling the stakes, and suddenly Eric knew. David had to protect his own hand from that stake, because *it would hurt him, too.*

"Son of a bitch," he muttered. "You're a vampire. You hunt vampires, but you're one of us."

David held his index finger to his lips. "Ssh. That's my secret." Then he reared back to jam the stake into Eric's heart one final time.

⊠⊠⊠⊠

Cicatrice dumped Jordyn on the floor with enough force to send her sprawling across the polished marble. She scrambled to her feet and whirled to face him, frantic. *Eric. Can you hear me? Are you okay?* Her hands were shaking. She couldn't believe she'd staked him. She should have been ready for Cicatrice to move. How had she failed so completely?

But she knew how she had. It was because at the last second, when Eric had stopped trying to keep Cicatrice from stealing his heart, she'd panicked, paralyzed by her terror of Eric dying. For that one moment, she'd been so utterly consumed by the horror of watching Cicatrice kill Eric that she'd lost her focus, and now he was out there, in the sun, dying, because of her.

"Come." Cicatrice strode across the room, slamming the shutters closed to block out the light. He swept his hand across the room, and a thousand candles burst into flames, perched in crevices, on the floor, on tables, on every piece of dusty, antique furniture in the room.

Jordyn surged to her feet, looking around the room for a weapon. She saw only a bed. A portrait. A... Her gaze swept back to the portrait. It was several feet tall, an antique oil painting with an ornate bronze frame centered above the massive headboard of the four-poster bed. The woman in the portrait was young and beautiful, with long brown hair swept up on her head. Her lips were blood red, curved in a half-smile. Her skin was porcelain, and a beautiful pendant necklace was her only jewelry.

Jordyn stared at the familiar pendant, awareness growing within her. "That's my grandmother."

"It is." Cicatrice strode across the room, his polished black boots making no sound on the floor. "I had that commissioned the day after I met her. She spent hours sitting for it. She was beautiful, my precious Bridgette."

"Your precious Bridgette?" She knew Oba's given name was Bridgette, but no one had ever called her that, except apparently her true love. The reverence in his tone jerked her back to the present, and she glared at him. "If she was so precious, why did you kill her?"

"Silence!" Cicatrice swept his hand at her, and her words tore from her throat. She opened her mouth, but no sound came out, her voice stripped away by the mere flick of his wrist.

Fear of the sheer magnitude of his power trickled through her as he turned toward her, giving her the first real look at the vampire who had hunted her for so long. His face was beautiful and poignant, as ethereal as the portrait of her grandmother. His clothes were those of an ancient lord, lush and rich, fitting his body to perfection. He moved with the grace of a predator, his muscles flexing effortlessly with each step he took. Along the side of his face was a jagged scar, still as raw and red as if he'd received it only recently. He touched it, his fingers sliding over it in a caress. "Your grandmother's present the day we met. She always regretted marring my beauty, but I will always cherish this as an eternal symbol of the passion that bound us." His voice was smooth and mesmerizing, just as it had been when he'd violated her dreams.

The scar on her breast began to burn, and she raised her chin, refusing to give in to the fear that he'd stoked in her for so long.

"Look at me, Jordyn." His eyes were bottomless and black, and she felt their pull the moment she obeyed him.

She immediately closed her eyes, cutting herself off from his allure. How could she possibly stop him? She had nothing to fight him with. Nothing except her mind. She thought of all the lessons her grandmother had given her, and she carefully, quickly began to weave the protections in her mind to block him.

A touch whispered across her throat, and she snapped her eyes open. Cicatrice was still standing on the other side of the room, but she could feel his fingers grazing along her neck and down her collarbone, a treacherous seduction. "Do you know how she was able to kill me?" he asked.

She brushed at her neck, rubbing the sensation of his touch away, even as she kept weaving her mental shields. "No. Tell me."

He smiled, sauntering across the floor toward the dresser across the room. A pair of gold rings sat there in a dish. "Because she was a NightHunter." He picked up a ring, and twirled it on his hand. "NightHunters aren't made. They're born." He watched the gold spinning, reflecting the light from all the candles. "They are the vampire's ultimate enemy, the only ones who are a true threat to the most powerful of us."

She watched him carefully, weighing his words. Her grandmother had always told her that she'd been born to take over for her, to continue her work. She'd assumed Oba was talking about magic. Was she a NightHunter? Was she one of the chosen few?

Cicatrice smiled and tossed the ring into the air, watching it spin with surreal speed before he snatched it out of the air in a lightning fast move. "Yes, you are. You've always known it."

Her heart began to pound. "How did she kill you?"

He extended a sinewy index finger toward her and shook it. "There's a special relationship between vampires and NightHunters, a symbiotic relationship." He picked up the other ring from the table and began weaving it through his fingers. "The reason she, and you, could kill me is because our magic is entwined." He began to walk toward her, still flipping the rings until they were moving with dizzying speed, the light from the candles bouncing off them. "But that also means you're the most powerful source of magic for me." He came to a stop in front of her. "You have the power to sustain me through any death, through any battle, through any lifetime." He held up the golden circle. "With this ring, I bind myself to you."

He jerked his shirt open, and then pressed the ring to his chest, above his heart. It glowed brightly, then sank into his flesh until it was a burning circle on his skin. Pain pierced her own heart, and she pressed her hand to her chest, in the exact spot where he'd carved his mark so many years ago. Icy panic tightened in her lungs. "No," she said. "You can't bind me."

"No? I can't?" He laughed softly. "Such innocence. I cherish the boldness of youth." He trailed his finger along her jaw, and she stiffened.

Her mind was frantic as she tried to find a solution. "That's what you did to my grandmother," she said, her heart pounding. "She didn't love you. You bound her to you. You trapped her. And yet somehow, she still managed to be strong enough to kill you. So it doesn't work."

He grabbed her by the neck and yanked her against him. Her chest hit his body. Solid muscle, and burning hot, not the ice cold she would have expected of a man who'd been dead for so long. "She loved me," he snarled. "As will you." She felt the push of his mind at hers, and she rebelled.

"No!" Instinctively, she jammed her fingernails into his chest. Her fingers closed on the hot metal, and she tore it out of his skin.

He screamed his rage and lunged at her, his face contorting with anger. She grabbed a nearby candle and shoved it into his face, right into the scar her grandmother had left. He screamed and tumbled, gripping his face as steam hissed out of the crevice. She leapt past him and raced to the window, throwing the shutters open. She searched the driveway where she'd last seen Eric, but he wasn't there. *Eric?*

Cicatrice grabbed her hair and yanked her backward. She twisted out of his reach and flung the ring out the window, shoving all her magic at it. She opened her mind to Eric, and wrapped her spirit around it, calling upon the magic of her grandmother, of the power that ran so deeply through her. She threw it all into the ring and sent it to Eric. *Take this ring, vampire, and bind yourself to me, your NightHunter.* For a brief moment, it rose, as if he was somewhere above her, and then Cicatrice lunged for it, snatching it out of the air and shoving it into her chest in a single move.

The pain ripped through her breast and she screamed, falling to her knees as the shock reverberated through her body.

She gasped, fighting for breath as she clawed at her chest, trying to pry it out of her flesh. It burrowed deeper, seeping into her body, anchoring itself to her very soul. Why couldn't she get it out of her own chest, when she could get it out of Cicatrice's? "No!"

"You can't get it out because you accepted it when you offered it to your lover," Cicatrice snarled. "But he's not going to get the other ring. I am." He grabbed her hair and yanked her head back, his eyes red and glowing. "And now, you are mine." He twisted her neck back, until pain shot through her. Then he held up the other ring. "It is done."

Then, with a flick of his fingers, he flipped it over so it landed on his bare chest. It floated there for a moment, hovering against the skin.

She lunged for him, trying to knock it free, but he jerked her back, pulling relentlessly on her hair as it sank into his skin. It sat there, glowing on his flesh, and she knew with sudden certainty, that she had to do something to stop it from sinking into his heart. Once it went inside, it would be too late to break it. She closed her eyes, and summoned all the spirits she could, raking them toward her with ruthless ferocity, tapping into her own magic, and the remnants of Eric that he'd left behind. His dark magic raced through her, hitting her full force, as if it had been waiting for her to call it. She felt her skin change, and the shadows tore through her, every bit the monster that had been trying to claim him before.

For a split second, she hesitated, realizing what was happening. His magic was hers, and it was there to claim her. If she released it, it would own her, just as it had tried to take him. Did she dare risk it?

In her split second of indecision, Cicatrice jerked her head back and slammed his teeth into her neck. She screamed at the invasion, and thrust Eric's magic at Cicatrice, but it was too late.

He drank her blood, and she became his.

CHAPTER 24

Eric. Jordyn's energy suddenly swept through Eric, galvanizing him.

He rolled to the right just in time, and David's stake slammed harmlessly into the roof deck by his shoulder. Eric kicked David's legs out from under him, and then tackled him as the man went down. He pinned David down and yanked the stake out of the roof. He elbowed David's head back into the deck, and pressed the stake to his chest. "Save my brother, you piece of shit."

David's eyes were wide, but they weren't red. Hate flooded his face. "He's a fucking vampire."

What the hell? "So are you, you hypocrite. Save him, or you die." He shoved the tip of the stake into David's chest, and the man's skin turned black. Energy was rushing through Eric, fierce, violent energy. His energy. Jordyn's. He could feel her presence within him, igniting his cells, firing up his very soul. *Jordyn!* He reached out to her, and felt a howl of emptiness, and the screams of thousands of voices. He went cold, realizing that his magic had taken her. "Shit!" He grabbed David's shirt and threw him up against the chimney. The red brick cracked, and David fell to the ground, still clutching his chest.

Beside him, Tristan lay still. "He's not going to save me," Tristan managed. "Can't you feel his hate?"

"He's the only one who knows how to save you. He's a psychopath, but he's brilliant." Eric felt another wash of his magic from Jordyn, and he knew he had no time. Somehow, she was empowering him, and he couldn't waste it. "We can't kill him." He slammed one of the less fatal stakes through David's shoulder, pinning him to the chimney, just as Tristan had been staked to the roof.

The vampire screamed, clutching his shoulder as black smoke poured from the wound, but he couldn't free himself.

Eric knelt beside his brother and put his hand on Tristan's chest, giving him some of Jordyn's energy. Tristan inhaled, and his body shuddered violently, and then he took another breath, a smoother one that didn't make his body convulse. He met Eric's eyes. "That's enough. Go get her. I'll be here."

Eric didn't waste time. He simply opened his mind to hers and followed the trail she'd left. He was in a full sprint by the time he crashed through the wooden deck door and into the house.

The scent of blood permeated the air as Eric raced down the attic stairs and through the ancient corridors. Dust was everywhere, and the plaster walls were cracked. He felt Jordyn's presence below, mixed with Cicatrice's, and the scent of blood was hers.

He tried to shift into mist, but he couldn't summon the strength. Already the energy that Jordyn had sent him was fading, and weakness was pervading his body. He ran harder, forcing his muscles to respond, knowing he had so little time to act.

He vaulted over the railing to the second floor, stumbling when he hit the Oriental carpet. He righted himself and then bolted for a set of closed French doors, knowing unerringly where Jordyn was. He rammed his shoulder into the doors, and they burst open under the force of his assault. The impact threw him off balance, and he crashed, skidding across the floor as he fought to regain his footing.

He leapt to his feet and whirled around, his heart freezing in his chest when he saw Jordyn limp in Cicatrice's arms, the vampire's teeth buried in her neck. Her skin was ashen, her body limp as she dangled over his forearm, as if she'd swooned in his arms. Her skin was shadowed, and he could see his magic coursing through her, trying to get a foothold, but she was unconscious, so it couldn't take her.

Cicatrice was in some sort of trance, entirely focused on Jordyn. He hadn't even noticed Eric's arrival. A small, golden circle was glowing on her left breast, in the same location that Cicatrice had marked before, and a matching one was blazing on Cicatrice's chest.

Shit. That couldn't be good.

Staying silent, so as not to break Cicatrice's trance, Eric palmed his hands and summoned the energy racing through Jordyn. It was his magic, and it leapt from her, tearing across the room toward him, greedily seeking his life force. It plunged into him and he turned it right back on Cicatrice in a seamless, brutal attack. It hit the vampire hard, flinging him backward and tearing him away from Jordyn. Cicatrice crashed through the massive window, careening out into the late afternoon light.

She slumped to the floor, still unconscious, blood trickling from the two pinprick holes in her neck. "Jordyn!" Eric raced over to her and swept her up in arms. "Jordyn, wake up. It's me—"

A claw slammed into his back, and he gasped, stumbling forward as Cicatrice's hand shot through his chest and locked around his heart. He staggered, and Jordyn slipped from his arms as Cicatrice's fingers closed around his heart once again. Eric reached behind him and grabbed the vampire's wrist, trying to keep him from tearing out his heart. Cicatrice's fingers closed tighter around the organ, his claws digging in as he twisted it.

Desperate, Eric threw energy back at the vampire. It hit hard, and he felt the vampire's grip loosen, but he didn't release him. Weakness seized him, but Eric kept firing magic at Cicatrice, slamming him again and again. He could feel the magnitude of the energy he was summoning, but he didn't stop. He could feel the howling abyss growing inside him, but he didn't dare cease his attack. Shadows swirled through him, taking root, and still he kept going. He had to get Cicatrice's hand off his heart.

Even as he thought it, he felt the claws dig in, and he knew he was almost out of time. Cicatrice would kill him within a split second, and if he did... Eric looked down at Jordyn, unconscious on the floor, the circle on her chest still glowing. She was utterly defenseless against a four-hundred-year-old vampire. Eric was her last line of protection, but if he lost his shit, she couldn't shield herself from him. She was helpless against his wrath, just like Jane had been when he'd killed her. She had no way to save herself from him. The dagger he'd given her was long gone. Despair filled him as Cicatrice tightened his grip on his heart. If Eric succumbed to his darkest magic, she would die. If he didn't, Cicatrice would kill him, and she would be left vulnerable and alone.

Her eyelids fluttered, and her eyes opened. She looked at Eric as he fell to his knees, no longer able to stand. His grip on Cicatrice's wrist was weakening, and he knew that he'd lose the battle within moments. She quickly took in the situation, and he saw her register how close to the edge he was. The shadows were raging in him—

Her energy swirled through him, warm and loving. *Do it.*

He met her gaze. *I love you, Jordyn.* As he said it, his words filled him with absolute rightness and conviction. He'd done everything in his power to never bond with another woman again, and yet, it had happened. She was so deep in his soul that he knew he would never take another breath without her being a part of it.

She smiled. *Do it.*

Her voice was so clear and steady that it filled him with resolve he'd never had before. What the fuck was he doing? Afraid he would hurt her? He knew there was no chance in hell of that ever happening. He loved her, for hell's sake. *He would never, ever hurt her.* Freedom exploded through him, the first sense of liberation he'd felt since the day he'd killed Jane. He couldn't hurt Jordyn. He could tap into his greatest powers, and she would be safe!

With a roar of fury, he dropped his shields completely. The rage came fast and hard, tearing through him, inciting a violence unlike anything he'd ever experienced. He sent it all at Cicatrice, hitting him so hard that the vampire screamed in agony, but still his hand stayed locked around Eric's heart. Swearing, Eric tried to twist around, still gripping Cicatrice's arm, but he couldn't turn far enough. He couldn't let go or Cicatrice would rip out his heart.

He hit him again, and this time Cicatrice slammed his

other hand through Eric's back, shattering his ribs as he grabbed Eric's heart with his other hand. Eric gasped, and reached behind him, gripping Cicatrice's other arm to keep him from being able to pull Eric's heart out. With both of his hands occupied, Eric couldn't throw any more magic, so he just let the darkness consume him from the inside out.

Lethal cold assaulted him, and his skin began to dissolve into fragments. He heard Cicatrice scream as the demon spirits began to flood him, reaching Cicatrice through their physical connection. Cicatrice began to fragment as well, and the pain assaulted them both, ripping through them as it shredded their bodies. But even as they both went down, Cicatrice's claws tightened in Eric's chest, fighting with all his strength to kill Eric before he destroyed them both.

They were all going to die.

⬚⬚⬚⬚

Jordyn lurched to her hands and knees, her body so weak she could barely hold herself up. Eric was half-disintegrated, but Cicatrice was in much better shape. Somehow, he was holding Eric off. Eric was going to lose himself before he killed Cicatrice.

Eric's gaze met hers, and she saw in them only bottomless depths of hell. The moment they made contact, the fragments of his being began to stream toward her, away from Cicatrice.

Shit. Eric's desperate gasp filled her. *They recognize you. Cicatrice isn't letting them in fast enough. They want to possess you.*

She struggled to her feet. *There's a ring embedded in Cicatrice's chest. I need it.*

Eric's face was pure smoke now, and his shoulders were starting to fade. He didn't question her or hesitate. *On three.*

She ran across the floor toward Eric, right into the stream of demons coming at her. It hit her in the chest, and she couldn't stop the scream of agony that ripped out of her. The cold was virulent, paralyzing her lungs. She went down on her knees in front of Eric, staying focused on his face. *Three,* she said. There was no time for a countdown. Three was now.

Eric vaulted forward, throwing his shoulders forward and jerking Cicatrice over his head. The vampire careened through the air, his arms outstretched for a split second, almost tearing Eric's heart out. Jordyn took advantage of the moment, and plunged her hand into Cicatrice's chest. Her fingers closed around the searing hot metal, and she ripped it free.

Cicatrice landed on his back, dragging Eric with him so Eric landed on top of him, his back crashing against Cicatrice's chest. As the two men came together, the force of it shoved Cicatrice's hand right through his body, bursting out of the front wall of Eric's chest. Eric gasped, and grabbed Cicatrice's wrists, keeping the vampire from pulling his hands back through and taking Eric's heart with him. *That hurt like a son of bitch.*

Fear tore through Jordyn at the extent of his grievous injury, and she tried not to panic. She palmed the ring. *Do you accept my love for all eternity, Eric? It will only work if you do.*

Eric met her gaze for a split second, and for a moment, she thought he was going to reject her. But he didn't hesitate. He nodded. *I'll love you until the end of time, Jordyn, and I accept your love in return. If you didn't love me, I'd just give up and die right now. I live for you, honey. Nothing else. Just you.*

His words were so heartfelt that tears filled her eyes. She pressed the gold ring against the blackened skin over his heart, and it sank instantly beneath the flesh. The gold band in her own chest glowed, and energy rushed through her. It was Eric's spiritual essence, filling her like a great burst of sunshine, locking them together. It was so different from when Cicatrice had bound them, and she knew now why she'd been able to take the ring from Cicatrice both times: because he hadn't loved her back. He'd wanted to possess her, but he hadn't loved her.

Eric did.

God, I love you, woman. He inhaled deeply, and then his magic exploded outward. It slammed into Cicatrice and the rest of the room in a violent explosion of smoke and ash, but it flew around her, parting like a split in the ocean. The assault was instant, and violent, a storm unleashed from the very depths of mother earth, and she felt it tearing him away from her, trying to take him.

"No! He's mine!" she shouted, summoning all the benevolence within her soul and holding it out to him. "Come back to me!"

For an agonizing moment, Eric's body continued to

disintegrate, spilling out into the room, and then she felt his soul reach for her. She lunged for him, wrapping her arms around his body, pulling him toward her as she opened herself completely to him, calling him back to her, just like Cicatrice had done to her grandmother for all those years. The pain howled through her, trying to rip her apart. *Eric! Accept me!*

Eric shuddered, and then his arm went around her, locking her against him. He buried his face in her neck, holding her desperately against him as the wind roared around them. NightHunter to vampire, and vampire to NightHunter, they solidified their bond and promised eternity. As they clung to each other, their energy mixed, two halves of a whole weaving together, balancing itself out until it had encircled them in a sphere of protection. The evil, howling spirits battered at them, tearing at their clothes, screaming in fury that it couldn't get past the barrier of their pure love. It spun away, searching for another victim...and then everything became silent.

For a long moment, neither of them moved. She was shaking violently, and she could feel that Eric was as well, but he was solid against her, and there was no more pain or cold. Slowly, she opened her eyes, and pulled back. Eric's face was ashen, and blood was trickling from the corner of his mouth, but his skin was solid.

They both looked around. The walls and ceiling were solid ash, held together by a whisper. Behind them, Cicatrice was hovering in midair, a shocked look on his face. Eric flicked his index finger, and everything simply disintegrated. The walls, the ceiling, and Cicatrice himself, leaving them in a room that was open to a sky filled with the oranges and yellows of a sunset. It poured onto Eric, but no smoke rose from his flesh.

He held her tightly, his fingers tangling in her hair, as if he was terrified she would disintegrate in his arms. "You bound yourself to me," he said, his voice raw. "You protected me with your love." He held out his arm, watching the sun glisten harmlessly across his skin. "You protect me even now."

"I know."

His gaze swept her face, as if searching for answers he couldn't fathom. "You're independent. You don't do things like bind yourself to men for all eternity. It's not your thing."

She smiled, tears filling her eyes as she noticed the gaping wound in his chest. "I'm entitled to make an exception for the man I love. Is that okay with you? I mean, I know you're a self-proclaimed player and all that—"

"Shut up, honey." He grinned and then kissed her. Hard, passionately, and emphatically, leaving her absolutely no doubt as to how he felt about it. She kissed him back without reservations, her entire heart singing with joy for the man in her arms.

After much too short of a time, he pulled back, brushing the hair back from her face. "Tristan," he said. "We have to get to him. He's on the roof."

At his words, they both looked up again, at the sunlight streaming through the missing ceiling. At the same moment, they both realized what the sun must be doing to his brother. Eric swore, and lunged to his feet. He staggered, and went down on his knees, his hand going to his chest. "Cicatrice's efforts are going to leave a mark, I think," he said.

"Battle scars are sexy." Her heart squeezing tightly at how bad a shape he was in, she slipped his arm over her shoulder. "Come on, big guy. You can do it. If you make it to the roof, I promise I'll have sex with you."

He cocked his head, studying her for a brief moment. "Did you use that line on me before?"

"I did."

He grinned, a lascivious light gleaming in his eyes. "As I recall, you fulfilled your promise, so yeah, that works for me." His arms tightened around her shoulders, and he surged to his feet, staggering only slightly. "Let's go get my brother."

CHAPTER 25

"Stop."

At Skye's sharp command, Jordyn and Eric froze as they stepped out on the roof.

Skye was crouched over David's body as if she were a predator ready to attack. David's skin was seared, and smoke was rising from his chest. Blackened blood was dripping from his shoulder, from which the stake still protruded. Tristan was on his side next to them, his eyes closed and his body still. There were holes all over Tristan, and a pile of bloodied stakes was on the roof beside him. There was white powder in his wounds, as if Skye had been treating them.

"Tristan?" Jordyn couldn't keep the fear from her voice. "Is he dead?"

No. I would be dead if he was.

But even as Eric said it, she felt his doubt. Was she so connected to Eric that she could sustain him now, even if Tristan died?

There was danger emanating from Skye, something so fierce that Jordyn felt it prickle over her skin. She looked nothing like the sweet child Jordyn had once known. She looked like a killer, poised to attack.

Beside her, Eric's muscles tensed, and he shifted his weight away from her, giving himself space to fight if necessary.

"Who hurt David?" Skye's eyes went back and forth between them, her body poised to attack.

"Skye. It's me. I'm not going to hurt you." Urgency

pulsed at Jordyn, and she began to walk across the roof. "We need to help them."

Skye didn't move. "Tell me what happened." Her voice was low and deadly.

"David stabbed both of us," Eric said, slowly moving alongside Jordyn. Despite his weakened state, he was keeping Jordyn slightly behind him, putting himself between the two women. "I needed to stop him to save Jordyn, but I didn't want to kill him. He's the only one who knows how to cleanse the poison." His voice was steady, but Jordyn felt his tension as he glanced apprehensively toward Tristan. "David's a vampire."

Jordyn sucked in her breath, looking sharply at Eric. "What? He *stabbed* you? And he's a vampire?" Betrayal rushed through her, and she stopped, staring down at the man who'd been her best friend. His eyes were closed, and his chest wasn't moving. "David?"

Skye nodded. "I know he's a vampire." She suddenly relaxed, and she sat back on her heels. "He's dangerous," she said, as she sheathed a knife that Jordyn hadn't even noticed she was holding. "I had to make sure what side Eric was on. My friend Richard and I have been trying to stop David for a while, but it's been impossible to get him in a situation where he was vulnerable. He's murdered so many," she said softly. "All in the name of honor, but terrible things nonetheless." She looked up at them. "Do you guys happen to know where Richard is? He never came by the house to check on me. I'm worried about him."

Eric cleared his throat, and Jordyn's throat tightened. "Skye, Richard's—"

Skye's face paled, and she held up her hand. "No." Her voice broke. "Don't say it. I can't hear that right now." She lifted her chin, but that didn't hide the glistening of tears in her eyes. "You bastard," she hissed at David. "How could you hurt him?"

"David was the one who attacked Richard?" She thought of the poor man and how crazed he'd been. David had done that to him? Her David, the one who had dragged her to safety so many times when her father had drunk too much, had hurt good people? Jordyn's chest ached with betrayal as she stared down at David. "What happened to you?" she whispered.

"What happened to my best friend?"

He didn't respond, but Skye stood up, her body lithe and muscular, and apparently entirely recovered from being almost dead. "Tristan needs earth," she said briskly, wiping the back of her wrist across her eyes. She looked at Eric. "And so do you."

Jordyn didn't move. "What about David?"

Skye and Eric looked at each other. "I think we leave him," Skye said.

"What?" Jordyn stared at her. "He's our friend!"

"He's not anymore. He hasn't been anyone's friend for a long time." Skye walked across the roof toward her, and Jordyn noticed that there were scars on her throat, old scars, not the ones David had healed. Terrible things had happened to Skye since the last time they'd met. "Some vampires retain their humanity. Many become crazed killers. And some..." she gestured at David. "Become worse."

"Worse?" Sadness filled her, and she knelt beside him, taking his hand. "David," she whispered.

"Get back." Eric's voice was heavy with warning. "Don't go near him."

"Jordyn." Skye knelt beside her, taking her hands. Skye's fingers were cold, too cold, making Jordyn realize that Skye wasn't actually in as good a shape as she'd first appeared. "This is a new battle for us," she said softly. "Your grandmother was a great NightHunter. She understood the nuances of vampires and creatures of the night. David believes that NightHunters should destroy all vampires. Once he became a vampire, he believed it was a gift from the NightHunters to enable him to destroy the vampires. He's merciless and cruel, and he's destroyed all values of what the NightHunters stand for."

Tears filled Jordyn's eyes. "How many people has he killed?" She had to ask. She had to know.

"Over a hundred that I know of. And not all of them were vampires. Some of them simply aided vampires. Some of them were great NightHunters who had been bitten so many times that their blood was mixed." She held out a note. "He came here to kill you, Jordyn."

Jordyn took the paper and looked down at it. The note

was scrawled in David's messy handwriting that she knew so well. *Skye, my beloved Jordyn has become like her grandmother. I have to destroy her before she bonds with Cicatrice or Eric and strengthens them. I've gone to your old house to find her. Prepare a burial site. My heart bleeds for what I have to do, but I will not stray from my mission.*

Jordyn crushed the paper in her hand. "He did read the rest of the book. He was waiting to see what side I would choose."

Eric nodded. *I love you, Jordyn. You are the bravest warrior I have ever met, and I will stand by you as you rebuild the NightHunters, as they were meant to be.*

Tears filled her eyes. *I love you, too.*

Skye wrinkled her nose. "Are you guys doing that mental telepathy thing? Because it's really rude, you know." Then she held out her arms. "Welcome home, Jordyn. We have a lot of catching up to do, including sorting out the mess that David has turned the NightHunters into."

Welcome home? Was she going to stay in the town she'd run away from so long ago? She looked up at Eric, who was using the side of the chimney to keep himself upright. He looked so handsome and dangerous, a lethal predator ready to wipe out any monster at any moment, despite the fact that she was pretty sure he might collapse if she sneezed on him.

I'm your predator. He grinned. *I can even do the magic without losing my mind, thanks to you. Why would I go anywhere else? You know you belong here, and so do I.*

Tears filled her eyes, and suddenly, all the tension she'd been holding in her body since the day she'd walked away so many years ago finally vanished. She was home, and this was where she needed to be. "Okay," she said. "I'll stay." She leaned forward to hug Skye, and out of the corner of her eye, she saw David move.

They both spun around as David drove the stake right toward her heart, his eyes etched with agony. "I'm so sorry, Jordyn—"

All three of them reacted, grabbing stakes from the pile by Tristan and throwing them. The three stakes hit him in quick succession, driving him back into the sunlight. His eyes rolled back in his head and he reached for her, as his skin caught fire. "Jordyn," he gasped. "Don't abandon me."

"He's too weak to withstand the sun," Skye said, her voice cold, but heavy with emotional pain she couldn't hide, because David had been her savior as well as Jordyn's when they were kids. "He'll die from it."

An overwhelming sense of loss filled Jordyn as Eric wrapped his arms around her, pulling her into the shield of his body. She leaned back against his warmth, tears flowing down her cheeks as she watched the man she'd loved so dearly writhe and twist in the sun. "I'm not abandoning you, David," she told him, her fingers burning from the stake she'd thrown at him. "I'm giving you back your freedom from the hate that's destroying your soul."

David caught fire as Eric's arms tightened around her. He drew her back into the shadows as the man who had once been her rock turned to ash and drifted away on the evening breeze.

With David's attempt to murder her, the cycle was complete. Every man she'd trusted had betrayed her.

Every man, except one, the man who had taught her what true love really meant.

❂❂❂

Jordyn paced restlessly outside her grandmother's old shack. It was past dark, and she was antsy. Eric had taken Tristan to ground somewhere in the depths of the swamp after they'd left the mansion, and he hadn't returned. He'd touched base with her mentally a few times, but it wasn't enough. She needed him to be with her. Badly.

Skye looked up from where she was sorting bottles of powders. "You need to relax, girl. He'll be here."

"It's been three days." She rubbed her arms, unable to shed the anxiety growing in her body. She felt as if a part of her was missing, stripped from her. "I'm not a patient person."

Skye laughed. "Maybe you should think about letting him turn you into a vampire, so you can go bury yourself in the earth with him."

Jordyn glanced sharply at her. "What? I could do that?"

Skye's smile faded. "You don't want to consider that, Jordyn. There's no way to predict how you'll react. David—"

"I know what happened to him." She sat down and hugged her knees to her chest. Her muscles were shaky, and she felt restless, unable to sit still. "I know he was a good man. He was my best friend."

Skye sat down next to her. "Jordyn, he was evil before he was turned into a vampire. The conversion didn't change him. He was that person all on his own."

Jordyn rested her chin on her knees, rocking back and forth as she digested that information. He had tried to kill her. There was no way to deny it. Whatever had happened to him had changed him irrevocably. "He was no longer the person I grew up with," she acknowledged. "There was nothing left of the David I knew." She picked up an old bone from one of her grandmother's long-abandoned altars, running her finger along the smooth surface. Talking about David helped distract her from Eric, but he was still in the back of her mind, her need for him radiating through her like a hunger that couldn't be sated. She hadn't slept since he'd left. Night had been the worst, when the grief of their separation weighed down on her so heavily. Even now, with dusk not quite here, the loneliness was sinking its claws into her. "Do you know what happened to David that made him change?"

Skye shook her head. "He was like that when I came back six months ago. I don't know what happened. I'm still trying to figure things out. Richard and I were—" She stopped, her voice breaking again.

Jordyn glanced at her. "Were you and Richard a couple?" Skye hadn't spoken of Richard since David's death, and she'd changed the subject every time Jordyn had mentioned it.

She shrugged. "I miss him," she said simply.

Jordyn nodded. "I'm sorry."

"Me, too." Skye was quiet for a moment, spinning one of Oba's gris-gris bags in her hand. "I have to tell you something," she said softly.

Jordyn glanced at her, alarmed by the edge in her friend's tone. "What?"

"I'm not sure he's dead."

Jordyn frowned. "Richard?"

Skye laughed softly. "I wish. No, I'm talking about David. Some of his vials were missing this morning. I know where I put them last night when I was sorting through his stuff, but this morning, they were gone."

Dread crept down her spine as she recalled the feeling of that stake coming toward her. "But we saw him burn up."

"I know. The logical explanation is that someone who was aligned with him is seeking to continue his mission." She hesitated. "But my gut tells me that something was off about what happened at the mansion. I'm not sure what. I've just..." She fisted the bag with sudden determination, and looked at Jordyn. "I've seen a lot of things since I started working with David, and having him affected by the sun wasn't one of them."

"But aren't all vampires affected?" But even as she asked it, she thought of Eric, who hadn't been touched by it since they'd used the rings. *Eric. I need you. How are you? How is Tristan?*

There was no reply, and she pressed her palm to her chest. The gold ring burned in her heart, easing some of the anguish.

"On some level, yes, but it varies." Skye chewed her lower lip. "I just have a feeling this isn't over, Jordyn."

Jordyn took a deep breath. "Of course it isn't over. It's just starting. Whether David's alive or not, there are still vampires out there killing people, and NightHunters who are on our side, and others who aren't." She swept her hand across the swamp, where the murky water was sitting in ominous stillness. "But I'm ready."

Skye grinned. "Me, too, girl." She hopped to her feet and picked up a jar. "I'm going to go experiment with this one." Her smile faded. "Tristan needs more than the earth. I need to find a way to help him, or he's going to be in trouble. He's too close to the edge to handle it on his own."

Jordyn stood up, eager for a distraction from her thoughts about Eric. "I'll help—"

"No." Skye shook her head. "I've got this. You keep searching your grandmother's stuff. The woman was a legend. She must have more information somewhere." She paused. "I'm glad you're back, Jordyn, and I'm really pleased that you believe that not all vampires deserve to die."

"Of course they don't." She met her friend's gaze. "But some do, don't they?"

Skye nodded. "Yes, they do." She paused, assessing Jordyn. "Are you okay? You want me to stay?"

"No, Tristan needs your help. You can go. I'll keep going through my grandmother's things. I'll find something." She put her hand over her heart again, needing that contact with Eric.

Skye smiled. "Okay. See you later."

"Good luck with David's lab." Jordyn hugged herself as she watched Skye disappear down the path leading to the house. Her friend moved with a grace that she didn't remember. Skye, like David, was more than she seemed, and more than she had once been.

David. She turned to look out across the swamp, glittering beneath the night stars. "If you're out there, David," she said to the night. "Find your way back to who you once were. We need you." As she said it, she couldn't suppress the whisper in her mind that if David was alive, he knew all her secrets. He could target her in a way no one else could. How much had he stolen of Oba's knowledge? Enough. With great sadness, she realized that as much as a part of her wanted him to still be alive and able to come back to her, she knew that in truth, she had to hope with every fiber of her being that he was well and truly gone forever.

The night was silent, but she felt the faintest prickle across her skin, as if a wind had drifted its ghostly fingers across the back of her neck.

She spun around, but saw nothing. Just the increasing darkness of the night, settling down around her like a thick blanket. But just as the chills started to seep into her body, she felt a sudden warmth brush across her mind. *Jordyn.*

Her heart leapt, and her entire body shuddered with relief. Just the sound of his voice eased the tension in her body. God, she missed him so much. *Eric? I need to be with you. When are you coming?*

"Now."

His voice drifted out of the darkness and wrapped around her as he stepped out of the trees. He was cloaked in shadows, moving with the same grace he always did.

Elation leapt through her. Her man had come back to her.

⌘⌘⌘

Eric's heart came alive at the expression of pure joy on Jordyn's face when she saw him. He caught her in his arms as she leapt on him, hauling her against him. She wrapped her legs around his hips, clinging to him as tightly as he was holding onto her.

He buried his face in her hair, basking in the scent he had missed so desperately when he'd been healing beneath the earth. Flowers, springtime, and warmth, along with the life that flowed so joyously through her. He kissed her neck, his body starkly hungry for her after being without her for so long.

She pulled back, desire flooding her eyes. "You want me."

"Yeah, you could say that." His body was aching, cramping with his need for her. He kissed her hard, his incisors lengthening as he deepened the kiss.

She clung to him, frantically kissing him back. Her need was as stark as his was, though hers wasn't mixed with bloodlust. The hunger was there though, equally forceful on both sides.

With a low growl, he backed her against a tree, using the trunk to support her while he gripped her hips. His cock was hard, straining against his jeans. He swore under his breath, trying to slow himself down. "Sorry," he managed. "I didn't intend to attack you. Shit. I need you so badly, Jordyn."

"I missed you," she whispered into his mouth as she slid her hands under his shirt, tugging it free of his jeans. Her hands splayed over his chest, searching for his wound. He winced as her fingers found the spot, and she pulled back, breaking the kiss. "You're not healed," she said. "Why are you here? You should to be beneath the earth."

"I can't heal without you," he said. "I need your kiss. I need to feel your spirit wrapped around me. I need the nourishment that only you can give me." He framed her face with his hands, struggling to put into words the depths of his need for her. "When I was underground beside Tristan, all I could think of was you. The sound of your voice. That expression you get on your face when you're about to tell me to shut up. The feel of your lips against mine. The way you make me feel complete, even though I shattered so long ago. You dragged me back from hell, Jordyn. You gave me the strength to manage my magic. And you gave me a reason not only to live, but to die."

Tears filled her eyes. "The last three days were the longest three days of my life," she whispered. "It was worse than losing Walter. Every part of my soul cried to be with you. I can't do it again. I can't sit here while you go below ground to heal." She pressed her palm to his heart, and her hand glowed gold as the ring buried in his heart reached for her. "I need you, Eric. You're a part of my soul. I'm incomplete without you."

Relief rushed through him at her words. "I thought it was just me. I think it's a vampire thing. It makes everything much more intense." He pulled her close and kissed her again, less frantic, but driven with the same, pulsating need for more intimacy, on every level. Physical, emotional, sexual, and that all-powerful bloodlust that was beating at him. "It's just you I want," he said. "I have to feed, but it's just you. Only you."

She pulled back, her hands tangling in his hair. "It better be only me," she said. "Seriously."

He laughed softly and palmed her buttocks, drawing her closer against him. "I'm a one woman guy now, honey. Only you." He felt like the world had shifted into alignment now that he was back with her. "I'm not going to the earth again," he said. "I need to be with you."

She pulled back, her eyes glittering. "You should go. You're still hurt."

"I don't care. I'll heal here—"

"Turn me," she said softly. "Since I'm a NightHunter, it should work okay—"

"No." He shook his head. "I'll never turn you into a predator." He kissed her again, tenderly this time, trying to convey how deeply he felt. "I treasure you exactly as you are. A warrior who can defeat anyone. A woman who will cry for the loss of those she loves. I don't want you to be like me, hon. I want you to be you. My entire being burns with the need to protect and treasure you, not turn you into what I am."

Tears filled her eyes. "I missed you too much." she whispered. "I can't do it again."

There was pure love in her voice when she said it, no fear of being so connected with a man again. Rightness filled his heart and flooded his body. "I'll never leave you again. I swear it. We'll find a way, one that doesn't involve you getting pointy teeth and an addiction to my blood."

She fisted his shirt. "You don't get to make my choices, Eric."

"I know." He kissed her knuckles. "We make our choices together now. Right?"

The independent woman he loved so dearly hesitated, making him laugh. "Okay, you make your choices," he conceded, "but I'll continue to make mine." He pinned her against the tree again, and sank his hips between hers. "You decided to become my vampire bride. I decided your teeth are too pretty the way they are now, so I'm not going to bring you over. So, it's a stalemate. Let's have sex and battle it out."

She grinned, her grip on his shirt tightening. "It's always about sex with you, isn't it?"

"Sex and bloodlust, yeah." He put his hand over her breast, thumbing over the scars Cicatrice had left there. "But also, I'll throw some love in there too, just because I'm that kind of guy. You good with that?"

She grinned and draped her arms around his neck. "Shut up and bite me."

He chuckled to himself and lowered his mouth to hers. "Oh, don't worry, I will." Then he kissed her, a long, slow, deep kiss that told her exactly how it was going to go.

She moved against him restlessly, trying to make him rush.

He planned to savor it.

He was looking forward to having Jordyn do her best to change his mind.

Ryland spun around, engaging all his preternatural senses as he searched the graveyard for Catherine. He knew she had to be close. He'd touched her backpack just before she'd vanished right in front of him.

"Catherine!" he shouted again. He'd been so close. Where the hell was she? All he could sense were the deaths of all the people in the graveyard. Women, children, old men, young men, good people, scum who had taken their demented values to the grave with them. The spirits were thick and heavy in the graveyard, souls that had not moved on to their place of rest.

They circled him, trying to penetrate his barriers, seeking asylum in the creature that would be their doom. "No," he said to them. "I'm not your savior." Not by a long shot. He was about as far from their savior as it was possible to be.

Dismissing them, Ryland focused more directly on Catherine, opening his senses to the night, but as much as he tried to concentrate, he couldn't keep the vision of her out of his head. He'd finally seen her up close. She'd been mere inches away, the angel who had filled his thoughts for so long. Her hair was gold. *Gold.* It must have been tucked up under a hat when he'd seen her before, but now? It was unlike anything he'd ever seen before. He'd been riveted by the sight of it streaming behind her as she ran, the golden highlights glistening in the dark as if she'd been lit from within.

Her gait had been smooth and agile, but he'd sensed the sheer effort she'd had to expend during the run. Another few feet, and he would have caught up to her easily, but she'd sensed him while he'd still been a quarter mile away, giving her a head start that had gotten her to the graveyard first.

Shit. He had to focus and find her. Summoning his rigid control to focus on his task, Ryland crouched down and placed his hand on the dirt path where he'd last seen her. The ground was humming with the energy of death, but again, he couldn't untangle her trail from all the others. He realized that she'd mingled her own scent of death with those of all the other spirits, making it impossible for him to track her. He grinned as he rested his forearm on his quad and surveyed the small cemetery. "I'm impressed," he said aloud. "You're good."

There was no response, but he had the distinct sensation that she was watching him.

Slowly, he rose to his feet. "My name is Ryland Samuels," he said. "I'm a member of the Order of the Blade, the group of warriors that you protect. I'm here to offer you my protection and bring you into our safekeeping."

Again, there was no answer, but suddenly threaded through the tendrils of death was the cold filament of fear. Not just a superficial apprehension, but the kind of deep, penetrating fear that would bring a person to their knees and render them powerless. Fear of him? Or of the fact he said he wanted to take her with him? Swearing, Ryland turned in a slow circle, searching for where she might be. "There's no need to be afraid of me. I would never hurt an angel."

The fear thickened, like the thorns of a dying rose pricking his skin.

Ryland moved slowly toward the far corner, and smiled when he felt the terror grow stronger. She might be able to hide death, but there was no cover for the terror that was hers alone. He was clearly getting closer to her. "Look into my eyes," he said softly. "I don't hurt angels."

There was a whisper of a sound behind him, and he felt the cold drift of fingers across his back. *She was touching him.* He froze, not daring to turn around, even though his heartbeat had suddenly accelerated a thousand-fold. Her touch was so faint, almost as if it were her spirit that was examining him, not her own flesh. Was she merely invisible right now, or had she abandoned her physical existence completely and traveled to some spiritual plane? He had no idea what she was capable of. All he knew was that he felt like he never wanted to move away from this spot, not as long as she was touching him. He wanted to stay right where he was and never break the connection.

He closed his eyes, breathing in the sensation of her

touch as her fingers traced down his arm, over his jacket. What was she looking for? Was she reading his aura? Searching for the truth of his claim that he would not hurt her? She would get nowhere trying to get a read on him. He never allowed anyone to see who he truly was, not even an angel of death.

But even as he thought it, he made no move to resist, his pulse quickening in anticipation as her touch trailed toward his bare hand. Would she brush her fingers over his skin? Would he feel the touch of an angel for the first time in a thousand years? He felt his soul begin to strain, reaching for this gift only she could give him.

He tracked every inch of movement as her hand moved lower toward his bare skin. Past his elbow. To the cuff of his sleeve. Then he felt it. Her fingers on the back of his hand. His flesh seemed to ignite under her touch. A wave of angelic serenity and beauty cascaded through his soul, like a breath of great relief easing a thousand years of tension from his lungs.

At the same time, there was a dangerous undercurrent beneath the beauty, a darkness that he recognized as death. A thousand souls seemed to dance through his mind, spirits lodged in the depths of her existence. Her emotions flooded him. Fear. Regret. Determination. Love. A sense of being trapped.

Trapped? He understood that one well. Far too well. Instinctively, he flipped his hand over, wrapping his fingers around hers, not to trap her, but to offer her his protection from a hell that still drove every choice he made.

He heard her suck in her breath, and she went still, not pulling away from him. Her hand was cold. Her fingers were small and delicate, like fragile blossoms that would snap under a stiff breeze. A hand that needed support and help.

Ryland snapped his eyes open but there was no one standing in front of him. He looked down and could see only his own hand, folded around air. He couldn't see her, but she was there, her hand in his, not pulling away. "Show yourself to me," he said. "I won't hurt you."

Her hand jerked back, and a sense of loss assailed him as he lost his grip on her. "No!" He reached for her, but his hands just drifted through air. "Catherine," he urged, as he strained to get a sense of her. "I—"

SNEAK PEEK: DARKNESS AWAKENED

THE ORDER OF THE BLADE
AVAILABLE NOW

Quinn Masters raced soundlessly through the thick woods, his injuries long forgotten, urgency coursing through him as he neared his house. He covered the last thirty yards, leapt over a fallen tree, then reached the edge of the clearing by his cabin.

There she was.

He stopped dead, fading back into the trees as he stared at the woman he'd scented when he was still two hours away, a lure that had eviscerated all weakness from his body and fueled him into a dead sprint back to his house.

His lungs heaving with the effort of pushing his severely damaged body so hard, Quinn stood rigidly as he studied the woman whose scent had called to him through the dark night. She'd yanked him out of his thoughts about Elijah and galvanized him with energy he hadn't been able to summon on his own.

And now he'd found her.

She'd wedged herself up against the back corner of his porch, barely protected from the cold rain and wet wind. Her knees were pulled up against her chest, her delicate arms wrapped tightly around them as if she could hold onto her body heat by sheer force of will. Her shoulders were hunched, her forehead pressed against her knees while damp tangles of dark brown hair tumbled over her arms.

Her chest moved once. Twice. A trembling, aching breath into lungs that were too cold and too exhausted to work as well as they should.

He took a step toward her, and then another, three more before he realized what he was doing. He froze, suddenly aware of his urgent need to get to her. To help her. To fill her with heat and breathe safety into her trembling body. To whisk her off his porch and into his cabin.

Into his bed.

Quinn stiffened at the thought. Into his bed? Since when? He didn't engage when it came to women. The risk was too high, for him, and for all Calydons. Any woman he met could be his mate, his fate, his doom. His *sheva*.

He was never tempted.

Until now.

Until this cold, vulnerable stranger had appeared inexplicably on his doorstep. He should be pulling out his sword, not thinking that the fastest way to get her warm would be to run his hands over her bare skin and infuse her whole body with the heat from his.

But his sword remained quiet. His instincts warned him of nothing.

What the hell was going on? She had to be a threat. Nothing else made sense. Women didn't stumble onto his home, and he didn't get a hard-on from simply catching a whiff of one from miles away.

His trembling quads braced against the cold air, he inhaled her scent again, searching for answers to a thousand questions. She smelled delicate, with a hint of something sweet, and a flavoring of the bitterness of true desperation. He could practically taste her anguish, a cold, acrid weight in the air, and he knew she was in trouble.

His hands flexed with the need to close the distance between them, to crouch by her side, to give her his protection. But he didn't move. He didn't dare. He had to figure out why he was so compelled by her, why he was responding like this, especially at a time when he couldn't afford any kind of a distraction.

She moaned softly and curled into an even tighter ball. His muscles tightened, his entire soul burning with the need to help her. Quinn narrowed his eyes and pried his gaze off her to search the woods.

With the life of his blood brother in his hands, with an Order posse soon to be after him, with his own body still recovering from Elijah's assault, it made no sense that Quinn had even noticed the scent of this woman, let alone be consumed by her.

His intense need for her felt too similar to the compulsion

that had sent him to the river three nights ago. Another trap? He'd suspected it from the moment he'd first reacted to her scent, but he'd been unable to resist the temptation, and he'd hauled ass to get back to his house. Yeah, true, he'd also needed to get back to his cabin to retrieve his supplies to go after Elijah. The fact she'd imbued him with new strength had been a bonus he wasn't going to deny.

But now he had to be sure. A trap or not? Quinn laughed softly. Shit. He hoped it was. If it wasn't, there was only one other reason he could think of to explain his reaction to her, and that would be if she was his mate. His *sheva*. His ticket to certain destruction.

No chance.

He wouldn't allow it.

He had no time for dealing with that destiny right now. It was time to get in, get out, and go after Elijah. His amusement faded as he took a final survey of the woods. There was no lurking threat he could detect. Maybe he'd made it back before he'd been expected, or maybe an ambush had been aborted.

Either way, he had to get into his house, get his stuff, and move on. His gaze returned to the woman, and he noticed a drop of water sliding down the side of her neck, trickling over her skin like the most seductive of caresses. He swore, realizing she wasn't going to leave. She'd freeze to death before she'd abandon her perch.

He cursed and knew he had to go to her. He couldn't let her die on his front step. Not this woman. Not her.

He would make it fast, he would make it efficient, he would stay on target for his mission, but he would get her safe.

Keeping alert for any indication that this was a setup, Quinn stepped out of the woods and into the clearing. He'd made no sound, not even a whisper of his clothing, and yet she sensed him.

She sat up, her gaze finding him instantly in the dim light, despite his stealthy approach. They made eye contact, and the world seemed to stop for a split second. The moment he saw those silvery eyes, something thumped in his chest. Something visceral and male howled inside him, raging to be set free.

As he strode up, she unfolded herself from her cramped

position and pulled herself to her feet, her gaze never leaving his. Her face was wary, her body tense, but she lifted her chin ever so slightly and set her hands on her hips, telling him that she wasn't leaving.

Her courage and determination, held together by that tiny, shivering frame, made satisfaction thud through him. There was a warrior in that slim, exhausted body.

She said nothing as he approached, and neither of them spoke as he came to a stop in front of her.

Up close, he was riveted. Her dark eyelashes were clumped from the rain. Her skin was pale, too pale. Her face was carrying the burden of a thousand weights. But beneath that pain, those nightmares, that hell, lay delicate femininity that called to him. The luminescent glow of her skin, the sensual curve of her mouth, the sheen of rain on her cheekbones, the simple silver hoops in her ears. It awoke in him something so male, so carnal, so primal he wanted to throw her up against the wall and consume her until their bodies were melted together in single, scorching fire.

She searched his face with the same intensity raging through him, and he felt like she was tearing through his shields, cataloguing everything about him, all the way down to his soul.

He studied her carefully, and she let him, not flinching when his gaze traveled down her body. His blood pulsed as he noted the curve of her breasts under her rain-slicked jacket, the sensuous curve of her hips, and even the mud on her jeans and boots. He almost groaned at his need to palm her hips, drag her over to him, and mark her with his kiss. Loose strands of thick dark hair had escaped from her ponytail, curling around her neck and shoulders like it was clinging to her for safety.

Protectiveness surged from deep inside him and he clenched his fists against his urge to sweep her into his arms and carry her inside, away from whatever hardship had brought her to his doorstep.

Double hell. He'd hoped his reaction would lessen when he got close to her, but it had intensified. He'd never felt like this before. Never had this response to a woman.

What the hell was going on? *Sheva.* The word was like a demon, whispering through his mind. He shut it out. He would never allow himself to bond with his mate. If that was what was going on, she was out of there immediately, before they were both destroyed forever.

Intent on sending her away, he looked again at her face, and then realized he was done. Her beautiful silver eyes were aching with a soul-deep pain that shattered what little defenses he had against her. He simply couldn't abandon her.

It didn't matter what she wanted. It didn't matter why she was there. She was coming inside. He would make sure it didn't interfere with his mission. He would make dead sure it turned out right. No matter what.

Without a word, he grabbed her backpack off the floor, surprised at how heavy it was. Either she had tossed her free weights in it, or she had packed her life into it.

He had a bad feeling it wasn't a set of dumb bells.

Quinn walked past her and unlocked his front door. He shoved it open, then stood back. Letting her decide. Hoping she would walk away and spare them both.

She took a deep breath, glanced at his face one more time, then walked into the cabin.

Hell.

He paused to take one more survey of his woods, found nothing amiss, and then he followed her into his home and shut the door behind them.

Sneak Peek: Ghost

Alaska Heat
Available Now

"What are you running from?"

Ben Forsett froze at the unexpected question, his hand clenching around the amber beer bottle. For a long second, he didn't move. Instead, his gaze shot stealthily to the three exits he'd already located before he'd even walked into this local pub known as O'Dell's in Where-the-Hell-Are-We, Alaska. He rapidly calculated which exit had the clearest path. A couple of bush pilots were by the kitchen door. They were large, rough men who would shove themselves directly into the path of someone they thought should be stopped. His access to the front door was obstructed by two jean-clad young women walking into the foyer, shaking snowflakes out of their perfectly coiffed hair. The emergency exit was alarmed, but no one was in front of it. That was his best choice—

"Chill, kid," the man continued. "I'm not hunting you. I've been where you are. So have most of the men in this place."

Slowly, Ben pulled his gaze off his escape route and looked at the grizzled Alaskan old-timer sitting next to him. Lines of outdoor hardship creased his face, and wisps of straggly white hair hung below his faded, black baseball hat. His skin hung loose, too tired to hold on anymore, but in the old man's pale blue eyes burned a sharp, gritty intelligence born of a tough life. His shoulders were encased in a heavy, dark green jacket that was so bulky it almost hid the hunch to his back and the thinness of his shoulders.

The man nodded once. "Name's Haas. Haas Carter." He extended a gnarled hand toward Ben.

Ben didn't respond, but Haas didn't retract his hand.

For a long moment, neither man moved, then, finally, Ben peeled his fingers off his beer and shook Haas's hand. "John Sullivan," he said, the fake name sliding off his tongue far more easily than it had three months ago, the first time he'd used it.

"John Sullivan?" Haas laughed softly. "You picked the most common name you could think of, eh? Lots of John Sullivans in just about every town you've been to, I should imagine. It'd be hard for people to keep track of one more."

Ben stiffened. "My father was John Sullivan, Sr.," he lied. "I honor the name."

Haas's bushy gray brows went up. "Do you now?"

The truth was, Ben's father was a lying bastard who had left when he was two years old. Or he'd been shot. Or he'd been put in prison. No one knew what had happened to him, and no one really cared, including Ben. "I'm not here to make friends," Ben said quietly.

"No, I can see that." Haas regarded him for a moment, his silver-blue eyes surveying Ben's heavy whiskers and the shaggy hair that had once been perfectly groomed. Ben shook his head so his hair hung down over his forehead, shielding his eyes as he watched the older man, waiting for a sign that this situation was going south.

He would be pissed if Haas turned on him. He needed to be here. He was so sure this was finally the break he'd been waiting for. He let his gaze slither off Haas to the back wall of the bar where an enormous stuffed moose head was displayed. Its rack had to be at least six feet wide, its glazed dead eyes a bitter reminder of what happened to life when you stopped paying attention for a split second.

Beside the moose rack was the battered wooden clock he'd been watching all evening. Adrenaline raced through Ben as he watched the minute hand clunk to the twelve. *It was seven o'clock.*

"What happens at seven?"

Ben jerked his gaze back to Haas, startled to realize the older man had been watching him closely enough to notice his focus on the clock. "I turn into a fairy princess."

Haas guffawed and slammed his hand down on Ben's shoulder. "You're all right, John Sullivan. Mind if I call you Sully? Most Sullivans go by Sully. It'll make it seem more like it's your real name."

Ben's fingers tightened around the frosty bottle at Haas's persistence. "It is my real name."

Haas dropped the smile and leaned forward, lowering his voice as his gaze locked onto Ben's. "I'll tell you this, young man, I've seen a lot of shit in my life. I've seen men who look like princes, but turn out to be scum you wouldn't even want to waste a bullet on. I've seen pieces of shit who would actually give their life for you. You look like shit, but whatever the hell you're running from, you got my vote. Don't let the bastards catch you until you can serve it up right in their damn faces. Got it?"

Ben stared at Haas, too stunned by the words to respond. No one believed in him, no one except for the man who had helped him escape. He'd known Mack Connor since he was a kid, and Mack understood what loyalty meant. But even Mack knew damn well who Ben really was and what he was truly capable of. Mack's allegiance was unwavering, but he did it with his eyes open and ready to react if Ben went over the line.

He had a sudden urge to tell Haas exactly what shit was going down for him, and see if the old man still wanted to stand by him.

But he wasn't that stupid. He couldn't afford for anyone to know why he was here. "I don't know what you're talking about," he finally said.

Haas raised his beer in a toast. "Yeah, me neither, Sully. Me neither." As Haas took a drink, another weather-beaten Alaskan sat down on Haas's other side. This guy's face was so creased it looked like his razor would get lost if he tried to shave, and the size of his beard said the guy hadn't been willing to take the risk. Haas nodded at him. "Donnie, this here boy is Sully. New in town. Needs a job. His wife left him six months ago, and the poor bastard lost everything. He's been wandering aimless for too damn long."

Ben almost choked on his beer at Haas's story, but Donnie just nodded. "Women can sure break a man." He leveled his dark brown gaze at Ben. "She ain't worth it, young man. There are lots of doe around for a guy to pick up with."

Ben managed a nod. "Yeah, well, I'm not ready yet."

"We gotta get him back on the horse," Haas said. "Got any ideas?" With a wink at Ben, he and Donnie launched into a discussion about the assorted available women in town and which ones might be worthy of Ben.

As the two old-timers talked, Ben felt some of the tension ease from his shoulders. In this small town in the middle of Alaska, he had an ally, at least until Haas found out the truth. Shit, it felt good to have someone at his back. It had been too damn long—

The door to the kitchen swung open, and a cheerful female voice echoed through the swinging door. Her voice was like a soft caress of something...damn. He realized he didn't even know what to compare it to. His mind was too tired to conjure up words that would do justice to the sudden heat sliding over his skin. But a seductive, tempting warmth washed over him, through him, like someone had just slipped hot whisky into his veins, burning and cleansing as it went.

Ben went rigid, adrenaline flooding his body. It was seven o'clock. Based on what he'd pieced together about her schedule and her life, she would be coming on duty now, walking out of the kitchen *now*. Was it her? *Was it her?* Her hand was on the kitchen door, holding it open as she finished her muffled conversation. She was wearing a black leather cord with a silver disk around her wrist. On her index finger was a silver ring with a rough-cut turquoise stone and a wide band with carvings on it. Her fingernails were bare and natural, a woman who didn't bother with enamel and lacquer to go to work. Her arm was exposed, the smooth expanse of flesh sliding up to a capped black sleeve that just covered the curve of her shoulder. She wasn't tall, maybe a little over five feet.

Son of a bitch. It might actually be her. *Come into the bar,* he urged silently. *Let me see your face.* He'd never heard her talk before. He'd never seen her in person. All he had was that one newspaper picture of her, and the headshot he'd snagged from her family's store website before it had been taken down. But her trail had led to O'Dell's, and he was hoping he was right. He *had* to be right.

The door opened wider, and Ben ducked his head, letting his hair shield his eyes again, but he didn't take his gaze off her, watching intently as the woman moved into the restaurant. Her back was toward him as she continued her conversation, and he could see her hair. Thick, luscious waves of dark brown.

Brown. *Brown.* The woman he'd been searching for was

blond.

The disappointment and frustration that knifed through his gut was like the sharp stab of death itself. He bowed his head, resting his forehead in his palms as the image flooded his mind again, the same memory that had haunted him for so long. His sister, her clothes stained with that vibrant red of fresh blood, sprawled across her living room, her hand stretching toward Ben in the final entreaty of death. *Son of a bitch.* He couldn't let Holly down. He couldn't let her down *again.*

"Are you okay?"

He went still at the question, at the sound of the woman's voice so close. She still had the same effect on him, a flood of heat that seemed to touch every part of his body. He schooled his features into the same uninviting expression he'd perfected, and he looked up to find himself staring into the face he'd been hunting for the last three months.

He'd never mistake those eyes. The dark rich brown framed by eyelashes so thick he'd thought they had to be fake, until now. Until he could see her for real. Until he could feel the weight of her sorrow so thickly that it seemed to wrap around him and steal the oxygen from his lungs. Until he looked into that face, that face that had once been so innocent, and now carried burdens too heavy for her small frame.

Until he'd found her.

Because he had.

It was her. Yeah, maybe she'd ditched the blond and let herself go back to her natural color, which looked good as hell on her, but there was no doubt in his mind.

He'd found her.

Son of a bitch.

He'd found her.

Sneak Peek: No Knight Needed

Ever After
Available Now

Ducking her head against the raging storm, Clare hugged herself while she watched the huge black pickup truck turn its headlights onto the steep hillside. She was freezing, and her muscles wouldn't stop shaking. She was so worried about Katie, she could barely think, and she had no idea what this stranger was going to do. Something. Anything. Please.

The truck lurched toward the hill, and she realized suddenly that he was going to drive straight up the embankment in an attempt to go above the roots and around the fallen tree that was blocking the road. But that was crazy! The mountain was way too steep. He was going to flip his truck!

Memories assaulted her, visions of when her husband had died, and she screamed, racing toward him and waving her arms. "No, don't! Stop!"

But the truck plowed up the side of the hill, its wheels spewing mud as it fought for traction in the rain-soaked earth. She stopped, horror recoiling through her as the truck turned and skidded parallel across the hill, the left side of his truck reaching far too high up the slippery slope. Her stomach retched as she saw the truck tip further and further.

The truck was at such an extreme angle, she could see the roof now. A feathered angel was painted beneath the flood lights. An angel? What was a man like him doing with an angel on his truck?

The truck was almost vertical now. There was no way it could stay upright. It was going to flip. Crash into the tree. Careen across the road. Catapult off the cliff. He would die right in front of her. Oh, God, he would die.

But somehow, by a miracle that she couldn't comprehend, the truck kept struggling forward, all four wheels still gripping the earth.

The truck was above the roots now. Was he going to

make it? Please let him make it—

The wheels slipped, and the truck dropped several yards down toward the roots. "No!" She took a useless, powerless step as the tires caught on the roots. The tires spun out in the mud, and the roots ripped across the side of the vehicle with a furious scream.

"Go," she shouted, clenching her firsts. "Go!"

He gunned the engine, and suddenly the tires caught. The truck leapt forward, careening sideways across the hill, skidding back and forth as the mud spewed. He made it past the tree, and then the truck plowed back down toward the road, sliding and rolling as he fought for control.

Clare held her hand over her mouth, terrified that at any moment one of his tires would catch on a root and he'd flip. "Please make it, please make it, please make it," she whispered over and over again.

The truck bounced high over a gully, and she gasped when it flew up so high she could see the undercarriage. Then somehow, someway, he wrested the truck back to four wheels, spun out into the road and stopped, its wipers pounding furiously against the rain as the floodlights poured hope into the night.

Oh, dear God. He'd made it. He hadn't died.

Clare gripped her chest against the tightness in her lungs. Her hands were shaking, her legs were weak. She needed to sit down. To recover.

But there was no time. The driver's door opened and out he stepped. Standing behind the range of his floodlights, he was silhouetted against the darkness, his shoulders so wide and dominating he looked like the dark earth itself had brought him to life.

Something inside her leapt with hope at the sight of him, at the sheer, raw strength of his body as he came toward her. This man, this stranger, he was enough. He could help her. Sudden tears burned in her eyes as she finally realized she didn't have to fight this battle by herself.

He held up his hand to tell her to stay, then he slogged over to the front of his truck. He hooked something to the winch, then headed over to the tree. The trunk came almost to his chest, but he locked his grip around a wet branch for leverage, and then vaulted over with effortless grace, landing in the mud with a splash. "Come here," he shouted over the wind.

Clare ran across the muck toward him, stumbling in the slippery footing. "You're crazy!" she shouted, shielding her eyes against the bright floodlights from his truck. But God, she'd never been so happy to see crazy in her life.

"Probably," he yelled back, flashing her a cheeky grin. His perfect white teeth seemed to light up his face, a cheerful confident smile that felt so incongruous in the raging storm and daunting circumstances.

But his cockiness eased her panic, and that was such a gift. It made her able to at least think rationally. She would take all the positive vibes she could get right now.

He held up a nylon harness that was hooked to the steel cord attached to his truck. "If the tree goes over, this will keep you from going over."

She wiped the rain out of her eyes. "What are you talking about?"

"We still have to get you over the tree, and I don't want you climbing it unprotected. Never thought I'd actually be using this stuff. I had it just out of habit." He dropped the harness over her head and began strapping her in with efficient, confident movements. His hands brushed her breasts as he buckled her in, but he didn't seem to notice.

She sure did.

It was the first time a man's hands had touched her breasts in about fifteen years, and it was an unexpected jolt. Something tightened in her belly. Desire? Attraction? An awareness of the fact she was a woman? Dear God, what was wrong with her? She didn't have time for that. Not tonight, and not in her life. But she couldn't take her gaze off his strong jaw and dark eyes as he focused intently on the harness he was strapping around her.

"I'm taking you across to my truck," he said, "and then we're going to get your daughter and the others."

"We are?" She couldn't stop the sudden flood of tears. "You're going to help me get them?"

He nodded as he snapped the final buckle. "Yeah. I gotta get into heaven somehow, and this might do it."

"Thank you!" She threw herself at him and wrapped her arms around him, clinging to her savior. She had no idea who he was, but he'd just successfully navigated a sheer mud cliff for her and her daughter, and she would so take that gift right now.

For an instant, he froze, and she felt his hard body start to pull away. Then suddenly, in a shift so subtle she didn't even see it happen, his body relaxed and his arms went around her, locking her down in an embrace so powerful she felt like the world had just stopped. She felt like the rain had ceased and the wind had quieted, buffeted aside by the strength and power of his body.

"It's going to be okay." His voice was low and reassuring in her ear, his lips brushing against her as he spoke. "She's going to be fine."

Crushed against this stranger's body, protected by his arms, soothed by the utter confidence in his voice, the terror that had been stalking her finally eased away. "Thank you," she whispered.

"You're welcome."

There was a hint of emotion in his voice, and she pulled back far enough to look at him. His eyes were dark, so dark she couldn't tell if they were brown or black, but she could see the torment in his expression. His jaw was angular, and his face was shadowed by the floodlights. He was a man with weight in his heart. She felt it right away. Instinctively, she laid a hand on his cheek. "You're a gift."

He flashed another smile, and for a split second, he put his hand over hers, holding it to his whiskered cheek as if she were some angel of mercy come to give him relief. Her throat thickened, and for a moment, everything else vanished. It was just them, drenched and cold on a windy mountain road, the only warmth was their hands, clasped together against his cheek.

His eyes darkened, then he cleared his throat suddenly and released her hand, jerking her back to the present. "Wait until you see whether I can pull it off," he said, his voice low and rough, sending chills of awareness rippling down her spine. "Then you can reevaluate that compliment." He tugged on the harness. "Ready?"

She gripped the cold nylon, suddenly nervous. Was she

edgy because she was about to climb over a tree that could careen into the gully while she was on it, or was it due to intensity of the sudden heat between them? God, she hoped it was the first one. Being a wimp was so much less dangerous than noticing a man like him. "Aren't you wearing one?"

He quirked a smile at her, a jaunty grin that melted one more piece of her thundering heart. "I only have one, and ladies always get first dibs. Besides, I'm a good climber. If the tree takes me over, I'll find my way back up. Always do." He set his foot on a lower branch and patted his knee. "A one-of-a-kind step ladder. Hop up, Ms.—?" He paused, leaving the question hovering in the storm.

"Clare." She set her muddy boot on his knee, and she grimaced apologetically when the mud glopped all over his jeans. "Clare Gray." She grabbed a branch and looked at him. "And you are?"

"Griffin Friesé." He set his hand on her hip to steady her, his grip strong and solid. "Let's go save some kids, shall we?"

Select List of Other Books by Stephanie Rowe

PARANORMAL ROMANCE

The NightHunter Series

Not Quite Dead

The Order of the Blade Series

Darkness Awakened
Darkness Seduced
Darkness Surrendered
Forever in Darkness (Novella)
Darkness Reborn
Darkness Arisen
Darkness Unleashed
Inferno of Darkness (Novella)
Darkness Possessed
Hunt the Darkness
Release Date TBD

The Soulfire Series

Kiss at Your Own Risk
Touch if You Dare
Hold Me if You Can

The Immortally Sexy Series

Date Me Baby, One More Time
Must Love Dragons
He Loves Me, He Loves Me Hot
Sex & the Immortal Bad Boy

ROMANTIC SUSPENSE

The Alaska Heat Series

Ice
Chill
Ghost

CONTEMPORARY ROMANCE

Ever After Series

No Knight Needed
Fairytale Not Required
Prince Charming Can Wait

Stand Alone Novels

Jingle This!

NONFICTION

ESSAYS

The Feel Good Life

FOR TEENS

A Girlfriend's Guide to Boys Series

Putting Boys on the Ledge
Studying Boys
Who Needs Boys?
Smart Boys & Fast Girls

Stand Alone Novels

The Fake Boyfriend Experiment

FOR PRE-TEENS

The Forgotten Series

Penelope Moonswoggle, The Girl Who Could Not Ride a Dragon
Penelope Moonswoggle & the Accidental Doppelganger
Release Date TBD

Collections

Box Sets

Alpha Immortals
Last Hero Standing

Stephanie Rowe Bio

Four-time RITA® Award nominee and Golden Heart® Award winner Stephanie Rowe is a nationally bestselling author, and has more than twenty-five contracted titles with major New York publishers such as Grand Central, HarperCollins, Dorchester and Harlequin, and more than fifteen indie books. She believes in writing stories where characters survive against all odds, fighting their way through to personal triumph, while discovering true love and sensual, hot passion along the way.

Stephanie is an award-winning and bestselling author of adult paranormal romance, and has charmed reviewers, receiving coveted starred reviews from Booklist for several of her paranormal romances. Publishers Weekly has also praised her work, calling her work "[a] genre-twister that will make readers...rabid for more."

In addition to her vibrant paranormal romance career, Stephanie also writes a thrilling romantic suspense series set in Alaska. Publisher's Weekly praised the series debut, ICE, as a "thrilling entry into romantic suspense," and Fresh Fiction called ICE an "edgy, sexy and gripping thriller." Equally as intense and sexy are Stephanie's contemporary romance novels, set in the fictional town of Birch Crossing, Maine

Stephanie is a full-time author who has been an avid reader since she was a kid (she even won the blue ribbon at her town library for reading the most books over the summer). She wrote her first book when she was ten, but abandoned that fledgling career when people started asking to read it. Fortunately, she now delights in people reading her work, and loves to hear from readers. With more than fifty completed novels to her name, Stephanie is well on her way to fulfilling the dream that started so long ago. Some of her favorite authors are Lisa Kleypas, Dick Francis, and Julie Garwood, but the list goes on and on

In her spare time, Stephanie loves to play tennis, take her rescue dog for walks in the woods, and to make up stories about the people she sees on the street with her daughter. Yes, the author's imagination is always at work.

Want to learn more? Visit Stephanie online at one of the following hot spots

WWW.STEPHANIEROWE.COM

HTTP://TWITTER.COM/STEPHANIEROWE2

HTTP://WWW.PINTEREST.COM/STEPHANIEROWE2/

HTTPS://WWW.FACEBOOK.COM/STEPHANIEROWEAUTHOR

www.ingramcontent.com/pod-product-compliance
Lightning Source LLC
Chambersburg PA
CBHW070307280626
47159CB00017B/357